This book is for

Lindsey and Connor,
who continue to not kill me in my sleep

THE DARK HALO

David Stanley

PAPER★STREET

Paper Street Publishing

Paper Street Publishing

Copyright © 2023 David Stanley

The moral right of the author has been asserted

ISBN (ebook) 9781916176362
ISBN (paperback) 9781916176379

www.davidjstanley.com
www.paperstreetpublishing.net

1

THE WINE BOTTLE LAY on its side, several feet back from the edge of the bed, like a finger pointing. He paused to squat down and study it. A thick film of dust covered the outside. An expensive wine no doubt, stored for years in a cellar. The dust was smudged around the middle where fingers had held it and a dark red stain had formed under the open end, spreading out across the pale cream carpet. Though the scene had already been photographed, Coombes was careful not to accidentally kick the bottle as he approached the body.

Milton Vandenberg was propped up on pillows facing the television, his face as still and white as a glass of milk. On top of the sheet, in the valley between his ancient legs, lay three empty pharmaceutical bottles. The pills, the wine. It told a story; one he'd seen play out many times before. A businessman, down on his luck, checks into an expensive hotel then checks out without paying. Only, Vandenberg wasn't down on his luck. Far from it. The man was senior executive officer at Pacific Pictures, notable for their *Stick Shift* driving movies. The latest in the franchise had recently crossed the billion-dollar mark at the global box office and showed no sign of stopping.

Vandenberg fit an emerging pattern; rich, powerful, and dead.

Coombes turned his attention to the containers in the old man's lap. He was able to read the label without having to move them. Diazepam, 10 mg. The drug was the generic form of Valium, an anti-stress medication that had been around for a long time. The label indicated that each bottle held a hundred tablets.

He shook his head.

Assuming they'd been full, three hundred was a lot to swallow. Even spread out over half an hour, it would be heavy going and require a strong desire to get to the end. Combined with the alcohol, 3000 mg would certainly be enough to see the old man over the rainbow bridge. This was no cry for help.

Grace Sato spoke behind him.

"What do you think?"

"Looks legit," he said. "No sign of force."

He avoided saying the word *suicide*, it bothered him.

"One less for us to worry about then."

"Maybe. I don't see a note."

"Come on, Johnny. Not this again. They don't all leave notes. Women leave notes, men not so much. Half the men I know can't write anymore. Maybe he sent a text or an email, that's more a man's speed. Quick, clean, no emotion."

Vandenberg didn't look like the type of man to send a text. Not at the end of his life, not ever. As for emails, he probably had people to send those for him. He was from a previous generation, one that used telephones to make calls. Someone that believed in the importance of the face-to-face. The shaking of hands. If anyone was going to leave a note, it would be this guy. Coombes could almost imagine the large, looping cursive a man like this would've produced, full of confidence and entitlement.

"This is the sixth in two months."

He'd finally said it out loud.

Grace paused, her eyes moving slowly over his face.

"You think there's a serial out there posing kills as suicides?"

It sounded crazy when she said it back to him. Maybe it was, but that didn't make it any less possible. The rich were dying, and not from the usual causes. He turned away from her gaze, back to the body. It was easier to look at Vandenberg's corpse than Grace's face right then.

She didn't buy it. The doubt was there, even some humor. She was treating it like a joke. Grace preferred to be the one with the oddball theory, he was the straight man. He was the senior partner. His job was to be the voice of reason, the hand on the leash.

He looked at the items on the nightstand.

A telephone, a lamp, and a hotel branded notepad. Next to that, the items Vandenberg had added. Theoretically, anyway. A large wine glass, a cell phone, an alligator skin wallet, and two silver dollars. Coombes didn't see a lot of silver dollars, but he'd found that people often kept hold of them like they were lucky charms. The coins hadn't done Vandenberg any good, that was for sure. Eisenhower looked off, unimpressed, toward the door. The glass had a small ring of wine residue at the bottom, but no visible trace of powder. Sometimes people would grind up pills and add them to a liquid to avoid the repetitive swallowing action which could cause vomiting. If you vomited, you were back to square one and may not have enough of the drug left to get the job done. It appeared the wine was simply a favorite, used to see out the remainder of his life.

What he saw was a classic scene, perfect in every detail.

A little too perfect, he thought.

Then there was the bottle on the floor, as if the old man had dropped it in the final seconds as life left his body. Perhaps knocking it off the nightstand in a panic after realizing what he'd done. That was the problem with suicides, he thought. You filled in what you didn't know with crude guesses and didn't care too much how well they fit the facts. As soon as you concluded it was a suicide, the job was to establish a rough narrative for what happened before washing your hands of it.

Homicide, that was his mandate. One person killing another. Suicides were free, they didn't appear in any unsolved figure, so no time was given to them beyond examining the scene and informing the next of kin.

He imagined himself stretched out on the bed.

If Vandenberg was drinking from the glass, he would've dropped that, not the bottle. But it wasn't the glass on the floor, the glass was safely on the nightstand. The wine bottle didn't track, and he was pretty sure that the stain on the carpet was the affectation of a killer, intended to look like a blood stain. If he test-dropped a hundred near-empty wine bottles, Coombes would lay money on none of them producing that type of stain. The shape of the bottle seemed to preclude it from happening.

Grace spoke softly.

"Is this because of Sutton?"

Theodore Sutton was a suicide they'd attended six weeks earlier. The father of a school friend, Sutton's death had felt personal. He'd spent a lot of time at the Sutton home growing up, and he'd looked harder at the case than he would otherwise.

But cases kept coming, and a probable suicide was soon forgotten.

"Yeah. Sutton opened my eyes."

"The man's old, Johnny. Maybe he had a terminal disease."

Coombes turned to face his partner. "He did. *Life.*"

A smile appeared on her face until she saw he wasn't amused.

He had no love or time for the entitled rich, but her attitude to the man's death was getting old. Worse, was the knowledge that her reaction would be as nothing compared to what he could expect from his lieutenant if he suggested adding six homicides to the unsolved total. A storm was heading his way, and his own partner didn't have his back. He walked past her. A man in his early twenties now stood in the doorway with a uniformed officer. Coombes read the name he'd written earlier on his notebook. Eric Lyle.

"You found the body, Mr. Lyle?"

"Yes, sir."

"You sat him up like that?"

"No way, man. He was like that already."

"You didn't move the body?"

"I didn't touch him, I swear."

Coombes leaned forward, crowding the younger man.

"You didn't check his pulse?"

"No sir, it was obvious he was dead."

"I see. How long did you study medicine before you got this job?"

Next to him, Grace laughed into her hand.

Lyle frowned; his face pinched with confusion.

"*What?*"

"Just a suggestion, Lyle, but if anyone else asks what happened here, tell them you checked for a pulse to confirm he was dead before you told the manager."

"I don't understand."

"That man was probably worth half a billion dollars. You don't want a family member or his company suing you because prompt action could've saved him. By the time you found him, it was too late. Yes? If he was in a coma your negligence killed him."

The youth's eyes grew wild and panicked.

"I checked his pulse, I forgot. He was dead."

Coombes nodded slowly. The kid was getting it.

"When you were at the bedside, did you touch anything else?"

The confusion was back. Lyle had zero poker face. He hadn't approached the bed at all, not to check the pulse, not for anything.

"No, sir."

Coombes pointed at the floor.

"Was that bottle like that when you found Mr. Vandenberg?"

"Yes, sir."

Coombes made a note of this in his notebook and resisted the urge to smile. Truthfully, he wished everyone called him *sir*. Working in a high-end hotel had conditioned the kid to be polite, it's where the high dollar tips were.

"Did you turn off the TV?"

Lyle looked surprised.

"Yeah. The volume was up crazy high, I could hear it in the hallway. That's why I found him actually, I was going to ask him to turn it down before anyone complained. When he didn't answer the door, I used my key. I thought he'd gone out and left it on."

"Where was the remote?"

Lyle pointed to the bench the TV sat on.

"Right where it is now. I put it back exactly where I found it."

Coombes glanced at Grace. Her head was tilted over. She saw it. Nobody would leave the remote there while they took an overdose. Not if the television was on. Vandenberg would have it next to his hand, or up next to his cell phone. Somewhere within easy reach. A lot of hotels glued the remote to the nightstand now, but not this place.

Then there was the volume to consider.

He was willing to accept the old man's hearing might not have been a hundred percent, but for Lyle to be troubled by it out in the hallway had to mean it was deafening inside the room.

"Did you adjust the volume before you turned the TV off?"

Lyle thought about it for a moment, then shook his head.

"I don't remember."

Coombes walked over to the console table and, holding the edges of the remote control in place with his gloved hand, pressed the on button. Sound filled the room. A news channel, KCAL9. An attractive woman doing a piece to camera, almost breathless with excitement. More about the shoot-out in Santa Cruz. He could feel the reporter's voice inside his chest.

He turned the TV off.

The only reason for setting the volume so high was to announce the body to the world. To lure someone in here, like bait on a fishing line. The killer wanted his latest masterpiece to be discovered. It could've been hours before Vandenberg was missed, and many hours more before he was traced here.

The killer needed the hit of exposure like any other junkie chasing a fix, and he needed it as soon as possible.

"Okay, kid, that's all. Remember what I told you."

Lyle nodded wordlessly and turned to go.

"Wait, just a second."

Lyle turned back, nervous. "Yeah?"

"You said your key opens this door. Does it open any door in the hotel?"

"Far as I know."

"All right, that's all."

He walked to the window and looked out.

When he visited crime scenes, he liked to take in what the victim had seen before they died. It was his version of walking a mile in another man's shoes. For a five-star hotel, the view was depressing. Parking lots the size of football stadiums and, next to them, the gray river of the 110 packed with pre-lunch traffic. It would make anyone want to end it all.

He took another look at the victim before he left.

There was little doubt in his mind that what he was looking at was staged, and because of that, it was a murder. No true suicide was this clean.

2

SATO WAS SILENT AS they left the hotel suite and walked down the hallway toward the elevator. The carpeting was thick, Coombes could feel his shoes sinking into the pile as he walked. It was something that would have offset the sound of Vandenberg's television, but the killer had taken no chances and set the volume to maximum. As they approached the elevator, he glanced up to scan for security cameras. He saw nothing. Either the hotel didn't have any, or they were well concealed. In his experience, cameras were rarely concealed, being visible was part of their function.

If you knew you were being recorded, you behaved yourself.

They got on the elevator and he thought through what would happen next. The hotel would be keen to push for a suicide narrative. It was bad for business, but nothing like the poison of a murder. They'd want the investigation to close down as soon as possible and would resist giving up security footage without a warrant.

The doors opened and they got out in the lobby.

A man with a pained expression walked sharply toward them, his small leather shoes squeaking on the marble. This would be the hotel manager, he supposed. Coombes leaned in close to Sato's ear and whispered what he wanted her to do before they could be overheard.

"Detectives. I hope we can make this as quick as possible, so that we can get back to normal. My name's Henry Dalton, I'm the day manager. Anticipating your arrival, I pulled the hostess who dealt with our...unfortunate guest from behind the desk so that she could speak with you. If you would come this way."

Dalton led them to a seated area on the opposite side of the lobby from the elevators where an attractive woman sat. She rose to her feet and looked vacantly between their three faces before settling on Sato's.

Coombes could hardly blame her on that front.

"This is Anna Lomax; she'll be able to answer your questions."

"Please sit down, Miss Lomax, this won't take long."

Lomax sat again, and Coombes sat opposite her. Sato turned to the manager.

"Would you be kind enough to direct me to the restroom?"

The manager grunted and moved off to the side then pointed toward the back of the hotel. Coombes took out his notebook and wrote Dalton and Lomax's names on it before he forgot.

"You checked in Mr. Vandenberg this morning?"

"Yes."

"How did he seem to you?"

She shrugged. "Fat."

Coombes laughed. The bluntness of youth.

"I mean did he seem happy, sad, worried, anything like that?"

"Oh," her face colored. "He seemed happy, I guess. Excited maybe."

Coombes nodded as he wrote in his notebook.

"That's good. Was he alone?"

"I think so."

"You're not sure?"

"No, but he's usually alone when he checks in."

"He's been here before?"

"Oh yeah, he's a regular. Every week. I know it's Friday when he checks in." Her voice trailed away to nothing. "I feel bad about saying he was fat before."

"That's all right. How long had Mr. Vandenberg booked the room for?"

"Officially, his departure time was tomorrow morning, but he never stayed later than 3 o'clock."

Coombes smiled, like they were sharing a joke.

"What do *you* think he was doing?"

"The first time he came here, there was a woman with him. She didn't come to the desk, she kind of hung back while he checked in. He kept looking back at her, as if to make sure she was still there. Then they got in the elevator together. I only remember because she was a real knockout, like a model."

"I assume this woman was not also in her eighties?"

Lomax shook her head, her face briefly showing irritation.

"Have you seen this woman since then?"

"Every Friday like clockwork, except today."

"What does she look like?"

"Five eight, slim, maybe 120 pounds. 25 to 28 years old. Long chestnut-colored hair with a curl in it. Sometimes she had her hair in a ponytail."

Coombes wrote this down. He noticed that Lomax didn't need to think before giving the woman's description, like she'd thought this woman many times before.

"You said she looked like a model; she wore expensive clothes?"

"No, nothing like that. Jeans and a T-shirt, running shoes, that kind of thing. I just meant she *could've* been a model, if she wanted. She did wear sunglasses inside the hotel though, like she was a movie star."

He noticed Sato approaching with a smile on her face.

"Okay, last question. Did you ever see this woman with anyone else, perhaps on days when Mr. Vandenberg wasn't a guest?"

"No, I would remember."

A red spot appeared on Anna Lomax's cheeks as she thought again about the mystery woman. She sighed, her eyes dipping to her hands, folded in her lap. He supposed she was realizing that she would never see the woman in the sunglasses again, whatever that meant to her. Coombes passed her his card.

"If you think of anything, give me a call."

He kept giving witnesses his card, telling them to call. But in all the years he'd been a cop no one ever had, not even to tell him they liked the color of his eyes. He stood, buttoned his suit jacket, and glanced toward Dalton who stood a short distance away watching them with a pinched, nervous look. When Lomax was gone, he turned to Sato.

"Turns out Vandenberg's been meeting a young woman here every Friday. Sounds like the old devil was having an affair, unless she's a pro. Either way, Vandenberg's wife is probably not going to like it. Our mystery woman didn't show today, which is an interesting coincidence, don't you think?"

"You think she's involved?"

"Probably not, but the timing's a little off. Did you get the security footage?"

Sato nodded.

"That security guy is disgusting. His office smells like underwear and burgers. Anyway, I told him the manager said it was ok for us to get a copy of today's security footage and he downloaded it all onto a thumb drive while he looked at my chest."

"We should leave before Dalton works out he got played."

"*Right.*"

They set off again, across the wide floor of the lobby.

"Any chance you to make your own way back to the PAB?"

"Where are you going?"

"I've got a dental appointment."

It was the same story he'd given his lieutenant and saw no reason to change it.

3

WHEN HE GOT BACK to the Police Administration Building, it was already 3:30. He hoped to avoid his lieutenant but found her standing in front of the elevator as the doors opened. Ellen Gantz had wild hair and piercing eyes that maybe you shouldn't look into for too long. Gantz glanced at the two cups of coffee in his hands.

"Good of you to join us, John. One of those better be for me."

He smiled and tried to make it worth something.

"Sure."

She reached out and he passed her one of the cups.

"Grace had an interesting story when she came back from that hotel. It sounded a lot like one of those internet conspiracy theories, and I want to make sure I have it right before I take it to the captain."

Coombes said nothing.

She took a sip of coffee and smiled.

"This is amazing! Is it from the place across the road?"

The LA Times building.

"Same as usual."

Coombes took a sip from his own cup and figured out why hers was so good. He'd given her the one that he'd topped up with Scotch. Gantz glanced at her watch, then at the still-open elevator behind him. *Get in,* he thought. Her focus drifted back to him and he knew he was sunk.

"Let's make this quick, I have another appointment."

They walked back through the detective bureau to her office in silence. He fell into step alongside her, but fractionally back. She liked people where she could see them, but she also liked to lead. It was a fine line to walk, but hardly difficult. Knowing the likes and dislikes of those around him was an important part of the job and any cop who thought otherwise probably wondered why he worked Robbery Homicide and they didn't.

They got to her office and he made the tactical decision not to close the door behind him. She sat on the edge of her desk and crossed her legs at the ankle. It was a position she used a lot and communicated that there was no desk between them, no rank. She took another mouthful of coffee and looked him over.

"How was it?" she said.

Her voice was soft, almost sympathetic. He shrugged.

"Just another crime scene. Pretty peaceful actually."

"Not *that*, the other thing."

"The dentist?"

Gantz sighed.

"You're wearing a black tie, John. You always wear navy. *Always*. Did you really think I wouldn't work out that you were at a funeral? I'm a little insulted by that dentist story. I *earned* this job, I didn't get it because of my winning personality and my great ass."

She'd known the whole time; he could see it. He nodded.

"The funeral was six weeks ago behind closed doors. This was supposed to be a public service...a commemoration." Coombes sighed, remembering. "It wasn't great. His son told me to leave, that I wasn't welcome. That's not a direct quote, he used shorter words."

"That's tough, I'm sorry."

He saw what was happening. The sitting on the edge of the desk, the sympathy. She wanted to kill his investigation.

"Listen, if you think that I'm-"

She lifted her hand to cut him off.

"24 hours."

"You think I can solve a serial in 24 hours?"

"No. That's how long you have to prove this isn't just a sad old man ending his life. And I better not hear anything about you working a serial killer case, am I clear? Your investigation is about Vandenberg only, at least as far as the department is concerned."

A day. What could he achieve in a single day?

"You know, in the movies, it's 48 hours. One time, it was 72."

"I'll split the difference. You still have 24 hours, but you can keep Sato."

That gave him nothing. He'd already assumed she would be part of his investigation since she was his partner. Gantz was burying the case by the back door. If he couldn't find anything, it was his fault, not hers. If it later came back to bite them, she'd insulated herself.

"And this arbitrary time limit starts tomorrow, right?"

She narrowed her eyes.

"*Fine.* But that's all I'll give you. Bring me something good."

She finished her coffee and dropped it in a trash can. Their meeting was over. As he walked back to his desk, Coombes realized that the narrow window of a day meant that Gantz hoped to hide the nature of his investigation from the captain. This was only possible because Vandenberg's wealth meant his family could afford the kind of legal counsel that could bury the Department if there was any hint of a rush to judgement. Grace Sato stood up and smiled at him when she saw him.

Then took his coffee cup out his hand.

Coombes was already familiar with photographs from the earlier suicides, despite having only worked on the Sutton case. His theory about a serial killer prowling the streets of L.A. hadn't just formed in Vandenberg's hotel room, but had been building over the previous two months.

He'd put the word out that he was interested in all suicides of high profile Angelenos since the beginning of the year and he had received a flood of emails, 143 total dead as of that morning. The number was higher than he expected, but he discovered that he could quickly dismiss most of them. There was a *sameness* about a true suicide scene that he could now recognize just from a couple of photographs.

Of the 143, only five stood out as suspicious, not counting Vandenberg. A small number in a bewildering number. Almost insignificant on the scale of things, yet he'd picked up the scent mostly from news reports or online newspaper articles. He'd looked at the photographs for over two hours, and all he could see was staged scenes, like someone had made them for their social media account.

He was too deep inside, he needed fresh eyes to see what he was seeing, and to know what it was. Coombes looked at Sato, scrolling through a list of names and numbers.

"What're you working on?"

"Vandenberg's cell phone records."

"They're through already?"

"Are you kidding me? Be lucky to get these by next month. I have a contact. One hand washes the other, you know?"

Sato turned from her screen and raised an eyebrow. Coombes smiled. Her brother worked at the FBI and her cousin for the IRS. Or maybe it was the NSA and CIA. He was convinced she'd given him different answers on separate occasions, perhaps deliberately. He didn't care, she was useful to have around.

"Uh-huh. Anything interesting?"

"Repeated calls to a cell phone registered to a veterinary hospital off Overland Avenue. Forty minutes to an hour and a half duration. All his other calls were sub five minutes. Vandenberg had no pets, not even a fish. I looked at their website and found this profile page for the owner, Kelly Taylor."

Sato switched apps on her computer to bring up her browser and angled her screen toward him. The page showed a woman in her late twenties with long brown hair. She was wearing green scrubs and was looking off camera like a stock photograph for a business report. She was a solid match for the woman described by Anna Lomax.

"The mystery woman," he said, nodding. "Good work."

"I called her. No answer."

Coombes sat back in his chair, thinking it over.

"Call her again."

Sato dialed the number without checking it against the screen. It was memorized already. From the number of times that she'd tried it, he supposed. She pressed a button and he heard the phone ringing on the phone's loudspeaker. No answer, no message, it just kept ringing. She gave it about 30 seconds and disconnected.

"What do you suppose it means?"

Coombes shrugged.

"She's in the wind."

His partner continued to look at him with a level gaze.

"I don't think she's dead, Grace."

"If you're right and this is a serial case, why not?"

"Because these guys always have a defined type, a specific target. They're careful, deliberate. Not opportunists. It's not about killing random people to them, it's like a game with rules. There's always a twisted logic behind victim selection. There's no way that logic is going to stretch from the head of a multi-billion-dollar movie studio to a veterinarian."

"What then?"

"She saw the media coverage and got out of town. Switched off her phone. It's what I'd do, wouldn't you? Go somewhere remote and wait for it all to blow over. If she believes what the news is saying, that he killed himself, then she might blame herself. For the guilt he felt about his family, about an argument they might've had, for not being there to prevent it. Survivors always think they could have stopped it, no matter what."

Sato looked like she was about to say something, then paused. He knew what she was thinking, it was there in her eyes. She thought that's why *they* were here, that he was doing all this because he felt guilty about the death of Sutton. There was probably truth behind it, he thought. He'd need to choose his words more carefully in future, particularly in front of Gantz or the captain. They'd either dismiss his theories because of his connection, or say it was a conflict and take him off the case.

"First of all, her cell's *not* off, it's ringing," Sato said. "Second, I don't think she's hiding somewhere remote. She's not a coyote with a wounded paw, Johnny, she's a grown-ass woman. We like to talk things through, not limp off to die in the woods. If she's alive, she's probably with her mom, sobbing into some home-cooked brisket."

Coombes frowned. "Am *I* the coyote here?"

"That a problem for you?"

There was a smile in her eyes. She was cheeky and he liked it.

"I guess not."

Sato turned back to her screen. "Figures."

"Any other interesting names on that list?"

"Far as I can see, mostly studio executives, lawyers, like that. Golf buddies, probably. However, one of the other names did catch my eye. A cardiologist at Cedars-Sinai."

Coombes sighed. "You think this doctor prescribed the Diazepam?"

"It's possible."

If Vandenberg turned out to be a genuine suicide, then his hunt for a serial killer was over before it started. He didn't know why, but the prospect depressed him.

"All right. We can circle back to that later if necessary. In the meantime, I need you to double-check some crime scene pictures for me. I've sent you a link to a folder on the server. I need fresh eyes and mine need a coffee."

He stood and pulled on his suit jacket.

"What about the veterinarian?"

As long as there was still a small chance she could be found hanging out of dumpster, he had to do something. *To protect and to serve.* It was more than just a catchy line written on the side of their vehicles. It *meant* something. This is how it often was, he reflected. Wasting time that he didn't have, on loose ends that went nowhere.

"I'll handle that when I get back."

"What am I checking?"

"Deaths of wealthy people in Los Angeles attributed to suicide since the beginning of the year. I want you to look for any that don't pass the smell test."

Sato groaned.

"Johnny, I want you to know something and understand. I gave up a third date to be here tonight and the third date...that's when the lock opens."

"Jesus, Grace."

She nodded.

"It's funny. I thought I'd hear that tonight, just not from you."

Coombes' face was scarlet when he got on the elevator.

Third date, he thought wistfully. He and his wife had dated for two months before any damn lock opened and recently, the lock appeared to have returned. As the elevator sank toward the street, he pushed thoughts of his partner to one side and turned again to the problem with the Vandenberg crime scene.

It was still fresh in his mind like he was looking at photographs on his monitor. As soon as he'd walked into the room, it hadn't felt right, but what was it that had made him feel that? Experience. Years on the job. His subconscious.

He made a mental list of the key findings.

The bottle on the floor.

The remote control that wasn't next to the bed.

The TV was on, the volume too loud.

The body's discovery by Eric Lyle.

Coombes had learned that a good way to develop a hypothesis was to work it backwards. To try to prove the *opposite* of what you believed. The weak point was Lyle, no question.

It wasn't hard to imagine the hotel porter knocking the wine bottle onto the floor himself after finding Vandenberg's body, his discomfort at seeing the dead man had shaken him deeply. The wine bottle had left a huge stain on the carpet, a stain that might never come out. The whole carpet might need to be replaced.

It was no great stretch to further imagine Lyle lying about the bottle to save his job. This explained both the bottle's odd positioning, and the fact that it was the bottle on the floor, rather than the glass. It would not however explain the position of the remote control, or the volume of the television that had lured Lyle into the room in the first place.

Coombes sighed as a new thought occurred to him.

Unless Lyle lied about that as well.

Lyle had a keycard that he claimed could open any door in the hotel. If Lyle assumed the room was empty because Vandenberg hadn't answered a knock at the door, he might've used his keycard in an attempt to steal something. A laptop, a tablet, drugs, perhaps even skim credit cards.

It was a big suite in a high-end hotel and the super wealthy were possibly less uptight about security for items that to them represented pocket change.

Having gained access to the room and found the dead body, Lyle might've panicked and called the front desk without thinking how to explain his discovery. Overhearing a loud television was the perfect justification for Lyle to enter the room when he had no right to be there. So he set the television volume high and put the remote back where he found it. The remote was never next to the bed, because Vandenberg wasn't watching TV.

Because he was already dead.

The narrative tracked well, disturbingly well in fact, except for one thing. In order for Vandenberg to be a suicide, Eric Lyle had to be a criminal and he'd picked up no vibe from him other than anxiety and disgust. Lyle had answered his questions quickly and naturally with no sign that he'd thought answers out in advance, the classic sign of a lie. He had also not mentioned the television to him until he was asked about it, if Lyle had planned to use it to frame his story, he would have mentioned it almost immediately.

Lyle was either the best liar he'd ever met, or it was all true.

Coombes had hoped that getting away from his desk would give him some kind of clarity and see an angle he'd missed but he was back to where he'd started, with a crime scene that could only be explained to his satisfaction by the presence of a third person. His killer. He was no further on but he knew that questioning himself always served two purposes: it forced him to examine his assumptions more closely; and it prepared him for questions later. If Gantz or the captain thought of an angle he hadn't, he'd look like an idiot.

A muscular African-American man pushed past him, almost knocking him over. The man twisted back toward him with his face twisted into a snarl.

"Watch it, man!"

The man glanced at Coombes' belt and the items attached to it. Gun, ammo, badge. This was the *wrong* street corner to be assaulting anyone in a suit. The snarl disappeared and one of his hands flared open in a calming gesture.

"Sorry."

Coombes glared at him and said nothing. This is how it was now, all the time. Anger bubbled under the surface wherever people met. It felt like the city was ready to explode and he couldn't say if it was just L.A., or if the tension spread out across the whole of America. Either it was getting worse, or he was getting old. Neither option gave him any comfort. The veterinarian might not want to run off to the woods and hide, but he sure did.

It's what any good coyote would do.

4

WHEN HE GOT BACK to his desk, he saw that Sato was fully immersed in the photographs he'd sent her. He placed a coffee on the desk next to her mouse and she nodded her thanks. She was in the zone and didn't want to be interrupted so he sat down and flipped through his notebook to where he'd written the number for the hotel. He should have done this earlier in person, and the only reason he hadn't was because of his play with Sato and the security footage. The Metro Grand was eight blocks away, a straight shot down the 110. He debated whether it was worth the drive, but not for long. Coombes called and asked to be connected to whoever dealt with security. There was a click and a man's voice answered immediately.

"Lawson, security office."

"This is Detective Coombes, LAPD. I have a couple of questions regarding the death of one of your guests this morning and about how you run things at the hotel."

"Like *what?*"

The man filled both words with hostility, a whole second-long gap between the words. Like a lot of hotel security, Lawson was probably a washout from the Police Academy with a chip on his shoulder. Coombes pretended not to notice.

"Eric Lyle, one of your porters, had a keycard that he said could open any door. I want to know if he was meant to have that, and how many keycards like that exist."

"Oh, sure." Lawson said, his voice relaxing. "All those guys have one of those. Otherwise, they'd have to keep coming down to the front desk to get a specific keycard which would be a huge waste of time. What was the other question?"

"How many of them are there?"

"Right. Current or archived?"

"What's an archived card?"

"One that's been reported lost or that we didn't get back from someone before they left the hotel. Both guests and employees do it. I think some people keep them like a memento."

"Can an archived card be used to open doors?"

"Nah. Guest keys expire automatically; staff ones are deactivated from my office."

Coombes sighed inwardly. The guy was wasting his time.

"The current cards then, how many?"

"Twenty-two."

"What stops an employee from using one of these cards to steal from guests?"

"Common sense. Each card has a unique code that identifies the owner. If they opened a door and stole some jewels or whatever, then we'd see their name in the door access logs. They'd get busted straight away. This is made very clear to all new employees in order to remove any temptation and to make them look after their cards."

This was the first he was hearing about door access logs.

"Can you bring up the log for room 1208?"

"Sure. Hang tight."

He heard some keys being pressed.

"Okay, Maria Torres prepared the room at 5:40, the guests enter at 9:21 and at 9:35, then we have Eric Lyle at 10:02 and I guess you guys showed up after that."

Coombes wrote this in his notebook, then frowned.

"Wait, the guest entered the room twice?"

"Different key. A guest gets two keys. Usually one for a husband, one for a wife."

Coombes ran his hand back through his hair. The killer must've used the second key, but why would Vandenberg give the killer his second key? It made no sense, not unless he knew his killer. Trusted him. He thought of the items tagged in the hotel room. No keycards.

Some people keep them like a memento.

"The guest in 1208, Mr. Milton Vandenberg, was a regular guest. Are you able to pull up previous door access logs for whatever rooms he stayed in?"

"Uh. Give me a minute."

There was the sound of slow keystrokes and Lawson humming to himself. A one-fingered typer. He pictured big hands, the same blunt finger stabbing down on a cheap keyboard, probably a crime-scene of food around the edges of all the keys. Coombes took a sip of coffee and looked at Sato working on her computer. She was now wearing huge headphones on her head, they completely dwarfed her.

"I have those dates onscreen, what d'you need?"

"All right. I want to know if the same patterns held true on previous occasions. He checks in, he opens his door, then a short time later the second keycard is used. A couple of hours after that, he checks out."

There was a pause, followed by small laugh.

"That's it exactly. You're good."

Vandenberg was a well-known figure, not just in Hollywood, but around the world. He checks into the hotel and goes up to his room alone, then after a discrete interval, a woman follows. The veterinarian. He gave her the second key then waited for her in his room. Giving her the keycard eliminated all risk of them being seen together. A young attractive woman standing at his door knocking would draw the attention of any other guest in the hallway. The old man answering the door with a smile, the whole gig would be up.

Therefore, the keycard. The carefully timed entry.

"All right, sir, that's all."

"Glad to help. Anything else, give me a call."

Lawson was ok once he warmed up, Coombes thought. Once he realized he wasn't being accused of something. It didn't sound like the earlier subterfuge with the security tapes had been discovered yet.

"Thanks."

Coombes hung up. The access logs backed Eric Lyle's story of when he'd been in the room. It remained a possibility that Vandenberg let him in. Lyle would know that the keycard would give him an alibi, but that thinking only tracked if he was the killer instead of a thief, and Lyle did not fit that profile in the slightest.

He took a couple of mouthfuls of coffee.

That only left the veterinarian as a loose end. Coombes opened his browser and went to Facebook. Typed in *Kelly Taylor Los Angeles* and hit enter. A long scrolling list of profiles appeared, both male and female. The list additionally included some Taylor Kellys and variations with other names.

He found the one he wanted in less than thirty seconds.

She was using the same picture on Facebook as she was using on her website. It was a professional photograph that had cost her money, so it made sense that she'd used it on both pages. He clicked on it and looked at her feed. Her last post was from the night before, a picture of a sad-looking dog with a cone on its head and a shaved patch on its front leg. Two likes, no comments. Nothing from her today, however a friend had posted asking her to message her privately.

Someone that knows about her affair, he thought.

Coombes didn't wonder why the person hadn't messaged Kelly privately to make contact. Applying logic like that to social media users got you nowhere. He scrolled down to the Friends section and saw a woman listed as her mother, a Susan Taylor of Glendale, California.

Susan Taylor was in the system. Four outstanding parking tickets all from a street in Highland Park. Likely on the street in front of her daughter's home address. Her license plate gave him her contact details and he punched the numbers into his phone.

"Hello?"

The voice was small, frightened. He glanced at the clock on his screen. After 10 p.m. Late for some people, not for others.

"Mrs. Taylor? I'm Detective Coombes with the Los Angeles Police Department. I need to speak to your daughter."

There was a brief pause, maybe a second.

"She's not here."

Even over the phone, he could tell when someone was lying.

"I *know* she's there, Susan. She's not in trouble, I just need to speak to her."

"Okay."

Jumping to first-name terms always unsettled the public. He heard her walking on a wooden floor, bare feet, not shoes. He'd prefer to do this in person, but it had been a long day and he hadn't been certain she was actually there.

"Can I help you?"

Kelly's voice sounded younger than he was expecting. Perhaps from crying all day, and pretending there was nothing to hide.

"I'm sorry for your loss," he said, and she immediately began to sob. She wasn't Vandenberg's wife but she loved him anyway, therefore he felt sorry for her. Since she wasn't hanging out a dumpster in some dark alleyway, he found his interest in her begin to wane. She was safe, she was unlikely to be the killer, therefore she was just using up his time.

"He didn't do it. He wouldn't."

The mother was standing close by, he could sense it. Listening in to the conversation, ready to close it down if necessary. Her presence was holding back Kelly and he needed to speak to her alone, he needed the nitty-gritty.

"Kelly, can you ask your mother to step away please, we need to talk in private."

There was a shuffling noise right in his ear, followed by muffled voices. He couldn't hear what was said, her hand was over the mouthpiece.

"I'm alone."

"Okay. Assuming that you're right, did Milton ever speak to you about being threatened by someone, anything like that?"

"If he did, he never told me."

It was what he expected. They had limited time together when they met so Vandenberg wouldn't want to waste any of that time talking about some nutcase who sent him an angry letter or email. There were probably hundreds of threats every year.

He made a note in his notebook: *movie studio - threats?*

"I need to know how it worked with the keycard."

"There's a flat rail in the elevator. After he checked in, he would stick the key around the back of the rail with a sticky pad. Same place every time, on the right-hand side. The control panel is on the other side so anyone getting on at the same time would go left. One of the studio's spy movies had used the same trick. It was perfectly safe; the cards have no room number on them. He'd send me a message with the number. I had to wait for the text, I wouldn't know what floor to get off at otherwise."

Somebody knew.

"You tell anyone about the keycard? A friend? Your mom?"

"No, never."

"Are you sure? Take a moment to think about it."

"I don't have to think about it. The only person I told was you."

"All right, tell me about this morning. Where were you?"

Kelly Taylor started sobbing again. She was falling apart.

"I was late. The night before I had to operate on a dog that got hit by a car. It was a long procedure and I was very tired by the time I got home. Usually, I turn in early and I ended up sleeping in. When I checked my cell, I saw no messages from Milton. None saying the room number, none asking where I was. I thought maybe something had come up at the studio or he'd forgotten it was our day, but I went to the hotel anyway. It felt wrong. He'd never forgotten like that before, no matter what was happening at work. When I arrived all the news trucks were there. I knew something had happened." She paused. "I knew he was gone."

The crying started again, louder than before. He knew there was little he could say that would ease her pain and the raw emotion in her sobs was heart-breaking. Coombes had never got used to the pain he encountered on the job. He thought if he ever did then it was probably time to call it a day. He took a deep breath and let it slowly out.

He'd take a dead body over live grief any day.

"I'm very sorry, we're nearly done."

He heard her blowing her nose.

"How was Milton, the last time you saw him?"

"He was happy. He said I made him happy."

Coombes said nothing. There had to be a 50-year age gap between them.

"It's not what you think. I hated all the sneaking around, it felt weird."

"*Weird?*"

"He didn't want our relationship to get out. His wife would divorce him, take half his money. I didn't want that. All I wanted was to spend time together, is that so much to ask?"

"You're hardly the first to have an affair, Miss Taylor."

"You don't understand. He's my father."

A long monotonous tone poured into his ear. She'd hung up on him. He sighed and did the same. Sato was looking at him, eyebrow raised, headphones off one ear.

"She's alive."

"I heard. I'm glad, you know. I hate the dumpster cases."

"She's his daughter."

"Ah." She frowned. "You don't think…"

"I really hope not."

Sato turned back to her screen and moved the headphone back over her ear with the index finger of her left hand. Back in the zone, returning to the suicide pictures. Where did that leave him? Back at the beginning? His two loose ends were tied off for now.

The two missing keycards were his only lead. Both had been used, one by Vandenberg, the other by the killer. If Kelly Taylor hadn't told anyone about the card drop in the elevator, and he couldn't imagine the boss of a movie studio telling his golf buddies about it, then the obvious take-away was that someone had witnessed the card being put into position.

The old man wasn't as smooth as he thought he was. But the kill had been thought out, it wasn't a crime of opportunity. The killer had a fatal dose of diazepam with him and he knew he wasn't going to be interrupted.

If the key had no number on it, the killer was either close enough to Vandenberg during check-in to hear what the number was, or else he got off the elevator with his victim and simply observed what room he'd gone into. Next to him, Sato sat back and looked away off over the top of her monitor, into infinity.

"You done?"

"Yeah, I'm done."

It had taken her one and a half hours to process the 143 crime scene pictures and the task seemed to take a lot out of her. She looked physically and emotionally shattered.

Running an investigation when you were exhausted was a waste of time, it was too easy to miss something important, and the danger was that once you'd processed it you never really wanted to do it again when you were more awake. As far as you were concerned, that task was done. Grace, like most women he knew, was a morning person. Something he was not. Either way, they were going to have to call it a night and hope that tomorrow was more productive.

"Don't keep me in suspense. Did any stand out?"

He watched the slow rise and fall of her chest and her peaceful, calm face. She looked like she was ready to fall asleep. After a moment, she turned her head toward him.

"Unfortunately, Johnny, I think you may be on to something."

"Sorry I ruined your night, Grace."

"If that's what you think happened, then you don't know me at all."

5

COOMBES WAS AT HIS desk the next day by 7:30, he didn't want to waste any time that was left to him before his lieutenant put him on another case. To save additional time, he'd brought a steel vacuum container of coffee from home. He poured a cup and got straight to it, pulling up the hotel's security footage Sato had retrieved the previous afternoon. It was a folder full of clips, close to 80 files. He was going to need that coffee.

His first task was to find footage of Vandenberg arriving at the hotel, checking in, then moving through the hotel to his suite. Once he'd done this, he'd broaden his search to look for likely suspects, first near Vandenberg as he arrived, then, more of a long shot, at any other time.

Three cameras covered the front desk. One pointed toward the desk from about twenty feet back, covering the whole width of the desk and the two people that stood behind it checking people in and out. The other two cameras were mounted high on either side, facing guests. Coombes set up the three feeds in separate windows on his computer then pressed play on each one.

He watched Vandenberg walk up to the desk and smile at Anna Lomax. As she stated in their interview, Vandenberg was on his own. There was no line behind him, there wasn't even a guest at the station to his left. The feed had no sound, so Coombes couldn't tell what was said. The two were familiar, friendly, even.

Vandenberg looked relaxed and happy, not the face of someone who planned on ending things a short time later. He had no luggage, though he did hold something in his right hand. Anna Lomax put a card envelope on the desk in front of Vandenberg.

The keycards.

He took the card envelope, thanked her and moved off toward the elevator. As he turned the shape of the object in his hand changed shape. It was a plastic bag with a wine bottle in it. No other guest had been close enough to him to hear what room he'd been given. Coombes let the desk footage continue to roll for a couple of minutes after Vandenberg left the shot, but still no-one appeared or followed after him.

From a single camera across the lobby, he watched Vandenberg press the button for the elevator then stand back and set the bag carefully on the floor between his feet. He was doing something with his hands in front of him, then he put one in his pants pocket.

Removing a keycard from the envelope to hide in the elevator.

To his surprise, Coombes found there were two cameras inside the elevator, one mounted above the control panel at head height, and another up high in the opposite corner. He was able to see Vandenberg get in, select the 12th floor then move to the side, his back to the wall. The doors started to close then opened again at the last second.

The feed went black on both cameras.

Coombes frowned, both clips were still playing. He paused them, then dragged the playhead back on both videos. One minute the picture was there, the next it cut out. Coombes dragged the playhead forward and the picture came back. Now the elevator was empty. He scrubbed back and forth. There was no picture for four and a half minutes. He scrubbed forward again, watching guests come and go. Kelly Taylor, the old man's daughter, was not one of them. Almost an hour later, the feed went black again. The doors opened on 12, the cameras died and when they came back the elevator was on the first floor and a young couple were getting on.

He searched through the folder of clips. There were no cameras in the hotel hallways, or on the space in front of each elevator. There was a camera facing each fire door on the stairwell, but from a quick skim, nobody had used the stairs all day.

Coombes sat back in his chair, vexed.

He'd expected nothing from the hotel security footage, but this wasn't nothing. The footage had been altered somehow. He had avoided looking at the footage the night before because he'd assumed it would just show Vandenberg going to his room without incident. Whenever an investigation flamed-out like that at the end of a day, the next day never recovered. It was better to go to sleep positive for the day to come than crashing and burning, at which point sleep would be impossible.

Now that he had the files he needed sorted and the timelines in place, he reset them all and played it all back from the beginning. This time, during the long shot of Vandenberg waiting he noticed what could be an elbow behind a pillar to one side of the elevator. Someone waiting and hiding from the camera. He kept the clip playing, after Vandenberg had got on and watched the doors start to close. The figure darted from behind the pillar to catch the door of the elevator. It took less than a second, and it was at the limit of the camera's range, almost out of shot.

It had to be the killer.

Coombes enlarged the long shot of the lobby and slowly scrubbed through the footage to see if there was anything usable. There wasn't, it was garbage. The picture degraded so badly with the enlargement, he couldn't tell if the figure was a man or a woman. He froze the best frame on screen.

It was worse than the Bigfoot clip from the 80s, it could be anyone.

He selected the video from the rear elevator camera and cued it up on the 12th floor, just before the picture went black the second time. The doors opened. No-one was standing in front of the doors waiting, he could see the floor. After a moment, the doors began to automatically close again. As before, a hand caught the edge of the door, interrupting the time-out. As soon as this happened, the cameras had gone black.

This, he suspected, was not a coincidence. The footage hadn't been erased; it hadn't been captured in the first place.

"Johnny. What did we get on the cameras? Is it Jack or Shit?"

He turned and saw Sato staring at his stubble like she wanted to touch it.

"Very perceptive. What we have is a ghost, let me show you."

She leaned in close as he ran through it. Watching the different feeds on screen, listening to what he said and nodding. It wasn't until after he'd finished that she spoke.

"So, either there's a fault with the elevator that cuts the camera when the emergency door release is triggered, or else our killer did something to it. If it's the former, he'd have to be a hotel employee past of present to know about it."

"Right."

"Can you go back to when the hand stops the door on 12?"

He reversed the footage to line it up.

"There," Sato said, pointing.

Coombes saw it for the first time and had to use the slow-motion control to get it back on-screen. The camera had captured four frames of video showing an arm reaching out, wrist extended, before cutting out.

"A diver's watch."

"A *Rolex*," she said. "That's a Submariner. It's iconic."

"Maybe...or a knock-off from a market stall."

"Let's suppose this *isn't* a hotel employee," she said. "After all, the hotel link only works for Vandenberg, not for any of the others. The most likely scenario is that the killer knows the victims, or moves in the same circles as them."

"If the Rolex is real, what does that get us?"

"It's something, Johnny. Isn't it?"

Someone killing off the rich and powerful would be unpopular upstairs without adding that the perpetrator might be another rich person. He turned to Sato. She was still leaning down next to him, her face close enough to kiss. He smiled awkwardly.

"Sorry, Grace. You're right, it's good. A start of a profile."

"Take a break, let me have a look at the video."

His wife hadn't been this close to him in two months.

"Sure."

With the security footage behind him, he was left with no new material to chase down leads so he spent the next half hour arranging for a tech to pay a visit to the hotel to look into the unfortunately timed camera failures. He was told that without an active murder case number it would likely take 10 days before it could be fitted into the work schedule and to call back if that situation changed. By the time the call ended the Vandenberg crime scene photographs were available and he began looking through them. The old man looked whiter than he remembered, like a store mannikin wearing a $10,000 suit.

Nothing fresh was coming to him so he decided to go back to the other cases he'd identified to see if anything new came to him in light of Vandenberg's murder. He pulled the pictures up again, not expecting much. The same grim scenes appeared before him. Rather than a physical print, the digital format allowed him to zoom right in on the smallest detail with only marginal loss in quality.

He sat close to the computer screen, zooming and panning.

The first picture, of Theodore Sutton, was the cleanest. It was just a man's body hanging from a ceiling in front of a panoramic window. The room was stripped bare for renovation work that might now never happen. A single chair lay on its side next to his foot on a wooden floor. Behind him, a cloudless blue sky. The floor was so deeply polished that he could see a partial reflection of the body hanging above it. Nothing else was in shot.

They called it a short drop.

It was almost always from stepping off a chair or a table, whatever first came to hand. Sometimes the drop was only two feet from start to finish. It was definitely not the way to go, Coombes thought. At a bare minimum, the drop should be equal to the height of the person before the fall is arrested. The goal was to fracture the second cervical vertebrae at the base of the skull, not suffocate slowly to death. A characteristic of short drop crime scene photographs, were the scrape marks that would be left wherever the victim's hands and feet could reach as they tried desperately to reverse their decision.

There was no sign of that here. Sutton's feet couldn't reach the floor, his hands couldn't reach the walls. He selected a close-up of Theodore Sutton's head and shoulders. Coombes would've expected to see claw marks around his neck as Sutton fought to relieve the pressure from his belt with his hands. There was nothing.

A possible explanation was that someone had strangled Sutton beforehand, then placed his dead body into the belt loop to frame it as a suicide. It was an explanation that made the most sense to him since there was considerable overlap in the injuries sustained by strangulation and those from hanging victims. Namely, crushing injuries to the structures of the throat and petechial hemorrhaging in the eyes and face.

Without taking his eyes off the screen, he picked up his coffee cup and drank half the contents. The belt was about an inch wide. Coombes reflected that manual strangulation by hands would produce finger marks wider than an inch. A garrote, on the other hand, might be too thin and leave narrower damage, inconsistent with the belt. Some other kind of ligature would have to have been used. It struck him that he was looking at it. The belt. If the killer had used the belt as a garrote, then everything would line up perfectly.

There was no evidence to support this theory, and even to his own ear it sounded fanciful. A belt would require more strength to apply. To be successful, the killer's arms and shoulders would be tremendous. A body builder, or a wrestler, that's the kind of body shape you'd need. He sighed. Anything he found regarding the death of Theodore Sutton would be tainted by their prior relationship. He'd be accused of seeing things he wanted to see because he didn't want to accept a far simpler truth.

That he'd killed himself.

A long time ago, the man in the picture had been a friend to him. A father-figure when his own father had been absent. Since Sutton's death, he'd thought many times about the two summers he'd pretty much lived in their house in Silver Lake. He remembered no signs of depression, or even sadness, but people changed. Life happened. A lot of times, people with depression hid it like it was something shameful or embarrassing. Yet as he looked at the scene there was something almost serene about it.

Sutton's demons, if he had any, were gone now.

He switched back to the wide shot and zoomed in on the knocked over chair that Sutton appeared to have used to climb up. His foot should've been able to reach it. Not enough to save himself, but enough to kick it farther away as they windmilled desperately beneath him. The chair was too close to the body, and Coombes thought it was an affectation, like the wine bottle in Vandenberg's hotel room. A prop, placed there to tell a story.

He moved on to the next suicide, Harry Ryan.

The scene was grim. A businessman sitting at his desk in a luxury leather chair looking straight into the camera lens. The top of his head was missing along the hairline, and the contents were on the wall behind him. Coombes had no sympathy for people who chose to shoot themselves knowing others would have to deal with the aftermath. That a family member could find their body. The visceral contrast between Ryan's death and that of Sutton's was jarring. It was hard to put the two together and see any link between them, and he hadn't. Not then.

Two high profile suicides weren't a pattern, they weren't even a coincidence. Rich people could be depressed the same as anyone else. Everyone had problems, and many weren't money-related. Sato's thought about ill health was a good example. You could be fine one day, then told you had six months to live the next. A dire prognosis made many want to skip to the end. No-one wants to suffer. But six suicides in two months was a high number in such a small section of the community.

A non-pattern, pattern.

Coombes moved the picture so that the top of the image was cropped off and he didn't have to look at it. The top half was so powerful, you saw nothing else. He zoomed in again, this time on the desk in front of Ryan.

The desk was busy and his eye moved slowly along it looking at each item. Left of center was a large iMac, a keyboard, a mouse, and a small wooden stand holding an iPhone at an angle. Along the front, were framed photographs. They faced away from the camera, but Coombes knew they were pictures of the man's wife and children. The two frames featuring Ryan's youngest children were face down on the desk, presumably so that he didn't have to see their faces as he emptied his brains onto the wall. Then there was a desk lamp, cordless headphones, and a large black mug overflowing with pens. He caught a glint in the corner of the image and tracked back for a better look. Hard to say what it was, the angle was all wrong.

He switched to high angle shot of the desk.

Two coins, one stacked on top of the other.

Silver dollars.

A shiver went down Coombes' spine. What were the odds the coins would appear at two suicides six weeks apart? Nobody used them as a form of currency anymore, though plenty remained in circulation.

He opened the file for Gordon Sellers.

The man sat on a floor with his back against a wall. Next to his body was a long gas cylinder, now empty. A hose led from the cylinder to a clear plastic bag that was drawn loosely around Sellers' head. It was known as an exit bag. The bag filled with an inert gas, in this case helium, displacing the oxygen the body needed to survive. Because there's no build-up of carbon dioxide the body suffocates without complaint.

It was a relatively peaceful scene, but Coombes gave that little attention. His eyes moved quickly over the image and soon found what he was looking for on the corner of a small table to the right of Sellers' shoulder. He double-checked all the crime scene photographs.

With the exception of Sutton, every scene featured two silver dollars. It was the killer's signature, and it was enough to take to Gantz.

Coombes opened a notepad app and made a list of all the so-called suicides, the date they died, and the cause of death. He included Sutton, despite the absence of silver dollars at the crime scene, then sat back on his chair to let his mind soak up the details.

Theodore Sutton	10/12	hanging
Harry Ryan	10/18	self-administered GSW
Gordon Sellers	10/25	inert gas exit bag
Simon Keehan	11/01	cyanide
William Morgan	11/15	drowning
Milton Vandenberg	11/22	drug overdose

After close to a minute, he pulled up his calendar and looked at the dates.

All the deaths occurred on a Friday, except for Sutton, who died on a Saturday. He sighed. A day out. Again, Sutton didn't fit. Teddy had been good to him and he wasn't ready to give up on him just yet. Coombes wondered why he preferred the idea of his friend's father dying by serial killer opposed to taking his own life. Surely a suicide was better than a murder?

There was something else wrong with the dates.

It was obvious that a name was missing between Keehan and Morgan.

6

PACIFIC PICTURES WAS LOCATED on a strip of land next to the L.A. River between Griffith Park and Glendale. There was no archway entrance, or Golden Era movie magic about the place, it was simply an industrial unit that could just as easily have been selling windshield wiper motors. He reversed his detective car, currently a Dodge Charger, into a space facing the office. A row of parked vehicles sat directly outside. Sixteen vehicles total, twelve cars, four SUV. Low-end Far East brands for the most part, the kind that ran for a million miles without complaint, with a couple of BMWs and Audis making up the rest. In Los Angeles, homicide cases always came down to automobiles in one form or another, and it was worth keeping an eye on what people were driving. Nobody took the bus to a killing. Nobody walked.

He turned to Sato.

"Is this what an eight-billion-dollar company looks like?"

"They look set to burn the building down for the insurance."

"You got that right."

Coombes cut the engine and the push of chilled air from the air conditioning came to a halt. He always waited until the last moment before turning off the engine. As long as the engine was running, he could sit in a car all day. The cool air and vibration relaxed him. He swung the door open and stepped out onto the asphalt. The surface was in poor condition, he could feel it through his shoes. He closed the top button of his suit jacket then walked toward the entrance, Sato taking quick steps to catch him up.

A man in his twenties with prominent Adam's apple and a piece of metal in his nose looked up. His eyes widened in alarm as he saw the two of them standing there. Coombes' suit jacket covered his badge and gun, but that never mattered. After eight years on the job, he might as well have LAPD tattooed on his forehead in inch-high letters.

He asked to speak to Vandenberg's assistant and was escorted down a hallway to a meeting room to wait. He guessed that the room was used for internal meetings only, for sure they didn't bring producers or actors into a place like this. A long table divided the room in two, one end piled high with what he supposed were scripts, and the other end had a prime view of the cars parked out front. Although there were plenty of seats, Coombes remained standing, his attention alternating between the window and the door. Sometimes people made a run for it, and it never seemed to be the ones he expected.

"What do you hope to get from this?" Grace asked.

"A confession."

She laughed. "And short of that?"

"The usual. Find a lead, eliminate dead ends."

"I just figure it's a bit of a long shot."

"A couple of years ago I heard a story about an actor. A famous one, not somebody you never heard of. Anyway, she was really beautiful, was always on those hottest lists in men's magazines, but she was never seen with any men. People started to talk, you know? Then she starts dating the plainest man you could imagine, looked like he might try sell you cheese in a deli. Guess why?"

"Because he asked her on a date?"

"Correct. Her looks had been scaring men off for years. Nobody thought they were good enough. The bottom line is, it's always worth asking. Maybe you don't get the answer you want, maybe it leads you in a new direction, but you can't do this job typing on a keyboard. Murder is a people business. You need to see their face."

"Johnny, look at me."

He turned and looked at her. There was a smile in her eyes, they had a sparkle. She was cracking herself up.

"What?"

"*It's always worth asking.*"

"You disagree?"

"In this case, no I don't. I like your story. Although I do wonder why she always waited to be approached, was she not able to talk to men first?"

"Is that what you do, Grace?"

"When the man is too stupid to recognize a flirt, you have to. But I like how special I feel when a man makes the first move. It's romantic. It makes me feel attractive and special."

She was making strong eye contact, which wasn't easy given her height. Her head was tilted way back looking up at him. He said nothing. He didn't know what she wanted.

"I'm guessing your wife made the first move, huh?"

The door opened and a woman walked in full of energy, like she had better things to be doing than talk to a couple of dumb cops. Her hair was piled up on top of her head in a neat bun and her clothes looked like they cost more than most of the cars through the window.

"I'm Carly Rogers, I was Mr. Vandenberg's executive assistant, which I guess means I drew the short straw."

She smiled pleasantly enough, like she was telling a joke, but he knew the truth when he heard it. He wouldn't be much of a cop if he didn't. They sat down. He took out a notebook and a pen and turned it to a blank page.

"All right. It took us longer than I would have liked getting here, and I can tell you've got other things to do, so if you don't mind, we'll get right to it. A bit of background first. How was Mr. Vandenberg to work for? Was he well-liked? Was he aggressive? I'm just trying to get an accurate idea of who he was in case that's relevant."

"He could be tough to work for sometimes, sure. He was the boss, there was a lot of pressure on him. He never said *please* or *thank you*, he never said *good job* or *you look nice today*. When you did well, he would sometimes give a small nod. That was it."

"Let me put it this way," Coombes said, repositioning his chair so he could cross his legs so that his left shoe was resting on his right knee. "When the news broke that he had passed away, were people smiling and laughing, or were they sad?"

"We were upset, of course we were. We still are. Truthfully, we're also worried about our jobs. The studio was close to collapse when he arrived. Everything we achieved is because of him. His investment, his leadership, the people he brought in. That's all at risk now."

"So, you never saw anyone happy by what happened?"

"No, never. We're like a family here."

Coombes looked around the room at framed posters for the studio's movies that lined the walls. Pacific Pictures' output was exclusively violent and most of the posters featured an explosion, not to mention actors holding guns. The posters for the *Stick Shift* movies dominated but another franchise about spies caught his eye. The inspiration for Vandenberg's hotel keycard switch. He debated whether such information was worth watching eight terrible movies to find out. He thought not.

Coombes turned back to Carly Rogers.

"Mr. Vandenberg was high profile and outspoken. I assume that a few people along the way sent him mail, threatening him."

He saw something in her eye, a flash of recognition. Disgust.

"He got mail like that. Mostly from people upset when they hadn't been hired. Some became angry, you know? We never passed stuff like that on to Mr. Vandenberg, he made it clear early on that he didn't want to know. Some got angrier when he didn't respond. I wondered if that was the best way to go, if a simple reply might have calmed them down. Nobody likes to be ignored."

"What did you do with this correspondence?"

"At first we just deleted it or trashed it, but one of our security people advised us to keep it, so for the last seven years that's what we've done."

"Good. We'll need to see it."

Her face twisted nervously.

"You don't think he killed himself, do you? Why else would you be here?"

"We're here to make sure we get it right."

Sato spoke for the first time.

"How many people work at Pacific Pictures, Miss Rogers?"

"About a hundred, indirectly. Most of the crew are self-employed, have their own LLCs, same with the scriptwriters. It was one of the changes that Mr. Vandenberg brought in. Studio runs like a production company, with a low fixed overhead. Unless we hire someone, they cost us nothing. Most end up being exclusive to us anyway, they like our flexibility."

"Is there more to Pacific Pictures than this one office?"

"What were you expecting?"

"You don't have a lot? Fake buildings, sets, studio space, tours?"

"Our movies are shot on location. Canada, South America, Asia. Our last was shot in South Africa. The locations are part of the movie. If we find a good location, we'll even write it into the script. There's no need for plywood buildings with a $200 million budget."

"Wow," Sato said. "That's a lot of money."

"We like to give people something worth the ticket price."

Coombes smiled to himself. Grace was an expert at drawing people in. Her process was always the same. She'd act dumb and the interviewee, usually male, would relax and enjoy filling her in. Then she'd hit them with the real question.

"Has anyone recently left under a cloud?"

Carly Rogers' face soured.

"About six months ago, one of our writers."

"Name?"

"Jake Curtis." She pointed at one of the spy posters. "He wrote all of the *Firestorm* movies. Our second-biggest earner, losing him was a big loss for us."

Coombes smiled. He liked Curtis for it already. The staging of Vandenberg's hotel room fit with the killer being a writer, someone aware of the importance of details and what they could tell you if they were presented in the right way. He took over the interview again.

"Why was he fired?"

"He tripled his price and wanted double digit points off the front end. *Nobody* gets points off the front end, never mind double digits. Mr. Vandenberg laughed him out the office, told him he'd go back to Olive Garden and find another writer. That's where-"

Her mouth popped open in a little O, remembering something.

"Let me guess," Coombes said, wearily. "He told Vandenberg he was going to kill him on the way out the door?"

She nodded, then began to sob.

"People say things they don't mean all the time, don't they?"

"Tell me what he said."

"I don't like to say, it was disgusting."

"Miss Rogers, there's nothing we haven't heard, okay? A good day for me is one where I don't stand in someone's brains by mistake. Harsh language I can deal with."

She took a moment to assemble the words in her head.

"He said, 'I'm going to f-word kill you, you f-word old c-word.'"

Coombes laughed. "Writers, eh? They're a colorful crowd."

She used the back of her hand to wipe tears off her cheeks and nodded again.

Grace angled her cell phone toward him with a picture of Jake Curtis. He was young, tan, muscular, and had a beard like a swarm of bees. Next to his name was his age, 26, and his estimated net worth, which was about 500 times Coombes' yearly take-home.

"Did Mr. Curtis send threatening correspondence?"

She looked like she was going to be sick.

"That would be one way of putting it."

"What did he send?"

"A pig's head."

"No kidding," Coombes said, impressed. "How'd you know he sent it?"

"He sent it by courier. His name was on the receipt."

He couldn't decide if Jake Curtis was an idiot or a sociopath. He'd made no attempt to hide his identity, even though he could safely assume they'd know who'd sent it. A pig's head. It was ballsy, for sure, but hardly likely to make Vandenberg change his mind about giving him more money. It wasn't a spontaneous act, either. It would take time to source the head, it wasn't like an angry e-mail that could be sent in a blind rage in a matter of moments.

"When was this? Six months ago, just after he left?"

"No. Last week."

He glanced at Grace and she nodded.

"Why would he do that after all this time?"

Carly Rogers thought about it for a moment, then flinched.

"We put out a casting call for the new *Firestorm* movie. First one he didn't write. I guess he found out and got upset. I should've thought about that before, but I didn't."

The issue was clearly still causing Curtis pain. In six months, it didn't seem like he'd moved on at all. The franchise was his baby, and it had been taken away from him.

Grace cleared her throat.

"Who replaces Mr. Vandenberg as CEO?"

"I guess Bud Kopek, he's second in command. The board will have to approve it first, then approve a new chief operating officer to fill his space."

Coombes uncrossed his legs and stood up. He'd heard enough. Corporate structure bored him. They had a strong lead and he didn't want to waste time on some suit moving to a different desk.

"We're going to need an address for Curtis."

"Of course."

They went back through to the front office. Carly Rogers copied down an address from memory onto a blank Rolodex card. While she did this, Coombes turned to look at the man with a piece of metal through his nose. It looked like shrapnel. Who would want something like that? It boggled his mind what people did to their bodies. Carly passed him the writer's address and he gave her his business card and asked her to send all of the threatening correspondence.

He paused in the doorway to put his sunglasses on, then stepped out onto the short path that led back to the parking lot and their vehicle. Next to him, Sato was silent.

"Jesus, Grace. Just say it, whatever it is."

"You shut me down, Johnny. I wasn't finished with her."

"What? The corporate stuff?"

"Yes!"

He unlocked the doors of his Charger and they got in. The car's interior was probably over a hundred and twenty. He started the engine and cranked up the air conditioning.

"You think this is about someone wanting the old man's job?"

"No. I think this is about you not wanting your friend's father to be a suicide."

"I'll give you that." he said, his fingers spread open in front of an air vent. "What I don't get is that it took her ten minutes to remember that someone threatened to kill Vandenberg. You'd thing that might've stuck more in her mind, wouldn't you?"

"Maybe people said it to him all the time. Look at the movies they make. People dying left and right. I bet he was a tyrant to work for. Staff were probably doing cartwheels down the corridor when they heard he was dead."

"I'll ask for a list of *everyone* who sent him a severed head."

"You're insufferable, Johnny. Do you know that?"

Coombes smiled. Other people had said the same thing, one of them had married him. Sure, he was prickly on the outside, but he was funny and that went a long way.

7

THE FIRST THING HE did when he got back to the PAB was run Jake Curtis' name through the criminal database. It was more out of habit than hope. Another box to check in a sequence that would no-doubt end with him being excluded from the investigation. As he hit enter, he visualized the message that typically appeared saying there were no results, but instead found himself looking at a long list of entries.

Coombes smiled.

Twelve counts of grand theft auto, four assaults, three of extortion, and one indecent exposure charge involving a girl of twelve. Despite all the evidence against him, Curtis had walked on every charge. The record showed he'd get arrested, charged, booked, held overnight, then get released within a day. None of the cases made it to trial due to lack of evidence or recanted testimony. It was a pattern he'd seen many times before. Every time a criminal got a free pass, they thought they were invincible and the crimes escalated until there was enough to put them away. Nobody got scared straight anymore, it was a myth.

Except he had never been convicted.

Curtis had moved from Miami to L.A. and reinvented himself. That was something he didn't see too often, certainly not the level of success that Jake Curtis had achieved. Fresh coast, fresh start.

Coombes began to look through the list of charges.

It appeared that Curtis and his brother Trent had run a classic car theft operation in and around Miami where there was both plentiful supply and demand for such vehicles. The cars were old enough not to be fitted with trackers or immobilizers, yet rare enough to maintain high residual values. The brothers' success brought them to the attention of law enforcement, and that scrutiny eventually made it impossible for them to operate.

Coombes picked up his phone and dialed the number for the Miami PD. The crimes were almost a decade old, there was a chance that the person he wanted no longer worked there. When the call connected, he asked if a Sergeant Gale still worked there. He was told she did, and was now a Lieutenant. He explained the subject of his call and waited to be put through.

"All right. What's that little shit done now?"

Coombes laughed. He liked Gale already.

"You remember him, then?"

"Oh, big time. For a while he was in and out the station every couple of weeks. I have relatives I've seen less often than that punk. So, what did he do?"

"He's a person of interest in a homicide."

Gale sighed.

"I guess it was only a matter of time before he killed again."

"Who did he kill in Miami?"

"His father. Pushed him down a flight of stairs."

"That's not in the database."

"He was a juvenile at the time and that stuff is all sealed or purged. Whatever you're looking at, half of it is missing, trust me. In the case of his father, he was brought in but not arrested or charged. He's one of those Teflon guys, nothing seems to stick. Whenever we arrested him before, he always hid behind his brother. Each would blame the other for their crimes, it was a reverse alibi setup. Smart for a couple of street kids. Instead of backing each other they did the opposite, choking the investigation. Each time it could've been either one, but not both. Back then, no one could tell them apart."

"All right. So, his brother was never a suspect?"

"His alibi was airtight. He was incarcerated at Okeechobee at the time."

"What was suspicious about his father's death?"

"He fell face-first down stairs. Typically, we see people fall backward going down stairs, forward going up. Also, it looked like his neck had been broken after the fall. Wade Curtis was a big man and he could easily have overpowered his teenage son. We figured Jake pushed him at the top then finished him off at the bottom while he was incapacitated."

"No alcohol or drugs in his system?"

"Actually, yes to both, but that was just who Wade was, he probably hadn't been sober for 30 years. In any case, the levels were not enough to make him blackout and fall to his death. Being honest, Wade was a piece of shit and probably beat both of his boys and their mom on a regular basis. He was also the main suspect in three ongoing rape cases."

"Did that influence the investigation?"

Gale was silent for several seconds.

"Yeah, I guess it did. Nobody was trying too hard to solve his case. The world was a better place without him in it, you know? The night he died, some of us hit a bar and had a few drinks. We weren't broken up at all."

It was a point of view Coombes could easily understand.

"Is the Wade case still open?"

"No. It was ruled accidental. One of his shoelaces was undone. It seemed plausible that he'd stood on his own shoelace and tripped himself up."

Gale wasn't reading anything from notes, this was from memory. He could tell by the way she was speaking. Remembering details from a case this old meant there was something about it that got under her skin. That something was wrong.

"You don't believe that?"

"I think Jake undid the shoelace after to make it look like an accident. In the crime scene photographs, the lace still carried the indentation from having been tied. If the old man had forgotten to tie it that morning then the indentation would have come out from being untied overnight. In fact, I'd imagine the lace would've snapped. Then there was internal bleeding. The M.E. estimated Wade bled for several minutes before he died, which doesn't track with him breaking his neck during the fall."

"Like Jake had a few things to say before he killed him."

"*Exactly.*"

He wound up the call with Gale and disconnected.

All the pieces were coming together nicely. Staging a death as an accident wasn't a million miles from staging one as a suicide. Fifteen years old, and Jake Curtis was already creating narratives for cops to follow. It was pretty impressive, and it was hardly surprising that Curtis had gone on to write movies.

Coombes made some notes from the call while the details were still fresh. He had enjoyed speaking to Gale, there was a warmth that had come down the phone line from her and he didn't want the buzz to end too soon.

8

Coombes sat on a barstool, staring into space. He'd arrived half an hour early for a meeting with Olivia Sutton and was using that time to sort through his thoughts on the investigation. Of the deaths so far, Theodore Sutton and Milton Vandenberg's deaths felt different to the others. Sutton's, because it didn't fit the pattern, and Vandenberg's because of the killer's rush to expose the death. Either one potentially indicating a personal connection between the victim and killer.

He looked up as Olivia stepped through the door.

She was wearing a white shirt, navy suit jacket, and a tight red skirt that showed the muscle of her thigh as she walked. She was stunning. He stood as she approached, a smile already on his face.

"Olivia. My god, you look amazing."

"And you look like shit, Johnny, but I always liked that about you."

He smirked. She'd never hidden the appeal of his wrong-side-of-the-tracks heritage. He made a show of checking his watch.

"I don't have to be back at my desk for a couple of hours if you want to take this somewhere private."

"Still a creep, eh? How's that working out for you?"

"I made Detective 3 last year. RHD."

"Robbery Homicide. That's a big deal, well done. I guess that's why I'm here, isn't it? Although I don't see how dad's passing is anything but his own fault."

"We'll get to that in a moment."

The bartender appeared. Young, long greasy hair, bad teeth.

"Help you, miss?"

Olivia ignored the bartender and made an awkward face at Coombes.

"I'm not allowed alcohol during work hours."

"Likewise," he said, his fingernail tapping a glass of Scotch.

"Water's fine," she said, her gaze shifting to the cooler units under the counter. "The Evian. Leave it in the bottle, unopened."

Coombes sighed inwardly. Meeting her in a bar close to her work was meant to put her at ease; the informal setting combined with the casual intimacy of a drink, was all supposed to make her open up. So far, it was for nothing. He might as well be interviewing in her office. Coombes paid for her water then guided her over to an empty booth he'd identified minutes earlier. He chose the far side of the table so that when she sat opposite, she was facing a wall and away from anyone that might recognize her.

He wanted her undivided attention.

She unfastened her suit jacket and lowered herself onto the bench seat and, after split second, he did the same. The top four buttons of her shirt were unfastened and he was treated to an extensive view of her cleavage.

She had never been more beautiful and it was obvious to him that she knew it. Four buttons. That was one too many, that extra button, that was just to mess with him. Remind him what he was missing, which was more than he remembered. *Possibly had work done*, he thought bitterly. She was certainly in the right window of age and wealth for cosmetic surgery.

Olivia straightened her back and light from the window fell evenly across her face. She had a dark halo around the pale blue irises of her eyes, a feature known as a limbal ring. He felt himself drawn to her once again, like he was tumbling into a black hole.

No man could resist those eyes.

"All right, Johnny, why am I here?"

"When was the last time you saw your father, and how did he seem?"

She nodded, encouraged by his businesslike tone and strong eye contact.

"It was two days before he passed. Just an ordinary day. He was having a problem with one of his contractors and was shouting a lot. Swearing. His face was red, sweaty. But he lived for all that. It was like oxygen to him, it puffed him up. I'd seen it a million times before, and didn't much care to see it again."

"Where was this?"

"At his office in Century City."

"When you heard what happened, what was your first reaction?"

"Shock. Denial. It wasn't true, it couldn't be true." She shrugged. "The whole cliché. As time passed, it seemed less and less surprising. I still didn't want it to be true, but if I got anything from dad it was the ability to see things the way they were, not the way I wanted them to be. Within a week, I'd accepted it."

Her answer seemed a little stale, but he wasn't the first cop she'd spoken to and he supposed she'd also talked about it endlessly with friends. Repeating similar lines over and over removed emotion that would've lain behind them first time around. He was coming to the party late. It was what it was. He changed tack.

"How was his health? Was he okay?"

"Johnny, you remember dad. If anything was wrong with him the last thing he'd do is tell me about it. Far as I know, he was as strong as an ox."

Coombes nodded. "How's Nicky?"

Olivia glanced over her shoulder as if her brother was somewhere in the bar. She took a deep breath, then let it slowly out, her eyes coming back to connect with his.

"I'm sorry for the way he came at you the other day. He was a lot closer to dad than I was. He worked with him 24-7. You can't imagine what that's like. He looks at this empty desk all day. Before it was like there was an angry tiger there, now, just silence. Nicky has not come to terms with it. He's so angry, he might never."

He sat back in his seat, like he was imagining the silent office, or the angry tiger, when really, he was reacting to was the way she spoke when she was talking about her brother.

"What happens with the business?"

Her gaze became, sharp, piercing.

"Split straight down the middle. Fifty-fifty."

Coombes said nothing. Nicolas Sutton already owned fifty percent of the business, the only person to gain from their father's death was sitting across the table from him. A darkness crept into her face; the mask of beauty forgotten.

"You don't think he killed himself, do you?"

"I liked your dad. He was good to me. Officially, there's no investigation into his death. I just took a look to make sure everything was as it should be. *Because we used to be friends.*"

He delivered the last line with extra emphasis.

Her cheeks turned scarlet; her teeth clenched tight together in an effort to control her curling lip. A fire burned inside her, and he could see it in her eyes. She stood abruptly and leaned across the table toward him, supporting her upper body on spread-open fingers. Her mouth barely opened as she spoke.

"Drop it. He killed himself, there's no goddam mystery."

She was inches from his face now, eyes filled with fury. Close enough, that her emotion could be mistaken for passion. The hairs on the back of his neck stood up as he remembered teenage Olivia and her intense physical demands. Her change in demeanor was both surprising and satisfying. Their interview wasn't for nothing after all.

She spoke again, loud enough for half the bar to hear.

"I know why you're doing this, John. I'm not stupid. You and me? *Ancient* history. I'm not interested, okay? Call me again and I'll file harassment charges."

She stomped angrily away, suit jacket spread wide on either side of her arms, a crackling bad energy surrounding her body. He wasn't the only person to watch her leave, her raised voice and stunning looks had guaranteed that. When the street door swung shut, faces turned back to him, the cause of the whole scene. One of them, a man about the same age as him, burst out laughing.

Coombes turned away to stop the anger rising.

He didn't like being told to drop a case. Not by his partner, not by his lieutenant, and not by a relative of the deceased who was probably fifty million dollars richer as a result of it. The Sutton property empire, the mansion in Silver Lake, the beach house...it all added up. But to what? Murder? He knew one thing for sure, Olivia could not have killed her father on her own. Teddy Sutton weighed 220 pounds minimum, there was no way she could've lifted him into that noose.

Had she mistaken his interest as a demand for some of the inheritance?

I know what you did, cut me in or I spill the beans.

He sighed and slowly rotated his glass of Scotch.

It had been a mistake to question her in a bar, alone. Whatever his thinking had been at the time, the scenario fitted all too well with her version of events, which she'd been kind enough to detail. That he was using her father's death to forcibly reinsert himself in her life, and that his investigation was little more than an excuse for the unwanted romantic interest of a predator with a badge.

The extra button.

Olivia hadn't dressed provocatively for his benefit. She'd done it to be remembered by other bar patrons. She'd come here with a plan to neutralize him, it hadn't just evolved because of the way the conversation had turned.

To gift wrap it, she'd caused a scene as she left that implied impropriety on his part. It was the kind of story that the media would eat up.

For now, his investigation into the Sutton suicide was over.

He left his untouched fifteen-dollar Scotch and Olivia's five-dollar water on the table and walked out into the street and the unforgiving Californian sunshine. His cell phone rang.

"How's your *hot date* going?"

Grace's voice dripped with amusement. Even his partner suspected his motivation.

"Not good. I forgot something about Olivia that was pretty important."

"What's that?"

"She's a lot smarter than I am."

Grace laughed and he closed his eyes, listening to it. He only heard her laugh properly over the phone, in person she covered her mouth with her hand like she was coughing or sneezing. He smiled. It was a beautiful laugh and it picked him up, hearing it.

"Anyway," she said. "Pacific Pictures came through for us on the threatening correspondence. Let's just say our suspect pool for Milton Vandenberg just got a *lot* longer. We're going to need some boots on this one, Johnny."

9

JAKE CURTIS'S HOME WAS hidden from view by a ten-foot wall and a metal gate made from inch thick bars with sheet metal sandwiched in the middle to prevent anyone from seeing inside. It was a fortress. Coombes sighed inwardly. Before he worked Robbery Homicide, the majority of his suspects had doors you could knock on. When they answered, there was no scope for hiding anything or fleeing the scene. *They were right there.* When you dealt with a home owner through a speaker, they had plenty of time to prepare. Get their story straight, hide the body, flush their drugs. Their properties were so large it was impossible to tell if they were occupied. Some speaker systems, the owners could answer using their cell phones from anywhere in the world.

The rich had it good.

Coombes had been watching the property since six a.m. from the driver's seat of his personal vehicle, parked on the outside curve of a turning circle opposite Curtis' gate. It was now close to eight thirty, and the only thing that had happened in that time was that two private security cars and a West Bureau SUV had approached him to ask him his business. After another ten minutes had crawled past, Sato arrived in a plain-wrap Ford Taurus from the motor pool. He parked his car on Franklyn Canyon Drive and hoped it would still be there when he came back for it.

When he returned to the Ford, he saw that Sato had moved over into the passenger seat and that her shoeless feet were up on the dashboard. He glanced at her feet as he got in behind the wheel. Sato had said nothing at all about Curtis since the day before, yet it was obvious to him that she did not share his suspicion.

"What are you thinking?"

"I know you've got a hard-on for this guy, Johnny, but Curtis is all wrong for this. He put his name on the receipt for that package, he *wanted* Vandenberg to know who sent it and didn't care what the consequences were. Do you really think he's going to kill him a week later? That's like confessing to the crime before it happened."

He nodded; he couldn't disagree with her.

"All I know is some people get lost in their anger, it consumes them. One week he figures the pig's head is enough, the next, only the old man's death will satisfy him."

"If we are looking only at Vandenberg, I could see it. But why would Curtis kill these other people first. If it was the other way around, you could argue that he got a taste for it. As it is you're either saying he killed four or five people *then* his true target *or* he happened to be a serial killer already, in which case the pig's head makes no sense."

"There's a lot of things wrong with the situation, Grace. We just follow leads wherever they go. If you've got some new investigative method, I'd love to hear it."

They were silent for a moment before Sato spoke again.

"You always say it's *never* the first suspect. It's your mantra."

Coombes looked across and saw she was angry.

"You actually listen to what I say?"

Her face relaxed. "Just enough to wing it."

He smiled. It was true, it was never the first suspect, not at their level. Cases where the killer was found covered in blood next to their victim were mopped up by local uniforms. They did happen, just not in Homicide Special.

The over-the-top nature of Curtis' mail package stuck in his throat. It was too much, it called attention to itself. Sato was right, it *was* like a confession.

But what if it was something else? The writer had to know he'd come to their attention, his threat to kill Vandenberg would be remembered. Sending the pig's head beforehand demonstrated that he was a buffoon, not to be taken seriously. He'd left his name on the receipt, no one that stupid could be responsible for flawlessly killing four or five people.

Wasn't it more likely that they were suicides after all?

Coombes could practically hear Curtis' lawyer in court, arguing for mistrial.

"What's the plan, Johnny? We can't sit here all day."

"Suppose for a moment that Curtis is the killer."

"All right."

"So far, he's made only one mistake, the TV remote control. The guy's good. All things being equal, he might not make any more mistakes, maybe that was it."

"Go on."

"I figure it's time to shake the tree, see what falls out."

"How does sitting here accomplish that?"

"Before you arrived, a local security guy came to chase me away. I badged him and told him to get lost, I didn't spare his feelings. A short while later, another guy appeared. Older, more senior, with pectorals like hub caps. Same story, he told me to leave or get towed. When the badge didn't work, I introduced him to my Glock and he left. The next guy was a real cop and the two of us had a good laugh at the rent-a-cops. Point is, Curtis *knows* we're here, I assume there's a camera somewhere, and he's trying to get us to leave."

"I'm just dying to know what we do now."

"Isn't it obvious? We leave."

He started the car and gunned the engine, foot flat on the floor. A cloud of smoke rose in the air and they shot off down the street. Sato gripped the door handle tight, her mouth hanging open. At the junction with Beverly Drive, he yanked the wheel to the left and the back of the Ford swung wide before the tires began to bite. He braked sharply and carried out a fast three-point turn in front of a driveway.

A silver Koenigsegg was parked at the side of the road and he pulled in behind it. Their vehicle was almost completely hidden by the sports car's huge rear wing, it was perfect.

Sato lowered her feet off the dashboard onto the floor.

"Jesus, Johnny. I almost pissed my pants."

He watched the end of Desford Drive, waiting for movement.

"I give him ten minutes."

"You're a certifiable lunatic, do you know that?"

He shot her a look and saw that her face was flushed and her hair was all over the place. She was breathing fast through her mouth, but it wasn't anger he saw in her eyes, it was something else. Something he couldn't place. He turned to look back through the windshield. After five minutes, the red nose of a Ferrari pushed carefully into the junction.

Curtis was leaving.

He let a moment pass before he pulled out and began to follow. The curving road helped mask their tail, though it also meant the Ferrari was out of sight for up to thirty seconds. Curtis drove slowly, like he was driving home after a night's drinking and wanted to avoid being pulled over. He was rattled, but the longer he drove without incident, the more confidence would return. Coombes overtook a pickup, then another two cars. He couldn't afford to trail behind the writer on city streets.

They cut slowly across to West Hollywood and joined the 101 heading south. The Ferrari could probably hit 200 mph, but in L.A. traffic it was lucky to do 50. Almost an hour had passed and they'd learned nothing. Coombes began to close up on him. They switched to the 110, then off, onto West 4th street. They needed gas; the needle was pointing at the last line of the gauge. The traffic ground to a halt. They were directly behind Curtis now. He didn't care if the writer knew they were there.

"He's going to see us, Johnny."

"I *want* him to see us. I'm shaking the tree."

Above them the light changed and they moved forward again. Slow and steady, 14 mph. The Ferrari was so close that he couldn't see the bottom of Curtis' vehicle. No more than a shopping cart width apart now. The writer's eyes moved between the road ahead and his rearview constantly. Coombes smiled, big enough for his teeth to show.

Next to him, Grace sighed, exasperated.

They were approaching City Hall now. In front, he saw Curtis talking in an animated manner, presumably over a hands-free cell phone. Maybe calling 911 to report his terrible driving. The idea of being pulled over by a black and white while trailing a potential serial killer amused him. Curtis finished his call and returned to the back and forth between the road and his mirrors. If he was the killer, he'd know why he was being followed.

That his pattern of kills had been identified.

Another light changed and Curtis began to slow, then stop. Coombes pulled up behind him. The writer was watching him carefully in his rearview. As soon as he stopped, Curtis hit the gas. In less than a second, he crossed the intersection. A second after that, the intersection was filled with vehicles from the cross street. In the gaps between passing cars Coombes saw that the Ferrari had disappeared. Grace snorted.

"You kind of had that coming, Johnny."

Coombes said nothing. He didn't care that much. The whole point of the exercise was to let Curtis know that they were on to him so that he'd start to panic, maybe make some mistakes. Because so far, he was doing a fine job running a masterclass in the perfect crime. The next step would be to bring him in and question him, now that he was softened up.

When they got back underway there was no sign of the Ferrari. There was nothing else to do but return to base and figure out the best approach for taking another run at Curtis. They continued on in silence for several minutes. It wasn't unusual for Grace to be quiet, but this time he sensed judgement. In her eyes, he'd made a fool of himself, of both of them, and she wasn't happy.

His cell phone rang. "Coombes."

"This is Block. What's your current location?"

"We're a minute out. Curtis gave us the slip."

"What a coincidence. He's sitting in my office."

"He lawyered up?"

"That's right. There's some kind of recording, you know the deal. Get back here and have Sato set up a laptop in the meeting room and let's see what we're dealing with."

"You got it."

Coombes disconnected and brought Grace up to speed while he parked. A recording. He knew what that meant, Jake Curtis had an alibi. Which in turn meant they were back to square one with no suspects. He found that he wasn't at all surprised. When something was too good to be true, it usually was. His mood nosedived anyway. He *wanted* it to be Curtis, it was like a hunger he couldn't feed.

10

WHEN HE GOT BACK to the detective bureau, five people were waiting for him in the captain's office; Block, Gantz, Curtis, and two others. Block turned to him as he entered the room, his face showing irritation at having to wait for him to arrive.

"Coombes, this is Deputy District Attorney Rachel Boyd, Jake Curtis you'll no doubt recognize, and William Fielding here is his legal counsel in this matter."

He nodded at Boyd and Fielding. The lawyer began to speak.

"My client has become aware of your interest in him and has surmised that it relates to the unfortunate death of Milton Vandenberg. We're here to make sure you don't waste any time pursuing the wrong man."

Curtis was the only person in the room sitting down. He was seated at a table the captain had at the back of his room; his hands folded together on top of it. He looked smug. Perhaps remembering the moment when he lost them at the intersection. Up close, the writer's beard was something to see and Coombes stared openly at it for a moment.

"You have a recording that gives you an alibi?"

He addressed Curtis directly, ignoring Fielding.

"That's right, from my home security system. The whole of last month. You can see where I was and when, it's all timestamped. The cameras roll 24-7, it's not motion-activated. After a month footage is archived, after two it's deleted. I am offering a month because a day's worth might not make sense."

"All right." Coombes said, turning to Boyd. "Where does the District Attorney's Office fit into all this?"

"There are certain *legal issues* arising from the footage that Mr. Curtis is offering that he wants set aside for the greater good."

"Specifically?"

Boyd sighed, her eyes drifting down to the floor.

"Use of a controlled substance, providing alcohol to a minor, and sexual activity with a person below the age of consent."

"You're kidding, right? You're going to rubber-stamp statutory rape?"

Her eyes zipped back up to meet his.

"The would-be victim was 21 days from legal age at the time, and Mr. Curtis claims he was unaware. You know how that goes. We'd be setting the City's money on fire trying to bring a successful prosecution. Of all the deals I'll have to make today, this will be the easiest, believe me. Bottom line, the deal's worth taking."

Coombes turned and glared at Curtis. The writer's face gazed blankly back, yet somehow there was amusement there, just beneath the surface. Curtis leaned way back on his chair, like he was sunbathing, his hands cupping the back of his head.

"If you prefer, you can reject the deal. I will then provide an edited version for the day in question only, then delete all the other data to prevent malicious prosecution. The edited version gives my alibi, but you're not going to like it too much."

"It's not Detective Coombes' decision," Block said. "We're taking the deal."

Jake Curtis ignored the captain and smiled at him. Coombes fought the urge to grab him by his hair and slam his face repeatedly onto the table.

Boyd placed some paperwork in front of Curtis and he signed.

Why did he think a month's worth of footage would be required?

The recording likely gave Curtis an alibi not only for Milton Vandenberg, but for William Morgan and Simon Keehan as well. That was why the captain and the DA's Office were so willing to take the deal; the *greater good* Boyd had already mentioned.

"All right," Coombes said. "Let's have it."

Curtis made a show of pulling two thumb drives out his jacket pocket, one had a red rubber band around it. The edited and unedited versions no doubt. He put the rubber band drive down on the table and put the other one back in his pocket.

"You'll have questions about what you see but I can't look at the footage, it upsets me. William knows my situation and can answer on my behalf."

Coombes took the drive and left the room with Fielding. They walked down the hall to the meeting room where Sato had set up the laptop, and the three of them gathered around to watch the footage. The drive contained a folder with 30 sub folders, each having 16 further sub folders. He recognized the system setup. Month, day, camera. He drilled down to the folder representing the day of Vandenberg's murder.

He turned to Fielding. "Which camera?"

"TV room."

Coombes opened the folder and found a single file for the whole day. He sighed. A raw feed. It would make it harder to navigate, but would at least make any edit obvious. He started playback. Midnight in an empty room. The picture was black and white with visible pixilation in the darkest areas. Infra-red. He clicked fast forward and sat back in his seat. This was going to take a while. At around five a.m. Curtis entered the room, naked except for a pair of briefs that extended half way down his thigh. Coombes reversed playback to the point that he appeared and clicked play. The writer crossed the wide space and paused several feet back from a floor-to-ceiling window. His head was dipped down, not looking out. After a beat, he lowered himself onto the floor then lay on his side.

Nothing happened.

Coombes frowned and hit fast forward again. Two times, five times, then twenty times fast forward. The view barely changed. Curtis appeared to shimmer as the playback speed exaggerated tiny movements of his body. As the light levels came up, the picture jumped to color, the resolution suddenly pin-sharp.

It looked seriously uncomfortable; the floor was wood. From the reddish tones, cedar. Coombes doubted he'd be able to lie on it for more than five minutes. After four and a half hours, a German Shepherd came over and lay down next to him.

Coombes looked at the timestamp. If Curtis killed Milton Vandenberg, he would already be in his hotel suite arranging the death scene. Curtis had his alibi. He turned to the lawyer.

"Why's he lying on the floor like that? Did he pass out?"

"My client is bipolar. When he's depressed, sometimes all he can do is...well, you can see. It cripples him in effect. He lies or sits and has to wait for it to pass. The world can overwhelm him. It's not physical. He could move, he just can't see the point of anything and shuts down. People use the word *depression* all the time, but most don't have it like this.

"When he's up, it's a different story. He's a live wire, the funniest guy in the room, a hit with the ladies. You name it. He can also do an amazing amount of work in this manic phase. He wrote the first *Firestorm* movie in three hours. But, as you can see, sometimes he's like this so maybe it balances out."

Jake Curtis was still lying on the floor. It had to be the most boring alibi in the history of the world. Three more hours had passed and all that had happened was that the dog had got up, cleaned itself at length, then walked out of shot. Coombes grabbed the play head with the mouse and dragged it rapidly along the timeline. The light dropped and a lamp came on. Coombes went back to see if he'd got up to put the lamp on. He hadn't, it was automatic.

"He's there all night, Detective. Most of the next day as well."

"You already watched this? Or he told you?"

"I watched it. He sent it to me this morning. Like you, I put it on fast forward. I left it playing like that while I ate breakfast and drank coffee. I knew what to expect, I've known him for years."

"What about the drugs and the under-age sex?"

"It's on a different day. I haven't seen that. I don't want to."

"Why include it if it's not on the same day? He already has his alibi."

"Because if you watch his behavior on the days before and after you can see the changes in his mental state, it shows the pattern. Eventually, we felt you'd want the extra footage so we thought we'd get out in front of the problem and make a deal while we had leverage."

Coombes rubbed his chin.

"Whose idea was the deal? Yours or his?"

"His, why?"

"No reason."

Curtis was smart, and this move proved it. Would they have asked for the extra material? It was possible, his behavior in the footage was certainly abnormal. In his experience, anyway. But was he really getting out in front of a problem, or was there something else going on? Something felt off about it.

Coombes opened the next day's clip and found the moment when the writer got off the floor. He did so slowly, like he'd forgotten how to move. The dog rushed forward, barking, tail wagging, overjoyed his master had come back to life. It reassured Coombes that he hadn't been looking at some kind of dummy.

He'd recently re-watched *Escape From Alcatraz* and Clint Eastwood's fake head was fresh in his memory. The man had really been lying there for thirty-six odd hours on a hard wooden floor. It wasn't eye-witness testimony, but it was hard to argue with as an alibi. Eye witnesses were unreliable in any case, they lied, they forgot dates and times. A good 50% of alibis were worthless and unverifiable.

He turned to face the lawyer.

"You know about the pig's head?"

Fielding nodded.

"A bad business. I can't condone it."

"You'll be telling me his *manic phase* is responsible for that?"

"I wouldn't insult your intelligence. Jake can be unpredictable. Sometimes, to be blunt, an asshole. But he's no murderer. The timing of the pig thing is poor, I agree. My client made Milton Vandenberg a lot of money and had merely asked for a better percentage. The way he was treated by the studio he helped build from nothing was appalling."

Coombes felt the tension go out of his shoulders.

As much as he disliked Jake Curtis, he had to admit that the case against him was weak and circumstantial. Vandenberg's murder was close to a perfect crime and that didn't fit well with someone who thought nothing about mailing a pig's head under his own name.

"All right. We'll need to study these recordings and verify they've not been altered in some way. I will also need access to a medical professional familiar with his case who can confirm this behavior as typical."

"We thought you might. My client has instructed his physician to give you whatever you need. If this really was murder, he wants the killer caught. Whatever made Vandenberg a target might make him one too."

Here's hoping, Coombes thought.

Grace ejected the thumb drive from the laptop, labeled it, and dropped it into an evidence bag. Then closed the laptop and put it in her case. When she was finished, the three of them walked back down the corridor together to Block's office.

"Obviously, Jake is keen that none of this ends up online or the nightly news. We're trusting you to keep a lid on this and not have copies spreading around. Can you do that?"

It's Jake now, when he's asking a favor.

"I work Homicide. Your client's interest in children will be ignored on this occasion, but tell him he won't get a second pass. He's visible to us now. If he even drives past a school, his life will take a turn for the worse. Make sure he understands."

The lawyer flinched and a dead silence fell between them. They re-entered Block's office, only to find that Block and Boyd had left, leaving Gantz to watch the writer. He nodded to his lieutenant and turned to Curtis. He looked diminished. Coombes had seen him at his lowest, lying broken on his floor for 36 hours, and he was clearly embarrassed by the situation.

"Can I go?"

"I wanted to ask you something first."

"All right."

"You know all the main players at the studio. Who'd you pick as a killer?"

"From the studio? Are you kidding? Not one of them has a spine, never mind a set of balls. You're barking up the wrong tree there, Detective."

Fielding passed him a business card and a sheet of paper with the address of Curtis' physician. They were done.

Coombes watched them walk down the corridor toward the elevator. As he was walking, the spring seemed to return to Curtis' step, and his shoulders began to pitch from side to side with exaggerated swagger. Either his confidence was returning, or the pretense was dropping away. He continued to watch them wait on the elevator. After a moment, Curtis turned and looked back at him, a smile on his face.

11

By Monday morning, it was clear to him that Vandenberg's threatening mail was a dead end, just as he'd imagined it was on Friday afternoon when he'd first seen it. Milton Vandenberg was simply one of those people that rubbed a lot of people the wrong way and after spending the weekend in a windowless room with Sato and four rookies, he supposed he might have that in common with the studio boss.

The majority of the mail was taken up by screenplays that had been saved as part of the security sweep of each of the threatening writers. These scripts were 90 to 120 pages in length, roughly an inch thick, and contained no information related to the threats.

The correspondence that followed confirmed only what he'd already established from Jake Curtis. Namely, that writers were an opinionated lot, who knew a lot of swear words and cool ways to kill people.

Given the type of movie the studio specialized in, none of this should've come as any surprise to staff at Pacific Pictures, and the entire pile of paper should've been moved to recycling where it belonged long ago.

This was true of every piece of correspondence, except one. Jake Curtis' parting shot to Vandenberg, the pig's head.

All that remained, were four photographs printed on cheap office photo paper, and the original consignment paperwork Curtis had calmly filled in, signed, and attached to the box for the courier. As both a homicide detective and combat veteran, Coombes had seen more than his share of dead bodies, but there was something still shocking about the photographs of the animal's head lying on the floor next to the wheels of an office chair.

He imagined Carly Rogers, Vandenberg's executive assistant, opening the package for her boss. Perhaps curious or excited about what the box contained, a half-smile ready on her face, cutting the tape and opening the cardboard flaps...then screaming loud enough to fill the building. The box then falling on the floor and the pig's head rolling out. The scene played vividly in his head every time he saw the pictures.

There was also a photograph of the inside of the box, which was stained black with blood, suggesting that the head had been attached to the pig's body not long before Curtis sealed it inside the box.

Alibi or not, he still wanted the screenwriter for the killings and nothing in the correspondence from Pacific Pictures had made him think otherwise.

———

IT TOOK LESS THAN five minutes to drive to the next murder on South Olive Street, but the area was already flooded with news crews and patrol cars. Coombes was used to arriving late. Every scene he attended was always processed first by at least one uniformed officer, a supervisor, and sometimes another pair of detectives. Delays were inevitable, but this time over two hours had passed before it was escalated to RHD.

The report that came through was that the victim was Haylee Jordan, a reality show actress, and that it looked like she'd slit her wrists in her penthouse hot tub. Other details were limited due to the belief that it was simply another routine suicide.

Finding nowhere to park, Coombes abandoned his Dodge on the street and left his card behind the windshield where it could be easily seen. The vehicle was fitted with light bars on either side of the rearview mirror, yet he'd still had it towed. A strong wind whipped around him as he stepped out onto the asphalt, and he paused to button his suit jacket while he waited for Sato to walk around the hood.

Another victim, it was a disaster.

And yet, from a certain point of view, another chance to get a lead and solve the case. So far, the case was going nowhere, they needed all the help they could get. Unfortunately, he didn't think the killer was going to be in a charitable mood.

Coombes glanced up at the building that towered over them, then moved toward the entrance and the waiting press pack. Cameras turned their way, already running. He ignored them and pushed on, forcing the crowd to open up and create a space. Reporters and journalists calling out questions, all of which he tuned out. They were almost at the police line when he heard his own name.

"Detective Coombes! Is there a link between the deaths of Haylee Jordan and Milton Vandenberg?"

His head began to turn automatically before he caught himself.

He reached the police line and ducked underneath the tape, holding it up for Sato. A man came under the tape with them while apparently recording the whole thing on a tablet computer, but was swiftly ejected by two officers. Sato looked at the man's incursion with alarm and he positioned himself to protect her in case anyone else came through.

There was a strange mood in the crowd that he didn't like.

They gave their name and badge numbers to a rookie in the entrance lobby. He noticed a lot of names and numbers already on the page, something he couldn't figure. The lobby was not where he would have stationed this cop, but he said nothing and walked onto the elevator and hit the top button, marked PH. Nothing happened, the panel was dead. A piece of paper hung down from its bottom edge on a strip of tape on the wall. He flipped it up to see the front, expecting it to say *Out of Order*.

Type 3439 on keypad for PH - LAPD.

Coombes noticed a small number grid like a pocket calculator next to the elevator controls. He typed in the code and the main panel lit up. Again, he pressed the button for the penthouse and this time the doors closed and they began to rise up through the building.

Sato spoke softly, as if they could be overheard.

"It's not going to be long before the press figure this out."

"You mean that it's a serial?"

"Yeah."

Coombes said nothing for a moment. It was the first time any reporter had recognized him, and it was somewhat unfortunate that it had happened now. She was right. Two high profile suicides little more than a week apart being investigated by the same detectives all but drew them a picture. The reporter almost had it already. It wouldn't last the day.

"At this point I'm wondering if we'll get to keep it."

"FBI or Block?"

He never answered. The doors slid silently open. The elevator opened directly inside the penthouse, and into a large reception room. At least twenty uniformed cops filled the space, apparently having gone to see the dead actress. Many of them were holding cell phones, their faces bright and animated.

"Hey!" Coombes shouted. "Get the fuck out of here! This is a crime scene, not a Lakers game. Someone is dead, show some goddamn respect."

Heads turned toward him, assessing his suit and then Sato. They didn't have to say what they were thinking, it was all over their faces. He knew well enough what it was like to be on the other side of a visit by RHD, giving orders.

"And I better not see anything posted online, or it's your badge."

They filed silently past, seething with anger. Only a third of them fitted inside the elevator at once and Coombes decided to stand and wait until they were all gone.

"Bloody tourists," he said. Sato was staring at him. *"What?"*

"You're fearless, Johnny. I could never have done that."

Coombes shrugged and walked on, Sato falling into step next to him. The floor was made of large high-gloss tiles and even without bending down he could see the shoe marks of all the cops that had walked through already. The room was beyond contaminated, and he had to assume that the crime scene where the actress was would be no different.

They entered a media room with a huge television and plush leather chairs. There was a low coffee table with a glass top, but it wasn't coffee on it, it was cocaine. Three bags of it, each as large as Sato's fist and next to them, a mirror with a partially rolled bill on top. A forensic technician was in the process of photographing the table and he glanced around as Coombes approached. His face darkened with embarrassment.

"I know what you're going to say, but I couldn't stop them. It was like a stampede. Soon as word got out it was Haylee, all bets were off."

"Where is she?"

"In the next room. Wear a mask, she's been there a while."

"Did you process the crime scene before it turned into Union Station?"

The man shook his head.

"We just got started. Photographed it, that's all. My partner's still in there but the trace evidence is probably worthless. None of those guys wore gloves or shoe protectors, and her boyfriend and responding officers had already been through there."

Coombes sighed. It was hard for him to be angry at the prospect of the FBI stealing his case, when his own team behaved so unprofessionally.

"What about the boyfriend?"

"He's in the bedroom."

Coombes nodded his thanks and walked toward the next door. Three boxes sat on the floor, all virtually untouched. Gloves, shoe protectors, masks. He and Sato put them on. To his surprise, the crime scene was not a bathroom, but a living area with another television, a bar area, and the hot tub mentioned in the dispatch. The smell hit him immediately and he pinched the top of the mask in tighter around his nose in an attempt to keep it out.

Haylee Jordan lay face down in the water. The hot tub was still on, water frothing around her naked body. In life, Haylee had been beautiful, her face appearing on magazine covers and an all-you-can-eat stream of news stories on the internet. Her wealth and status were built on her looks, famous family, and her loud mouth. Her abilities as an actress, not so much. Coombes had no time for reality shows, or the vacuous opinion that people like Haylee shoved down America's throat, but none of that mattered.

The way he saw it, she was someone's little girl and he was going to catch the person responsible for this and make them pay.

"I appreciate the sentiment, but it's too damn late."

Coombes turned and saw a woman in white coveralls. The hood was pulled up around her head, cinched in tight around her face which had a mask over it. He realized she was talking about the shoe protectors and gloves.

"Those mouth-breathers are nothing to do with us."

"I guessed that much, Detective."

Coombes walked around the hot tub, keeping his breath shallow so as not to draw in too much air. The exposed side of the actress was already decomposing and the side in the hot bubbling water wouldn't be any better.

The tub was partially sunk into a raised deck and was octagonal, at the corners was a triangular space. On the left side triangle was an open straight-edge razor; on the right, a television remote control, an empty cocktail glass, and two silver dollars.

He stepped back, aligning himself so the tub was centered in front of him. The razor, the tub, the view of Los Angeles through the window beyond, and the cocktail glass. Another tableau from their killer. Suicide by slit wrists. He took a couple of photographs on his cell phone for quick reference, then moved closer again, looked down into the water and frowned.

"Where's the blood?"

He was talking to himself, but the woman in coveralls answered.

"Tub cleans the water while it's running. Probably took two days to clear, but it's all gone now."

"No kidding."

It was a detail that the killer would not have anticipated and would doubtless find disappointing. He could imagine how the tub would've looked filled with bubbling blood.

Coombes saw a pair of sandals on the floor and what he took to be a satin nightdress next to them. It looked like she'd slipped out of the dress then half-kicked it to the side with one foot. He'd seen his wife do the same thing many times. It looked real, not neat and carefully positioned like the other items. The killer could have changed it, used a pair of high heels and a fashion dress from her closet to make the scene more Hollywood. Instead, he'd chosen to leave it. To let them know she got into the tub willingly, with intimacy in mind.

He thought about how it must have happened.

She would've got in the tub first, her back to her visitor as she lowered herself into the water. Haylee had felt safe with him, confident. That's when he'd get the knife out his pocket, perhaps then hiding it under an item of his own clothing. He could've killed her at any point, but he wanted it to look like a suicide. To do that, he had to get into the water with her and hold her in place as the life drained out of her.

Anger twisted Coombes' face under his mask.

Afterward, the killer would've been covered in blood. There should be a trail of it from where he'd walked across the floor, except all he could see on the polished marble was shoe prints from the cops that had walked through the scene.

The killer had cleaned the floor.

A trail of bloody footprints didn't fit with a suicide.

"Be sure to process the bathroom and shower stall. He washed before he left."

The forensic tech turned to him.

"Do I tell you how to kick down doors, Detective?"

"I guess not."

"Bathroom is next."

Sato came over, taking pains not to look at the corpse. He could tell from her eyes that she was struggling to hold it together. This one was bothering her, either because of the smell, or who the victim was, it was hard to say.

"What do you think it means, Johnny? First time he's killed a woman, first time an African-American. It's unusual, isn't it? Changing victim selection like this?"

Coombes moved to the window and stood looking at downtown L.A. It was a stunning view, but he would bet his last cent that Haylee Jordan had spent more time looking in a mirror than taking in a view that had probably cost her $12 million.

"I think he's killing people who meet some criteria, or fail some personal test. To him, these people are somehow all the same. Like they are choosing themselves as victims."

"You aren't seriously suggesting he doesn't get off on this?"

"Sure, but the challenge of the act itself. *That's* what he likes."

"This is a game to him?"

"He's laughing at us. Look out the window, what do you see?"

"Downtown. The Civic Center. Tell me."

"*Us.* We could've walked here, Grace, this is four blocks from our house. Look," Coombes pointed through the glass, ticking them off. "The PAB, City Hall, the DA's Office, the US Courthouse, the Criminal Justice Centre, over there is the federal building..."

"A coincidence. This is just where his target lived."

"Maybe. Or maybe, like a cat, he's dropping dead bodies on our doormat to dispose of. It feels to me like the victim was chosen by location as part of his tableau."

Sato was silent. It was how she disagreed with him, with silence.

"Let's see what the boyfriend has to say," he said.

On the other side of the apartment, Randall Jones was sitting on the edge of a heart-shaped bed staring into space. Jones had thick, muscular arms and wore tight sports clothes like he was about to go to the gym and work out. The ends of his sleeves were darker than the rest of his top. Still damp from being in the water.

Coombes opened his notebook and found a blank page.

"Why don't you tell us about the last time you saw Haylee alive."

A deliberate slow ball with no backspin, to get them started. Despite this, Jones looked at him nervously, the white of his eye visible all the way around his irises.

"It was Thursday. We had a big fight; half the crew saw it. Haylee accused me of something and didn't want to hear my side of it. She told me we were done."

"She broke up with you?"

"Yeah."

The word was filled with doom. Things didn't look good for Jones, and he knew it.

"What was it she thought you'd done?"

"She thought I was seeing someone else. A friend of mine. It wasn't true. How do you disprove something that isn't true? Someone got to her, twisted my friendship in her mind, she couldn't hear my words."

Coombes nodded, his head down as he made notes.

"Your friend's name?"

Jones sighed. At every step he'd held a piece back, hoping not to get here, yet knowing the whole time it was pointless.

"Mike Black."

Coombes glanced up.

"Uh, huh. What do you do, Mr. Jones?"

"Are you kidding? I'm an actor. Me and Haylee work together."

"That show in Beverly Hills where women talk shit about each other?"

He saw fury in the other man's eyes.

"Yeah. *That* show. It's got the 14th highest ratings on US television."

"I see. Who do you play in the show?"

"Haylee's boyfriend."

Coombes laughed, causing Jones extreme irritation. It looked like Sato was about to cut in, so he shot her a warning look. He was on a roll here, and didn't want the flow interrupted with alternating questions.

"Why don't you tell us the truth? After your bust-up on-set, you decided to come here and continue the fight. Haylee was fed up being your meal ticket and was going to have you fired. You lashed out. Happens all the time, right? Side effect of the testosterone shots for your arms. Mood swings, problems with your rage. You slap her about to make her *hear* you, only this time, she knocks her head against something and suddenly she's got no pulse. She's dead. You panic, everyone on the show saw your fight, they'll know you did it. So you strip her, dump her in the hot tub and open her wrists. Is that about right?"

"No! None of that is right! I would never hurt her. I loved her."

The man's big shoulders shook as he sobbed.

It didn't look particularly real to Coombes. If it wasn't for the silver dollars and the staged crime scene, Jones would be prime suspect. The man was such a bad actor he couldn't even sell something that was true. Coombes glanced at Sato who stood with her mouth hanging open, shocked, then back to Jones. He wondered where you'd get hold of a heart-shaped bed, and if they made fitted sheets for it. Not a practical shape, he thought. It was large, with only a small usable space in the middle to sleep on.

His wife would push him right out onto the floor, no question.

"Say I believe you, Mr. Jones. Who else knew the code for the elevator?"

"She had parties all the time, everyone on the show knew the code."

"You think one of them killed her?"

"No way, without her there's no show. She's the heart of it."

"Then we're back to you?"

"Oh Jesus. I didn't kill her. Lots of people had her code, that's what I'm saying. It's the last four digits of her cell number, it's the only way she could remember. She never worried about security. There are cameras everywhere and a guy in the lobby 24-7. Her whole life was public. The show, her parents, she didn't...she didn't see things the same way."

Randall Jones' face became tight.

"What does *that* mean, Mr. Jones?"

Jones hands formed into fists between his knees.

"She had a fantasy a fan would come here while she was sleeping. Tie her up, gag her, do things to her, you know? Sex stuff. She liked all that. Loss of control, danger. It excited her."

"Did she ask you to roleplay that for her?"

Jones' head dropped and he stared at the floor. "Yeah."

"How did you like that?"

"I *didn't*. She was imagining having sex with someone else while she was having sex with me. It wasn't sexy. She would beg me to stop, tell me I was hurting her, the whole routine. It was messed up and it got old fast. I did it because she liked it, because I loved her."

"How often did she ask you to do this?"

"Since August? Every time we made love. After the first time, it was the only way she wanted it. I thought she'd get bored with it and move on if I waited long enough."

Coombes had never heard a man say *made love* before and he made a note of it. He got to the bottom of the page and turned to a new one.

His handwriting was getting worse, it was almost illegible.

"You have your own place, Mr. Jones?"

"Yeah, and it's nothing like this."

"How often were you here?"

"Three, maybe four times a week."

Coombes was silent a beat.

"Which was it usually? Three or four?"

"Three."

"You ever think she was seeing someone else those other days?"

Jones' face pinched with pain like he'd been shot through the heart. He looked away. For all the strength in his body, he couldn't say the words out loud.

"Do you think she broke up with you to be with someone else?"

Jones nodded.

"I came here to confront her. I thought there was going to be a guy here, I thought-" Jones paused to recompose himself. "Anyway, I got out the elevator and the apartment was silent, the lights in the outer room off. They were *never* off, not even when she was out of state. I looked in the bedroom first, I had to know if she was there with some guy. It was empty, so I go through the rest of the apartment. I saw she'd been hitting the coke. She swore blind she'd kicked that stuff last year, but there it was. I stood looking at it, wondering if that was why she was being so paranoid, and I smell something weird. Something disgusting. I follow it into the next room and there she was in the hot tub. I didn't figure it right away, that *she* was what I was smelling, I didn't even know that thing was her. I touched it, I turned it over, saw her face. Oh Jesus, her beautiful face, it's gone."

Coombes let him get a grip of himself before he spoke again.

"All right, Randall, we're nearly done. Any idea who she might've been dating? Someone on the show, someone new hanging around that you hadn't seen before? A Hollywood-type?"

Jones shook his head. "If there was someone else, I never figured out who it was and I *looked*."

He nodded and took Jones' contact details then gave him his business card in case he thought of anything. He walked back to the elevator, Sato trailing behind him.

"I didn't recognize you in there, Johnny."

"I disgusted you."

"Yes."

They got on the elevator and he hit the button for the first floor. Coombes watched the floor numbers change, his focus fixed on the panel.

"He was closed down, my questions opened him up. It's not our job to be anyone's friend. He was holding details back through the whole interview. Sometimes you have to stand on a few toes to get people to open their mouth."

Sato was silent all the way to the first floor.

12

MOST OF THE SOUR-FACED cops he'd rousted from Haylee Jordan's apartment were milling about the lobby area like they were waiting for him to leave so that they could go back up. They glared at him all over again. While they watched, he went over to the rookie with the list of names and badge numbers and took a picture of it with his cell phone. It was pretty easy for a list like that to go missing, so he wanted to cover his bases. One of the uniforms held his nose, a gesture normally saved for a cop who has betrayed another to Internal Affairs.

The atmosphere was highly charged and Sato moved with him like a shadow as they walked to the front desk. A large man wearing a security guard costume stood waiting for him, a happy smile on his face. Coombes guessed from looking at him that he wasn't the sharpest tool in the box.

"What's your name?"

"Huck."

"No shit. Take a seat, *Huck*, we have questions for you."

The man sat back down in his chair. He looked between Coombes and Sato, apparently puzzled by their serious faces, like the death of his top guest didn't justify that on its own.

"Explain to me how the security here normally works."

"How'd you mean?"

"Say I'd come to see Haylee. Do I talk to you first?"

Huck cracked a smile. "No..."

"You don't control who gets in or out?"

"I'll be honest with you, Detective. Haylee had people coming and going all the time. Friends, family, business. It was impossible to keep track of everyone and it's not really my job. I figure if they know her code for the elevator then they're meant to be there."

"Wait," Coombes said. "What *is* your job?"

"Building security."

"Isn't keeping track of people *exactly* your job?"

The man's happy-go-lucky act vanished, his face hardening.

"This is a private residence, not a prison."

"The elevator opens *inside* her apartment. You're letting anyone in off the street and you don't see a problem? Even if she knows the person, she could be asleep, or in the shower. Aren't you meant to call up when she has a guest?"

The guard's head pitched from side to side.

"We're *supposed* to call, but Haylee didn't want that. She got so many visitors that answering the internal line became a hassle, so she told us not to bother. Anyway, there's a lock-out on the elevator in her apartment. When activated, the elevator won't accept her code. *That's* her security, not me, not her pin code, not the cameras. The lock-out keeps people in the lobby."

Sato leaned in over the counter.

"Does your computer log when owners apply the lock-out?"

"Yeah, hang on." He poked at his keyboard with one finger. After a couple of seconds, he sat back, a heavy line across his forehead.

"She never used it, did she?" Coombes said.

"Apparently not."

He thought about what Randall Jones had told him about her fantasy, and her love of danger. Someone had come for her, just as she'd always wanted, but it didn't turn out the way she'd imagined. In her final moments, she would've known that she'd brought it on herself.

"All right," Coombes said. "We need a print-out of every time someone entered her number into the elevator for the last seven days. Then we need security footage coinciding with those times."

"Oh, man. That will take forever."

"A woman is dead."

The guard looked up at him, confused.

"She killed herself, didn't she?"

Coombes shook his head marginally from side to side. The man got it then, his eyes opening wide. It was the appeal of suicide, he thought. As soon as you think it's not murder you immediately relax. With murder, it could be you next.

"How many cameras do you have here?"

"One above the main entrance facing the sidewalk, three in the lobby, three in the parking garage, and one covering the entrance and exit to the garage."

"Motion-activated, or always on?"

"Always on. Look, don't get excited. The system is 40 years old and the resolution is about the same as a VHS tape. There's no infra-red, so it's worse at night."

"Haylee's boyfriend said she relied on those cameras to keep her safe and you're telling me that they're basically just for show?"

The guard's face turned red, either with anger or embarrassment.

"Camera upgrades have been blocked by the board of residents every year for the last decade. Maybe now they'll change their minds, but that's not on me."

"Fair enough. How long to pull the footage together?"

"Half an hour, maybe less. I never did what you asked before."

"I'll let you get right on it then."

As he stepped back into the main lobby area his cell phone beeped. A text message. He saw it was from Gantz and simply said *CALL*. The display of his iPhone showed one bar. It likely meant that his cell had lost service while he was inside the security station and she had been unable to connect. He moved closer to the entrance and called her back.

"John, where are you?"

"Still at Haylee Jordan's building."

"Should I assume that she fits the pattern?"

"Yeah. Our friend left us the usual pocket change."

Gantz sighed.

"Well, that's why I called. The TV networks have been looping a clip of you entering that building for the last 20 minutes. The press has it, John. You're officially working a serial killer case, congratulations. Get back here as soon as you can, we're going to build a team. Block's all in. Whatever it takes, he says. Chief's promising to suspend the overtime cap."

Coombes had never led a team before and his back stiffened.

"Is it still mine, Ellen?"

"A hundred percent. We're only where we are because of you."

She disconnected and his focus drifted through the doorway into the street beyond. The crowd had doubled in size since they'd arrived. As he watched, a small section broke away to surround his Dodge. A white sheet opened out between them with a message written on it.

JUSTICE 4 HAYLEE.

He decided to check the parking garage while they waited.

13

BLOCK WAS WAITING FOR them with Gantz in her office. It looked like he'd been there a while and that neither of them was too pleased about it. The office was hot and the captain's face was pink, his stiff shirt collar appearing to bite into his fleshy neck. Coombes held his hands up in a calming gesture as he came through the door.

"Sorry. We were waiting for security video, took a little longer than anticipated. It should have the killer on it so we wanted to get hold of it as soon as possible."

Block was still bristling, but his chest was slowly deflating.

"You think we'll be able to pull an ID off it?"

Coombes took off his suit jacket and began to roll up his sleeves. He figured Block for the type that would associate this action with getting a job done.

"The security system is from a period when dinosaurs still roamed the Earth. Most likely, the killer's own mother won't recognize his face. I'm hopeful we'll get a partial description, which is still more than we have at the moment."

He found himself thinking about Curtis' beard.

No matter how bad the resolution, it would show up on camera.

"That's too bad, Coombes," Block said. "We need to get out in front of this, the coverage is already wall-to-wall. This is national now, maybe international. Haylee Jordan was a big deal; people are going to expect results."

He wondered if he should tell Block about the contamination of the crime scene but decided against it for now. He'd mention it to Gantz when he had her alone.

"Ironically, the age of the camera system might help us out. Previously, the killer glitched the system at the hotel somehow. He's smart, knows technology. But *this* system is so old that this won't have been possible. We'll see the killer, just not very clearly."

"All right. Now, the task force. Chief Jackson has authorized three teams of detectives to work the case, plus as many uniforms as you want for donkey work. It's your case so you and Sato will lead, with Wallfisch and McCreary, and Davis and Newman."

Coombes glanced at Gantz and saw from her face that she played no part in the choices. Wallfisch and McCreary were idiots pure and simple, and worse, Wallfisch was the same rank he was so the chain-of-command within the team would not be clear.

"I was thinking of Becker and Gonzalez."

Block made a face. "Becker's past it. He's four months from retirement."

"Becker worked on Night Stalker and Grim Sleeper. He's the only detective in RHD with experience working a serial. Gonzalez is good with technology and is also, I hate to say it, a woman of color. All your picks are white men except Sato."

The room became painfully silent and Coombes was careful to avoid looking at either of the women, his focus fixed on Block whose eyebrows were knitted together.

"Shit, you're right. Okay, Becker and Gonzalez instead of Davis and Newman."

It was clear he wasn't getting rid of Wallfisch.

He turned to Gantz. "Anything else?"

"The meeting room has been upgraded to a command post. Laptops, whiteboard, television, phone lines. Did I mention the tip line? That's already up and running, news channels are showing the number. Hopefully we'll make the coverage worth something."

Coombes could imagine the crazies who were likely to call in with tips, and what they were worth to the investigation. They'd probably spent the morning waving a sheet demanding justice.

"If that's everything-"

"It's not," Block said. "You're scheduled to address the media downstairs at 2 p.m. and I think you can expect it to be well-attended. People are losing their minds over this and I need you to calm things down. You need to communicate that we have this under control and that the LAPD is taking it seriously. I want people to think that you're close to arresting someone. Serial killers are bad for business and Christmas is almost here. Am I clear?"

"I'll see what I can do, Captain."

The meeting broke up and he and Sato left the room. As they walked back to their desks, she grabbed his elbow and spun him around.

"That's how you see me? Included for representation?"

"He's a politician, Grace. I spoke to him in a way he understood. You're the best damn cop I ever worked with, not to mention my best friend."

"I'm your only friend, Johnny."

He shrugged.

"Best *and* only friend."

Her head was tilted back to look at him and her lips had opened, the tips of her teeth showing. He glanced at her mouth and after a second, he saw a smile spread across it.

The task force room, as it now was, had three laptops set up on either side of the large rectangular table that only hours before had been covered in Vandenberg's mail. Another table had been added to the back wall and above that, a huge television.

Wallfisch and McCreary walked in and sat without turning their heads to acknowledge him. The way the room was structured, this took a lot of effort and it told him all he needed to know about the two detectives. Either they didn't want to be here, or else they thought they should be in charge. Of the two, he thought the second was more likely. It had taken him 14 years less time than Wallfisch to make D-III and it burned the other man like napalm.

Coombes turned to Becker.

"Mark, I understand you're due to come off rotation. Is this a problem?"

Becker glanced at Gonzalez and back.

"Are you kidding me? The chance to work another serial? We're good, John. One hundred percent, you got nothing to worry about."

"All right. Depending on how long this takes, we're going to have to figure out a way to have days off or we'll all get burned out. You two will be at the top of the list."

"Appreciated."

"I'll bring everyone up to date with the case in a moment. First, we've got security footage from Jordan's apartment that I want to look at, see if there's anything we can use. Block has arranged a press conference for 2 p.m. and I'm pretty low on good news."

They all nodded, except for Wallfisch and McCreary, who glared at him like teenagers. He sat in front of one of the laptops and plugged in the thumb drive. It was a 15-inch laptop, they wouldn't all be able to see.

"Anybody know how to use the big screen?"

"I got it," Gonzalez said.

He moved to the side and she leaned in, setting up the laptop. Up on the big screen, there was a burst of light, then the layout of his desktop icons and his cursor appeared. Like Wallfisch, the screen was large and not very bright. He saw that Sato was already at the light switches. He nodded and the overhead lights shut down.

Coombes opened the thumb drive and pulled up the files.

According to the print-out the security guard had provided, the last time Jordan's elevator code was used prior to Randall Jones arrival, was at 10:34

on Friday night. He brought up the security clips that the guard had put together and played them back in the reverse order he expected to find anything, saving the parking garage cameras and the back of the lobby camera for last. Sure enough, all the other clips were clear. He pulled up the clip covering the entrance to the garage. The camera was positioned to capture the face and license plate of someone driving in, but nobody drove in. He walked.

"Here we go," Coombes said.

The camera didn't get much, it wasn't optimized for pedestrians walking on the sidewalk and ducking down under the control barrier on the road. The man was on-screen for less than two seconds and he was wearing a hooded top. He rested his hand on top of the barrier, but it appeared that he was wearing dark gloves.

It was useless.

There was a tense silence in the room as Coombes cued up the next clip, taken from next to the stairwell, pointing back at the entrance. They saw the figure duck under from the other side and walk straight toward the camera. The garage was lit by fluorescent tubes spaced wide apart, the light level on screen poor. The killer was well-built and rolled his shoulders from side to side like a boxer as he walked.

Muscular, like Randall Jones.

It occurred to Coombes that the killer might have dressed and walked in a way likely to implicate the actor, perhaps even selecting clothes he knew Jones owned. If true, it would mean that the killer had spent time on-set and might be familiar to the rest of the cast.

The figure was half-way down the screen now.

Each time he approached one of the fluorescent tubes he dipped his head forward and walked with his eyes down by his feet, before coming up again. His hooded top cast a shadow across his face, lighting only the tip of his nose. Coombes turned between the smaller higher-resolution image on his laptop, and the screen that filled the opposite wall. Looking for something, anything.

He couldn't even see a beard.

"He's jerking us off," Wallfisch said.

Coombes nodded in the dark. "You got that right."

The rest of the clip was no better. The killer walked right up under the camera position, his head lowered, and entered the stairwell that led up to the first-floor lobby.

Coombes closed the clip and the room became dark while he cued up the first-floor lobby camera. Compared with the parking garage, the clip was brightly lit. To his astonishment, the camera was so badly positioned that when the door from the parking garage opened it obscured the camera in the lobby until the door closer pulled the door shut automatically. As the door cleared the shot, all they saw was the killer half-on, half-off the elevator which had been sitting waiting. There were groans from around the room.

"Goddammit!" Coombes said.

He scrubbed the slider forward and back, but it got him nothing. All they had was a left hand swinging back with no wedding band, a pair of blue jeans, and some sneakers. Coombes didn't bother viewing the inactive cameras for the next batch of recordings, which were timed at around 12:45, Saturday morning. He assumed the killer would exit the same way he entered, and he wasn't wrong.

Walking backward, using a raised cell phone to see behind him, the killer exited the way he had arrived via the door to the parking garage. It looked like the previous video being run in reverse. The door opened, cutting off the camera as the killer left.

"Son of a bitch," Becker said.

"That guy knew exactly where the cameras were, Coombes."

The playback froze onscreen and he stared at Wallfisch.

"He's been there before," Coombes said. "Knows the code for the elevator, the placement of the cameras, the angles. He *knows* her. An old friend, a lover, whatever."

Wallfisch nodded his fleshy head in the gloom.

"That's what I'm saying."

"So, there's going to be *older* footage where he *doesn't* hide his face? Maybe even looking up at the camera to see where it is."

Wallfisch paused, sensing a trap. "I guess that follows."

"That's a good lead, Tommy. As soon as the press conference ends, I want you and Don to go back to her apartment building and scoop up all footage like this going back three months. Then I want you to isolate every man that uses her elevator code and use these clips as a baseline for comparison."

"Coombes, you can't be serious. That'll take days."

"Maybe we should go back *six* months to be on the safe side?"

The room was silent while he and Wallfisch stared at each other in the half-dark. He couldn't back down. He had to put down a marker to show who was in charge so there could be no doubt. Not for the first time, Coombes evaluated the other man's fighting capacity. Wallfisch carried a lot of weight and there was an outside chance that there could be muscle under it somewhere. He got ready to kick the chair back and stand, in case Wallfisch charged him down.

"He was in her apartment for over two hours. Doing what?"

It was Sato, still standing by the light switch. Her words caused the tension to dissipate. If she ever got bored being a detective, she could transfer to the bomb squad.

"I think he brought the cocaine. Haylee had broken up with her boyfriend and might've been in the mood to celebrate, or take her mind off things. Let's say they got high together. She was an addict, perhaps he was her supplier from way back and that's how he knows her code. After a while, they decide to continue their evening in the hot tub where, instead of making out, he guts her like a tuna. Her blood should've been all over the window and across the floor, but it wasn't, so I'm guessing he held her under the water until she was empty."

Silence returned to the room for a long moment.

"I have a suggestion for you, Johnny," said Gonzales. "If it comes up at the press conference, don't say any of that. Literally, *none of it*. Not unless you want to see Block's head explode and four million Angelenos assemble outside this building carrying pitchforks."

"Duly noted."

Coombes started the last clip, of the killer leaving through the parking garage. His shoulders rolled from side to side as before, like a wannabe gangster. Like Jake Curtis had as he left their office the week before. The killer was less than two feet from the concrete above.

The killer was tall, about the same height he was.

He had no idea what he was going to tell the press, never mind how he was going to catch the killer. All they knew for sure was that he was a white male, between six two to six four with a muscular build that probably put him between 180 and 200 pounds. He'd additionally guess that the man was between 25 and 35 years old from the easy way he walked.

It was a profile that fitted him as well as it fit Jake Curtis.

14

HER NAME WAS MARY-LOU Daniels, and she had shoulder-length blonde hair and a flower print dress. She'd called the tip line to report that she'd been on Olive Street early Saturday morning, and that a large man in a hooded top had run past her.

Coombes smiled as he approached her, trying to look friendly.

She was small, less than five feet, which made him at least a foot and a half taller than her. Mary-Lou did not smile back at him, instead, her eyes widened in what appeared to be alarm and she glanced at the doors behind her. It wasn't unusual for eyewitnesses to re-think their involvement, which could happen as late as the second they stepped into a courtroom to give evidence. People could become forgetful at the worst possible time.

"Miss Daniels, I'm Detective Coombes, thank you for coming in so quickly. If you'd like to come this way we can get started."

She looked like a deer caught in headlights. He put the smile away and let his face relax. Sato would be better at this, he thought, a situation he intended to correct as soon as possible.

As they stepped onto the elevator, she shrank into the far corner away from him. He sighed. Being in a building full of cops wasn't for everyone. The doors opened and he gave her plenty of space as he led her to Block's office and got her seated. His captain was tied up elsewhere for the rest of the afternoon and the office was quiet with large windows. A good place to give her statement and work with a sketch artist.

"I think I might do this another time if that's okay."

Her voice was shaky, barely louder than the air conditioning.

"Best to do this while the details are still fresh."

The door opened and a man called Gibson came in carrying a leather satchel. Coombes was pleased to see him; he wasn't sure how long a wait Daniels could've taken. The sketch artist had a natural sympathetic way about him, and he launched immediately into a story about his sister-in-law's pet poodle while he took out his drawing pad and charcoal pencils.

The tension disappeared from Mary-Lou's face as the story unfolded, her shoulders relaxing. Gibson had been telling the story of his sister-in-law's poodle for years and it seemed to get better with every telling. The basics were simple; a ladder had tipped over, covering the unfortunate dog in a gallon of blue paint. In a panic, it charged around inside a neighbor's home leaving a trail of devastation.

Coombes stood and straightened his suit jacket. He knew the story well enough to know when it was time to leave.

"Can I get you anything to drink, Miss Daniels?"

"I'm okay, thanks."

Her voice was louder now, less shaky. He nodded and left the room.

Sato was at her desk looking through transcripts from calls from the tip line. The line had been open for eight hours and had already received over two thousand calls. Aside from Mary-Lou's call, they were all junk. Callers either demanding justice for Haylee, or else stating that she deserved it.

"Anything interesting?"

"Not so far. How's the eyewitness?"

"Terrified. Any chance you could babysit and take her statement?"

Grace turned to face him, eyebrow raised. "Swap?"

"All right."

He moved his chair over to her workstation and began to read the next transcript. It was easier than logging in and trying to move through the stack to where she'd got to. Four uniforms were answering the calls, and he didn't envy them at all. After a couple of minutes, he got to the point where he was able to quickly scan text and assess if the caller had any information before moving on to the next. It was mind-numbing and time passed slowly.

His cell phone rang. "Coombes."

"You're a hard man to get hold of, Detective."

Lieutenant Gale. He'd heard her whispery voice only once before but it was instantly recognizable. He sat back in his chair. It was 5 p.m., which made it 8 p.m. Miami time.

"What can I do for you, Lieutenant?"

"Several things come to mind if I'm being honest."

He laughed; not certain he was understanding her correctly. The reason why she was calling was easier to understand.

"I guess you saw the press conference."

Coombes heard ice moving in a glass. She was drinking.

"Yeah, but I'm not calling about that. I have something that might interest you. Trent's gone missing. His PO hasn't seen him for six months, which means next time he pops up he's headed back to Okeechobee to finish his sentence with interest on top."

"Sorry, *Trent?*"

"Jake Curtis' older brother. After we spoke before, I decided to check on his whereabouts. Everything came up dry. He's used an alias in the past, but I'd still expect him to check-in with his parole officer. Not doing that is a big deal, there's an arrest warrant out for him."

"You think he's in L.A.?"

"That thought did occur to me, yes."

"What was Trent doing time for at Okeechobee?"

"He fire-bombed a loan shark's SUV. The man was inside the vehicle with two of his associates at the time. They all survived, if that's what you want to call it. Trent stood and watched as they tumbled out on fire and rolled around on the ground screaming."

Model citizen.

"And he got paroled?"

"He claimed to have accepted Jesus into his life. The background is that there were some overcrowding issues in his unit and they were looking for prisoners they could kick loose. Him and fifty-four others walked."

The justice system in action.

"You think Trent could be the guy we're after?"

"What? No. *Jake* is the guy you're after. I think Trent's helping him."

"As much as that works for me, Jake Curtis has a cast-iron alibi for more than one of the killings. We have him on video elsewhere at the exact time victims died."

There was a long silence and he thought she'd disconnected when she spoke again.

"Dig deeper, Coombes. It's him, trust me. His alibi is bullshit."

Then she really was gone.

Gale had dropped the ball investigating the death of Jake's father and had grown to regret it. Now, she hoped he would be able to correct her mistake and put him behind bars. He'd seen this before when detectives fixated on suspects they believed had escaped justice, and could understand why she could fall victim to the same thing.

Curtis' alibi *was* bullshit.

Since he'd stopped work on the tip line transcripts anyway, he decided to call it a day. He'd gone through 382 calls for no reward, and the total number still to be processed had gone up, not down. People were still calling it in. He decided to check his emails before returning to Block's office and was rewarded with an email from TID.

A partial fingerprint had been found on Haylee Jordan's shower door.

Coombes smiled. Finally, a mistake.

The print was made from blood, so the chance it belonged to anyone but the killer was remote. Photographs were attached to the email; a wide shot of the bathroom, the shower door with a marker indicating where the print was found, then a shot through the glass door at the bloody print on the interior surface of the handle.

He could see why the killer had overlooked the print during his clean-up operation, it was hidden by the handle. The door was hinged, causing it to fold in on itself as it opened, further hiding the print. It occurred to him that the tech had to have climbed into the shower stall and closed the door on herself. It was a great catch.

Do I tell you how to kick down doors, Detective?

Coombes smiled again, thinking of her comeback. He looked for her name on the email and made a note of it. Carrie Dupont. He liked to know the names of people he could rely on to do a good job, and people to praise in his own reports.

There was no match in the fingerprint database.

He returned to Block's office and found Mary-Lou Daniels gone. Sato and Gibson stood looking down at a charcoal drawing that lay on the table between them. Coombes moved over to join them. A dark figure with a hood pulled up, like a comic book character. The top half of the face was heavily shaded, the features above the eyebrows almost gone. Tufts of dark hair pushed out below the ears, held in place by the hood.

"That's it?"

It was hard for him to keep the disappointment out his voice.

"Yeah, I hate the hooded ones. There's so little to work with."

Coombes studied the drawing again.

The man had a wide jaw covered with a coarse, dark stubble like grains of black pepper. Unkempt for sure, but by no means a beard. The mouth was slightly open, no doubt the result of the suspect running as he fled the crime scene. As always with a sketch, it lacked the spark of life that he could get excited about. The eyes dead, with nothing going on.

He looked back up at the artist.

"This could be a drawing of me."

"Oh shit, you're right. Could be she described you because you'd just met?"

"Maybe."

"She really thought it was a good likeness."

"Thanks, Gibson. Might still turn out to be something."

He waited until the artist left before he turned to Sato.

"What do you think?"

"You're better looking than that, Johnny. This guy's a mess."

"Grace-"

"Well, it's true. What's the cop-partner way to answer?"

"I was *asking* if you thought it could be Curtis."

"You still like Curtis for this? What about his alibi?"

"That alibi stinks and you know it."

"Don't they always? Innocent people don't know they're going to need an alibi. If cops asked me to produce one it's almost always going to be me sitting alone in front of a TV watching murder shows. Who's that going to convince?"

"Nobody's going to believe you were alone, Grace."

She smiled and dimples appeared in her cheeks.

"Anyway, the witness said nothing about a beard."

He had a theory about that, but he wasn't ready to share it with Sato because he knew it sounded desperate. Ridiculous, even. That Jake Curtis' beard was fake and always had been. No more than a prop he'd been using for years to make himself more memorable. Without it, the writer would all but disappear and became something close to invisible.

Coombes tapped the desk next to the drawing.

"Unless this isn't our killer. It would explain why he let her live."

"The clothing, the physical description, the location, the time frame...they all match our suspect. You might not think about this, Johnny, but lone women walking down a street after midnight do not make eye-contact with *any* man, never mind one with jacked-up muscles and a hooded top. Daniels probably glanced at him then focused really hard on the sidewalk, hoping he didn't attack her. She didn't need to know he was a serial killer to be afraid of him, she's probably been afraid since she was 12 years old."

"Damn, Grace."

"Welcome to *my* world."

15

JULIE'S CAR WASN'T IN front of his home when he got back and all the lights were off. He sighed. It was getting hard for him to remember what his wife looked like. He'd seen her only four times in the last two weeks and each time she'd been asleep. Coombes locked his car and walked to his front door, one hand getting his keys out, the other carrying a paper sack of Korean take-out. He dumped the food on the kitchen counter and separated the containers, sorting them into his and hers, then took his through into the living room. He watched TV while he ate, flicking through different news channels to catch coverage of the case.

After the press conference, Gantz had told him to smarten himself up. She was right. He looked like a hobo on camera and he resolved to do something about it. The public needed to have faith in his investigation and he was giving them no reason to have it.

One channel had a section where they asked Angelenos on the street what they thought about the killings. Predictably, Haylee Jordan was the only victim anyone cared about. Two interviewees believed that there *was* no killer, that they were just suicides. This was a theory he'd seen trending online and it seemed to be gaining traction. Because only the rich were being targeted, there was no fear or demand for justice from anyone being interviewed.

When they cut back to the studio, the news anchor spoke with a tone normally reserved for feel-good stories about surfing piglets or skateboarding dogs. The murders were being viewed as a form of entertainment, he thought.

The killer had tapped into something big. If they didn't solve it soon, it could be the start of something far larger.

The next story about a flu outbreak in China didn't much hold his interest, so he shut off the TV and stared for a moment at the black rectangle.

Jake Curtis' smirking face came to him again.

Coombes wanted the writer for this, he wanted it in his bones.

It was 10:30 and Julie still wasn't home. He got up and walked into the kitchen and looked at the front of the fridge. They used to leave each other notes there when they first got married. Sometimes they were funny, but mostly not. Now all they said was *we're out of milk*, or *recycling tomorrow*. Not new notes, the same two over and over. There were no notes. He walked over to the wall calendar and found the right day.

Spin class. Drinks with R.

Coombes looked out the window into the dark rectangle of dust that was his back yard. Seeing the worst in everyone was essentially his job, he couldn't turn it off when he got home. He pulled out his cell phone. They had an app that allowed them to track each other. Julie had insisted he install it, suggesting it somehow made him safer on the job. He selected the app and it showed two round markers for him and Julie.

According to the app, she was inside the house.

He walked through to the bedroom and turned on the light. The bed covers were all rucked up. A mess. He walked around to Julie's side and flattened the cover. Her cell was on her nightstand behind it, charging. A twitch started in his face, like a string was pulling just under the skin. Julie took her cell phone everywhere with her. At any given moment, it was normally in her hand, whether she was using it or not.

He sat on the bed and leaned over near her pillow.

He could smell her perfume and the musk of her naked body. Coombes felt a slight breeze on his face and glanced to his right. She'd left the bedroom window locked part open, something she used to do after they'd had sex.

He closed his eyes and concentrated on his breathing.

It was just a window; it didn't mean anything.

Who was R?

Coombes went back through to the kitchen, and the wall calendar. He looked at the other entries. All of them were Julie's, he never wrote on the calendar. Either he was working, or he was here. A lot of the time when he was here, he was also working. He supposed he didn't have a lot going on. There were four other entries that included R that month. No name other than the letter.

He took out his cell phone again and opened Facebook. He found Julie's profile and scrolled down her page. Julie posted constantly, about everything and anything. Eventually he got to the day of the previous meeting with R and was rewarded with a photograph of his wife standing next to another woman in a bar laughing. Coombes recognized her as an old friend of Julie's called Rebecca.

He felt some of the tension go out of his chest.

He'd never heard Julie call her anything but Becca, but he supposed it was possible she'd still shorten it to R. The other woman was tagged in the picture, so he clicked on her name, taking him to her profile. Rebecca had posted less than twenty minutes earlier, a photograph of her and her husband at a casino in Vegas. Their fifth wedding anniversary. Coombes closed his eyes for a beat and swore, a bubble of angry energy inflating in his chest. He grabbed his keys off the kitchen counter and headed for the door. Walking back through the living room, he decided to leave his cell phone down the side of his chair. Two could play that game. He didn't know what he was doing, but he couldn't stay in the house and he couldn't do nothing. It was better to be moving, even if it got him nowhere.

SOMEONE WAS FOLLOWING HIM. Twenty-five, maybe thirty feet back. Coombes kept walking at the same pace, resisting the urge to turn around. Since the parking garage, he thought. He walked on a couple of seconds more. Steady footsteps, followed by a burst of quick steps close together. No, not the parking garage, he thought. Someone had followed him there first in a vehicle, then been forced to continue on foot when he got out his car. He approached the glass walls of Julie's gymnasium. Anyone on the sidewalk could look right in at the people exercising, like animals at a zoo.

He heard the quick steps behind him again, someone struggling to keep up. Someone not as tall as he was, with shorter legs.

Julie liked to spin, so he walked around to where bikes were set up. His eyes scanned the room as he walked and he knew before he got to the bikes that she wasn't there. Not on the bikes, not on the rowing machines, not anywhere.

He turned his head, looking along the glass at the figure behind him. A woman. She had shoulder length brown hair and his sudden interest in the gym had caught her by surprise and she'd frozen up, not wanting to get too close.

He walked on. She was familiar, but he couldn't place her.

Why would anyone be following him?

Coombes thought instinctively of Internal Affairs. He figured that any number of people from the Chief down might have concerns about his ability to handle a case of this size and have IA audit his personal life. Looking for potential problems, areas where they could experience personal blowback. He came to a crosswalk and got straight across, stranding the brunette on the other side. He realized it was the wrong play, he needed to confront the woman now, or he'd waste time thinking about her and who she might represent.

A bar came up on his left and he walked inside.

The interior was dark and it suited his mood just fine. He made his way to the front and sat on one of the bar stools. It was polished leather, and it was still warm from the last occupant. He folded a twenty-dollar bill lengthwise and held it out between thumb and forefinger, waiting for the bartender to notice him. There was a mirror behind the bar and he stared at himself in it. He didn't look good; it was no wonder he wasn't getting served. Stubble, wild hair, crazy eyes. Same as it ever was. He used his free hand to get his hair pointing in the right direction. A television was mounted high up on the bar, angled directly at where he was sitting. A sports channel. He sighed. At least it was muted.

Coombes thought about Julie not being at the gym. On its own, it meant nothing. Something might've come up, a friend needing help. A flat tire. She could've just been in the gym's locker room, or in the showers. More likely, she'd actually *told* him she wasn't going to the gym and he hadn't been listening. Rebecca's trip to Vegas could've been a last-minute surprise by her husband, causing Julie to change her plans.

Causing her to forget her cell phone.

Behind him the doors clattered open again.

Coombes glanced around and saw the brunette standing framed in the doorway. She paused for a beat, eyes searching for him in the dark. He recognized her; she wasn't IA, she was a journalist. Not one of the main players, some kind of junior position. Always on the periphery, watching. Hungry for a case that would launch her career, which explained why she was following him. She saw him and gave no reaction to the fact that he'd seen her, walking straight over and sliding onto the stool next to his, like they were old friends.

"Mind if I sit here?"

"And if I say yes?"

She gave a small laugh.

"It was a rhetorical question."

"How do you figure?"

"I'm wearing a push-up bra and a low-cut top."

Coombes glanced at her and nodded. She was, as advertised.

"I feel like I owe you dinner and a movie and we just met."

"You're kind of old fashioned, huh?"

He knew *old fashioned* was code for *sexist,* or worse.

The bartender came over and stood in front of the brunette, ignoring him. The journalist asked for a double vodka on the rocks and a drink suitable for a Neanderthal. When the drinks came, she gave the bartender the folded twenty from between his fingers and told her to keep the change. The woman didn't check if that was okay with him, or thank him for the tip. Coombes took a sip from his Bud, his gaze fixed on the brunette's reflection in the mirror.

"I'm curious if you want me to hit on you and try to get the information that way, or if you're going to be up front and introduce yourself like a professional."

"You recognize me."

"I've seen you about." He shrugged. "We get our coffee in the same place."

"That's embarrassing."

She wasn't embarrassed. People who said they were embarrassed never were.

"How about we start over," he said.

"Monica Sullivan, *LA Times.* "

"No comment."

She laughed again. "You're funny, I didn't expect that."

Coombes left that alone, his eyes returning to the television above the bar. He didn't feel funny. He felt the opposite of funny, whatever that was. His wife was having an affair, he was in no doubt. He wondered if this was the first time, or simply the first time he'd noticed. Things hadn't been right for a long time; he'd known it and done nothing.

The TV was showing an ice hockey game. He'd never taken any interest in the sport before, but the presence of the journalist made now seem like a good time to check it out. After a couple of minutes, commercials came on.

"You know it was insulting being ignored when hockey was on, but now they've cut to commercials I'm getting pissed off."

"I didn't come here looking for company, quite the reverse."

"Tell me about the coins."

Coombes forced himself not to react. He stared at his drink, wishing he'd stayed home. It was bad news that she'd uncovered the coins, but it was no great surprise either as they had been mentioned in daily briefings to cops all over the city. It was almost Christmas and cops had gifts to buy same as anybody else.

"You know I can't comment on an active investigation."

"All right, but I already know about the coins. We're going to run the story anyway, with or without you."

"And I suppose nothing will convince you to sit on it?"

"The information's out there to be found, Coombes. If I don't publish it, someone else will. A journalist, or some fearless blogger wearing sweatpants in their bedroom. You know the score, there's no sitting on information anymore."

"So, what do you need from me?"

"I need to know what he does with them."

"With the coins?"

"Yes."

Coombes took another drink from his beer, an idea forming in his head. Perhaps they could help each other out. As she'd stated, they were going to run with it anyway, he couldn't stop that, but he could do something. Add a twist they could use to filter out copycats and fakes. He turned to face her and saw for the first time how attractive she was close up. Sullivan had her eyes wide, her body leaning in like she was interested in him.

"Whatever I say is off the record, right? I can't be a source."

Her eyes twinkled. "We can do that."

She leaned in even closer, her mouth parted like she was ready for a kiss. Her lip gloss made her mouth glisten in the semi-dark of the bar. Coombes guessed a lot of men fell for her act, maybe some women too. He spoke softly, so that no one overheard.

"He puts the coins on their eyes."

The reporter nodded, a blush spreading across her cheeks.

"Of course."

He frowned, his mind trying to make the same connection.

"Because of the eye on the dollar bill?"

"No, no. In ancient Greek literature, coins were placed on the eyes of the dead to pay Charon to transport them across to the otherworld."

"Ahh. My knowledge of ancient Greece is a little spotty."

She smirked. "I'm sure."

"Did the Greeks ever place coins anywhere else?"

Like on hotel nightstands, he thought morosely.

"Sometimes on the mouth, or *inside* the mouth."

"And you know all this how?"

Sullivan said nothing and tilted her head to one side. She was still flirting with him. Perhaps she liked the feeling of control it gave her, or maybe it was just habit. She was wasting her time; she wasn't his type. Yet, he reflected, he was talking to her. If a male reporter had approached him like this, he would have told that reporter to get lost.

"This Sharon, who was she?"

She smiled. Her teeth were perfect.

"Charon with a C. He was the Ferryman."

He got a flash of an old movie. A figure on a boat crossing sea taking coins with a skeletal hand. It was too bad he'd made the whole thing up, it worked well. It was the kind of lie that would survive the truth. When a detail like that was strong enough, it didn't matter what would come later, nobody would want to believe it.

"Want a word of advice, Coombes?"

"And if I say no?"

She swatted that away like a fly.

"Shave. Brush your hair. Better yet, get a haircut. The shorter the better, this isn't the 60s. Nothing longer than an inch, you'd suit it. There's a nice face under there, the kind of face you could make room for in your life."

"You sound like my lieutenant. The first part anyway."

Sullivan slid off her bar stool and emptied her untouched vodka down the back of her throat. He watched her larynx pulse up and down as she swallowed, her crotch pressed casually against his knee. He realized she *was* his type after all. She put the glass down on the bar and smiled, their eyes locked together.

"*There* you are, and just as I'm leaving."

She pressed against him harder than ever. The heat from her body restored him.

"What if I have more questions about ancient Greece?"

Her smile turned into a half-snarl.

"I'm sure you'll figure something out. You *are* a detective after all."

He liked her better like this, when she needed nothing from him. He supposed he liked all women better that way. Strong, independent. If someone who didn't need you spent time with you, it meant something. Of course, she *wasn't* spending time with him. Now that she had what she wanted, she was leaving. He wasn't sure he didn't find that attractive too.

"I'll see you around, Sullivan."

"No doubt."

Coombes watched her walk away and was still looking when she reached the door and turned back, catching him. He knew she was going to look back and felt no shame at being caught. In his opinion, the back was as good as the front. He raised his beer and she smiled again before she continued on through the doors.

In the past, he would have gone after her and made a fool of himself trying to make something happen. But that was a lifetime ago and he'd learned his lesson.

Besides, he had a beer to finish and it had cost him 20 bucks.

16

It took Coombes almost two and a half hours to find the problematic areas in the mountain of footage that Jake Curtis had provided. Twenty days before Curtis took his long rest on the floor, he was doing lines of coke off the underage girl's glistening bare chest with a rolled-up $100 bill. It looked like a scene from one of Pacific Pictures' retro action movies, and he thought that was pretty much what it was.

In real life, cocaine sticks to sweat and begins to dissolve, something that immediately happened in the footage. Curtis laughed and began to lick the dusting of the drug he'd left behind. Coombes shook his head. Not only was the scene offensive to him given her age, it was clumsy and over-the-top. He noticed Sato silently watching his screen.

"What are you thinking, Grace?"

"He's acting out for the camera."

"Agreed, but to what end? Maybe that's why he had the cameras put in. To record all his conquests. Dollars to doughnuts he's got a folder of the good stuff saved away somewhere."

Sato ignored this; her attention fixed on the screen.

The underage girl was Tammy Watkins, a student from a wealthy family in Pasadena. She was petite, and when she wasn't giggling, she was talking. It seemed to Coombes that words never stopped tumbling out of her mouth, and every one of them was drivel. He'd muted the playback pretty quickly. It was obvious to him that she was underage and, in his opinion, it didn't even look close. She looked fifteen. Curtis' claim that he didn't know her true age, while not a legal defense, wasn't even credible based on the video.

"How old would you say she looks?"

Grace shrugged. "I don't know."

"She looks underage, doesn't she?"

"How old would you say *I* looked, Johnny?"

Coombes felt his face turn scarlet and he turned to face her.

"What?"

"I'm not too big myself. Breast size does not indicate age."

"Look at her. She's wearing no makeup yet her lips are red, her cheeks flushed."

"Yeah? So are yours."

"Come on. I wasn't-"

"Fuck that. Say something nice to me right now or we're done."

He wasn't sure how this had become about her, or what it meant that it had. He glanced around to see if anyone was watching but the detective bureau was quiet. He beckoned her closer and spoke softly.

"Grace, if I had footage like this of you, I'd keep it forever. I'd erase my *wedding pictures* to make room for it. You're perfect, okay? Absolutely stunning."

She laughed, her hand up over her mouth. He'd shocked her and she'd liked it. It was there in the light of her eyes, the continued proximity of her body. For whatever reason, the case was changing the way they were together and he couldn't say why.

"One day, Johnny, that mouth's going to get you in a lot of trouble."

"I think that ship's sailed."

Coombes liked the way she was looking at him and he turned back to the screen before it became obvious to her. In Jake Curtis's bedroom, Tammy was now drinking from a can of beer. It was the final thing he'd been waiting for, *providing alcohol to a minor,* and he made a note of the time so he could find it again if he needed to.

He tilted his head over to the side, thinking.

"What is it?" Grace said.

"The way this camera system is set up, each camera records a single file all day. Midnight to midnight, right? As far as I can tell, everything that was waved under his deal with the District Attorney is on this file. All there is on the other cameras are shots of this girl arriving, sitting next to the pool sunbathing, and leaving again. Nothing illegal. There isn't even an angle of them going into the bedroom on any of the other cameras."

"You're saying he only needed to delete one file?"

Coombes shook his head.

"No. If he deleted it, there'd be a gap. We'd know he'd deleted it. What I'm suggesting is kind of the reverse. Remove *all* the bedroom camera footage from the files he gave us and we'd never know it was missing. We only know there are 16 internal cameras because that's what he gave us. The bedroom's not part of his alibi so we'd never get a warrant for it, and if he deleted it no warrant could bring it back anyway."

"You're right. So why didn't he do that?"

"That's the real question, isn't it?"

A silence fell between them.

Curtis had an alibi for the day of Vandenberg's death, but his alibi stuck in Coombes' throat. It was a stupid alibi, in his opinion, and it stank. There was something wrong with it, beyond the underage girl. It was too neat, too clever. Rather than make him believe they had the wrong man, it did the opposite. He believed more than ever Jake Curtis was their killer.

Monica Sullivan had published her story about the coins and it had exploded across the media spectrum. The coins changed the mood music for a very simple reason. The killer now had a name, a name he himself was responsible for giving him. It was catchy, and everyone had immediately adopted it.

His phone rang. He paused the video playback. "Coombes."

"This is Franklin. You got a Walter Ford to see you."

He frowned. The name didn't ring a bell.

"Yeah? What's he want?"

He heard the desk sergeant repeat the question, but he didn't hear the reply.

"He said to tell you he's the Ferryman."

WALTER FORD WAS HUGE, probably close to seven feet tall and three feet wide. His shoulders tapered up to his thick neck and his arms looked like they could rip Coombes apart. He walked along the corridor swinging from side to side like a bear that had been taught to walk on its hind legs, his head tilted down to avoid the ceiling. Four uniformed officers escorted him, one with his hand resting on his sidearm.

The man was bad news and everyone felt it.

Coombes and Sato hung back while he was led into an interview room, then watched via the camera from the monitor station as he was seated and handcuffed to the table. The giant was placid, without a care in the world. It was a look Coombes had seen before from killers when they confessed. Whatever turmoil had been going on inside their head, they knew it was almost over. Gantz appeared next to them, her eyes wide.

"Jesus, look at the size of him!"

Coombes nodded. "He barely fits behind the table."

"What do you think, John? Is this our boy?"

"He looks like a killer, but he doesn't feel right for this."

"Be careful in there."

Coombes and Sato filed out, leaving Gantz watching the monitor. They glanced at each other as they put their sidearms in lockers. Normally this didn't faze him, but he was uncomfortable facing such a big opponent unarmed. Grace was putting on a show, her brave face, so he winked and she flashed a smile at him. They walked into the interview room and closed the door. Ford's eyes skated right off him to look at Grace.

"You Chinese?"

"I'm American, same as you."

Ford snorted. "Yeah, right."

"Okay, Chief, settle down," Coombes said, sitting opposite Ford. "We're here to talk business not trade insults, yes?"

The big head swung toward him.

"That's right. Business."

"I'm Coombes, this is Sato-"

"I know who you are, I saw you on the news."

"My wife thinks I look fat on TV, what do you think?"

A frown appeared on Ford's head, puzzled by the comment. For the first time, Coombes noticed that there was a cut in the skin near Ford's hairline and his hair was matted down with blood.

"You look the same I guess."

It was notable that people confessed to crimes, and there were a lot of them, always expected the conversation to be about them and dealt badly when conversation shifted elsewhere. Coombes smiled humorlessly.

"What happened to your head? I see you've got an injury."

"I hit a door. Not the first time."

"Okay. This is all being recorded, so right off the bat I've got to ask you if you want to have a lawyer present, or if you want to waive your rights."

"I don't want no lawyer. I'm here to tell you what I did."

"Tell us about the death of Theodore Sutton."

The confusion returned to Ford's face.

"I don't know who that is."

"No? All right. What about Milton Vandenberg?"

"I killed him in that hotel room. Forced him to eat all those pills. Told him I'd kill his kid if he didn't do it. Said I'd do some stuff before I killed her, you know? He got the picture."

"How did you get into the room?"

Ford shrugged. "I knocked; he opened the door."

"Okay, so he ate all the pills, did you bring the wine?"

"He had that already. I let him drink it, helped him swallow the pills."

Coombes nodded, making notes in his notebook. It was all being recorded, but he liked being able to pull out points at the time or refer to something again during interviews.

"Tell me about the pills. Where did you get them?"

"I broke into a retirement place, they had loads of pills. I chose them."

"When was this?"

"Last year. They were still in date, I figured they'd work."

"Then what? Did you wait for him to die, or did you leave before?"

"I waited. Didn't want him calling for help."

"And if he wasn't dead, you wouldn't be able to leave the coins on his eyes."

Ford nodded is big head emphatically. "*Exactly.*"

"So he's dead, you've done the coins, then what?"

"I left."

"You do anything else before you left?"

The brow came down again as he thought about it, before brightening

"I knocked the wine onto the floor. Made a big stain. Looked like blood."

"And then you left?"

"Yes."

"Did you take anything from the scene? Some guys like mementos."

Ford's mouth turned upside down.

"Not me. That's evidence. I'm too smart."

"Yet you've come in here today, confessing."

The big man scratched the side of his face.

"It was a game back then. Cat and mouse. I always wanted to be caught, but you guys were getting nowhere. The game stopped being fun."

Ford was a tourist. He only knew what had been reported. He didn't need to ask about the other deaths, Ford was wasting his time.

"You're not our typical walk-in, Mr. Ford. Those guys are small, nerdy. You know the kind. They live with their mom and maybe she's still alive, maybe not. Point is, you could snap 'em like twigs. They're here to prove something, what are you here to prove?"

"That I killed those people. They had it coming."

"Can I call you Walter?"

"Sure."

"Here's my problem, Walter. If I ask cops here ten years from today if they remember that big guy that came in to confess to the Ferryman killings, every single one of them is going to say yes. You're kind of memorable. The Ferryman sneaks in and out, nobody sees him. He's like a ghost. Some claim he doesn't even exist. You, I could track from space."

"Son of a bitch!"

Ford struggled to his feet, a task made more difficult by the chair and table being fixed to the floor and his handcuffs pulling him forward. Coombes forced himself to stay calm.

"Sit down and relax."

To his surprise, his voice was as cool as an airline pilot and the big man instantly responded to it, slumping back down. Ford hung his head. Rather than push him again, Coombes let the words come to the other man. It took a couple of minutes.

"I got nothing, man. No job, no girl. My truck's in the shop and I can't afford to fix it. I took the bus here. I saw this guy on TV, a murderer, killed three women in Texas. He's engaged. Women write him letters every day. They're going to make a movie about him."

"That's what you wanted?"

Ford nodded, then shrugged his big shoulders.

"I wanted to be famous. Be on TV, like you."

Coombes closed his notebook.

"I don't know if you thought this through or not, Walter, but prisons are not made with people your size in mind. You think it's hard out here? Write to someone on the inside, ask them what it's like. Better yet, go speak to one of them. They're coffins for the living. If I had a dog, I wouldn't treat it like that. Don't waste your life, don't hurt someone because you think there's a conjugal visit or a movie deal in your future. It's not like that."

"What do I do?"

"This world's bad enough. Try making it better, not worse."

"It's too late for me, I can't be that guy."

"Sure you can."

He stood and walked away. As he got to the door, Ford spoke again.

"That Ferryman, he's making the world better."

Coombes sighed. He needed a coffee.

17

Maxwell Rollins had one of the biggest desks in the department. It contained an ultra-wide screen that at first glance looked like three screens pressed together. Unlike most of RHD, Rollins' computer was state of the art, never more than 6 months old. Coombes walked up casually behind the tech and stood there, hovering. The other man hated being watched, and had attached a blind spot mirror to detect people standing behind him.

"Something I can do for you, Coombes?"

"A suspect gave us video footage as an alibi. I want you to check it out."

"I heard. A film director."

"Screenwriter."

"Whatever. I'm a little busy."

It was always the same with Rollins. He was too busy to breathe most days, and he expected everyone to be super grateful for the slightest attention he might give them. Coombes leaned over, into the smaller man's space. He was not above intimidation.

"Too busy for a serial killer. Wow. These must be super important *traffic cams* you're looking at here. What happened? Your mom get popped running a stop light?"

Rollins sighed. "Give me the drive."

Coombes smiled and handed it over. Rollins plugged it into his computer and opened the folder. He looked at the files, hummed to himself, then opened a new program. The screen filled with windows. All of the cameras running together, synchronized. At the top of the page was a larger playback of camera 1. Of course, Coombes thought, this is how it would show on Curtis' system. Not as a list of separate files, but as a whole. The cameras were showing just after midnight on the first of November.

"Help me, Coombes. What are we looking for?"

"I need to know that the dates on these files haven't been changed. That each camera is showing the same day, and that we're looking at is a genuine calendar month, not different days stuffed into a folder. Basically, anything that points to his alibi being bullshit."

"You realize, Detective, that the timestamp is displayed *over* the footage?"

"So what?"

"Well, if he changed the date of the file, it wouldn't change what appears *on* the recordings. That's encoded at the time of the recording."

"At the movies I've seen aliens and dinosaurs. I've seen actors and singers perform after their death. I figure a timestamp is small beer."

"All right, let's think about this. First of all, you'd have to remove the original timestamp and generate new pixels to fill in where the numbers were. There are 16 cameras running 24 hours a day for a month in 4K resolution at 30 frames per second. That's a *lot* to retouch, even using an AI. Then you'd have to go back and drop in the new timestamp which is no breeze either because it's semi-transparent." Rollins paused and shook his head. "If he was really going to do that then for sure he'd *only* give you footage for the day of, not for a whole month. The amount of extra work that adds is off the charts."

Coombes nodded. He had already calculated that there was almost 12,000 hours of recordings. Even watching it would take too long, retouching it would take forever.

"What about metadata?"

Rollins smiled. "Well look at you joining the twenty-first century. This program actually uses the metadata to play back these files, that's how they're synchronized. Up here it shows the date and time, which is the same for all cameras. If your guy changed the date on one file then that camera would freeze and a red box would appear around it."

"So, in your opinion, this is all legit?"

"Put it this way, Coombes. Your guy didn't alter these files after the fact. I am 100% certain of that. What's on them, happened just as they were recorded. If he's on camera here, then I guess he isn't your killer."

Coombes had a new idea and had the tech bring up the 22nd, the day of Vandenberg's murder. Because he'd watched it already, he was able to get Rollins to advance it in a matter of seconds to just before Curtis first appeared. This time, because all the cameras were playing, he was able to watch Jake Curtis move from one camera to the next as he walked through his house before finally curling up on the cedar floor next to the window.

"Could he have looped this footage over and over somehow? He's like that for almost 36 hours."

"Like the bus video in *Speed*?"

Coombes hadn't seen that movie for a very long time, but he knew immediately what Rollins was talking about.

"Yes! Could he have done that?"

Rollins stroked his chin.

"Not for 36 hours. The problem is the light changing through the window during the day. Even if he only did it for two or three hours so he could whack your guy then come back, there'd still be a jump when it changed. Which, by the way, is what happened in *Speed*."

"Okay, how about this. What if he'd lain in that spot for the right amount of time on a different day, all that lighting stuff would match up. Then superimpose it onto the recording later and edit out the joins."

"In that case, it would be simpler to swap out that whole camera feed and fix the timestamp. Of course, he would then need to alter the other cameras so that he could leave the house and kill your guy, then alter the cameras so he could get back in, then alter the cameras again to line up with the dummy recording. You see the problem, Detective? The amount of work just balloons and balloons. The man's rich, no? It would be easier for him to pay an escort to say she'd been with him the whole time on some yacht in the Catalinas. You might suspect her story was bull, but unless you could prove it, he would have an alibi."

That much was certainly true.

"All right. Thanks anyway."

Rollins gave him back the thumb drive and returned to his previous screen looking at street cam footage of an intersection. Closing programs was a form of goodbye in Rollins' world and he knew better than to wait for the man to say any more to him. There was a divide between them, he had a badge and a gun; Rollins had a laminate ID. It was a divide that would never close. Rollins wasn't a cop and never would be.

He headed back to his desk on the other side of the floor.

Truthfully, running anything past Rollins was always the last step before moving on. You knew something was junk, you took it to Rollins who told you it was junk, and then you forgot all about it. He sighed. Even before he knew about the underage girl, Coombes had wanted Jake Curtis in the box for the murders. There was just something about him and his ridiculous goddamn beard. His wealth, his attitude, the way he carried himself. Everything about him irritated Coombes. Obviously, there was the pig's head incident, and there was no doubt in his mind that he could charge him for that. Whether it could be escalated to some kind of extortion or threatening behavior charge wasn't clear. The main problem would be that Pacific Pictures neither retained any of the evidence beyond a couple of photographs, nor had they pressed charges at the time.

His cell phone began to vibrate. Grace Sato.

"Tell me something good."

"It's not good, Johnny. You're in some deep shit."

When he got back to his desk, he found Block standing there, hands on his hips, leaning over Sato who was seated in front of her computer. Block was not a small man and his position over her was outrageous and totally crossed the line. Coombes stood over him, just to see how he liked it.

"*Captain.*"

Block jumped and twisted out from under him.

"Coombes, what the fuck have you done?"

The captain's breath came at him like a wild animal, all garlic and spices. His fleshy face was red with anger, his eyes bulging.

"I don't know what you're talking about."

"You two clowns are the only people who had access to the footage, and let's be honest here, Coombes, this move has your name written all over it."

He still didn't know what Block was talking about, but he was getting an idea what it might be. He turned and looked down at Sato's computer and saw an LA Times web page. The headline filled much of the screen; he could read it without any difficulty. *Firestorm Screenwriter Caught with Underage Girl.* A large edited screenshot lay underneath for those who needed help with the words. This was what Rollins had referred to without him realizing it. He hadn't given any thought as to how the tech knew about the video, but this explained it.

"I didn't do this," he said.

In hindsight, he wondered why he hadn't.

"Come off it, Coombes. Put yourself in my position, what would you think?"

He looked into Block's eyes and made it worth something.

"Honestly, I had nothing to do with it. I don't like the guy and it wasn't my idea to agree to that deal. All I've done is try and establish if he's our killer. Unfortunately, it's a wash. I'm just back from seeing Rollins and he can't see how the alibi video could be faked."

The anger was still there in Block's face, he wasn't ready to give it up.

"That's too bad. Because if he sues us, we're going to be looking at the wrong end of a multi-million-dollar payout."

"No jury's going to award a payout to a rapist."

"That's a real weight off my mind, Coombes. I'll tell Jackson that you think we're in the clear, I'm sure he'll appreciate that."

Coombes' patience was wearing thin.

"Look, Captain. I didn't do it. I know Grace didn't either, which means the leak came from somewhere else. The facts are simple. Curtis can't prove where it came from and he'll want this to go away as soon as possible, which is the exact opposite of a trial."

"You really don't know, do you?"

"What?"

"The video is out there too, totally unedited. This isn't going anywhere."

Coombes said nothing for a moment, thinking it through.

"All right. This girl, Tammy Watkins. I doubt she's his first. There's an old charge on his file for exposing himself to a minor, that's the pattern of a predator. Get sex crimes to look into him, see if they can dig something up."

"That's not bad, Coombes. I'll do that."

Block turned and walked off. As he did so, Coombes noticed that some of the other detectives were standing, watching the show. Smiling. They all knew about the story, and they all thought he'd leaked it.

"Jesus, Johnny. What did you do?"

He sighed. "Et tu, Grace?"

She tilted her head over, studying his face.

"I like the haircut, Johnny. Just enough to flick through my fingers."

"It's funny, that's exactly how I asked for it."

He imagined Grace running her fingers through his hair. Pulling it. Her delicate face close to his, her breath landing on his cheek. A shiver went down his spine. What the hell was he doing? Sato was still looking at his face, smiling.

His cell phone rang again and this time he saw it was Gantz. More blame, he supposed, for the leaked video of Curtis or his enthusiastic back-and-forth with Block.

"Coombes."

"We got another body, John, and it's a bad one. Don't eat anything you don't want to see again."

18

As THEY DROVE TO the crime scene, he found himself thinking again about the Jake Curtis video, and how it might have found its way online. It hadn't put itself out there that was for sure and he could see how Block would think it was him. Viewing it objectively, he was the most likely candidate. More likely than Sato, or any of the others on the task force. He had also noticed that the article had been written by Monica Sullivan and it was common knowledge in the task force that he'd used her to plant the false coins narrative. It made him wonder if he wasn't being framed for it.

But who would benefit from it, except Sullivan?

Clearly there could be a financial motive, but he didn't figure that any payment would be worth that much. Not enough for a serving cop to risk a serial killer conviction. It was more likely personal.

Personal to him, or personal to Curtis?

It was conceivable that he could be removed from the investigation and someone else would have to step in. Another D-3. He thought of the other detectives that had been standing, watching him and Block go at it. *Wallfisch*. His face had been split open with a grin like a Halloween pumpkin. Wallfisch wanted to lead the investigation bad enough and was certainly not above a move of this kind.

Then there was Curtis' lawyer, William Fielding. He had access to the video footage before he had and he appeared to be both disgusted and upset to be in a position of defending his client's behavior regarding the girl. Was it possible that he'd copied the contents of the thumb drive and sent it on to Sullivan?

Traffic had slowed to a halt, there was some kind of obstruction ahead. He saw Sato reading her tablet. A white page with a lot of text on it. A Wikipedia page. He could tell by the formatting, and the margins.

"That the vic?"

"Yeah."

"Tell me."

"Long version or short version?"

He glanced at her and said nothing.

"*Right*," she said.

Sato skimmed the article again, mentally summarizing the contents, her fingers zipping through the page, which seemed very long and require a lot of scrolling.

"Anthony Price Junior, 65. Ran a hedge fund worth tens of billions in New York for close to two decades. Left for Los Angeles after 9/11 in search of a new life, yada, yada, yada. Bought the restaurant in '04, apparently as some kind of joke and that's pretty much all she wrote. Charity work, the usual rich white guy routine. Trying to buy his way into heaven with cents on the dollar."

"You're starting to sound like me, Grace."

"I can live with that."

"Did it say how much he was worth?"

"No. Hang on, I'll Google it."

The traffic moved forward again and he saw a CHP officer ahead directing traffic. It occurred to him that the crime scene *was* the obstruction. He pulled his badge off his belt and held it in the palm of his right hand. Next to him Sato whistled.

"Seven point eight billion."

She used a hard *b* so there was no room for doubt. Coombes groaned. Things were about to take an unpleasant turn, that was for sure. He held his badge up to the windshield and the Highway Patrol officer waved him toward a gap between the two Mustangs parked across both lanes.

He drove slowly between the vehicles.

The Beverly Hills PD had taped off a huge section of street around the restaurant where the murder took place and two adjacent properties. It seemed like overkill to Coombes, but he'd encountered this before. It meant that what was inside was going to be bad. The worse it got, the farther the crime tape seemed to be positioned. No doubt signaling a desire of the officers involved to get away from what they'd seen.

He parked up next to a couple of BHPD SUVs and ducked under the tape a uniform was holding up for them. There was a box of disposable gloves and slip-on shoe protectors next to the patrol cops at the door and Sato and Coombes gloved up first, then bent down to pull on shoe protectors. He turned his head toward her and saw her face was tight with fear. They stood up and looked at each other.

"Grace, why don't you hang back here?"

"And do what, Johnny? Hold your coat?"

The conversation was going as well as he imagined.

"Just giving you the option."

"I'm a homicide cop, same as you. Don't dick-block me, okay?"

Her nostrils were flared with anger, her jaw clenched shut. She had a point, but it didn't feel right to not offer her a choice. He held up his hands in surrender.

"I will try and keep my dick out of your way."

"Let's not be hasty. I might need that thing one day."

The uniformed officers laughed. There was a desperate edge to it, like they were thankful for the levity. Sato walked into the restaurant and Coombes followed her inside. He was shaking his head, a smile on his face. Dark humor was a good sign, she only needed to get used to the sight of dead bodies and she was all set.

They walked through the dining area toward the back. He glanced about. The place looked expensive, the furniture, the decor. Everything he saw told him that steak and fries would cost him three figures. It was the type of restaurant that put wine glasses out on empty tables, then took them away again as soon as they seated you.

Not his scene, that was for sure.

According to the initial report, Price was found in the kitchen by Sarah Brooks, the bar manager, who was opening up. Brooks, who also happened to be his ex-wife, noted a strong smell as she entered the premises and made her way to the kitchen to investigate. Expecting to find a backed-up sewage line, she instead she found her ex-husband sitting in a chair, murdered. Brooks passed out and hit her head on the corner of a steel-coated island unit and spent the next twenty plus minutes unconscious on the floor. When she came around, she was able to call for help using her cell phone, before passing out for a second time.

Over to their right, he saw a young LAPD forensic tech called Vogler talking to his BHPD counterpart next to cases of equipment. They nodded at each other. The smell was becoming hard to ignore, it was like a soup, the air was saturated with it. Sharp, acrid. Strong chemicals mixed with body fluids. His eyes watered. Sato took a cloth out her pocket and held it over her nose and he did the same.

His smile was long gone, like it had never happened.

Sato fell back as they approached the kitchen doorway so that they arrived at the same time. Despite their conversation, he had his left arm ready to catch her in case she decided to follow the lead of the bar manager. Her pride notwithstanding, he'd be damned if she was going to contaminate his crime scene.

They walked into the kitchen and swore loudly.

Anthony Price was sitting in an office chair next to a meat counter. He was wearing a pale blue shirt, black suit pants, and slip-on dress shoes. The blue shirt was unfastened and spread wide, exposing the full horror of what had happened to him.

His throat was gone, leaving a deep hollow space where it had been and, further down, a ragged hole a foot long had appeared in his abdomen. On the floor between his $1,000 shoes lay his intestines, or what was left of them, in a semi-liquid pink slurry. Both his hands were slick with blood, and a knife lay on the tile under his right hand.

Four bottles of drain cleaner sat on the counter, next to two silver coins.

Another grim tableau from the Ferryman.

He glanced at Sato. She had one gloved hand against the wall to brace herself, the other still up at her face. Her eyes did a slow blink, her head tilting down toward the floor like she was falling asleep, then she seemed to recover. Her chest inflated and her head came back up, eyes wide. She nodded that she was okay, so he turned back to the victim. He moved forward to get a closer look, taking care where he placed his feet.

Why the office chair. Why not one of the dining chairs?

Wasn't that a better message?

He slid Price's shirt cuff up his right arm and saw dark bands around his wrist. Coombes had seen it more times than he could count during his career in law enforcement. Price had been bound with steel handcuffs while the Ferryman had forced the corrosive down his throat. He nodded to himself, understanding.

The office chair had arms, the dining chairs did not.

Coombes stepped forward, between pools of blood, then pivoted his hips to close in on the other man's right shoulder. *Where the Ferryman must've stood.* He tightened the cloth over his nose and leaned in close. The victim's mouth was badly blistered from the liquid that had passed over it. Industrial strength drain cleaner, designed to break down fat and oils, and all the other things humans are made from. He pulled back, giving himself some space.

"What's your take, Johnny?"

There was a patch of blood in Price's dyed black hair. Coombes used his thumb and forefinger to part the hair around it. There was some kind of mark on the skin, a contusion, long and rounded at the edge.

"Victim was struck over the head here, with something like a baseball bat or a pipe. Once subdued, our killer sat him here and handcuffed his wrists to the chair arms. Probably his ankles too. When our victim came to, these bottles were emptied down his throat, one after the other. The cuffs were then removed and he was either handed the knife or it was left nearby, within reach."

"You think Price cut himself open?"

Coombes nodded.

"He was dissolving from the inside out. It must've felt like he was on fire. I'm sure he just wanted it to end, and get all that stuff out of him as fast as possible. A pretty pointless goal when his throat was being eaten away."

When he was speaking, he had to hold the cloth back from his mouth and nose. The smell was disgusting, he needed fresh air. He reversed his previous movement to get back over to the doorway. He looked at the corner of the metal unit that the bar manager had struck with her head, then at the pool of blood she'd leaked onto the floor. There was a lot of it, maybe as much as a pint. It was a serious injury; she was lucky to survive. He froze. There was a pattern in the blood, the tread of a shoe. It distorted the straight lines above. He moved his head back and forth, up and down. The pattern appeared and disappeared.

He went through into the restaurant and waved the forensic tech over.

"There's a shoe tread in the secondary blood. The bar manager's. You can only see it from some angles. See if you can get a photograph of it, I think it's the killer's."

Vogler's eyes lit up and he nodded enthusiastically.

"You bet."

"Put some kind of scale in the shot, so we can calculate a shoe size."

The tech nodded again and entered the kitchen. Grace frowned.

"I don't understand. How could blood from the bar manager have the killer's shoe print in it if she arrived after the killer left?"

"It's like a latent fingerprint. The prints are there the whole time, but it needs some kind of reagent to make it visible. In this case, it was the way her blood pooled on top of it, and maybe the fluorescent tube above it casting a flat light."

"You think we'll get anything else?"

"No, I don't. This wasn't a mistake, this was luck." He paused, looking at her. She still wasn't right. It was fair enough; Price was hardly looking his best. "It's early, Grace, but do you want to get lunch somewhere? I'm starved."

She laughed a little, despite herself.

"You fucker!"

"I really could use some chili right now. Or meatballs in a nice, thick gravy."

There was more color in her face, she was coming out of it.

"You're disgusting," she said. Then, after a beat, "thank you."

19

It wasn't exactly on his way home, but Coombes decided to pay another visit to the Metro Grand and see if he could speak to Lawson, the security guy there. There was something about the keycards that he couldn't put his finger on. Removing the cards after the kill did seem like a memento, as Lawson had suggested, but what if it was something else? What if the reason the two keys were taken was to hide something? As far as he knew, no other mementos had been taken from any of the other Ferryman crime scenes, and removing them called attention to the fact that it wasn't a suicide.

A blandly beautiful woman smiled at him as he approached the front desk. He explained who he was and that he wanted to speak to Lawson, or whoever was on duty. Her off-the-rail smile disappeared in a blink of his eye, replaced by something else. Disgust, maybe. *He was here about the murdered guest.* She made a phone call in a hushed voice, then told him to take a seat and wait.

Five minutes passed before a man approached.

This would be Lawson, he thought. He was older than he was expecting, but pretty much everything else matched the mental image he'd compiled. Either these jobs attracted a certain type of man, or the man changed because the job required it. Form follows function. Lawson was heavyset from sitting all day, eating candy and burgers, then going home for some brewskis.

Coombes stood as the other man spoke.

"Help you?"

"I'm Detective Coombes, we spoke on the phone."

Lawson nodded. "Sure, I remember."

"I had a couple of follow-up questions and I was in the area."

"No problem. Come into my office."

He followed Lawson back the way he'd come. The big man dragged his left leg a little and his rounded shoulders had a strange movement as he moved his left foot forward. A knee injury, Coombes thought, and not a new one. They came to a door with SECURITY written on a silver plate. Lawson held the door for him and he walked through, around the other man's belly, into a windowless space filled with computer screens.

Coombes glanced around the room. The hotel's grandeur hadn't made it past the door, that was for sure. This was a blind spot, something the public weren't meant to see. The room smelled of sweat and fried food. He could practically taste the air, and by proxy, Lawson himself. The place was a mess. Whatever Lawson had been doing during the five-minute wait, it wasn't cleaning up. A power play then.

Make the detective wait, show him who's boss.

A faded calendar hung on the wall, a Playboy-type image of a young woman in a swimsuit next to a pool. By modern standards, tame. It was dated July, 1967. The calendar was older than he was, which made the model in her seventies.

He turned to see Lawson holding up a mug.

"Get you a coffee?"

Coombes didn't like to judge, but he was pretty sure the mug had never been washed since the day it had been bought.

"I shouldn't. It's a long drive home if you know what I mean."

"Trust me, I know. Take a seat."

They sat, and he pretended not to notice what appeared on Lawson's screen when his big hand nudged the mouse. He instead put his head down and peeled back his notebook to the page he had about the hotel security as the other man quickly closed his browser.

"This won't take long, just a couple of questions."

Lawson said nothing. Coombes continued.

"Okay, you said before that the locks on the doors were computerized and there was a record. A door access log." Coombes looked up. "Who opened the door, what time?"

"That's right."

"Is that every time the door opens and closes?"

"No, only when you unlock it and enter the room."

"If a guest opens the door for room service, that wouldn't be logged?"

"That's right," Lawson said again.

Coombes nodded and wrote *unlock only* in his notebook.

"If a guest loses their key during their stay, you issue them with a replacement?"

"Of course."

"How do you control replacement keys?"

"We ask for the credit card used with the booking, but there was no replacement key with your victim. Our system logs replacements and your dead guy didn't have one."

"That answers my next question. You said previously that these keycards are only active for the duration of a guest's stay, right? They don't open that door after that?"

"God no, you can only imagine. That would be a security nightmare."

"The cards that you get back, from guests or staff leaving, they're recycled?"

Lawson nodded.

"If they were never stolen, we'd get an easy ten years of use out of them. What tends to happen is that we change our branding so all the old keys get trashed and we get new ones made with new logos or what have you."

"The cards come back, you change the code and they're good to go again?"

"That's it exactly."

Coombes said nothing for a moment, watching Lawson carefully.

"And who does that?"

Lawson straightened, his mood changing in a heartbeat.

"I get the cards back, I blank them out, wipe them down then pass them through to the front desk. When they need a key they run them through the machines up front."

"But you can do them here as well, right? On this computer. The staff keys are done here, correct? Not at the front desk."

"Listen, pal-"

Coombes held up his finger.

"Take it easy. You've seen the news; you know what's going on here."

"Yeah, and you're not going to pin it on me."

"When you make staff keys, do they come into this office?"

The question seemed to derail Lawson.

"Yeah. I make the key, explain that their codes are logged every time a door opens, all that. So they don't lose them or think about stealing something. There's also this welcome pack for new employees and they sign for everything at the end so they can't turn around and say they never got the key or something."

"Make a key for me right now. Pretend I'm a new employee. At the end we can cancel it out, I just want to see the process."

Lawson still looked angry but he nodded anyway. He opened his top drawer and pulled out a rectangular box and removed the lid. It was full of plastic key cards. He took one out and placed it just in front of his keyboard and brought up one of the programs already running on his computer. The way the screen was angled, Coombes could see what Lawson was doing. There was a square box in the middle of the screen with different form fields for name and address, employee number, cell phone number. There were two tabs at the top Staff and Guest, and three buttons down the side that said Erase, Print, and Cancel.

"I need your details."

"Fill in anything, it doesn't matter. You can delete it all after, right?"

"Of course."

It was what he thought. Everything could be changed later, it was digital.

Lawson filled in the form with random keystrokes and numbers, then moved the mouse over to Print. He clicked it, then picked up the keycard and ran it down a slot on the side of the monitor. A small green LED pulsed in the corner. He put the card on the table between them. Coombes picked it up by the edges and turned it over. There was a magnetic stripe on the back. It was not a complex task. A child could do it. He saw that the keyboard's keys had a surface texture, not counting the food and other substances Lawson's fingers had added. The crime lab would get nothing from the keyboard except diabetes or an STD.

"Is that it?"

"That's it."

He looked at Lawson with a level gaze. The security man didn't see a problem with his setup. It was a joke.

"What's your first name, Lawson?"

"Bret."

"Bret, I'm going to need you to dump these cards into another receptacle. I'll be taking this box, it's evidence now. The same goes for your mouse. You will also need to have your fingerprints taken for elimination purposes. Tomorrow's fine."

"I don't understand."

"Your door wasn't locked. The drawer where you keep the cards wasn't locked. Your screensaver has no password. Odds are, the Ferryman came in here while you were taking a comfort break, printed himself a card then came back after and deleted it. With a bit of luck, his fingerprints are on that box."

Lawson glanced at the box like it was a severed hand.

"Is this cop humor?"

"No."

He called dispatch and had patrol come to pick up the evidence. He signed the chain of custody form while a young officer sealed two evidence bags with the box and the mouse. He decided it would probably also be worth getting a tech to fingerprint Lawson's door handle, the edge of the door, and the underside of the drawer handle.

The security office was in a semi-public space. In order not to stand out, the Ferryman might have avoided wearing gloves. He'd have a limited window to get in the office, print the card, and get out before Lawson returned. On tight timelines, mistakes were made, fingerprints were left behind. Coombes smiled to himself.

It felt right.

He looked through the glass in the lobby at the evening traffic outside. Long lines of light in all directions. It would be solid for the next two hours, minimum. He had a good feeling about the box, and he decided to stop in the bar to celebrate.

20

It was after ten when he parked up in front of his home and it depressed him to see it was all lit up and Julie's car was parked at the door. Days when he needed her to be there, she was gone, days when he didn't, she was there. They just couldn't catch a break. He went inside and heard music playing at the back of the house. *Thump, thump, thump.* She thought it was music at any rate. He didn't know what it was, some kind of Euro pop, or techno. The month before she'd gone through a death metal phase where it sounded like singers had the microphone lodged in the back of their throat and were choking on it.

Because of the music, she didn't hear him come in and he was able to walk right into the bathroom where she was having a bath, her right leg hanging over the edge, dripping water and foam onto the mat beneath. Her eyes were closed and she was smoking the end of a joint like her life depended on it. He turned and looked at the music player that sat on the closed lid of the toilet. It was plugged into an extension lead that ran in through the open door to an outlet in the hall. He turned and looked back at her face and saw that her eyes were open.

"Do it," she said. "Throw it in the water. Maybe I'll feel something."

"It's a stereo, Julie, not a time machine."

She sniggered. Whatever she was smoking, it was good.

"I guess I should congratulate you on your big break. It's good to know our marriage isn't being destroyed for nothing. Maybe soon we'll be able to move out of this shit hole and into a place where the air conditioning works."

Most of the foam had gone from her bath and he could see her naked body beneath the water. It was the first time he'd seen her naked in three months. He frowned.

"What big break?"

"The film director, the one killing all these people."

Coombes felt the blood go out of his face.

"You mean *screenwriter?*"

"Shit, Johnny, he's your suspect. Jake something. The one that likes little girls."

"It was on TV?"

"You think I started buying a newspaper? Of course, on TV. It's been on all night. Why, did I get it wrong? Is he not a suspect?"

The pounding music stopped and Coombes turned to the stereo, surprised. The music started up again. A different track, but somehow identical to the last. *Thump, thump, thump.* On another day, when he hadn't seen a man melted with chemicals, he might have laughed. It was like listening to one of those TV stations that showed nothing but home renovation shows. Someone was taking out a wall with a jackhammer, in his bathroom.

He looked at his wife sadly.

"I miss the days when you listened to The Beatles and Fleetwood Mac."

"That's old people music, you got to update. You want one of these?"

He saw that she had a whole line of joints set up on an abalone shell next to the bathtub. For a second, he wondered if it might not be such a bad idea, what with the image of Anthony Price still burned into his brain. Then he remembered what she'd said about the news and Jake Curtis. He might need to be sharp.

"Thanks, but I'll take a pass."

He turned for the door and she spoke again.

"Why didn't you do it?"

"What?"

"The stereo. Why didn't you throw it in?"

He shrugged. "The house has a circuit breaker."

"Wow," she said. "I thought it was because you loved me."

Coombes nodded slowly, then left without saying anything. In the living room, he switched on the TV and changed it to a news channel. A mafia man who'd been murdered several days earlier in Marina Del Rey was still getting coverage and the news anchor was trying to pretend like she cared without causing lines to form on her perfect face.

Finally, it cut to a piece about Jake Curtis. Coombes stood and watched, his suit jacket still on, his hand with the remote frozen in front of him. A caption filled the screen from one side to the other in capital letters.

DISGRACED HOLLYWOOD SCREENWRITER JAKE CURTIS LEAD SUSPECT IN 'FERRYMAN' SLAYINGS.

Another beautiful woman stood across the street from the PAB, like a twin of the news anchor, talking about his case.

"My sources have confirmed that the shocking details of Jake Curtis' sexual exploits with seventeen-year-old Tammy Watkins came to light as a *direct* result of the investigation into the so-called Ferryman killer. When asked what link there was between Curtis and the killer, my source said simply *none, they're the same person*. Andrea, my head is exploding. This is a huge break in what was otherwise seen as a stalled investigation. I have tried to speak with the lead detective, John Coombes, but with no success. Clearly, a very busy man tonight."

He frowned and took out his cell phone.

There were 86 missed calls. He muted the TV and called his lieutenant's cell. She answered immediately.

"What's going on, John? All hell is breaking lose."

"I've no idea, I just got home and saw the news."

"Block's been riding my ass all night, you got to give me more than that."

"That's some visual, Ellen, but I don't know what to tell you. Curtis alibied out. We are not looking at him at all, not even for Tammy Watkins."

"Block's talking about putting Wallfisch in charge."

"Oh Jesus."

"He thinks *you* are the source, Johnny, and that you leaked the previous story about the girl to that *Times* reporter."

Coombes sighed.

"I did speak to Sullivan, but not about this."

Gantz' voice became tight. "Go on."

"She knew about the coins. I don't know where she got it from, but she was going to publish it anyway. I told her the killer puts them on the victims' eyes."

"*John!*"

"I know, but it worked. Think about it. Every person that walks in off the street claiming they did it, they all talk about putting the coins on the eyes. Remember Walter Ford, the big giant? They all swallowed it. Only us and the killer know the truth."

Gantz was silent for a moment, thinking it over.

"You didn't leak anything else?"

"I didn't leak anything *at all*. I diverted something that was coming out anyway. You think I would bust my ass on a case, then at the same time, potentially destroy it? Come on, you know me. I grind 'til nothing's left. I hate the press. I'm a cop's cop."

"Yeah, I know that. Sorry, Johnny."

It was the first time in a long time she'd called him Johnny. He walked from his living room to his kitchenette diner. He was hungry, he'd eaten nothing since lunch. He opened the fridge and looked at its contents grim-faced.

"I don't know who's leaking information about Curtis, but their information seems to be a little out of date so it's probably not someone on the task force. That lawyer that came with Curtis, I got the feeling that he didn't like representing someone that had sex with a minor. Killers are one thing, but that's something else. That crosses a line."

"You can't be serious, his own lawyer?"

Coombes took out a quart of milk and closed the fridge door.

"I don't know, he was definitely uneasy. He had possession of the footage. But you know what it's like, a juicy tip like this might pay for someone in the department to get a new cell phone or a tablet. Money's tight."

Again, Gantz was silent.

"You think you can hold off Block?"

"Already done."

The call disconnected.

Coombes pulled down a bowl and poured out some Cheerios. He could think of someone else who would gladly throw Curtis under the bus, someone that would contact the press if that's what it took. She lived in Miami, Florida, and she was a lieutenant.

He carried his bowl of cereal through to the living room and sat down. Using his tablet, he searched for Gale online and soon found a photograph and a first name, which was Alisha. The picture was a group shot and he pinched-zoomed tight on her head and shoulders. She was attractive but the resolution of the picture was low and it degraded badly with enlargement. He switched to Facebook and found her in a couple of clicks. There were many more pictures of her, and his first assessment did not change.

He pulled up a picture of her on a yacht. She was smiling, long blonde hair blowing behind her. He ate his cereal, eyes fixed on Alisha Gale. It wasn't a chore. By the time his bowl was empty, he had decided that he didn't much care if she had thrown Curtis under the bus. It was where he deserved to be.

21

Coombes craned his neck, looking up at the smashed window on the 13th floor of the Capitol Records Building. He could make out a small dark space below one of the sun shades that projected out from the side of the building. He then zipped his eyes down fast, as if he'd been there at the time, to where Steve Ellis lay crumpled on the sidewalk.

It wasn't how he'd choose to go; it didn't even make the shortlist. Sure, you might not have long to think about what you'd done, but time had a way of drawing out when you least wanted it to. Plenty of time to change your mind as the sidewalk approached. He shook his head as if to clear the idea and walked across the street.

Hollywood Division SUVs had closed Vine between Yucca and Hollywood Boulevard and, closer in, a secondary police line had been erected to keep pedestrians at bay. A sizable crowd had assembled and more seemed to be arriving all the time. He knew social media spread news fast, but this was ridiculous. Coombes and Sato approached the body together in silence, hands up near their mouths, just in case.

Ellis had landed flat on his back, his feet toward the building. The impact had forced his brain to partially liquify and push out through his eye sockets, his nose and his mouth. It was bad. Splats were always bad. It was like he had sneezed a strawberry milkshake all over his own face.

Coombes glanced down the length of the man's body. Ellis was naked and there was a lot of it. Alive, the man had been larger than life, in death, this continued. His skin had stretched out on the sidewalk, melting in. They'd need a high-pressure washer to get him off the asphalt was his guess.

An autopsy of Ellis would be hard to read. Organs got distorted or mashed together, and he knew that some parts would simply not be found. It didn't matter much from an evidentiary point of view, it was clear what killed him.

"I think he landed on Garth Brooks."

He looked up and saw Billy Lass standing there, a big cheesy smile on his face. Billy had been his partner when he'd worked Hollywood.

It took him a moment to understand: *The Hollywood Walk of Fame.*

"Still with the laughing and the joking, eh?"

"You got it. They told me you guys wanted to take a look as part of your Ferryman case that's all over the news. I gotta say, I think this one is definitely a candidate."

Coombes realized he could smell Ellis and took a step back. His stomach clenched, and for a second, he felt his breakfast start to come back up.

"What makes you say that?"

Lass glanced briefly at the building, at the exit point.

"We're too far out. It's not physics that made him land there. Not gravity alone in any case. You have to see inside, it's going to blow your mind."

"Like this guy?"

His old partner laughed. The problem with a guy like Lass, he reflected, was that he had a way of quickly lowering you to his own level. Being partnered with Sato had made him a more professional cop, not to mention a nicer person. A change that was, apparently, not permanent.

He turned to her.

"Grace, this degenerate is Billy Lass, my old partner. I took the credit for all his work and moved to RHD and left him here to rot."

She nodded as Lass laughed, her face frozen with disgust.

"Seen enough?"

"More than," she said.

Her face was pale, her eyes wide. He guessed his own face looked much the same. Sometimes experience was no protection. They walked around the body, toward the entrance. When you walked around a splat, you gave it plenty of space. Before he entered the building, he looked at the crowd of people watching, cell phones recording. Capturing this moment of history.

Two men, in effect, lay on the sidewalk behind them. Steve Ellis, father of four; and Helmut Grady, soft rock singer of power ballads and occasional actor. Without the police line, Coombes was certain the crowd would encircle their hero and photograph his smashed body.

When you were a celebrity, death was your final performance.

He'd never been in the Capitol Records Building before and the architecture was something to see. The circular shape had defined everything inside it. Lass led them across to an executive elevator and they rode up to the top floor. Lass changed his posture, and it seemed like a different person appeared.

"You hear I have a kid now? A little boy."

"Billy, that's fantastic! What's his name?"

His old partner's eyes sharpened again.

"John. Just like you."

"That's...great."

The elevator doors opened and Coombes got out.

Their partnership had been tight before he moved to the elite Robbery Homicide Division. At the time, Lass had been upset about being left behind, but now he realized it had nothing to do with the job. Lass was upset that he was losing a friend. He felt awkward. After the first week at RHD, his thoughts had never returned to Lass, or any of his other coworkers. His final case at Hollywood had been mired down by the acrimony of his colleagues and he'd decided it was easier to cut ties altogether. His old partner was crude, but he was as loyal as a Labrador and had clearly never forgotten him.

They walked in silence down the heavily curved hallway to where a uniformed officer stood guarding a door. Coombes kept the pace fast, fearing that if he slowed Lass might ask if he had any kids of his own yet, and how things were between him and Julie. The second question would've answered the first question, and for sure he didn't want to get into that with a clown like Lass.

Inside the room, a long table had been turned sideways, filling it from side to side. The end went right up to the space where the window had been, like a runway. Next to it, sat a chair with a neatly folded stack of clothes on top, and a pair of dress shoes next to it on the floor. There was a fussiness to the precision of the folding that made him pause. He'd never seen a man fold clothes so neatly.

A fabric of some kind hung down on either side of the window and rested on the surface of the table. Coombes frowned and walked over to examine it more closely, prodding it with gloveless fingers. It was some kind of elastic, a bungee cord. It was anchored top and bottom on either side of the window by industrial bolts. He turned toward Lass, still standing in the doorway.

The big grinning face was back.

Coombes shook his head in disbelief.

"It's a fucking catapult."

"I knew you'd like it. There was an office chair in the middle of the street when I arrived, it didn't make any sense until I saw this. This guy of yours fired Ellis' fat ass out the window like a cannonball. I'm certain he was aiming at the Walk of Fame. It's a statement, isn't it?"

Coombes said nothing.

There was another bolt at the other end of the table, with some kind of ratchet attached. This would be to pull Ellis back against the force of the bungee cord.

"He's escalating," Grace said. "This is out in the open now, he's not even pretending that Ellis did this to himself."

He nodded. It was exactly what he was thinking.

"I think he's pleased with himself. He wants us to know how he did it."

"Why do you think Ellis was naked?" Lass asked.

"A lot of splats take off their clothes, it's like they're going out of the world the same way they came into it. I'm guessing the killer was keeping it real, showing us his insight."

"*Splats?*" Grace said.

"Yeah. Jumpers...splats. We hardly ever see the jump-"

She held up her hand to stop him.

"All right, I see that," Lass said. "What's your take on why Ellis sat in that seat as it was being pulled back toward the wall. He had to see what was coming, right?"

Coombes nodded. "There's only one explanation. He had no choice. The way I see it, Ellis was forced to climb up on the table then into the chair at the end of a gun, and our guy gave him some kind of tranquilizer like an epidural to stop him escaping. Probably did it right through the back of the chair."

"You think Ellis was conscious?" Grace said.

"Of course. All this set-up? The killer was drawing it out. If he wanted, he probably could've just pushed him out the window but that would have been too quick."

Nobody said anything for a moment. Lass stared at him like a screensaver had come on behind his eyes. His old partner had lost a lot of weight but gained some gray hair. Fatherhood, he supposed. Lack of sleep.

John. Just like you.

"What about the bolts?"

"Installed yesterday by someone wearing a high-visibility vest and hard hat. Nobody could provide a description. It's a dead end."

This was something he'd come across many times before. The more someone looked like they were meant to be doing something, the less they were questioned about it. Among certain trades, including his own, they fell so far below the radar that they were effectively invisible. Coombes sighed, guessing what was coming.

"Cameras?"

Lass shook his head.

"I'll get what they have sent over to you, but it's worthless, I'll tell you that for nothing. Most of these systems are. How many times did we close a case based on security footage?"

"Not once."

Coombes turned and looked out the glassless window frame. Air came in through the opening, moving his hair around. It was a fantastic view. He leaned over and looked down onto Vine and saw close to 500 people looking back up at him. Among the crowd now, news crews.

He directed his attention to where Ellis lay on the sidewalk. To the left were some trees, to the right, a longer angle to the sidewalk. The Ferryman craved publicity. If Lass was right about the *Hollywood Walk of Fame*, then this would be the only office capable of hitting it.

"I assume those are for you?"

Coombes looked where Lass was pointing.

Two silver dollars, one on top of the other.

When they got back outside, four men were gathered around Ellis' body wearing coveralls and full-face biological masks. One of them appeared to be holding a snow shovel, no doubt to help scoop up loose globules of fat, brain, and other material scattered across the sidewalk. They had a public health hazard on their hands, and from the way they were standing, none of them knew quite where to begin.

Coombes and Sato gave them a wide berth, heads turned away. They'd seen all they wanted when they'd arrived. He glanced across at his partner and saw her face was frozen and pinched. The sun had got to work on Ellis' remains and the smell pushed past the hand he held over his nose and mouth.

The old rock star was slowly cooking.

About the only way to survive some of the things you saw in homicide, was to start thinking about victims as evidence, not people. Steve Ellis might've walked into the Capitol Records Building a happy family man, but Coombes couldn't think of the mess on the sidewalk in the same way. It wouldn't help his investigation to get immersed in Ellis's final moments and what was left of him. Bringing his killer to justice wouldn't undo what happened but it would give him some satisfaction, he'd give himself that.

"Your old partner is something else."

He shot a look at Grace.

"That's a generous way of putting it."

"It's the best I can do."

A position he could understand.

Billy Lass wasn't for everyone. When he thought about Lass, it was like thinking about a version of himself that had taken a left turn when he'd taken a right. They'd got to about the same destination, but Lass's route had taken something from him. His partner had become both bitter and political, and it seemed to him like Lass was never happier than when he was complaining about something.

The world was against him, and that was just how he liked it.

They reached the car and climbed in. He'd parked in full sunlight and the interior was like an oven. Coombes started the engine and kicked the AC up to max, his hands resting on top of the wheel, fingers spread open so that the chilled air blew between them.

The crowd had turned to watch them leave and he returned their interest. The Ferryman might be right in front of him. Killers were often thought to stand in the crowd, watching the police process their kills, getting a second high from it. To be seen, and not seen.

The killer knows who I am, he thought.

Perhaps, where I live.

He'd been in the media spotlight before, but never a serial case. If it looked like they were making too much progress, the killer might see them as a threat.

"I've been thinking about Sutton," he said.

"How so?"

"I think he's another victim."

He turned to Grace, to see her reaction. She was frowning.

"Didn't we discount that? There were no coins."

"I know, but a killer's M.O. changes and evolves over time. With every kill he gets better at it, adding little flourishes. An artist perfecting his craft. Perhaps the idea for the silver dollars came later, inspired by something random. A late-night TV show, his kid's book report, it could be anything. If Sutton *was* a victim, then you'd have to conclude that there could be others. People that don't match our original search parameters. Let's face it, we only know about Sutton because he was our case, he didn't come up in the computer results."

She looked doubtful and he continued before she said anything.

"Okay, here's what I'm thinking. The Ferryman hasn't replicated a single kill method, right? Pills, exit bag, all the others. It's like he's checking them off a list. Isn't it surprising that he *hasn't* used hanging as a method if Sutton wasn't one of his? Doesn't that seem like a strange omission? It has to be one of the simplest ways possible."

"All right, say we discover this dirtbag killed another ten or twenty people before we thought he started, what does that get us in terms of getting closer to catching him?"

"Maybe nowhere, Grace, but a lot of these guys start close to home, people with a direct connection. The first victim was real, these others are just because he likes it. Celebrities, the rich. There's going to be no connection, that's what I think. We're pissing into the wind looking for something that just isn't there. All that links the victims so far, is that they're rich and powerful. The top of the food chain. It's no sport hunting bums sheltering under a bridge, that's too easy. You could do it without getting out of your car. Taking out these Alpha predators, making it look like they did it themselves, that's a challenge. A sport."

They were silent for a moment, thinking it over.

"If we looked at all suicides," she said, "we'd drown in cases. This is a hard town and it breaks a lot of people. Depending on the time frame and search radius, we could potentially be looking at hundreds of cases. You're also looking at limited evidence collection. You know the drill; if it's not murder it's not our problem."

"I know it."

"How's your friend doing anyway? Nicolas, right?"

He felt his face color. He didn't know if she was asking out of interest, or to highlight the personal connection between him and the Sutton family, it didn't matter.

"Honestly, I've not been in contact since the memorial. If I reached out to Nicky now, he'd assume I had something new to tell him and I don't. The death is filed as a suicide and the city wants to keep it that way. In any case, I'm not sure he'd welcome the news his father might be the victim of a serial killer. Who wants to hear that?"

Sato said nothing.

When it came to Theodore Sutton, he couldn't think in the same detached manner he could for other murder victims. Sutton's death *bothered* him on an emotional level. Even though he hadn't seen him in a long time, Coombes' memory of him was clear and detailed. Sutton had a dirty joke for every occasion, and what he remembered most about him was the times they had all spent together laughing. The man had given him his first Scotch, his first cigar, and his first paying job. He *owed* him, and his son had basically said as much the last time they'd met.

This debt was a blind spot he couldn't see past.

He put the car in drive and pulled away from the curb.

Time to get back and write up Ellis while the details were still fresh. They approached the police tape and he slowed to allow a uni to lift the tape and let him drive out. He saw two Hollywood detectives he recognized canvassing the crowd. Richter and Williams. They'd been partners for close to twenty years and, for most of those years, they'd hated each other.

As he drove away, Richter turned toward him and held his hands palms-up, the universal sign for *what the hell?* Coombes shrugged and shook his head. There were no words for what had happened and he shared the other detective's dismay.

After a hundred feet they came to a red traffic light.

He slowed to a stop, the only car in line. A man in his thirties walked out into the street, lifted a camera and stood there taking pictures of them through the windshield. Coombes sighed. If the light didn't change soon, he knew others would join this bozo. They were part of the story and everyone wanted a piece. His partner turned to him.

"What do you suppose it means that the killer didn't hide how he killed Ellis?"

He thought about it for a second. The answer was obvious.

"I think it means he's finished."

"I agree."

Coombes said nothing.

"Like he had a list of people he was working through and he reached the end."

He glared at the man taking their photograph.

"Even Santa's got a list," he said.

"Have you ever made a list of unrelated things?"

His breath caught in his throat and he turned to Sato.

"Say it."

"If there's a list of names, there's a link between them."

And for the first time, he believed it.

22

COOMBES STUDIED THE LIST of victims he'd started on the second day of the investigation. Their name, the way they died, followed by the date. It helped to give him an overview. Not trying to assess each crime, but rather to see where they fitted together as part of a whole. He had chosen to start with Theodore Sutton, despite the fact that he didn't fit the pattern. If Sutton was the first, it made sense that he didn't fit the pattern. The killer had perfected things as he went on, that's what you did when you did anything again and again. If Sutton's death *had* matched up perfectly, he'd want to look further back, to find the one with the rough edges.

Nobody was perfect first time.

And yet, he reflected, each kill *was* a first time.

The Ferryman used a different method every time, no duplication. The killer could take little experience from one kill to the next. Changing the cause of death was a huge risk for the killer, as it increased the level of exposure and the chance of something going wrong. Sutton had been found hanging by his own belt from a steel beam in his house. As methods went, it was straightforward and required little in the way of advanced planning. Compared to later kills, it was a walk in the park.

Why not keep it simple?

At the beginning, the change in m.o. hid the fact that the deaths were kills at all, rather than suicides. Despite that, the killer had felt compelled to apply his signature, the two silver dollars. To Coombes, this seemed like a desire by the killer to take credit, and that couldn't happen until the deaths were seen for what they were. The mistakes, as he'd perceived them, might turn out to be no more than breadcrumbs left on purpose.

His telephone rang.

"Coombes."

"This is Dennis Chen at the crime lab. I've processed your fingerprint evidence on a keycard box, a computer mouse, and films lifted from a door."

His trace evidence from the hotel.

"That was fast, normally it takes two or three weeks."

"Chief Jackson told us to move your case into the priority line. Unfortunately, the only prints on the keycard box matched those provided for elimination by Bret Lawson. The mouse gave us nothing but partials, all Lawson's."

"Shit. And the door films?"

"I ran them through AFIS and got four hits, I'll email their details."

The technician's voice wasn't hard to read.

"Honest opinion?"

"I don't have access to the NCIC database, Detective, but my read of the IDs is that we're looking at hotel staff with plenty reason to be going in and out of that office."

He caught a floral scent and saw Gantz standing next to him.

"All right, Chen, thanks anyway."

Coombes hung up.

"My office, John. You too, Grace."

He followed the lieutenant and braced himself for what was certain to be a tide of harassment. Gantz sat behind her desk and waited for Sato to close the door. She didn't ask them to sit down, so he remained standing.

"Your face doesn't look like it's going to tell me good news any time soon."

"I just need more time, we're close."

Gantz's eyebrows shot up. "Really? Because my reading of the situation is that you're no further forward than you were when you started. What have you got so far?"

Inwardly, Coombes sighed. When the pronoun shifted from *we* to *you*, things never took a good turn. The message was clear; this is your neck, not mine.

"He's white. Dark hair. Tall, between six one and six three. Athletic. 180 pounds. We have a partial fingerprint, which we believe is from a right middle finger-"

Gantz laughed, but there was no humor in it.

"Oh, I'm quite certain that it *is* the middle finger, John."

He shifted uncomfortably and she continued.

"So, a white athletic man, around six feet, and one eighty pounds. This description hardly narrows it down, does it? I'm looking at a perfect match right now. Do you have anything to say before I book you?"

He felt his face become hot.

"We're still pursuing active leads. I'd like to reinterview the witness who saw a man running along the sidewalk a block from Haylee Jordan's apartment. I'm going to get Becker and Gonzalez to take a copy of the artist's sketch and show it to people in the area see if they get a hit. Staff in convenience stores, gas stations, the whole works. I'm also waiting for Detective Lass at Hollywood to send over security footage from the Capitol Records Building, but I'm not hopeful. Looks like there's nothing there. This guy's a step ahead of us, he always knows where cameras are located, so we get nothing."

"Back up, Coombes. Did you just say Lass?"

"Yeah, why?"

"*Billy* Lass?"

Gantz was looking at him in a strange way. Around ten thousand people worked for the LAPD, he was surprised she'd even heard of Lass.

"Yeah, Billy. He and I worked together down there."

"Lass hasn't worked for six months, he's suspended."

"Well, he's working now."

Gantz shook her head.

"Not a chance. He kicked Captain Hurst in the balls at a charity function, then spat on his face while he writhed on the floor in agony. Jesus Christ couldn't come back from that."

"Lieutenant, I don't know what to tell you, he was there. He showed us the crime scene, he gave us a walk-through. He knew everything about the case..."

His voice trailed off and it felt like the floor dropped away beneath his feet. Gantz sat back, fingers pressing together in front of her mouth as if in silent prayer.

Coombes pictured Lass as he'd first seen him, standing on the sidewalk on the opposite side of Steve Ellis's smashed body. Wearing the same old suit, the same cheesy smile. He'd looked up, and seen his old partner. It wasn't a coincidence that Lass should be assigned to the case, Hollywood was his patch. There were no alarm bells at all.

There'd been something close to a twinkle in his eyes as he'd spoken to him, which he'd figured was because they hadn't seen each other in such a long time. A reunion, two old buddies. He tried to remember the rest of it; the walk into the building, the elevator, the curved hallway, then, finally, the crime scene. Lass had never turned his gaze toward Sato, it had been fixed on him.

Gauging his reaction. Soaking it up.

I knew you'd like it.

I'm certain he was aiming at the Walk of Fame.

It's a statement, isn't it?

Coombes sat heavily in the seat behind him and let out a long sigh. Anthony Price had been restrained with handcuffs; a tool familiar to Lass.

Sato looked back and forth between them.

"I don't get it," she said.

Gantz looked at her. "You don't?"

"No," she said. "Not unless...oh."

Not unless his old partner was the Ferryman.

It occurred to him that he and Lass had held numerous conversations over the years about the rich and famous. Notably, about how they were keeping all their wealth to themselves, and the crime they witnessed daily was the direct result. Hollywood rubbed your face in the divide between rich and poor, it was impossible not to have a position on the subject.

Coombes recalled his old partner's position without any difficulty. Lass believed that at some future date, those with nothing to lose would rise up to take back the wealth, and as during the L.A. Riots, the LAPD would do nothing to stop them.

Gantz laid her hands flat on the table between them and stared straight up at the ceiling for a moment, before looking back down at him. She used this gesture frequently, to indicate she was thinking about the Chief of Police.

"Nothing would spoil solving this case more than finding out the killer is one of our own. We're looking at a public relations black hole of gargantuan proportions. This would be ten times worse than Rodney King, and it took us over a decade to recover from that debacle. This? This would sink us."

"I know it."

"That being the case, I'd like you to be very careful. Do *not* bring Lass in for questioning under *any* circumstances. Is that understood? We can't lose containment. Find a way to dig into his activities that won't tip him off, can you do that for me?"

Coombes nodded.

"He told me he has a child now, a boy. I could use that as a pretext for getting back in touch with him. We used to be friends." He paused for a beat, an awkward grimace forming on his face. "I think he named his son after me."

Gantz looked at him, incredulous, her eyes piercing.

"Is this going to be a problem for you, John?"

"No, but I still hope it's not him."

"From your mouth to God's ears. Okay, until I say otherwise, the three of us are the only ones with Lass's identity. We can't afford for it to get out, I don't even want to hear we've got a *suspect*, are we clear?"

"Yes, Lieutenant. What about surveillance?"

Gantz shook her head.

"Difficult. We don't have probable cause, that's what I need you to dig up. Something we can take to a judge to get a warrant."

He ran his hand over his chin, thinking.

"Are IA investigating the Hurst incident?"

She smiled. "Nice. I see where you're going. We can piggyback off their investigation and get SIS to start around the clock surveillance. Hurst himself will sign off on that."

Internal Affairs to the rescue. First time for everything, he supposed.

He stood up. "If that's everything."

"Keep me in the loop, John. Every detail."

"You got it."

They turned to leave, but Gantz wasn't finished.

"Grace? Hang back a moment."

Coombes walked out of the office and closed the door behind him. This is how it started, with private chats behind closed doors. It was lunchtime and the detective bureau was quiet. He stood next to an empty desk and waited for the lieutenant to finish with Sato. She wasn't long, a minute later she appeared looking embarrassed and avoiding his eye.

"I'm hungry," he said. "You want to grab something to eat?"

She nodded and they walked to the elevator. There was no-one else standing there, but she looked around to double check they couldn't be overheard.

"You really think it's him?"

The more someone looked like they were meant to be doing something, the less they were questioned about it.

"Yeah," he said. "I really do."

23

Billy Lass lived in a bungalow in Culver City. He'd bought the property in cash with earnings he'd made as a technical advisor on a TV cop show that never aired. It was a surprisingly common Hollywood story, and one that amused his old partner no end. Coombes parked across the street from it in the shade of a walnut tree and gathered his thoughts. He wasn't sure what kind of reception he was going to get, or if Lass was smart enough to work out why he was really here. It was a risk he'd have to take.

He'd decided not to call ahead because he wanted to gauge the other man's natural reaction. Sometimes, those first unguarded seconds could tell you more than an hour-long interview ever could. His smart watch had a voice memo app capable of recording audio within three or four feet and he started the recording. Nothing recorded with it would be admissible, but it was something.

A short flagstone path led up to the front door. He pressed the doorbell, then stepped back so that he wasn't crowding whoever opened the door. After close to thirty seconds, he heard locks being turned. Coombes put a slight smile on his face, like he'd just remembered a joke, and hoped it would pass for friendly. The door swung open and Lass stood there like a wild animal, his eyes burning bright.

"Johnny! My man! How are you?"

"You know how it is. Knee-deep in the dead. They're like a tide that keeps rising."

"Sure, sure. Come in, we're in the yard."

As he passed Lass, the narrow doorway forced them both to turn sideways to make room. For a second, they were eye to eye, toe to toe. Lass' eyes were wide, like he was on drugs. Without knowing why, Coombes smiled.

"Sorry it's been so long. Barely see my wife, never mind old friends."

Billy Lass shrugged like it was nothing.

"Are you hungry? We were about to have lunch. We've got plenty of food."

He had timed his arrival with this exact scenario in mind.

"That'd be great."

Coombes walked down the hallway into a breakfasting kitchen. It was three years since he'd last been here, and it had changed a lot in that time period. Some kind of renovation, a wall missing. Something big. He looked around, trying to figure it out. When he turned back, Lass was standing next to an open fridge.

"Can I get you a beer?"

"I'm good, thanks."

Lass stiffened. "Are you on the program?"

"Not in this lifetime."

Lass reached into the fridge and pulled out a six pack of Coors.

"Don't you love it when people quit drinking then can't stop talking about it? It's as if they want a goddamn medal. Like, if that's who you are sober, do the world a favor and have a goddam drink."

Coombes said nothing.

For the first time, he noted Lass' physical appearance. At the crime scene, he'd been wearing a shabby old suit, same as always. It'd been a bit on the baggy side, but he hadn't paid too much attention to it with everything that was going on. But today, he was wearing a tight T-shirt, knee length shorts, and flip-flops. There was no hiding it, Billy Lass hadn't just lost weight, he'd totally rebuilt his body. His arms looked like the belonged to an Eighties' action star, they were enormous. Coombes imagined the strength required to deadlift a drugged Steve Ellis into position on the conference table in the

Capitol Records Building. It wasn't the way he'd imagined it, but it was possible. Definitely possible.

Lass seemed to notice the way he was looking at him.

"Are you on the job?"

"Nah, man."

"What, then?"

Coombes smiled. "Are you kidding? I'm here to see your boy."

The tension vanished from Lass' face.

"I thought that was it when I saw you at my door!" He shook his head ruefully from side to side. "I tell you something, Johnny. I love that little guy. He's got fat sausage arms and legs, but he's the cutest thing I ever saw. Come on, let's go out back."

He followed Lass into his yard, which was huge by L.A. standards. A deck area with a grill and some seating backed onto the house, and beyond that lay a faded rectangle of grass. Despite the cool December sunshine, Lass' wife lay topless on a towel next to her child.

Coombes looked away, embarrassed.

"Sofia, look. We have a guest."

"Johnny!"

His wife squealed with delight and ran toward them. Sofia was a very well put-together Latina in her late twenties. She barreled up the steps to the raised deck area and wrapped her arms tight around Coombes' waist like they were old lovers. His face turned scarlet. He could feel the warm press of her breasts through his thin cotton T-shirt.

He glanced at Lass and saw him grinning from ear to ear.

When Sofia's hug ended, she looked up at him with a face just as flushed, he guessed, as his own. Coombes had always found her attractive and motherhood had changed nothing. She smiled at him with such warmth that he could feel it in his bones. He'd almost forgotten what that felt like. Her smile faded and she frowned.

"Where have you been, Johnny?"

Her voice now had hard edge. She punched him in the ribs.

"You bastard! What happened to you? We *missed* you."

She continued to punch him. They weren't play punches; they were the real deal. Her face was intense, her dark eyes full of anger and something else. *Fire.* He'd heard Latinas could be passionate, but had no experience of it until now.

"All right honey," Lass said. "How about you put a top on?"

She tilted her head over at an angle.

"You don't like my tits, Johnny?"

He flinched. "I'm...trying not to look."

"It's true! He doesn't like them!"

"They are spectacular, Sofia. Really."

She beamed up at him, her eyes bright.

"Spectacular! I like that."

She turned and skipped back down to where her son sat and picked up her bikini top. He hadn't remembered Sofia being so kooky, but she was a delight. Lass lifted one eyebrow at him and nodded his head slowly, as if to say *you see what I'm dealing with?*

"You're a very lucky man," Coombes said, quietly.

"How so?"

"I totally just destroyed my shorts."

Lass threw back his head and laughed.

"I don't doubt it. Her hormones are all over the place right now. She could land a 747 with the signals she's giving off."

Sofia returned with her son in her arms. The boy stared at him with unblinking curiosity. Despite his young age, the child already had a thick swatch of dark hair.

"Johnny, meet John." She smiled. "Do you mind that we named him after you?"

God, it was true.

"I'm honored. Can I hold him?"

He had learned that this is what new parents expect you to ask and she happily handed the infant over to him. John wasn't a small baby and was surprisingly heavy. Coombes looked into the child's dark eyes and found himself smiling. He rocked John from side to side. There was something pleasing about the child's weight. *What am I going to do if I find out your dad's a serial killer?* It would be a disaster. A guy like Lass, he wouldn't give himself up. He'd fight till his last breath. If it came to it, would he put him in the ground?

"He likes you," Sofia said.

"Smart kid."

"You got one of your own yet?"

The rocking stopped and he passed the child back to his startled mother. "No."

Lass laughed again and clapped his hand down on his shoulders. "Lighten up, Coombes! It'll happen, believe me. And not when you expect, that's for sure. Now, let's get some burgers on the grill, I'm starved."

Sofia moved back over to her spot on the grass with John, and he and Lass moved over to the large grill at the end of the deck. It looked like the grill had been on for some time, and the heat distorted the air above it. He'd embarrassed himself and he decided to stay silent for a while. He watched Lass set out a huge pile of food across the surface of the grill. Burgers, hot dogs, corn cobs. It seemed to go on and on.

"I don't know if you've got enough food for all of us, Billy. You want me to go pick something up?"

Lass turned to him, a long two-pronged fork between them.

"You know, Sofia's right. We *have* missed you."

He nodded, awkwardly.

"I heard you had some kind of beef with Hurst, you ever get that sorted out?"

"No, man. It's still going on."

"What's the real story? All I heard was that you assaulted him."

Lass nodded and seemed to gather himself for a moment.

"We were at a charity dinner for sick kids. Five grand a plate if you believe that. I was standing in for my L-T who bailed at the last minute, so it was all paid for. Everything was going fine. The booze was flowing and the food was fantastic. Not my usual gig, but it was cool. How the other half live, you know? Men in ten-thousand-dollar tuxedos, women in fifty-thousand-dollar dresses. It was something else, like being at the Oscars maybe.

"Anyway, Sofia had to keep going to the restroom and I see Hurst approach her three different times as she came and went, trying to hand her his empty wine glass. He saw her, and he saw a servant. Three times! She was eight and a half months pregnant, John. I didn't catch on at first what was happening, but soon as I did, I kicked his balls into the back of his throat and I don't regret it for a second. Nobody treats my girl like that."

Coombes sighed. None of this surprised him in the slightest.

"I'm sorry, Billy. That's tough."

Lass shrugged and drank some beer. His body had become tense, his memory bringing the anger back. Coombes moved a little closer and dropped his voice.

"I kind of wish I'd seen that fight though."

Lass looked him in the eye.

"It was *fantastic*. I felt like a god. I could've kicked him all night long. It was the best rush of my life seeing that racist cracker cowering on the floor. I shouldn't say this, being a cop, but some fools need to be called out for their behavior, it's the only way they'll learn."

Lass's eyes shone like they'd been polished. There was a spark there, the same kind of crazy energy he'd noticed at the front door.

"I hear that," Coombes said. "The man's had it coming for years."

"That's what I'm saying. *Thank you*."

Smoke started to rise from the grill and Lass began to flip burgers.

"Is that beer still on offer?"

Lass smiled. "Help yourself."

Coombes took a can, opened it and took a long drink. It was still ice-cold from the fridge and it felt good going down. He watched Lass work the grill in silence. The altercation with Hurst predated any of the Ferryman's kills. It was conceivable that the fight had been the trigger event for everything that was to follow. Either the enjoyment of the violence itself, or the suspension from duty that stemmed from it. He moved his beer can into his left hand so that his watch could better capture conversation.

"I've not been in a fight since my early twenties, but when you mention that buzz...I can remember it like it was yesterday. Sometimes, words just don't get the job done."

"I knew you'd understand, Johnny. We come from the same place, you and me. We're the same. But you know how the system works, the elite close ranks. We *all* get passed the empty wine glass, my friend. We're just dirt on the soles of their feet."

Lass played the victim card all wrong. For him, it was like a superhero's cape that he wore around his shoulders with pride. By playing the part of victim none of his circumstances were his fault. He understood Lass' attitude to a racist like Hurst, not to mention his desire to protect his wife, but did it stop there or had Lass taken it somewhere else? With the right mindset, Lass could use these beliefs to justify almost anything.

"I take it Hurst is pressing charges?"

"Actually, no. From my reading of the situation, he can't. If he presses charges then the whole thing will come out. He knows he can get away with being racist in a one on one, but he's smart enough to know it's career poison out in the open. He's refusing to take part in the investigation, so the whole thing's dragged on for months."

Lass began to scoop up burgers and put them into buns he had sitting open. He put two patties per bun, each one 3/4s of an inch thick. When he was through, he added a serving of ketchup and mustard, a plastic bottle in each hand like a production line and then sat the top bun in place. Coombes saw Lass was smiling as he worked and he found himself smiling along with him. It had been a while since they had been friends but some things never change. There was a bond of some sort between them even now, with the thought of the murders in the background. Lass passed him a plate towering with food.

"Do me a favor, Johnny. Don't talk about this in front of Sofia."

"No problem."

He stayed for almost two hours. Eating, drinking, and talking. It was as though nothing had happened, their friendship picking back up where it had left off with no bad blood. By the time he got up to leave, it was obvious to Coombes that his partner's life had turned out better than his, and the only cloud on the horizon was the business with Hurst. As far as he could see, Lass had too much to lose to be killing off the city's rich. He was a family man now. He'd struck out at the captain to protect his wife, that was all. Coombes had gone back and forth over this problem the entire time and every time he'd decided he'd reject the idea, he'd catch a hint of darkness or rage in Lass's eyes or the curl of his mouth.

Lass walked with him, down his path to the street.

"You're taking a lot of heat on this Ferryman thing."

This was the first time either of them had mentioned the case.

"It's going to get worse before I'm through."

They crossed the street and stood next to the walnut tree.

"At your press conference on Friday, you said that you had several promising lines of enquiry. Is that true?"

"Yeah."

"So, you've got nothing?"

Coombes laughed.

"Not a goddamn thing, brother. The guy's a ghost. A real pro."

He watched Lass' face closely. His eyes dipped down to the ground and the corners of his mouth came up. Tiny movements. Micro-expressions. He was no expert, but it was clear to him that Billy Lass was pleased his case was going nowhere.

Coombes unlocked his car and got in. It was cool inside; the walnut tree had done its job. He started the car and lowered the window so he could sign off with Lass. Billy put his hands on the door frame, his muscular body leaning over him.

"That coins on the eyes thing, I assume that's to detect copycats and fakes?"

"Correct. I didn't know I was gifting the guy a name."

Lass nodded and was silent awhile, thinking.

"No link between the victims?"

"None we can find. We're still looking, but I think it's a bust."

"Random then? An opportunist."

"The *method* is his thing, the challenge of it, rather than the victim. You saw that damn catapult. At the end of the day, the victim is just meat."

He still hadn't asked Lass why he was at the Capitol Records Building, and he could see that there was no easy way to get to it. If he broached it head-on, it would be obvious to Lass why he'd come here and that would end their friendship. There'd be no going back, and he needed to keep Lass on-side so that he could continue to sniff around.

"Billy, thanks for lunch. It was great to meet John. I meant to bring him something, a gift, but the time got away from me. Next time, I'll do better."

This wasn't true. He'd deliberately not brought anything to give him another reason to come back. Lass appeared to notice that his hands were on the paintwork and without batting an eyelid, took a cloth from his pocket and wiped down the door frame.

"Call me anytime if you want to bounce some ideas off me about the case. I need a project to work on to keep my hand in the game, you know?"

"I might just do that."

24

COOMBES SAT IN THE task force room staring at the wall. Not the wall they'd covered with information, but the blank wall above Grace Sato's head. The room affected his concentration in a way he couldn't define. He preferred to work alone or, at most, with a partner. Being part of a large group didn't work for him. It wasn't that he couldn't delegate, it was that the small apparently insignificant steps that were part of every investigation were actually part of his process, and often where a case broke. To notice inconsistencies in data, one person had to view all of it.

His eyes dipped and he saw that Sato was watching him.

She's quite beautiful, he thought. Grace held his eye contact until he looked away. His interest in her was shifting from professional into something that should never exist between partners.

Coombes stood and left the room.

He needed to be moving, to feel like he was getting somewhere, because it was obvious to him that he wasn't. The Ferryman case was going nowhere. He rode the elevator down to the street and stood at the entrance in the still air in front of the building. At one time, when it had been legal, cops had been able to go outside for a smoke and think through their cases. Coombes had never smoked, so he did the next best thing, and set out for a coffee.

When he got back to his desk, he was about halfway through a cup of coffee the size of his head. One day soon, he was certain they'd serve coffee in popcorn buckets. He was ready for that day, he'd been ready for years. He decided to finish the cup before he returned to the task force, on account of the coffee he hadn't brought for anyone else.

The phone on his desk rang.

"Coombes."

"Detective, this is Officer Fleet out of Hollenbeck. We met a couple of times when you worked Hollywood station, and briefly again last year."

Coombes leaned back in his chair and looked at the ceiling.

"Fleet," he said, trying to remember. He pictured a kid in his twenties that looked like he hadn't started shaving yet. "Are you the snot-nosed punk that contaminated my crime scene on the Lilly Nichols case?"

An awkward laugh came down the line.

"Uh. Officer snot-nosed punk, reporting for duty."

"What can I do for you today, Fleet?"

"I read about your case in the *Times* and thought of something that might be related."

"All right."

"A few weeks ago, I attended a fatal accident. One Adrian Blackstone out of Bel Air. His car took the Fourth Street exit of the I-5 in excess of 100 mph and hit the side of an RV that was crossing the intersection. We figured he fell asleep and his car drifted onto the exit lane. There were no skid marks until he was almost at the traffic signal, which is when we assumed he woke up. At that point, there was no chance of stopping his car."

"Okay."

Not an unreasonable assumption.

"That intersection is less than a mile from our station and the whole thing happened in front of my vehicle as we headed back out after an arrest. It was close, another two seconds and he would've hit me. The accident happened too quickly at the time, but we have it all on dash cam. On playback you can see he's terrified."

No shit, Coombes thought.

"And how do you think this relates to my case?"

"Blackstone had two silver dollars in the center console."

It was pretty much what he'd expected Fleet to say.

"Any other change in there?"

"No."

It felt right, like it belonged on the list. Coombes opened his notebook to where he'd written down the timeline with the dates.

"Let me guess, was this November eighth?"

Fleet paused, no doubt looking at his own notes.

"Yeah, how'd you know? Around two in the a.m."

Somehow, the press had yet to notice that the kills had all occurred on a Friday. He supposed this was due to the way the story had unfolded, like a dam opening. Coombes felt no desire to share this information with Fleet.

"Lucky guess."

He picked up his pen and wrote *Adrian Blackstone* into the blank line he'd left between Simon Keehan and William Morgan. He'd always known there was a name missing. Known enough, to leave a space for it.

"Any sign the car was tampered with?"

"Far as I know, it was never checked. You got to understand, the vehicle was totaled in the accident. That compartment with the coins was about the only part of it that still moved. Our primary focus at the time was trying to save his life. A fire crew spent fifteen minutes cutting him out his car, but he died at the scene. I'd say *sadly died*, but it was the smart move on his part, his face was burger. His airbag hadn't deployed."

"Who investigated it?"

"That's what I'm telling you, Detective. There *was* no investigation. It was an open-and-shut accident. We saw it with our own eyes, and we have it on a recording. There was no room for doubt."

His chest filled with anger. The situation wasn't Fleet's fault, yet the persistence of the accident angle grated. Clearly, it was not an accident, and the fact that Fleet had called him was a belated recognition of that fact. Still, the incident had happened at 2 a.m. and at that time in the morning no one is thinking clearly. By the time it gets passed from the graveyard shift to the day crew, detectives would be looking for cases that could be quickly closed out to minimize their inbox.

"You guys still have the dash cam footage?"

"Sure. I'll send everything we've got over to you."

Blackstone was the first victim to have survived, if only for a short time.

"Did he say anything before he died?"

"The man was breathing and had a pulse, that's it."

Coombes sighed in frustration.

"What was Blackstone driving?"

"Tesla Model S. Such a waste, I'd love one of those."

"What happened to the coins?"

"No idea. Unless they're needed for evidence, personal effects are returned to next of kin as soon as possible, so my guess is that his widow has them. I tell you something for nothing, Blackstone was seriously rich. He was wearing a watch worth four million dollars, I recognized it immediately."

"Four million? *For a watch?*"

"Oh yeah. A Patek Philippe 5004T. If there's one thing I know, it's watches."

Coombes sighed. How the rich chose to spend their money was a frequent source of irritation to him. Once again, there was zero physical evidence for him to work with, it was like working a twenty-year-old cold case. There'd been no fingerprints left on any of the other coins and there was no reason to think the killer would start making mistakes now.

The Tesla, however, was different.

Adrian Blackstone of Bel Air almost certainly had life insurance in the tens of millions. Perhaps more. Coombes had no idea what the ceiling was for the super-rich. In any case, the insurance agent would want to examine the car before approving any claim. The vehicle would not yet have been destroyed.

"All right, Fleet, have a good one. If you think of anything else let me know."

"You got it."

He cut the call. The shot-nosed punk wanted to be on the task force, he could tell.

Blackstone fitted the pattern of the Ferryman almost perfectly. Rich, killed on a Friday, and the two silver dollars left at the scene. What didn't fit so well, was that this appeared to be an accident, not a suicide. If they had to look into accidental deaths as well, then their workload might've just doubled.

He opened his browser and typed in *vehicular suicide* then clicked the search button. He got nearly a million hits. Some of the links were purple, because he'd already been on those pages researching the other suicide methods.

It made for grim reading, and after only a short amount of time, he closed the four tabs he'd opened. One article mentioned how the vehicle's brakes would often be applied before impact, as the last flicker of survival kicked in.

This replicated what Fleet had told him about Adrian Blackstone's crime scene, and held out the possibility that the killer had somehow been in control of the car and had applied the brakes late to further his twisted suicide agenda.

Another elaborate tableau from the Ferryman, churned gracelessly underfoot by tired LAPD officers convinced they'd witnessed an accident. The subject left a bad taste in his mouth and he fed in a stick of gum to clear it out.

Walter Ford had viewed the dead with amusement when he'd confessed and he sensed a similar dry humor from Fleet describing the victim's wealth. Nobody cared when the poor died, but when it came to the rich, a lot of people were borderline delighted. As if the death was some kind of cosmic correction to balance out the good fortune they'd experienced up until that point. Coombes walked back to the task force room.

He couldn't take any pleasure from what was happening. The Ferryman was no hero redistributing wealth, he was a sick serial killer and his victims deserved justice the same as anyone else. Inside the meeting room he found all five members of the task force sitting around the table working on laptops. They looked up and watched as he entered the room and walked to the large whiteboard mounted on the wall. He picked up the eraser, wiped out the top four names on the list and moved them up to make room for the new name.

Theodore Sutton	10/12	hanging
Harry Ryan	10/18	self-administered GSW
Gordon Sellers	10/25	inert gas exit bag
Simon Keehan	11/01	cyanide
Adrian Blackstone	11/08	car crash
William Morgan	11/15	drowning
Milton Vandenberg	11/22	drug overdose
Haylee Jordan	11/29	slit wrists
Anthony Price	12/06	ingestion of corrosive liquid
Steve Ellis	12/13	fall from height

When he finished, he stepped to the side so they could see.

"Oh, man," McCreary said.

Sato sat back on her seat.

"Well, Johnny, you always said there was one missing."

He nodded.

"On the other hand, it seems obvious from the date alone that Sutton doesn't belong on this list. As much as I hate it, I have to conclude his was a suicide all along. Unless any of you think otherwise, I'm going to take his name off the board."

Coombes looked at each of them, all shook their heads. Sato was the only one who gave him eye contact while doing so. She knew that Sutton wasn't just a name on a list. He picked up the eraser again and slid it back across over his name. When he was done, there was still a trace of Sutton's name there, like a ghost, at the top of the list. Nobody had believed his theory about Sutton being the first victim, but they'd gone along with it because that's what you did. You worked the case and you ground away, until only the truth remained.

"One piece of good news," he said. "It's the 21st today."

Five blank faces looked back. Coombes pointed at the last date on the timeline.

"He's stopped."

25

COOMBES HELD A BOWL of cereal up near his face and shotgunned the contents into his mouth, crunching and slurping. The most important meal of the day, gone in thirty seconds. He wiped his chin then took his coffee over to the breakfast bar where his tablet was propped up.

He had mirrored a lot of the murder books' content onto his tablet, along with key images from each crime scene so he could pull them up and work on them when he had the time or an idea drifted through his head. Taking documents home was against official policy, but he didn't know of a cop that didn't do it. There was no telling when you might get an idea and he knew from experience that if you didn't immediately run it down it was likely to be forgotten long before you got back behind your desk.

He pulled up photographs first of the Vandenberg scene, then of Steve Ellis. It was hard to believe there was any link between them. A blue-blood movie producer and a renegade rock star. Then he remembered that Ellis had developed a sideline in acting. Not cameos as himself, but playing proper roles. Small budget indie movies mostly, a couple of high-budget Hollywood movies. Coombes made a note to check if Ellis had ever worked for Vandenberg's studio. There was a creak on the floor behind him.

"Oh, Jesus! Put that away."

His wife's face was screwed up, her head angled away from his tablet.

"I'm working, Julie."

"Not here you're not. Not *that*. Read your notes, or news stories, or whatever, but not pictures. I don't want to *see* it. I don't want that in our home."

Coombes sighed and flicked the cover closed on his iPad.

"I don't much want to see it myself; it makes me remember the *smell*."

Julie held up the palm of her hand. Too much.

"Do you really think you can swim in the same water as this psychopath and not be contaminated by the darkness? In case you haven't figured it out yet, all this," she pointed at his tablet, "it's not normal. It's *sick*."

It was part of their old relationship dynamic that she'd test him with an argument because how he responded told her how he felt about her and how much he valued their relationship. He didn't have time for games.

"You know what? You're right. I'm sorry you saw that, okay?"

It was a skip-to-the-end answer and her lip curled with anger. She didn't *want* to be right; she already knew she was right. She wanted to be *valued* and he just couldn't get there.

"When will this end, Johnny?"

"When I catch him."

"There's always going to be someone who needs to be caught."

"I should quit? Let this guy continue to kill?"

"Why not? Someone would replace you. When this guy's caught, someone will replace him. People are crazy, Johnny, you can't stop that. Is this all you want from life? Looking at someone's brains over breakfast? Our last vacation was five years ago. Five years! You might as well be dead for all the difference it makes to me."

Coombes nodded, like he was agreeing with her, instead of spinning his mental radio dial to another station. He opened a kitchen cupboard and pulled out his travel mug. Her eyes fixed on it, clear about its significance. That he'd rather drink his coffee alone as he drove to work, than listen to her.

Coombes tipped his coffee into it, held it up like he was toasting her health, then scooped up his iPad and walked out the room.

"Johnny! We're having a *conversation* here."

"Yeah? Let me know how it turns out."

He pulled the front door shut and heard something thump against the wood next to his face and crash on the floor. When he solved Ferryman, he was going to be back here listening to this for two weeks minimum. He got into his car and pulled away fast, like he was fleeing the scene of a crime.

No matter how bad things got, he'd never once considered leaving the job. It was all he'd ever known. Even in the Army, he'd been a cop. What would he be if he wasn't a detective? The thought went around and around as he moved through Fairfax. He knew cops who'd punched out early. Some had gone on to work as security consultants, some little more than bodyguards to the rich. More money, regular hours, no corpses.

It didn't appeal to him at all.

His cell phone rang and the screen displayed a photograph of Grace Sato. He hadn't added a photograph to her contact details, yet there it was. It was a selfie, and it appeared she'd used his phone to take it. He found himself smiling as he took the call.

"*Grace.*"

"Hi, Johnny. Are you on your way in?"

"Yeah, what's happening?"

"I'm at Theodore Sutton's home in Silver Lake. Someone set it on fire last night and they weren't messing around. The building's gutted and part of the roof has fallen in."

He felt a space open up inside him, something important.

"Anyone dead?"

"Nobody seems to know. The fire investigator just got here."

"All right. I'll be there in fifteen."

Twenty-eight minutes later, he parked and stepped out onto a packed street. Because of her size, it took him a moment to locate Grace Sato. When he did, he saw that she was looking straight at him and probably had been the whole time. Instead of being irritated by this, she looked amused by his confusion.

"You remembered me being taller, huh?"

"Grace, I forget what you look like from one minute to the next."

Her jaw fell open and she smacked his arm playfully with the back of her hand. It was no Sofia Lass *punch*, yet he felt it just the same. Her eyes were dark and intense. They weren't hard to look at, yet some primal urge made him turn and face across the street to where a man was standing watching them. Nicolas Sutton. The other man's hands were balled up into fists inside a warm-up jacket, the muscles across his shoulders stretched tight with tension.

Coombes' smile flattened out.

Whatever friendship they'd once had was long gone, replaced by something close to hatred. He'd failed to catch Teddy's killer and now here he was at the burned-out scene of the crime with a big smile on his face. Coombes made what he hoped was a more compassionate expression and threw in a small nod. Sutton spat on the asphalt and walked away.

Coombes sighed and turned back to Sato.

"What do we know so far?"

"Neighbor woke around 4 a.m. Thinking something woke him up, he looked out his bedroom window. One time he saw a coyote on the street and he keeps hoping to see it again. Anyway, this time, he sees a figure running out of Sutton's gates. By the time the neighbor got out front, the building was on fire. He called it in. Fire Department got here in five minutes; our guys took twenty-two. Needless to say, they found no trace of the arsonist."

He flinched at the twenty-two minutes.

It made little difference. Whoever did this would be inside a car in less than a minute, and a mile away several minutes after that. There was little chance of catching the perpetrator of a crime when the crime itself consumed much of the evidence left behind.

"He saw *a figure?* That's what he said?"

"That's what he said. I pushed him to see if he might go one way or the other, but he said it was too dark to be sure. I have a feeling his eyesight isn't the best. He was wearing these *Mr. Magoo* glasses with thick lenses. They made his eyes look like they were lit up."

"*Great.* Any security footage?"

"I checked houses on the street before you got here and none have cameras angled outward. There *is* helicopter footage of the fire. That's why I came actually, it was on the news while I was eating breakfast."

"Probably didn't capture the arsonist though."

"That would be my guess."

Silence fell between them and he turned to look back to where Nicolas Sutton had been standing. There was no sign of him, yet Coombes still felt the energy of the other man's anger directed at him. As a cop, he was used to being the recipient of hostile emotions by people who thought they knew who he was. Who assumed he was an oppressor, some kind of fascist puppet of the government. It all rolled off his back unnoticed.

Nicky was different.

He *did* know who he was, better than almost everyone.

Despite this, it seemed Sutton now personally blamed him for both the fire and the death of his father. His mind turned back to the investigation. The two events had to be linked, it didn't seem likely that the home would be randomly targeted, it had to be part of the Ferryman case. Fires were typically set in order to file an insurance claim, erase evidence, or with the intent to kill someone trapped inside.

"Okay," Coombes said. "Say the Ferryman took out Teddy Sutton. Let's also say this was his first murder and because of that it's special in a way the others aren't. He thinks about it a lot, around and around, like a happy memory. First kiss, first touchdown, first kill. Like that. Suddenly he realizes he made a mistake. A moment he wasn't wearing a glove; or that he'd been in the house before, socially. That his DNA is everywhere. He decides on a permanent solution."

Sato nodded. "Nobody burns down a house to cover up a suicide."

"*Exactly.*"

"It's like he *wants* us to know we screwed up, Johnny. That we missed some piece of evidence. He's rubbing it in our faces and laughing."

"A tableau of a different kind."

"I see that, but I mean it feels forced, doesn't it?"

Coombes said nothing and turned to stare at the destroyed building. He'd spent much of his teenage years here with the Suttons, like he was an orphan they'd adopted. The building was barely recognizable. He wondered if it might be a relief to Nicky that the place where his father died had been cleansed, that it would likely now have to be fully destroyed. After a couple of minutes, the fire investigator emerged from inside the blackened building and walked up the driveway toward them, his eyes moving over their suits.

"Slow day at RHD, detectives?"

"Not quite. This location was previously the scene of a possible homicide. What can you tell us about the fire?"

"All right. I can confirm it was deliberate. Starting in the front doorway, it swept quickly through the rest of the building. An accelerant was involved and I'm going to go with gasoline based on residues left behind and the burn pattern on the wall next to the staircase."

"Anyone inside when it went up?"

"Doesn't look like it."

"You can't be sure?"

"There's usually something left behind and I didn't see anything."

"What about coins?"

"*Coins?*"

"Specifically, two silver dollars."

"*That's* who you are! The *Ferryman* detective, I thought you were familiar. I didn't see any silver dollars, but gasoline burns at 1,878 degrees. That's hot enough to melt silver and copper, so it's possible they didn't survive. Strange to think a human body could outlast a metal coin, isn't it? You want my *two cents?*" The investigator paused to smile. "This was just a bored teenager with a can of gas and a bunch of matches."

Coombes put on his sunglasses.

"Two cents doesn't buy as much as it used to."

26

COOMBES FOUND A STACK of emails waiting for him from Officer Fleet when he started his computer. It impressed him the way the young cop had broken down the information by content type and split it across multiple emails rather than mashing everything together on a single long email, as a lot of cops did.

He opened the email containing the dash cam footage first.

There were links to around fifty files on the server. The filenames showed three different call signs representing the different patrol vehicles that attended the crash. All the clips were five minutes long and each was time stamped to show they were unedited.

He played the first clip, which showed Fleet's vehicle pulling away from their station house and cruising along near-empty streets. A light rain was falling and the asphalt was wet, a fact that doubtless played into what happened next. The clip ended before the incident and he supposed Fleet had included it to support the timeline in his report. He moved on to the next. Almost immediately, the big patrol SUV turned toward the I-5. In front he saw the RV Fleet had mentioned during their call.

This was it, the clip that would have it all. The others were just noise. Coombes glanced to the left side of the screen toward where Adrian Blackstone's Tesla would appear. Above, in the distance, a stop light changed to green and they moved forward, quickly building speed. The patrol vehicle, the RV, and a car in front of that he couldn't make out.

It seemed like nothing was going to happen right up until the last second, when the Tesla appeared almost out of nowhere and hit the RV. The closing speed made it look like a missile strike, and even though he was expecting it, he was still shocked.

The RV was sheared in half by the collision.

Adrian Blackstone's Tesla spun around after the first impact, hit Fleet's SUV, then spun the opposite way, popped up over a curb until it came to rest against a fence. The car appeared to be relatively intact, except that the front section had crumpled up and the side windows were now gone.

Almost four seconds passed before Fleet and his partner exited their vehicle and ran to provide assistance. Coombes could clearly see their hands shaking from the shock and adrenaline spike. The partner called it in while Fleet bent to look inside the Tesla. He then moved sharply to the right and vomited at the side of the road.

It was the smart move on his part, his face was burger.

Coombes shook his head and sighed. You don't throw up at the crime scene, you just don't. It was like the first rule in police work. The man couldn't stop contaminating his crime scenes. It was a hard job, and they can't prepare you for what you will see, but still.

The clip came to the end and rather than go on to the next one, he played the beginning again, slowing down the impact sequence and advancing frame by frame. As the Tesla entered the shot, Adrian Blackstone's face was illuminated by the headlights of the SUV. His mouth was frozen open in what Coombes could only assume was a scream, his eyes wide with horror.

Blackstone saw his death coming and it was no suicide.

He moved to the next email, which contained photographs of the scene taken from every angle. The intersection, facing up each cross street; the three vehicles involved, including Fleet's SUV; shots of the fire crew cutting the Tesla open; and lastly, shots of Blackstone himself. Coombes picked up his lunch and dropped it unopened in his trash can. A minute later, he was in the washroom splashing water in his face.

He'd looked down on the young cop for being sick, but he owed the man an apology. The Blackstone crime scene was right up there with Steve Ellis' at the Capitol Records Building. It was as bad as anything he'd seen in his entire career and it was seared into his brain merely from a photograph of it. He leaned over the sink and looked at his face in the mirror.

It was white as a ghost.

The door popped open and his least favorite person in the department came through it. Detective Wallfisch. Ruddy face, bad hair, and a body that was almost completely spherical. He was mid-laugh as he came in but the laugh died on his lips when he saw him.

"Damn, Coombes. What happened to you?"

"I just saw a man smashed to pulp in an auto wreck."

Wallfisch nodded, like *that would do it*, then walked toward one of the stalls.

"There's a pint of *Wild Turkey* in my drawer if you need it."

Coombes looked at the other man's broad retreating back with surprise. It was the first decent thing the detective had ever said to him. His desk temporarily infected by what he'd seen on his computer, he decided to go to the task force room and make some notes about the fire. He found Sato in there, her face inches from her laptop screen.

Coombes moved around the side to see what she was watching and saw it was the Haylee Jordan parking garage footage. The killer walking toward the camera, his head dipping as the strip light approached, then coming back up after it was behind him. The whole sequence was over in seconds.

She rewound to before the head dip and paused it.

The Ferryman was looking directly toward the camera but all they could see was shadow and pixel grain. She turned up the brightness on her screen, trying to make a face appear out of the darkness, but all that happened was that the shadows washed out and the white unshaded tip of the killer's nose became a blown-out sun.

Sato sat back in her seat.

"He's like a ghost, Johnny. The more you look at him, the less he exists."

"The camera is junk. The brand went out of business 30 years ago. Rollins said it's equivalent to $1/6^{th}$ of a megapixel, we'll get no ID from it."

Sato tapped her screen.

"He hides his face. He knew the cameras were there and that we'd look at this footage."

"Of course."

"But he's still framing Haylee's death as a suicide, like she did this to herself."

Coombes nodded, getting her meaning.

"He likes the press attention the kills give him. The coins, the suicide, it's all part of his signature. He's captured the public imagination."

"It only became a signature later. At the beginning, the suicide had a function, to hide the fact that these people were being murdered."

"Was he hiding the murders from us, or the other victims?"

Sato's mouth dropped open in surprise.

"Wow, I hadn't thought of that."

"Families don't like suicide. Funerals become private with no publicity. From a social point of view, it's like the victims have disappeared. Robbed not only of their life, but a celebration of that life and what they achieved. A guilty secret that no one talks about. People outside the inner circle might not find out for weeks or months."

"And if he's killing one a week-"

"They could all be dead before any of them realizes what's happening."

The door opened and Gonzalez came in with a big smile and a lot of positive energy. She put an evidence bag down on the desk in front of them. Inside was a circuit board with wires coming out of it. He glanced back up.

"What's this?"

"*That* is an Arduino microcontroller board. We pulled it out of the Metro Grand elevator. It was hooked into the power, emergency door release, and security cameras. I'm sure you know what it does."

"It cuts the cameras."

"That's right. Now tell me the clever part."

Coombes looked at the circuit board. Even without removing it from the bag he could see it was covered in dust and that one of the chips had a darker corner from heat build-up.

"It's been there for ages."

Gonzalez smiled.

"32 days before Vandenberg was killed, the elevator was out of service for approximately five minutes. It worked perfectly afterward so it was never investigated."

"Let me guess. The hotel only keeps recordings for 31 days."

"In fact, it's only 14, but the default set-up is 31."

"Our guy installs this in advance. He knows he'll be recorded while he hooks it up, but he also knows it won't matter. By the time its purpose has been discovered, the old footage has been automatically erased and he's back to being the invisible man."

"That's it."

Coombes studied the circuit board.

"How difficult is it to make one of these?"

"Not difficult at all. It's off-the-shelf, you program it to do what you want and you're all set. The hard stuff is done by the elevator, this is essentially a switch and a timer for how long to cut the cameras. It's probably only around 20 lines of code."

Gonzalez seemed pretty pleased with herself. He'd given her a puzzle and she'd solved it. That's how she looked at the situation, not about what it meant for the investigation.

"What you're saying, is this gives us nothing."

"Well, not *nothing*. We know whoever did this doesn't work at the hotel. Everyone I spoke with knew precisely how long recordings were kept."

Coombes tapped the evidence bag.

"You think a member of staff, smart enough to do this, wouldn't realize the 14-day period was inside knowledge? That they'd be implicating themselves? Maybe the killer *allowed* the extra days to get us to look the other way. That's what I'd do."

Gonzalez' face fell. "I never thought of that."

Sato glared at him. A warning. He could speak to her like that, but not Gonzalez. He made his voice softer.

"Sorry, Carla. That didn't come out right. This is good stuff, maybe the geek squad will be able to get something off it. Fingerprints, DNA, some kind of digital marker. A serial number that we can trace to a purchase would be nice. For the record, I don't think we're dealing with a hotel employee. You don't shit where you eat, even wild animals know that."

Sato was still giving him the look after Gonzalez left.

27

COOMBES ARRIVED EARLY FOR his meeting with the Tesla technician at the impounded vehicles lot that was operated by the Sheriff's Department. Although he had seen both videos and still pictures of the vehicle, he had yet to personally inspect Adrian Blackstone's car and he wanted to be as familiar with it as possible. Walking around the outside, the damage fell into two groups; catastrophic, and none at all. The rear half was ready to be rolled back into a showroom, while the normally streamlined front was scrunched up to what Coombes took to be about a third its normal size.

He walked around to the front and crouched down so his eyes were just above wheel height. The car had struck the RV off-center and the result was that the right side was significantly more damaged than the left. He assumed this was the result of Blackstone attempting to steer away from the other vehicle.

He stood again and walked to the driver side.

The door was missing, cut off by first responders in an attempt to free Blackstone from the wreckage. The door was propped against the intact back section of the car. A clear plastic seat cover had been left on the driver's seat by the evidence collection team and he turned and sat down on it.

Inside, blood was everywhere.

Misting, pooling, and cast-off arcs from the fast, jerking movement of Blackstone's head. It was as if he'd been repeatedly beaten with a hammer, except the hammer was the car. It was a grim scene, almost as bad as Harry Ryan's supposed self-administered gunshot wound, but the time delay had robbed it of its visceral impact. The blood had dried black, and like Blackstone's corpse, the smell of death had gone.

Coombes saw movement through the starred windshield and when he stood, he saw another Tesla drive past and park next to his Dodge. A man with large glasses and a smile walked toward him, shoulders swinging. It reminded him of Jake Curtis' swagger after the farcical meeting with the Deputy District Attorney. The tech was taller than Curtis, but shorter than himself.

It was important to keep score.

"Sean Bostic."

"Coombes."

Bostic smiled, like he'd remembered the punchline to a joke.

"I hate seeing them busted up like this, it's upsetting."

They walked side by side toward Blackstone's wrecked car.

"You think this is bad, you should see what happened to the driver."

"Can I?"

Coombes glanced at Bostic with a frown. "No."

"I recognize you from the news. Is this part of the *Ferryman* case?"

"I can't comment on active investigations."

"That's too bad, I love all that true crime stuff."

He watched Bostic setup his laptop and begin typing on the keyboard. Multiple screens opened up on the limited screen real estate. Bostic hummed quietly to himself, looking at the screen, typing on the keyboard. The keys were made of rubber and made a muted tapping sound rather than a clicking.

"You said you didn't want the insurance agent present, how come?"

"Well, Coombes, *no first name*. My company wants to help you catch whoever is responsible for killing our customer. That's our priority here, not worrying about some lawsuit or bullshit federal investigation."

The facts, with no sales pitch or careful phrasing. How refreshing.

"*John*."

The side of Bostic's face pulled up in a smile, and there was a small nod, but he didn't turn from the screen. He was like Sato when she was in the zone on her computer, her headphones on. A minute passed, then another. Coombes looked around the lot. There were close to a hundred cars, mostly mid to low-end. Blackstone's Tesla was the only wreck he could see. Vehicles that had been totaled would be held for insurance or criminal investigation, then destroyed elsewhere.

"Holy shit. That's cold, man."

"What you got?"

"Looks like someone connected remotely and took control. Changing lanes, accelerating to 122 MPH, then returning control for the last two seconds before impact."

"That explains the brakes at the end."

"That's kind of the problem, Detective. It shouldn't be possible. Safety systems overrule everything else, and the brakes are like a vice. If you've never driven an EV before, you won't appreciate how quickly they can stop."

Sounded like he was getting the sales pitch after all.

"Obviously it *was* possible, Bostic. Whoever took control, turned off all that stuff, right?"

"That's beyond the horizon, I never saw that before. Those systems are protected."

"I'm Homicide, I don't care about anything else. If this crash is the result of some glitch in your software tell me now and it stays between us, okay? I have a killer to catch and I don't want to get sucked down a tunnel of bullshit."

"I swear to you, that's what the data says."

Coombes straightened from his bent-over position pretending to understand what the laptop's screen showed. He looked again around the rows of cars, trucks, and SUVs that filled the lot. It was perfectly still with no movement. He took a deep breath and let it out again. He ran his eyes once again over the crumpled front of the Tesla.

"I'll give you this much, Bostic. This car took some punishment. A bit longer on the brakes and your customer might have made it."

"Oh, you're right about that. I'd guess he was maybe four or five seconds from being able to walk away from this. I'm done here, you mind if I look inside?"

"For what purpose?"

Bostic smiled and shrugged his shoulders. "To see."

The tech was a ghoul who wanted to be where a man had died, a crime committed. His first instinct was to tell him where to go, but he decided to see where it went.

"All right, but no selfies. I don't want this on social media."

"That's not me, you've got nothing to worry about."

Bostic walked around the side and slid into the driver's seat. Coombes followed to see what Bostic was doing.

"The airbag didn't deploy."

"Right."

Coombes hadn't registered the airbag failure, even though it had been in the report. He'd been too busy looking at the comet tails of blood spatter that filled the interior like a Jackson Pollock. Bostic smiled at him, his whole face lighting up.

"That thing about the coins is bullshit, isn't it?"

"What are you talking about?"

"Like I say, I follow the case you're working on. The Ferryman. I figure that if you're working *this* case, it has to be part of *that* case, they're not giving you extra work to pad out your day. Therefore, this is a Ferryman victim. Judging by the door's removal, the victim survived the initial impact and they were trying to save him."

Coombes looked calmly at him and said nothing.

"If he was still alive, there were no coins on his eyes."

He'd underestimated Bostic, but again he decided to let it continue.

"I can't comment on active investigations."

The tech laughed. "That deadpan delivery, I love it!"

Bostic returned to looking around the destroyed car's interior. The man's eyes crawling slowly over everything like he was trying to memorize it, his huge glasses like retro TV screens. By his own admission, he was a true crime fan, this would be a fantasy come true for him. His head came to an abrupt stop as he looked at something.

He straightened his arm, his finger pointing.

"Detective, look. A camera. That's not one of ours."

Coombes squatted down next to Bostic and looked along his arm. There was a small black dot on the passenger side door. It looked like a drop of dried blood, only it was way out on its own, away from the other spatter. He took out his pocket flashlight and shone it toward the door. The lens shone. The car had been processed, but nobody had caught the lens.

Bostic had a good eye.

"Shit, you're right."

"It's pointed at the driver. You think someone watched him die?"

Coombes nodded, disgusted.

He walked back to check the door that had been removed, but there was no sign that a camera had been added to it. Too close to the driver, he supposed. Or too visible. Bostic climbed out the car. He looked excited by the discovery of the camera. Coombes was tempted to show him a picture of Blackstone's face, see how funny he found the situation then.

Coombes pulled out his notebook and pen.

"Who could do this, control the car remotely?"

"A half dozen people at the company, maybe a couple more former employees. Then you have state actors like Russia, China, Israel, Great Britain, and the US of course. Spy shit."

He nodded and wrote it all down.

"How close would our guy have to...connect like this?"

"To the car? Anywhere in the world, it's like a cell phone."

A moment went by after Coombes had written this into his notebook. He was missing something. All computer people were alike, they lost the ability to speak to humans the more they interacted with computers.

"Why did you ask if I meant the car, what else would we be talking about?"

"The camera. Some of our models have built-in cabin cameras on the rearview, but this one didn't. I'm guessing it's wired into the power for the door mirror to get an angle on the driver, but there's no link to the network there and it might not have the bandwidth to support video anyway. Got to punch through a lot of metal there. I doubt it could transmit more than half a mile, probably less."

The Ferryman had been close.

It figured. He'd have to be able to see the off-ramp exit.

"How long would it take to add the camera?"

Bostic tilted his head over, eyes turned up to the left, imagining it.

"Open the door, unfasten the panel, pop it open. Drill the hole, mount the camera, wire it in, pop the panel back into place, double-check the lens alignment on a monitor while sitting in the driver's seat. That's it. Ten minutes?"

"What about keys, alarms, all that?"

"If I was going to do this, I'd use the driver's own key after it had been valet parked. Somewhere I might also be able to get a little privacy."

Coombes smiled. "Nice."

He wrote *valet parking* in his notebook and drew a heavy box around it.

The technician folded up his laptop and returned to his car. In his own way, Bostic carried out his own investigations, only of machines that had gone wrong. Coombes wondered how much he earned, and what his life was like driving around in a sports car, pressing a couple of keys solving a puzzle right there, then driving away someplace else.

No corpses, no grieving family.

It was the kind of job Julie would choose for him.

Bostic's Tesla pulled silently alongside and the window powered down.

"Coombes. The guy you're after knows EVs like the back of his hand. *Really* knows them, you know? You're looking for an engineer."

He supposed that EV was *electric vehicle*.

"Someone like you?"

Bostic grinned. "I wish. I could do the camera, sure, but I couldn't highjack the OS like that. I'm strictly debug-only. The guy you want? If he did this alone? He's a genius."

He nodded morosely.

"Tell me something I don't know."

"Have a better one, Detective."

The Tesla powered smoothly away, leaving him standing on his own. One thing was for damn sure, Billy Lass didn't remotely control a car, he had problems picking up emails.

He made a call to arrange for the car to be re-processed and for the whole passenger door to be taken to the crime lab for disassembly and forensic analysis. He imagined a nice juicy fingerprint carelessly left behind on some interior surface by the Ferryman, waiting to be discovered. He disconnected and began to walk back toward his Dodge. His cell phone rang before he could return it to his pocket. It was Sato's cell.

"Hi, Grace. What's up?"

"I'm downtown at City National Plaza. You're going to want to get here as soon as possible. Olivia Sutton's been abducted. There's blood, Johnny, it could be our guy."

28

OLIVIA HAD BEEN ABDUCTED from the parking garage on her way to work, which was a corporate law office nestled high up in the building above. No doubt a nice corner office with a view across the city. As he understood things, Olivia Sutton was a multi-millionaire with a vast personal fortune and chose to work because she enjoyed it.

That must be nice, he thought.

He parked his Dodge as close as he could get to the taped-off section and sat there for a beat looking at his right hand. His fingers were shaking. He clenched his hand into a fist then straightened them out again. The shaking persisted. An image came to him of Olivia in the bar that day, the extra button undone, her cheeks flushed with anger.

Goddammit.

He picked his iPad off the passenger seat and got out the car. The weight of the tablet as he carried it was enough to stop his hand from shaking, a trick he'd learned while serving in Afghanistan. He gave his name and badge number to a uniform with a clipboard and made his way toward a towering African-American in a three-piece suit. Jed Hollings. Coombes recognized the detective due to his height, which barely fitted in the parking garage. There weren't many cops he had to tilt his head to look in the eye and he didn't much enjoy it.

"I don't like waiting around for people, Coombes, and I don't see how this connects with your serial. This is an abduction, not a murder."

"Relax, Hollings. This is your case and that's not going to change. That said, there is a potential overlap with my case that could help both of us."

"Oh yeah? What's the overlap?"

"Olivia Sutton's father is potentially the first victim of my killer."

Hollings was silent for a moment while he thought this over. Coombes didn't bother to mention that he knew both victims.

"That must've been months ago, why come back for her now?"

Coombes shrugged.

"I don't know, but I don't like the timing. Her father's home in Silver Lake was set on fire last night. It's where he apparently killed himself, so obviously I'm wondering if it was to destroy evidence missed at the first crime scene."

"Your killer tying off loose ends?"

"Seems that way."

Hollings' face softened, perhaps thinking he could backdoor into solving a serial and the effect this might have on his career.

"What do you want me to do?"

"Work the case as normal, anybody that comes to your attention loop me in. I'm assuming there's been no contact, no demand?"

"Not as far as I know."

If Coombes was right, there would be no ransom demand, because money was not the motive. He turned to the section of the parking structure where Sato stood looking down at the smooth concrete. If he was right, Olivia Sutton was already dead.

Something inside him clamped together.

He'd barely seen Olivia for years, yet feelings for her persisted. Some people were like that, they remained a part of who you were long after they left your life.

He saw Vogler, the young forensic technician that had worked the Harry Ryan and Anthony Price scenes. Coombes finished up with Hollings and walked over.

"We'll have to stop meeting like this, people will talk."

"This one's a friend, Vogler. No jokes."

"Okay. How did you get on with that shoe print?"

"Still working it."

Coombes looked at the dark splashes of blood on the concrete and wondered what it meant. It appeared to be a small amount, from a minor impact. The tension across his chest began to ease. Olivia hadn't died here.

The blood was at the end of the parking bay, between her Range Rover and the spot next to it, which was empty. She'd parked in her private space, marked on the wall in front of her for all to see, then walked to the rear of her SUV where her abductor was waiting. Perhaps hiding behind the bulk of her own vehicle, ready to grab her up, into a waiting trunk.

Her cell phone lay next to the SUV's rear wheel. It looked like it had been stamped on repeatedly, it was destroyed. A lot of energy, a lot of anger. Silver-gray scrape marks led across the polished concrete to the blood trail. It seemed that the cause of the blood loss was from being hit on the head by her attacker to control her. He thought about Olivia, filled with fire and attitude. She was athletic, bordering on muscular. She was a fighter.

Coombes imagined a new scenario.

This time, instead of hitting her, her attacker grabs her from behind, pinning her arms around her waist before lifting her off her feet and carrying her toward the open trunk. Olivia would do what anyone would. She'd arc her head backward into her abductor's face, into his lips or nose, causing the drops of blood.

Making it *his* blood, not hers.

Either way seemed just as likely. What was less likely, was that the Ferryman was in CODIS, the FBI's DNA database. They'd be able to use it to match or eliminate suspects later, but that wouldn't do her any good now.

"I'm sure she's okay, Johnny."

Coombes turned and saw Sato watching him, head tilted to one side. He nodded, lacking the conviction to agree with her. It made no sense to abduct Olivia and keep her alive.

"How did your thing go, with Blackstone's car?"

A subject change. Sato read him like a book.

"Someone took control of his car remotely and accelerated it into the other vehicle. The technician thought it was the work of an engineer and a genius, so Billy Lass is in the clear."

"I don't get it, Johnny. The killer wants Blackstone dead, fine. Why go to all this effort when he could just shoot him?"

"I've been thinking about that. Blackstone's wife said he used to spend all his time in that car. She said something like *she was a widow long before he died*. Each death is somehow tailored to the person. Harry Ryan was a gun nut, Gordon Sellers a diver, and so on. There's some twisted logic at work here, but the main reason is because he enjoys it. It's a challenge."

Her eyes lit up while he was speaking.

"Grady had that song *Falling for You*."

"Ellis."

"Right. I keep thinking of him by his stage name."

A decade earlier, the song had been everywhere. It had been impossible to turn on a radio without hearing it. A significant portion of Steve Ellis' fortune probably came from that song alone. He nodded. It aligned perfectly with his theory, almost too perfectly. In the world he now lived, catapulting a man from the top floor of a building was perfect.

Vogler was now hunched over on the concrete with a jewelers' magnifying rig attached to his head, and was swabbing the dried blood onto cotton buds and placing them into test tubes for analysis. A tube for each drop, in case they were from separate people. Vogler was a good kid. Thorough. If they had any chance at all of finding the Ferryman on CODIS, this forensic technician was the one to make it happen. Coombes heard a disturbance behind him and saw a large man in a bright shirt trying to push his way past a couple of uniforms. He turned away.

"Let's get out of here."

"Why? Who is he, Johnny?"

"Thomas Garvy, Olivia's husband. We are not on good terms."

"What a surprise."

Coombes said nothing.

He thought about Olivia's cell phone. There would've been a tight window to pull off the abduction, but her attacker had found the time to spend ten to twenty seconds ramming his shoe repeatedly onto her iPhone. That felt personal. Why not put it in front of his tire and drive away over it?

For the first time, the Ferryman had shown emotion.

29

THEY CAUGHT A FAVORABLE flow of traffic and were in Culver City in less than twenty minutes. He spent the whole drive thinking about Olivia, and if she was still alive. The idea that she was a fighter took turns giving him hope, then causing despair. Was strength a quality that made her more likely to survive, or to get her killed? He parked in his usual spot under the walnut tree and asked Sato to wait in the car for a moment.

Sofia Lass opened her front door. She looked exhausted. Beautiful, but exhausted. A big smile spread across her face.

"Johnny! What a lovely surprise."

"I'm looking for Billy, is he here?"

"Oh, no. He busy working."

She angled her head, a confused look in her eyes. It was as if she was saying *But surely you know this?* The penny dropped and everything became clear to him. Either Lass hadn't told his wife he'd been suspended, or else she thought it was all behind him. Sofia thought he was back on the job and that they were working together again.

She thought Billy was working the Ferryman case.

And where would she get an idea like that?

"Sofia, I'm a little embarrassed. The truth is, I knew Billy wasn't here. What it was, was my partner and I were in the area and we got to talking about how you guys had kind of named your little boy after me. My partner, she loves kids, is there-"

"She wants to see John? Of course!"

Sofia looked around him toward his car.

"Where is she? You left her in car like suitcase?"

She punched his arm, hard. He laughed, what else was he going to do. Coombes had a feeling she liked hitting him, it was something she'd always done since they first met. He didn't know what lay behind it, and for sure he wasn't going to dig into it.

"I'll be right back."

Sofia was smiling harder than ever.

Coombes returned to the Dodge and explained the situation to Sato in a lowered voice. He expected her to be angry at the way he'd represented her, but he found no trace of it on her face. She immediately understood the play, and her part in it. Back at the front door, Coombes noticed that Sofia had pulled her hair back into a ponytail and was now wearing shoes. He introduced them, and Sofia led them inside.

"I put John down but I think he's still awake."

Sato made a show of looking around.

"You have a beautiful home, Sofia."

Sofia giggled. "Thank you."

They walked down the hall to a door he'd never been through before. The master bedroom. Sofia opened the door and the three of them stood in the doorway looking in. The room was half-dark, the shades drawn. He saw the Lass' bed and, next to it, a child's cot with flat wooden bars all the way around.

In the darkness, the child laughed.

Coombes found himself smiling.

Sofia had evidently been waiting for a sign John was awake, because she moved forward into the room and started fussing over him. After a moment, she lifted the infant out the cot and held him against her chest, where he tried to feed automatically, his small mouth ranging back and forth, searching for a nipple. She spoke Spanish under her breath.

You're eating me alive, little one.

Coombes felt uneasy. Now that he was certain Lass had no part in the killings, it was clear to him that what he was planning to do crossed the line. All the same, he still needed to confirm his theory and dismiss Lass as a suspect for good.

"Sofia, could I use your bathroom?"

"Of course, Johnny."

Coombes backed out the room and along the hallway. The doors to the bathroom and Billy's den faced each other. He turned on the bathroom light, which also activated an extractor fan, then turned to face the den.

He eased the door open and moved carefully inside.

The room had changed completely since his last visit. Billy had previously used it as a place to unwind and drink beer. Now, it was a home office with a desk, chair, computer, and laser printer. It all looked new, and there was the fresh smell of new electronics in the air.

Another desk sat against the wall to the right. There were nine folders lined up next to each other, and he could guess what they were. Billy's version of murder books. He moved over for a closer look. A name was written in capital letters on the front of each. Because he lacked official access, the books were thin. The folders were in chronological order. He walked down the line and saw that the name on the first folder was Theodore Sutton.

Like him, Billy thought he was a victim.

Coombes felt validated by this, that with no input from him, Billy had come to the same conclusion. He frowned. If there were nine folders including Teddy, then someone was missing. It took him a moment, since all the names were right. Adrian Blackstone. His car crash had never been publicly linked to the Ferryman, so Lass didn't have it.

Coombes took out his cell phone and photographed the line of folders, then the summary pages at the back of each folder where Billy had condensed his findings.

A crash came from the master bedroom, followed by laughter.

He looked up at the sound and saw for the first time that the wall next to the door had a whiteboard screwed to it. Billy's evidence and thought process, right in front of him. Coombes took pictures of that too. Wide shots, close ups. When he was done, he stepped into the bathroom across the hallway and flushed the toilet.

When he returned to the bedroom the shades were open and the room was full of light. Grace was holding John in her arms and making baby talk. It was disconcerting to see his kick-ass partner this way and he could only stand and watch in amazement. Her face was scarlet with emotion and when she looked up at him he felt his heart surge.

"Johnny, you've got to hold this little guy, he's amazing!"

She wasn't saying it as part of their play, it was for real. He leaned in close as she passed him the baby. Their hands touched for a prolonged moment and their eyes connected as he took John.

Sofia glanced between them.

"So...how long have you been partners?"

"About eight months," he said.

"It's been well over a year, Johnny."

The baby looked deep into his eyes. Coombes smiled and made a funny face. He didn't want John to start crying, not with Sato watching. It was like a test, and he always seemed to break babies. The infant watched with a serious expression, then sneezed. Snot lay in a thick trail down the child's face. He'd broken it. Less than thirty seconds, a new record.

Coombes looked up at Sofia, helpless.

"Ooo! Someone's done a gloop!"

A cloth appeared and little John's face was cleaned up.

They finished up a short time later, with Coombes promising to visit again another time. He wondered how that would go. She would obviously mention their visit to Billy, who would see straight through the reason for their call. The two of them had done the partner-going-to-the-bathroom routine so many times there was no tread left on the tires. It was the oldest trick in the book.

Sato waited until they were inside the Dodge.

"He's running a parallel investigation?"

"Oh yeah. Like you wouldn't believe."

"I guess that explains why he was at the Capitol Records Building."

Coombes nodded and said nothing. He started the car and drove off down the street. It seemed so impossible now that he ever thought Billy could've been the Ferryman. He was a loudmouth with a few bad jokes up his sleeve, that was all.

"What's he up to do you think?"

"Simple," Coombes said. "He's trying to get his job back."

30

THEIR ROUTE BACK TOOK them past the Metro Grand. He could've taken any number of routes, but his subconscious had chosen this one. As they approached the turn lane, he recalled his conversation with Bret Lawson, the head of security. Lawson had talked about guests and former workers retaining keycards as mementos. It was something that had hit home for him. He'd stayed in a few hotels himself, and had on more than one occasion kept a keycard. You didn't have to be a serial killer to want a keepsake of a holiday, or of time you spent with someone you loved.

It seemed plausible, and it was a narrative he'd returned to when his theory that the Ferryman had accessed Lawson's computer came to nothing. Yet it bothered him. As far as he was aware, no other mementos had been taken on any of the other kills.

He put on his turn signal and drifted into the turn lane.

"What are we doing back here, Johnny?"

"Working a hunch."

"I figured that much out on my own."

"We've been assuming the killer used the spare key that Vandenberg left in the elevator for Kelly Taylor and then took both keycards with him, right?"

Sato nodded, her face brightening.

"We never looked!"

"That's right. And the way I figure it, it's still there."

It took them an easy five minutes to travel the short distance across the road and get parked. He hated wasted time, but the time passed quickly, as it always did when he felt he was approaching a break. They walked into the lobby and across the marble floor toward the elevator. Grace hurried to keep up with him.

Before he could hit the call button, the elevator doors opened and two businessmen got out. Coombes walked in and pulled on a pair of nitrile gloves. He stared at the rail and licked his lips. His heart was beating fast, he knew it was there. *Sensed it.* Why had he not thought of this before? It was so obvious. The doors closed again and the elevator rose up through the hotel.

He glanced at Sato, then dropped onto his right knee and ran his hand along the back of the rail. His small finger bumped against a crisp edge and a keycard fell down onto the floor. He continued to move his hand along behind the rail.

A second keycard fell down.

He looked up at Sato and saw she was open-mouthed in shock.

"What the hell? How did you know there would be two?"

"Because someone's playing a game," he said, picking up the cards.

The elevator stopped and the doors opened. He was still on one knee, Sato now standing in front of him. Her crotch was right in front of his face and he couldn't imagine what it looked like from behind. He glanced over his shoulder. A woman with white hair stood awkwardly waiting.

"Well? Did she say yes?"

Coombes felt his face go red as he got to his feet. He put the two keycards together and pulled his right glove off around the cards to protect them, then passed the bundle to his left and put his hand in his pocket before turning around.

"Not yet, ma'am. But I'm not giving up."

Grace filled the elevator with laughter.

"You shouldn't. She obviously likes you."

"I hope so."

"Are you going down?"

"Most likely."

Next to him, Sato almost lost it.

The woman frowned, then got into the elevator, pulling a case with a pull-up handle. She pressed the button for the first floor, the doors closed and they began to descend. Coombes turned to look at Sato and saw she was looking back. She had stopped laughing, but her eyes were alive with it, the laughter pulled inside for now. It was a good look for her, he thought. It was the kind of look that made life worth living.

The woman turned to him.

"My late husband proposed to me in Union Station, surrounded by people. Did the same thing you did, got down on one knee. Said he couldn't wait any longer. I would've preferred an elevator, believe me."

They stopped and the doors slid open. The first floor.

"How long were you together, ma'am?"

"Fifty-two years."

A small smile crossed her face, then she gave a curt nod and walked across the lobby toward the reception desk, her luggage rolling along behind her, like a dog on a leash. He followed her off the elevator and stood to the side to wait for Sato. He took off the glove that was still on his left hand and returned it to his jacket pocket.

"That's what I love about you, Johnny. You make me laugh."

The amusement was still there in her eyes, like an insect trapped in amber.

"You know what I love most about you, Grace?"

She smirked, her head tilting over at an angle.

"My hot Asian body?"

He made a gun with his hand, then made a *click* sound.

When he spent time with Grace he felt himself relax. She could be serious, she could be funny, but she didn't talk non-stop about nothing like Julie. Sato was happy to exist in a silent space, as she did then as they walked back to the car. Their friendship was closer to friendships he'd had with men, built on mutual interests and the job. Now, because of the woman with the white hair, things had once again taken a strange turn between them.

He needed to get it back to where it was meant to be. Coombes knew how the situation developed, either it got serious or it stopped being fun and turned bad. He was married, there was no scope for things to get serious. It was an amusing joke they were both riffing off, but he didn't want to lose her as a partner, they worked well together.

"You mind driving back? I want to get things straight in my head."

"Sure."

Coombes passed her the key and walked around to the passenger side of the Dodge and got in. There was over a foot height difference between them, so they went through the routine of swapping their seat positions to get comfortable. When he was done, he took out his notebook and left it sitting on his knee, waiting for Sato to ask her question.

He knew it was coming, she couldn't help herself.

"Did you go down on one knee when you proposed to Julie?"

"No."

"How did you do it?"

She started the car and reversed out the space one handed, the other hand cranking up the air conditioning. He was silent while she did this. He was silent as she drove around the lot and still silent as she waited to pull out of the hotel's narrow exit. She glanced at him, a slight frown on her face. He decided to tell her the truth.

"What happened was she told me she was pregnant. I'd just closed a big case and I'd had a couple of beers and I was feeling pretty good, so I asked her to marry me. That's what you do, right? It wasn't exactly romantic. The TV was on and I didn't even mute it. I didn't want to miss the end of the movie. That was probably a sign right there, not muting the television."

Sato sighed.

"I'm sorry, Johnny. I didn't know you'd lost a child."

"Yeah, well. That came later. The first time, she made it up. She wanted me to propose, she even borrowed a friend's pee stick to sell it to me."

"Oh, man. That's messed up."

"I think the only reason we're still married is because my health plan covers her dental bills. Julie also got really interested one night when I mentioned what she'd get if I died in the line of duty. She's got that money spent, I can tell."

Sato turned to him, her normally calm face torn with emotion. He'd forgotten what it felt like to see someone look at him this way. He turned away and looked out the side window. He didn't want her to cry, or try and hug him, yet there was a feeling of release that he'd told her, told someone.

He thought of the giant, Walter Ford, and his need to confess.

They drove in silence and when Coombes was able to put his conversation with Sato behind him, he opened his notebook and began flipping through the pages, hoping something would pop out at him. Often, he'd make a note of something and it wouldn't mean anything when he wrote it down, but when he went back to it later it fitted with something else. A pattern would emerge. But a quarter hour later he reached the end of his notes without any revelation, so he took out his pen and made some notes about the keycards instead.

How did you know there'd be two?

His partner hadn't seen the angle, but he did. The killer was having fun. It was a callback to the movie *Dial M For Murder*, he was certain of it. The killer was winking at him, showing him how clever he was. He'd taken Vandenberg's spy movie keycard play and changed it to suit his needs.

He looked up from his notes and saw they were approaching a drive-thru.

"Bit early for lunch, isn't it?"

"It's nearly one, Johnny."

"Nearly *twelve*. Where are you getting one from?"

"The dashboard."

He laughed and turned back to his notes.

"That clock's an hour out half the year, no one changes it."

They sat in silence for a while before Sato spoke again.

"Johnny, describe Jake Curtis' alibi to me."

"You mean him lying on the floor like a corpse for 36 hours?"

"But that's not his alibi, is it?"

Coombes looked up from his notebook.

"The timestamp. I asked Rollins about that, he said it was a big deal to change it on all the footage. Taking out one date, putting in another. I got tired just listening to him."

"All right. But what if he didn't *have* to change it because it was already out?"

Inside him he felt something drop, like an airplane hitting turbulence.

"Jesus, Grace. That's perfect! *That's* why he included a whole month. He used the underage girl and the deal with the DA to distract us from the most obvious thing. We were looking at old recordings."

She had a big smile on her face. *"Right?"*

He thought back on what the writer had given them.

"Before he gave me the thumb drive, Curtis said his system kept recordings for two months before being automatically deleted. I thought nothing of it, storage always limits how long footage is kept. Suppose, however, he's changed the date on his security system. He knows he'll need an alibi for Vandenberg in November and comes up with the plan involving the girl. It's a fresh angle, fresh enough that we didn't catch it. He needs a whole month's worth of footage as set-up, but it leaves him exposed. If we ask him for *October's* footage, it wouldn't exist because November's *is* October's. He'd have to run two months ahead just in case. It would also provide alibis for the first killings if he ever needed it and the number of days in the month would match up."

"You really think he's got another month's footage up his sleeve?"

"He's smart, Grace. If we thought of it, be sure he did too."

"The footage he gave us is from September?"

"It would have to be, otherwise he'd be absent during the earlier killings." She nodded.

They reached the restaurant's order station and their conversation ended while they each placed their orders. Grace didn't eat beef and was sensitive to the smell of it, so he ordered chicken and she did the same. Relationships were built on mutual respect, which cost absolutely nothing. They crawled slowly toward the serve window.

"Okay," she said finally. "Where does that leave the girl, she'd have to be in on it, wouldn't she? She'd have to lie about the date, and also about her age at the time."

Tammy Watkins.

After calling her cell twice without success, he'd forgotten all about her. Lass had become the primary focus of the investigation and Jake Curtis had fallen away, an early mistake. Calling her back was merely routine and there was, he thought, no need to hear her side. He'd accepted the alibi at face value and he'd seen for himself everything that had transpired that day on the footage. She wasn't there on the day of Vandenberg's murder, so what did it really matter what she said later?

But it did matter, for a reason he hadn't thought of at the time.

"What are the chances she really went to her friend's cabin in Big Bear?"

"Oh, Johnny, don't say that."

He stared through the side window at a homeless man pushing a shopping cart of junk down the sidewalk. He looked like he was 200 years old.

"If Jake Curtis is the killer, she has to be dead. His alibi relies on it."

31

J AKE C URTIS OPENED THE front door of his seven-million-dollar home wearing floral shorts and flip-flops. Coombes had seen him wearing less on video, but up close and personal there was something disturbing about the way the writer's beard seemed to travel down his thick neck and join with the hair that spread across his muscular chest. It looked like he was transitioning into a werewolf and he found himself flashing back to the scenes of Curtis and the underage girl in bed.

"Detective Coombes! I must admit I've been waiting for you."

"Is that a fact?"

But Curtis had already turned his head.

"Who is *this* beautiful creature?"

"Detective Sato," Grace said. "And spare me your sexist bullshit."

Curtis nodded for a couple of seconds, then laughed. If he was worried about being arrested, he didn't show it.

"Well, detectives, I guess you should come in."

Curtis led them down a hallway lined with framed movie posters. They were for old movies, not ones he'd written himself. Stars from a different time; Humphrey Bogart, Lauren Bacall, James Cagney, and Veronica Lake. Coombes had only seen one of the movies before, the original *Cape Fear* with Gregory Peck and Robert Mitchum. He didn't see one for *Dial M for Murder*, but that might be elsewhere.

"See anything you like, Coombes?"

"This isn't a social call."

Curtis smirked. "No doubt."

They came out in a wide-open space with floor to ceiling windows that showed the pool area beyond. He recognized it from the footage, it was through this window that Tammy Watkins had been recorded sunbathing in her bikini. He turned his head and found the camera position, a white plastic casing against a whitewashed stone wall. It was almost invisible, only the black circle of the lens showed. When he turned back the other man was seated on a wide oatmeal color chair in front of the glass, a large unlit cigar in his hand. For the first time, he noted the presence of Curtis' German Shepherd asleep at its master's feet.

Coombes sat opposite on a sofa that seemed to swallow him. There were a lot of cushions piled up on the arms on either side so when Grace sat next to him their legs were pressed together from hip to knee. He expected her to reposition herself, but she did nothing. He glanced at her and saw the corner of her mouth turned up. He couldn't tell if she was amused at the way the chair was pushing them together, or by his reaction to it, but either way she didn't seem to care.

"You still think I killed the old man and all those others?"

Coombes took out his notebook.

"We can start there if you like."

Curtis ran the cigar back and forth under his nose, smelling it.

"I like you, Coombes. You're like one of those dogs that bites your leg and won't let go. You set your sights on something, and that's it. Total commitment. The jaw locks, the teeth buried deep in your prey. No escape. I admire that, it's a good trait to have as a cop, but a little myopic considering I already have an alibi."

Coombes decided to cut to the chase.

"We're having trouble locating Tammy Watkins. The last time her cell phone was active was right here in this room fifty days ago. *Fifty days*. I've met teenage girls that can't last fifty minutes without an internet connection.

First of all, they go pale, then their body goes limp like they have no energy, then finally...coma. It's very sad."

A grin spread across Curtis' face.

"That's funny. So I killed Tammy now too?"

"You tell me."

"She forgot her iPhone and the battery went flat. No mystery. It's in a drawer somewhere until she comes by to pick it up."

"That's pretty weak, Curtis. You need cutting tools to separate a teenager from a cell phone. My bet? Our forensic techs are going to come in here with a black light and find glowing patches on the floor where you used bleach to get out her blood."

Curtis turned to Grace. "Is he serious? Tell me this is a joke."

"Is that what you think, Mr. Curtis? That we spent an hour in lunch traffic to come tell you jokes?"

"I could've told you this with a phone call, saved you the trouble."

Coombes cut in again.

"People that kill in the heat of the moment, I can understand that. Losing control for a split-second, doing something you never dreamed you could. Anyone could do that. That alibi of yours for Vandenberg, that blows my mind. The preparation involved is amazing."

Curtis sat back on his chair.

"You've lost me now. All I did was give you my security tape. The tape proves I didn't kill him, I was right here the entire time."

"Sure you were. *In September.*"

Curtis stared at him for several seconds before the smile returned bigger than ever.

"Oh my god! You think I changed the date on my security cameras months before the crime to establish an alibi. That's actually pretty good, I might use that in a script."

"The recordings are for real, that's what you're saying?"

"That's what I'm saying."

They stared at each other in silence. Curtis looked sincere. He'd pushed him, expecting him to be smug. To tell him that there was no way for him to prove it, then rub his face in it. But he hadn't done that, and for the first time, Coombes felt doubt grow inside him.

"Why give us the whole month? You only needed an alibi for the day of Vandenberg's death. If you'd done that, we'd have known nothing about the girl. That thing with the DA, all that pointless noise, what was that about?"

Curtis cut off the end of his cigar and made a big show of lighting it with a match, puffing blue clouds of smoke into the air around his head.

"I saw an opportunity. I knew that *month thing* would mess with you. The girl was just the icing on the cake. In the right place, at the right time. My medical condition never worked so well for me. It wrapped the whole thing up in a pretty bow."

There was almost a sparkle in Curtis' eyes. Suddenly the leak made sense.

"You released that video online yourself, didn't you?"

"That's right."

"And the story about you being a Ferryman suspect...you released that too?"

"Of course."

Coombes wanted to punch the man in the face. "Why?"

"This is Hollywood, Detective. I was fired from Pacific Pictures and with the shit they were spreading about me I'd never work again. That's how this town works, word of mouth. The old boy network. Conversations on golf courses, sauna rooms, AA meetings, back rooms you don't know exist. Once word goes out, you're done. I wasn't going to take it lying down, I needed to change the story.

"So that's what I did. Since this Ferryman thing started, my career has gone into the stratosphere. The *Firestorm* script Pacific rejected I sold elsewhere with minor changes, I sold five elevator pitches that aren't even outlines, and

I sold all the scripts I wrote when I was at USC. Everyone wants a piece of me, and it's all thanks to you."

Coombes sighed. "And Tammy Watkins?"

"Is alive and well. She's not at Big Bear, she's staying at my ranch in Topanga Canyon with a bunch of her friends. I can give you the address if you like. It's registered through my LLC so you probably won't find it."

"You realize that while you were playing your little game the real killer has been free to move around and kill again?"

The writer yawned.

"Nobody cares about the people he's killing. Well, except for Haylee. I had a lot of time for her. We met a couple of times at parties, she was a riot. Funny as all hell and sweet, you know? Not like she was on her show, that was just for ratings."

Coombes was overcome with a powerful need to hurt Jake Curtis. His body become tight, the muscles preparing themselves for a sudden burst of energy. His jaw clenched together, his teeth grinding. Curtis was shorter than he was, but he was highly muscled. A fight might not work out the way he wanted. Woken by some kind of primal instinct, Curtis' dog got to its feet and stared at him, a low growl coming from its throat, teeth bared.

Grace leaned in, her hand on his arm.

"It's what he wants, Johnny. He's baiting you. Don't you see? We're on camera. If you hit him, he'll sue the City for a million dollars, maybe more. Roll it up with a harassment charge. We already know he's connected at City Hall. Let's just go, this guy's a waste of time."

She'd spoken softly, but he could tell Curtis had heard.

Another cloud of blue smoke, another grin.

He had nothing left to say to Curtis, they'd reached the end. The point where words didn't get the job done anymore. He recalled his conversation with Lass about the physical release experienced after a fight. In nature, that's what would happen now, they'd hit each other like dumb animals, but at the end the static that had built up between them would be gone.

"You should listen to her, Detective. She's a smart cookie."

He stood and walked toward the door.

The thing that had always bothered him about the recording of Curtis was that he lay for so long on a hard cedar floor. *Even the dog knew to lie on the rug.* It was the one truth in the video that he couldn't accept, because once you accepted it, there was nowhere left to go. If Curtis lay there for 36 hours without the rug, without any attempt to make himself more comfortable, it was because his disorder was real and because he was innocent.

At the door, he let Grace walk to the Charger alone so he could have a last exchange with Curtis. Strangely, there appeared to be no security camera covering the entrance.

"I guess this is goodbye, Coombes. It's kind of too bad, I've enjoyed leading you astray. Maybe I'll write you into a story sometime then invite you to the premiere."

"You think you're so clever, but the way I see it, it won't be long before the two of us meet again. Only next time, you'll be dead."

"Threats, Detective? I expected more from you."

"You pretended to be the Ferryman. I don't know how *charitable* a killer like that is going to be. Are you aware that your home is on Google for anyone to find? A big pin appears on their maps showing where you live. That's *before* you consider that interiors magazine you had in here taking pictures. All that stuff is online, just a click away. Those people that you say don't matter, how much do you differ from them? Aren't you *exactly* the type he kills?"

Despite the thick beard, he saw Curtis swallow repeatedly. It reminded him of something, but he couldn't put his finger on it.

"But he's finished killing now. I read that."

"I think we both know that a guy like that never stops until he's caught, or until he's dead. He kills because he likes it. Probably all that happened was he ran out of coins; it was the only reason we recognized the pattern in the first place. His little signature. Suicides are at an all-time high, Mr. Curtis. We'd never notice one more. At my next press conference, I think I'll say we've made a huge break in the case, then thank you at length for all your help." Coombes smiled. "That ought to help you sell some more scripts, right?"

Curtis said nothing, his face frozen into a grim mask. Coombes walked back to his car, his smile widening. Grace stood next to the passenger door, her gaze shifting back and forth between him and the writer. He unlocked the doors and they got inside.

"What the hell did you say to him, Johnny?"

"I simply wished the man well with the rest of his life."

"He looks like he just soiled himself."

Coombes nodded as he put the gear selector into reverse. The parking area was tight, Curtis had so many vehicles that there wasn't much room for anyone else. It seemed like a metaphor for the man's life. His smile faded as they approached the metal gates that protected the property. He'd had one suspect when he arrived, and none when he left.

They were back to square one.

32

WHEN THEY GOT BACK to the PAB, Coombes avoided his desk and instead headed toward the task force room. There were two main reasons for this; the first was that he was embarrassed that he'd been fooled by Curtis yet again, and second, that his lieutenant was less likely to look for him here. Now that he was back to the beginning anyway, it would seem like a no-brainer to have a change in leadership, get some fresh ideas. It wasn't Gantz' style, but she would be under a lot of pressure for the results he'd failed to deliver.

Barring some kind of miracle, he would be out.

Wallfisch was a D-III, same as him, he'd be given control. Gantz would figure he was already up to speed, something he was not. The switchover would kill what little momentum remained in the investigation and the Ferryman would never be caught.

When he got to the room he found Becker still there, he hadn't gone for lunch yet. He had one of the blue murder books open and, next to it, a laptop with a web browser full of text. A *Times* story. Coombes was disappointed he didn't have the room to himself, but exchanged a nod with the older detective.

Becker, he could deal with. He was the human equivalent of elevator music and most of the time you didn't realize he was even there.

Coombes stood at the whiteboard at the end of the room, reading the list of victims, the suspects, key locations. Hoping some hidden pattern would jump out at him. After close to a minute, he took a red marker and drew a line through Jake Curtis.

Becker gave no reaction; he was deep into something on his laptop.

Coombes picked up the murder books on Vandenberg and Ellis. The two kills differed from the others and he thought they offered the best opportunity for a break despite the amount of time he'd already expended on them. With Vandenberg, the killer had effectively announced himself to the world, while Ellis was the over-the-top last kill, the killer's final statement. The Ellis kill had been sloppy, an artist bored with his creation.

He opened the Vandenberg book to the property report, re-reading the same information he'd read before. The list was less than half a page long, yet when he got to the bottom, he found that he'd forgotten what he was looking for, the process of opening the binder to the right section and re-reading had allowed the idea to escape.

"John."

Coombes looked at Becker across the table.

"I've been working the shoe print from the Price crime scene. I have a match."

"Yeah, it's a rare Nike, Sato already ran that down."

"No. A match for an owner, but you're not going to like it."

Coombes rubbed his chin. "Hit me."

"Nicolas Sutton."

"You're kidding."

"Sutton bought a pair of these shoes at auction for $27,000 in 2010 and I found no evidence that he sold them again or gave them away. Same size, everything."

There was no way Nicky could be the Ferryman.

There wasn't was there?

"You did just say $27,000 for a pair of sneakers, right?"

"It was for charity. Apparently, he and another man consumed several bottles of Champagne before the auction and were trying to impress their guests by winning."

Coombes shook his head.

"Let me ask you something, Mark. If you had one-of-a-kind shoes, would you take them to a crime where you planned to use chemicals to melt some poor sap all over the floor? Or would you put on an old pair you didn't care about that couldn't be traced back to you?"

"Depends."

"Really? On what?"

Becker smiled, embarrassed.

"When I was younger, I had a pair of shoes I wore to dates. The first time I wore them, I got lucky. To me, the *shoes* were lucky. So I kept them good and wore them to every date I went on from that point on. The luck continued." Becker shrugged. "Maybe they just gave me confidence, but in my head, it was all down to the shoes."

"The Nikes are special to our killer, so he wears them to all his kills."

Becker nodded.

"None of the early kills were messy, so he never thought about it before. After that, it's a uniform. Every time he wears them, he gets away with it. They're *his* lucky shoes."

He liked Becker's thinking.

It wasn't a logical position for anyone to take, least of all a homicide detective, yet it had an *emotional intelligence* that simply worked. He was prone to thinking in the same way on occasion, like buying a lottery ticket on a day when he'd experienced luck elsewhere.

"What happened to your date shoes?"

"I was wearing them when I met my wife. Been married for 20 years."

"You throw them out?"

"God, no. I keep them in a box under our bed. If I got rid of them, she might realize she made a mistake. Without her I'd eat my gun inside a month. Hell, I'd probably die of hunger first. I'm too old to learn how to cook, Coombes."

"*Right.*"

He sat back and looked at the ceiling tiles, trying to get his thoughts in order.

Imagining Becker's date shoes was a way of allowing himself not to think about what had led to the conversation in the first place. He tilted his head back down and saw Becker was still looking at him, waiting for what came next.

If Teddy Sutton was the first victim as he'd originally thought, then didn't it make sense if it was someone close to him? Someone that worked with him day in, day out? Both men were tightly wound.

Was it so unlikely they got into an argument that went too far?

Then, after, seeing how quick the LAPD were to dismiss it. Labelling his father's death a suicide and moving on. Perhaps getting the idea that anyone could be killed if it looked enough like a suicide.

It all fitted together.

His thoughts returned to the fire, and the abduction of Olivia.

Fire could be effective at getting rid of evidence, particularly if you weren't sure where you might have left it. Assuming Theodore Sutton *was* the first victim, it was no great stretch to imagine his killer had made mistakes early on, mistakes he might only have thought of later as he perfected his craft.

Olivia was where the wheels came off. He couldn't see Nicky ever doing anything to hurt her, not even if he *was* the Ferryman. The two were close, they always had been.

Sato walked in and glanced between them.

"What did I miss?"

"How do you like Nicolas Sutton for the Ferryman?"

"Wow. Seriously, what did I miss?"

He motioned for her to come in and close the door before he continued.

"Sutton owns a pair of those rare Nikes, same size."

"Damn. You think it's him?"

Coombes glanced at the whiteboard, to the description of the killer.

"His height, build and hair color match the eyewitness' statement. He's rich enough to move in the same circles as the victims, it's possible he knew them. I never saw him wear a Rolex, but that doesn't mean he doesn't have one. People like that have about ten watches, all of them expensive. He's linked to the house in Silver Lake, and to Olivia, who we assume was abducted by the killer. If he's not the Ferryman, that's a lot of coincidence."

"Why would he abduct his sister?"

An answer came to him all too quickly.

"She just inherited half his business, maybe the house in Silver Lake too."

"You think she's *dead?*"

Coombes looked at Sato, wishing she hadn't said it.

"I hope not, but why else would he take her?"

"Even if she inherited everything, killing her wouldn't undo it. The business and the house would become part of *her* estate. Her husband would get it."

"I know that, Grace. Maybe he's angry, not thinking straight. Hell, we *are* also saying he's a serial killer so maybe his elevator doesn't go to the top floor."

"It's too neat, isn't it?"

"Yeah, but that doesn't mean it's not true."

Coombes stood and walked to the whiteboard. A copy of the artist's impression was taped to the edge for quick access. He took it down and set it on his desk then used his tablet to bring up photographs of Nicolas Sutton. There were a lot to choose from. Sutton was rich, single, and attractive, Google had a warehouse filled with his face. Coombes found an image of Nicky looking slightly to the left like the suspect in the drawing and sized the image on screen to match. The three of them stood and looked down at the two images side by side.

Again, he found it hard to get past the dead charcoal eyes.

"I don't know, Johnny." Sato said. "I honestly don't think that drawing looks like anyone other than you on a really bad day."

He ignored this comment and pointed to the suspect's mouth. On the drawing, one of the front teeth was squint.

"Sutton's teeth are straight."

"Still though," Becker said, "nose and jawline are close to perfect."

That much, he had to agree with.

If he was being objective, Sutton was a better fit for the Ferryman than Jake Curtis ever was, even excluding the shoes. The eyewitness had never mentioned the suspect having a beard and nobody who'd seen Curtis would forget that. He'd entertained the idea that the beard was fake, and that Curtis simply removed it before carrying out any of the kills. Now that he accepted the writer was not the killer, he could see how desperate that really was.

"All right. Let's dig into Nicky's life, see what we find. Health, financials, relationships. See if we can match the partial fingerprint from the Haylee Jordan crime scene and if we can nail down his location during any of the kills. Perhaps that shoe print had been in Anthony Price's kitchen for a while-"

Sato cut him off.

"Johnny, aside from what Price and the bar manager left on the floor, that thing was spotless. You could've eaten off it. There's no way Sutton walked through there a month before and his perfect shoe prints were still there. The kitchen staff would walk over that spot all night; you'd get like thirty overlapping prints in ten minutes flat."

Coombes glared at her.

"Did you check if the shoes had been reported stolen?"

"A pair of Nikes? No."

"They cost him $27,000. If someone stole them, he's going to have reported it to claim on insurance, I guarantee it."

Sato's eyebrows shot up at the price, but she skipped over it.

"And if he *hasn't* reported it?"

Coombes sighed. The logic of it was inescapable.

"Then either he doesn't know they're missing, or he's the Ferryman."

33

WHEN HE STUCK HIS head around his lieutenant's door, he found her slumped forward, holding her desk phone to her ear like a gun. She jumped slightly, startled by his appearance, having apparently not heard his knock. Coombes held his hand up to apologize and leave, but she waved him in impatiently, bracelets jangling.

The Nikes *hadn't* been reported stolen, which came as no surprise to him. Sato had also found a memorabilia website with photographs of the shoes in a glass display case, apparently shot in Sutton's own home. It looked like the case was mounted to the wall like a painting, to the side of a very large television. Not in a drawer, or a safe deposit box.

It was impossible to see a scenario where Sutton hadn't noticed the shoes were missing unless he was on vacation the whole time, which he was not. It remained a possibility that the shoe imprint came from a different shoe of the same size and type and that the other links between Nicolas Sutton and the case were merely coincidental. He'd counted them up; it would be a total of eight coincidences if Sutton was *not* their man, and that wasn't something they saw a lot of in Homicide.

Gantz finished her call and looked at Coombes with real interest.

"John. I'm hoping you're about to tell me Christmas is a day early this year."

"It's kind of a good news, bad news situation."

Gantz sighed and sat back in her chair. "Please tell me it's not Lass."

Coombes smiled. He'd already forgotten about Billy Lass.

"We think its Nicolas Sutton."

Gantz frowned. "Sutton. Why do I know that name?"

"His sister was abducted from a parking garage yesterday."

"Right. Is her abduction related?"

"Looks like it."

"And the bad news?"

"Nicky and I were friends in high school, I practically grew up in their home. If you recall, his father's suicide was actually where I started to piece this together. I also dated his sister for about six months."

"Shit. Shit. Shit."

Gantz turned away from him and looked off into space, her left index fingernail tapping out a staccato beat on a leather mat that was spread out in front of her computer.

"Who knows of your friendship?"

"Everyone on the task force."

She turned to look at him. *"Wallfisch?"*

He nodded again. If Wallfisch knew, then Block knew, they were tight. Since he was a useless piece of skin, he'd assumed from day one that the captain had pressured Gantz into installing Wallfisch on the task force so he had a man on the inside.

"Does Wallfisch know Sutton's a suspect?"

"You think I'd tell that buffoon anything before I told you?"

"Right now, who knows?"

"You, me, Sato, and Becker."

"Keep it that way. Telling McCreary is the same as telling Wallfisch."

"What about Gonzalez? Becker won't like keeping it from her."

"It's your ass, John. You trust her?"

"A hundred percent."

"All right. Have Wallfisch and McCreary chase rabbits and beat the grass while the four of you tie this thing up. We don't need forever. As soon as you're ready to arrest Sutton, you can clue in the clown car and by then it's too late for any damage."

The clown car.

Combes smiled, it was a perfect description of Wallfisch and McCreary.

"You got it."

"I suppose you realize that it's going to look like you let Sutton continue to kill because your friendship made you blind to his guilt? The press is going to have a field day, John, I don't even want to think about lawyers."

"The facts won't back that up. Nicky and I haven't been friends since we were teenagers and I can hardly be held accountable for the actions of every person I've known."

"I'm not sure that's going to matter, you know what this town's like. Make it a good arrest, you understand? Flawless. And for God's sake, stop calling him *Nicky*, it sends the wrong message."

When Coombes returned to his desk, he found a Post-It Note in Sato's handwriting stuck to his keyboard. A phone number and the word *Tesla*. Grace was on her computer, headphones on. *Maybe I should get a set of headphones*, he thought. Coombes pulled off the Post-It, scrunched it into a ball and fired it into his waste basket. Sean Bostic wanting another true crime fix no doubt. The Ferryman was a big case and Bostic probably figured he had his foot in the door.

The note reminded him of Bostic's idea about Blackstone's Tesla being altered while in a valet parking lot. It was an idea worth checking, not to mention a perfect task for Wallfisch and McCreary, as he suspected it would take the rest of the day to run down.

He found Wallfisch at his desk with a tablet in his hands. It looked to Coombes like the detective was playing poker, which in his experience was played for money, not for the hell of it. He pretended not to notice and positioned himself so that the screen was facing away from him.

"I've got something for you and Don."

Wallfisch stared at him with dead eyes and said nothing.

Coombes outlined what he wanted and heard in his own voice how much it sounded like busy-work, rather than what it was, a solid avenue of investigation.

"Sounds like a job for a couple of rookies to me."

Coombes smiled like he'd got the answer he wanted.

"All right. I'll tell Gantz that you and Don want off *Ferryman* so she can return you to rotation for new cases. Maybe you'll get another serial killer, maybe it'll be a rich kid with a bumped knee. We'll see."

Wallfisch sighed. "Give me ten minutes."

"Sure, finish your game. You got that *two pair*."

"I'm on my goddamn lunch break, Coombes."

He smiled again and returned to his desk.

There were two types of detective, he thought. Those that worked their lunch around a case, and those that did the opposite. He knew the only reason Wallfisch hadn't fought the assignment harder was because it offered him the chance to work at his own pace, which was similar to that of a tortoise.

With Wallfisch and McCreary dealt with for now, Coombes thought about the best way to proceed with Nicolas Sutton. So far, all they had was circumstantial evidence, none of which was strong enough to get a search warrant. He decided to do what all cops did in this situation, and checked the criminal database.

As with Jake Curtis, he expected nothing. As with Jake Curtis, he was wrong.

Fourteen entries, ranging from bar fights to a DUI. It appeared that Sutton's aggressive nature was not improved by the presence of alcohol in his blood stream. The most recent altercation was six months earlier, when he knocked a man unconscious with a beer bottle. The man was hospitalized by the incident, but Sutton escaped jail time in favor of court-mandated anger management sessions and a fine of $10,000.

Coombes sat back on his chair and sighed.

One law for the rich, one law for the poor.

It was an assault with a deadly weapon charge and his booking prints were therefore on file. He frowned. Even the partial fingerprint from the Haylee Jordan crime scene should've been good enough for a match. That left three possibilities: Sutton was innocent; there was a problem with the print; or the print was the boyfriend's, not the killer's.

He pulled up the photographs of the bathroom and the hinged glass shower door where the print had been recovered. The door had a curved metal edge that you pulled to open the door. The print was found on the back of the edge, facing into the shower stall. He enlarged the picture so that the front of door filled the screen. An idea came to him, and he reached around the desk divider to tap on Sato's desk. She pulled off her headphones.

"Grace, check this out."

She wheeled herself around next to him on her office chair.

"What you got, Johnny?"

"All right, this is Haylee's shower door where we got our partial print. Here's my question, how would you open that door?"

Sato reached out her left hand, fingers cupped into a C-shape as if to hook into the fold of metal. She then pantomimed moving it to the left as if the folding door was opening.

"Like that I guess?"

Coombes smiled, but said nothing. Sato frowned.

"Why, how would you do it?"

"The print was processed as coming from the killer's right hand, but even a right-handed person would open that door with their left hand. Nobody would twist their right hand 180 degrees and pull across the whole of their body, it's not natural."

Sato looked at the screen again, then back.

"Okay. So, the lab scanned the wrong side of the film?"

"I think so, yes."

"Then we have a left fingerprint, not a right. Does that help?"

"We've been trying to ID someone by the wrong hand. Sutton's in the system. If he's our guy, all we have to do is flip the print and run it through AFIS again."

She nodded. "I like it. Call the lab."

He got bounced around before he was put through to the technician who had processed the original evidence, a man called Harry Flynn. Coombes laid out what he suspected happened in a neutral tone without mentioning that people had died as a result of the mistake, keeping those nukes held back in case Flynn became difficult.

"Detective, I'm looking at the film right now, it was *not* scanned backward. The print you have is correct."

"Do me a favor, Flynn. *Indulge me.* Flip the print, run it through AFIS."

"All right, but you're wasting your time."

He heard a *clack* and realized Flynn had placed the phone on his desk while he worked on his computer. The tech was angry at the suggestion of a mistake. Coombes turned to Sato.

"He's going to run it flipped."

"Why is Sutton in the system?"

"A bar fight over a woman, he put a man in hospital."

There was a shuffling noise as the phone was picked back up.

"I don't understand, Coombes, but that got a hit."

"Give me the name."

"Nicolas Sutton. N I C O L A S, no h. I'll send it over."

"Thanks for your help, Flynn."

"Look, Detective. It shouldn't have worked. The film *is* the wrong way around."

He didn't know what to do with that.

"What hand is the print from? The left?"

"Just a second," Flynn said. "No, the right."

Coombes disconnected and shook his head. Again, with the right. The original forensic technician must have correctly identified the hand from the wrong side of the film. But why would Sutton have used his right hand to open the door? Perhaps the fingerprint itself was the clue. His hands were covered in Haylee's blood. There might have been more blood on his left hand and he was simply trying to avoid touching surfaces.

He supposed he'd add this to his list of questions for the Ferryman.

"Well?" Sato asked.

"It's time to have a word with Sutton."

34

NICOLAS SUTTON LIVED IN an upscale neighborhood south of Mulholland Drive. A thick, twenty-foot-high hedge grew around the property, the only accessible view of the house being a wide driveway and a car port projecting out from the side of the building. Coombes parked across the exit and looked at the car that sat on the concrete apron.

A silver Hyundai.

The vehicle was heavily rusted and it didn't look like it had been washed in at least a decade. Not the type of vehicle he figured belonged to Sutton. A car like this wouldn't help him sell million-dollar properties, he'd want something high-end. *Aspirational*. A big SUV, or a sports car.

The only use he'd have a car like this, was to move a body.

Coombes stepped out the Dodge and walked down the side of the Hyundai. A small sign close to the ground listed a security company that claimed to monitor the property, but he saw no cameras as he approached the door. Sometimes, a sign alone was enough. He knocked, then stepped to the side and drew his Glock. After a moment, a middle-aged Latina came to the door wearing a blue apron. She was short and heavy-set, with eyebrows like caterpillars. Her head tilted up to look at him, fear already on her face.

"Yes?"

"Who are you?" Coombes said.

"Romina. I clean for Mr. Sutton. Are you police?"

Coombes re-holstered his weapon.

"LAPD. Detectives Coombes and Sato. Is he here?"

"No sir, just me."

"We need to come in, Romina. Won't take long."

"I'm not allowed to let anyone in."

Coombes took off his sunglasses, folded the legs with exaggerated care, and put them in his shirt pocket. He said nothing, and instead clenched his jaw as if anger was building inside him. Her eyes darted about. He leaned closer to her, crowding her personal space.

"I suppose it's okay," she said. "Since you're police."

He smiled at her, but put no light in it and she shrank away from him. He saw enough monsters to know how to look like one. She backed away from the door and he pushed his way inside before she could change her mind.

The interior was sparsely furnished, with white walls and no decoration. A man's home, with no feminine touches. He had no doubt that Nicolas Sutton brought women back here, but none stayed long enough to soften up the way it looked. Surfaces were empty, like a home dressed for sale, or a hotel room. He turned to Romina.

"How often do you work here?"

"I come Tuesday and Friday afternoons while Mr. Sutton work."

"When did you arrive here today?"

"Ten minutes ago."

"You're a fast worker, the place is spotless."

"No, no. I show you, come."

She walked through the house and they followed along behind. They reached a door made from a dark brown wood and she opened it for them. Inside, was a large bed in the middle of the room. The end didn't touch a wall and there were no night stands.

"I make bed for him last time, see? Turn down corners, fix pillows. Today, it's not messed up, it's the same. He must be tripping. He gone."

"You think Mr. Sutton is on vacation?"

"*Sí, sí*. On vacation. Usually, he tells me not to come."

He glanced at Sato and she took over.

"When you came on Tuesday, did the place look normal or messy?"

"Normal."

"No sign of a struggle? Blood?"

"Oh, no! Nothing like that."

There was a tone shift, and Sato caught it.

"But it *was* different?"

"I don't know if I should say."

Grace smiled. "We're trying to help Mr. Sutton."

"He'd been drinking, there were bottles everywhere."

"Alcohol?"

The woman nodded. Coombes took out his iPhone and brought up a photograph of Olivia taken from her law firm's website. He held it up to Romina.

"Have you seen this woman?"

"No, sir."

It was what he expected her to say, but it never hurt to try. There would be no trace of Olivia here, he was certain. If Sutton hadn't been here since Tuesday, then he'd likely taken off shortly after the abduction, or shortly after he'd disposed of her.

Finished with the maid, Coombes walked off through the house to the media room. He saw the television and the presentation case mounted on the wall. The case was empty.

He swore out loud.

If the shoes had still been there, the chance of Sutton being innocent were higher. There was only one reason for taking the shoes, and that was because he was the Ferryman. The latent shoe print had never been revealed by the press, only the task force and the killer knew the significance of the Nikes. On the other hand, if the shoes were never recovered it might be difficult to use the evidence against him.

He photographed the case using his cell phone. First showing the television setup, then close-ups. There was no security lock, it just hinged open. The clear plastic provided no security, it was merely for displaying the shoes. As he moved closer, he noticed the top was misted with fingerprints from all the times Sutton had opened and closed the case.

For a pair of sneakers, they sure were important to him.

A sliding glass door was open at the back and he went out and stood next to a pool. The late-afternoon sun hit his face and he stood for a moment with his eyes closed letting the warmth of it fill him up. He could imagine sitting next to the pool with a beer, relaxing.

If Sutton had all this, why was he getting into bar fights?

Why kill at least nine people and abduct his own sister?

What was missing from his life that all this wasn't enough?

Coombes walked back into the house. It could be a trap for a detective, trying to make sense out of something that made no sense. Some people did what they did with no more idea why they were doing it than anyone else.

He found Grace in Sutton's home office, digging through his desk. They didn't have a search warrant, and exigent circumstances didn't exactly cover the contents of a desk. Olivia wasn't in a drawer. A defense attorney might not like it, but there would be another way to get the information, once they knew what it was. Sato closed the drawer and opened another. Almost immediately, she held up Nicky's passport and he found himself smiling for the first time in several hours. Whatever hole Sutton had crawled into, it wasn't in a country with no extradition treaty. It was right here, in the US.

"Good work, Grace."

She looked up at him.

"He's got a whole room back there where he keeps his clothes. Rails and rails of suits, it's like a goddamn Armani outlet. The two of you are about the same size, you should go see if there's one you like. He'll never notice it's gone from a prison cell."

Coombes couldn't tell if she was joking and he liked that.

"I don't suppose you found a Rolex?"

She shook her head.

"Sutton has 19 watches in that dressing room, each more expensive than my car. It looked like one was missing, so I guess he's wearing the Rolex."

He'd imagined the search would have led to Sutton's arrest and, not long after that, to charging him with multiple counts of murder. So far, the search hadn't even located Sutton himself, never mind any evidence against him.

"Did you find out what banks and cell carrier he uses?"

"Yeah."

"Then I think we're done here."

"What about the Nikes?"

"Gone."

"Pity. I wanted to see what $27,000 sneakers looked like."

They made their way back outside, the mood between them flat. The Ferryman had been one step ahead of them the entire time, now it appeared that he was almost a whole week away. But what would prompt Sutton to run, and why would he leave his passport?

His cell phone rang. *Becker*. His spirits lifted.

"Mark. What's the news from Century City?"

"Sutton Realty is closed. I spoke to someone in the unit next door and he said there's been no sign of activity since the middle of last week."

"Shit. Same story here. Looks like Sutton's in the wind."

"No doubt," Becker said. "What now?"

"Now we pray he left his cell phone on."

35

FOR THE FOURTH TIME in two months, Coombes stood before the Sutton home in Silver Lake. The fire that had raged here for almost an hour had robbed it of its grandeur and stripped it back to a darkened shell that looked like it was ready to be bulldozed. The security gates sat wide open, with nothing left to protect.

He began to walk along the short driveway, his eyes probing the dark, glassless spaces of the windows. His flashlight in his left hand tight next to his firearm, ready to go.

Sutton's cell phone had been switched off for the last five days. Since before the fire, before Olivia's abduction. Now, it was back, pinging within the walls of the building in front of him. The only logical reason for Sutton to turn it back on was to lure him here and have the end come, however that went. For Nicolas Sutton, the game had changed, he was now the one being hunted and being hunted was no fun at all.

Coombes stepped through the stone archway where the front door once stood and paused to let his eyes adjust to the darkness. The interior still smelled strongly of smoke and of everything the fire had consumed. He glanced at Grace next to him and indicated with his hand that he wanted her to go left, up the stone staircase. They hadn't discussed tactics, and she shook her head. She didn't want to split up. He made the same hand movement again and she reluctantly moved off.

The upper floor needed to be cleared and Grace was half his weight so it made sense for her to do the sweep upstairs. He went to the right, along what had been a hallway lined with oak panels and oil paintings. Beneath the trimmings, the building was cinder block and poured concrete with no more soul than a parking structure. Coombes felt nothing that it had been destroyed by fire, it was all it deserved.

Grace was wasting her time, he knew where Sutton would be. If this was to be the end, he had to be where it all started. His shoe crunched on glass. It was spread out across the floor; his eyes could just make it out.

Broken light bulbs.

An old trick from a cheesy movie, but effective at announcing his presence. He used the side of his shoe to brush the glass aside. Since his position was compromised anyway, he turned on his Maglite and swept the flashlight and pistol together.

Nicolas Sutton stepped out of the shadows holding a revolver.

"Johnny. I hoped it would be you. More poetic this way, don't you think?"

The killings hadn't touched him at all. He was the same as he'd always been.

"I never liked poetry. Too much like someone laughing at their own jokes."

"Nothing wrong with that. I crack myself up every day."

"No doubt."

"Where's that *little bird* of yours?"

Sutton squinted into the flashlight beam to search the hallway behind him.

"Come on little birdie, out you come. Flutter, flutter."

"She's not here. I told her you'd want privacy. She's at the end of the driveway with some friends of mine. You and me are going to have a conversation, then we're going outside to get everything straightened out. Okay?"

"These friends of yours, do they have shotguns and bulletproof vests?"

"I told them you were a gentleman, that you'd be unarmed."

Sutton glanced at the gun in his hand.

"Alas, there are so few of us left. Put yours away, perhaps I'll do the same."

"You first."

"All right." Sutton put the gun in his pants pocket, grip hanging out. "Happy now?"

There was a manic edge to Sutton's voice, like he'd taken something. Coombes decided to play along to calm him down, perhaps get close enough to take his weapon. No need to rush him outside to face the music. Coombes holstered his own gun and nodded.

Sutton was watching him closely.

"I love what you've done with the place, Nicky. Very modern."

"It has something, doesn't it? Like a good Scotch that bites you on the back of the throat as you swallow."

They were in the room where Theodore Sutton had taken the short drop. All trace of that day was gone, but they both glanced at where he'd been, like he was still hanging there. Seconds ticked by before Sutton spoke again.

"He did it in front of me you know."

"You never mentioned that before."

Sutton shrugged.

"I walked in and it was all set up. The noose, the chair. He wanted me to see. He stepped up and slipped the rope over his head. He looked me in the eye. I thought it was a joke, like that kid in *Harold and Maude*. I laughed. Next thing, he's swinging back and forth, his feet pumping. I went to him and held him tight until he stopped."

"Why not help him?"

"I *was* helping him. It's what he wanted."

Sutton's eyes dipped briefly, before coming back.

"Why do you believe that, Nicky?"

"Because I told him something he couldn't handle. He'd rather be dead."

"You told him you killed people?"

Sutton shook his head.

"This was before all that."

It hit him what the look in Sutton's eyes meant, where he'd seen it before.

"You're gay."

Anger flashed over Sutton's face.

"No. *Not* gay. Why does everyone use that word? I hate it."

"I thought-"

"Just you, nimrod, nobody else. You were the only one that could've stopped it and you never saw me. Not then, not now. All you saw was my sister and her perfect little C cups. I never stood a chance."

This was the reason Sutton had taken Olivia captive. Not because she knew his identity as the Ferryman, but because two decades earlier, she'd dated his best friend.

"This was all for you, John. I needed you to see me."

Again, he said nothing. If he took Sutton at his word, his childhood friend had murdered nine innocent people because he was in love with him. Coombes had no way to process that, except to think it was a detail he'd be leaving out of his report.

Sutton turned and looked at the glow of the Los Angeles skyline beneath them. He showed no concern at the possibility of being picked off by a police sniper on one of the rooftops below. As long as Olivia Sutton was missing, nobody could touch him.

Coombes closed the gap between them.

He needed the revolver out of commission.

"My dad, for all his faults, gave me everything I wanted. I never had to take some dead-end job to make ends meet. When I held him on that rope and felt him fighting to live, I never felt more alive." Sutton sighed. "Some people never find out what their true purpose is, you know? What they're good at. What shallow, empty lives they lead. But you found out, and so did I."

Sutton turned back. He gave no reaction to Coombes' closer proximity.

"Tell me, John. Does she know?"

"What are talking about?"

But he did know. He knew exactly what Sutton was going to say.

"Little bird. Does she know you're in love with her?"

He flinched. It was likely that Grace was close enough to hear them, she wouldn't be much use as backup if she wasn't.

"We're partners, Nicky. That's it."

Sutton nodded sadly.

"Then you do know what it's like to be next to the thing you want most in this world and for them to know nothing about it. You should tell her, you could be dead tomorrow."

He wondered how Sutton had managed to pick up on his feelings for Grace, when he wasn't sure of them himself. He decided to change direction. He glanced up, as if at the still-hanging body of Theodore Sutton.

"Your dad, he did it wrong. The drop was too short."

Sutton looked at him, his gaze piercing and bright. *Conspiratorial.*

"I know. No matter, he showed me the way. He showed me that nobody takes any interest in suicides, not the LAPD, not his friends, or the press. Everyone assumes the worst, that the person did it to themselves. Except you, old friend. Why did you take an interest?"

"His passing upset me. I liked your dad."

Sutton bared his teeth.

"Then you didn't know him. Nobody knew him like I did."

There was no mistaking the anger in his voice, the hurt. Instead of imagining what lay behind it, he imagined Grace's likely position in the building. It was dark in the burned-out hallway. Grace would be there, gun out in front of her in two-handed grip. There was just one problem, he was between the doorway and Sutton.

"Why the coins?"

"I guess you don't remember how my dad got started."

There'd been rumors for years about Theodore Sutton's business practices. Taking over housing intended for the poor, clearing them out and replacing the buildings with more expensive properties. In later years, the process was known as *gentrification*, but back then there was no name for it. If something happens often enough, they give it a name to make it acceptable.

Some said thugs went door-to-door dragging people out into the street, while others claimed unexplained fires had a habit of burning down properties that stood in his way. He'd heard rumors of buildings being set on fire with the people still inside, but he'd never believed it. That didn't reflect the man he'd known.

He took stock of the fire-ravaged room he stood in.

"Is that why you torched the house?"

"I'm not talking about the fires, man. I'm talking about the coins."

He said nothing.

"It was his favorite story. He started with a single apartment that his old man paid for, which he sublet to someone else. Instead of using that rent money to pay for an expensive hotel room, he used it to rent a slightly smaller space, and sublet that as well. He said he was able to do that four times before the money ran out. At the end of the first month, he had four properties, and he was homeless. All he had left, was two silver dollars. He claimed to have eaten out of a dumpster more than once."

Coombes realized he'd heard the story before, at least once.

"Rags to riches, huh?"

"It was grade-A horse shit. I got him drunk once and he told me the truth. That he dressed as a waiter and stole tip money from tables in upmarket hotels and restaurants. One time, there were two silver dollars and he kept them, never spent them. He had them in a frame in his office to remind him how far he'd come. He started to collect silver dollars whenever he saw them, put them in a jar in his office doorway."

"He never sublet his apartment?"

"There never *was* an apartment. My grandfather was a deadbeat, split from my grandmother when my dad was two years old. The whole thing was fiction. He was nothing more than a common thief." Sutton held his arms wide. "He built this with stolen tip money."

"Little late to take the moral high ground, isn't it?

Sutton laughed. "For sure."

"This funny to you?"

"I did nothing but rid this world of parasites and you know it. I should get a medal for taking these people off the board."

"If you really believe that, why stop?"

Sutton held out his left hand and unfurled his fingers.

"Because I only have two left and I'm going to need those."

The moonlight caught on the metal in his hand. Coombes frowned. Sutton clenched his hand into a fist again around the coins. A split second later, he pulled the revolver out of his pocket with his right. It came up awkwardly between them as if in slow motion, the long barrel catching on the hem of his pocket.

Without hesitation, Coombes drew his Glock and fired twice. Sutton flew back, his body slamming against the wall with a heavy thump.

Coombes ran forward, pistol aimed low.

He kicked the revolver out of reach then kneeled next to Sutton. The damage to his chest was catastrophic. Blood rolled thickly over his collarbone and around both sides of his neck and onto the charred concrete floor.

It looked black in the moonlight.

Sutton swallowed repeatedly and Coombes reached under his head to tilt it so that blood inside cleared the windpipe. Sutton looked dully into his eyes.

"Goddamn, this hurts."

"Where's Olivia?"

"Outside. Trunk of my car."

"Why, Nicky? Why'd you do this? Why kill all these people?"

"Because I had to have something that was mine."

Sutton's head went slack and his left hand opened. The two coins rolled across the floor and curved around in a spiral until they hit the blood, then they fell over.

36

COOMBES SWUNG HIS FLASHLIGHT around until it caught Grace standing in the doorway holding her gun. The automatic remained level with his chest for a couple of seconds before falling away, back down to the concrete floor.

"He made you shoot, didn't he?"

"Yeah."

Coombes looked at the last two coins.

"The final tableau, suicide by cop."

"Lass is upstairs," she said. "He's banged up pretty good, I already called it in. He's unconscious, but breathing okay. I think this piece of shit broke all his fingers, torturing him for information."

"Jesus. How did he even get here?"

"I guess he's a decent cop, after all."

He should've known what Sutton had planned. It was obvious in hindsight. The fumbling way he'd pulled the revolver out of his pants pocket, a blind man could've put two in his chest. The gun was a prop, just like the wine bottle in Vandenberg's hotel suite. Coombes felt in Sutton's pocket for his keys. There was no key fob, just an ancient metal key with a Mercedes logo on it. The old man's car. It was probably older than he was. He stood and made his way toward the door.

"Come on," he said, "let's go."

She hesitated; her eyes locked on his.

"What he said...is it true?"

"Grace, you're a knock-out but I'm married. You're my partner and my best friend. Are we good?"

"Yes."

He noticed he didn't say that it wasn't true.

They ran out through the building. Now that Sutton was dead and any threats posed by him vanished, the building seemed to shrink and they were quickly back outside. The driveway was empty, no cars. He wasn't surprised, they would have noticed the car when they arrived. On a modern car he could have pressed the unlock button and looked for flashing turn signals, but the car he was after didn't even have central unlocking. He peered down the drive at the security gates and the cars parked on the street.

"Do you see an old Mercedes?"

"No," she said.

He remembered a space at the side of the house where the Suttons had parked extra cars during parties and took off in that direction. His brain still mulled over what Sutton had said about Grace Sato. Nicky had always cut to the chase, except apparently about his own sexuality.

The Mercedes was where he'd pictured it, down the side of the building. He put the key in the lock and turned but before it could fully open Grace put her hand flat on the trunk to stop it opening.

"Johnny, if it's true we talk about it, okay?"

Coombes sighed inwardly. She'd forget this conversational thread soon enough, but it wasn't going to go away as soon as he liked.

"But I'm *not* transferring or changing partners. I like working with you, John, we're good together. If I ended up with Wallfisch, I'd die every day."

"Likewise," he said.

He opened the trunk and a small yellowish light came on.

Inside, curled up in the fetal position, lay Olivia Sutton. She was stripped to her underwear and had a clear plastic bag fastened around her head with thick copper wire. Her body was emaciated and her skin appeared hollowed out between each of her ribs. She'd been dumped here and left to die. Rage boiled inside him. How could Sutton do this to his own sister? It was impossible. The man he knew was incapable of this, of any of the killings.

A smell rose to meet him, but it was not the smell of decay, it was the smell of sweat turned cold. Of fear. He swallowed and leaned closer; his eyes narrowed. Studying the bag around her head. The inside of the plastic was heavily misted with condensation, almost obscuring her face. He realized he was holding his breath.

The bag's shape changed.

"She's alive!"

Coombes tore the bag open, then scooped her out of the trunk and laid her sideways on the driveway in the recovery position. He got on his knees and put the tips of his fingers to her neck. Her skin was cool to the touch and it took him a moment to find her pulse. It was weak, like the beat of a clock that was about to stop. He leaned close to her face, like he was going to kiss her. His eyes were tearing up. He'd assumed she'd been dead the whole time and that her life had been no more than a final tragic death of a sick killer.

"Olive, it's me, Johnny. Wake up."

Her face was like a doll's in the moonlight. He held the back of his hand in front of her nose and mouth. Her breath was barely detectable. The only thing worse than finding her dead would be to lose her in front of him. She needed oxygen. He heard an approaching siren. It would be the ambulance Grace had called in for Lass, but it wasn't going to arrive in time.

Coombes slapped Olivia's cheek, hard.

"Johnny!"

He ignored Grace and slapped her again. Harder. Hard enough to leave a mark. Her head would've spun right around, except she was lying on the ground, trapping it. His hand stung from the impact. For a second nothing seemed to happen, then there was a gasp and Olivia Sutton's chest began to rise and fall. He spoke softly into her ear.

"Follow my voice. You're safe. We've got you."

Olivia's eyes flickered open. "John?"

Her voice was slurred, like she was drunk.

He smiled. "Olive."

"Nobody calls me that anymore."

"Sure they do. *I* do."

The ambulance parked at the end of the driveway and doors slammed as medics rushed out from inside. The siren had stopped, but the strobes continued to pulse through the night air, washing their garish colors across the scene. Her eyes moved over his face, reading it.

"Nicky's dead, isn't he?"

"I'm sorry."

She nodded. "Help me up."

"Maybe we should wait until you're checked out first."

"I had a bag on my head, Johnny, it's not a spinal injury."

Coombes lifted her up. Her right arm swung wide and hung limp, her legs remained half folded. She wasn't ready to stand by a long way. He walked her over to the old Mercedes and they sat on the edge of the trunk. He slipped off his jacket and wrapped it around her shoulders. She leaned into him. They'd sat like this many times as teenagers but that was a long time ago.

He looked up and saw Grace watching. Their eyes connected and something passed between them, something he couldn't explain. *Desire.* He wasn't sure what was happening, only that it was going to be a problem. She smiled on one side of her face, then turned and ran toward the medics.

Olivia lifted her right hand up to her cheek.

"What the hell happened to my *face?*"

37

BILLY LASS WAS STRETCHED out on a hospital bed in front of Coombes. His head was turned away from the door and it gave him a moment to look at his old partner unobserved. The extent of Lass's workout regime was there for all to see, he was massive. A powder blue nightshirt was stretched to breaking point around his biceps, deltoids, and pectorals. It made him feel inadequate to see so much muscle and yet, he reflected, it hadn't done Lass much good in the end. Finally, his eyes moved down to Lass's hands, which sat like white boxing gloves on top of the sheet. Layer upon layer of gauze and tape simultaneously showing and hiding the damage caused by the Ferryman.

"How're they treating you, big guy?"

Lass turned sleepily toward him. He had a broken nose and two black eyes.

"John. Good to see you."

"I wish I could say the same, old friend. You look like shit."

Lass laughed, then winced with pain.

"Don't sugar-coat it, buddy. Tell me the truth."

Seeing Lass in this condition bothered him more than he would have predicted and he didn't want it to show on his face. He glanced around the room with a fixed smile as if he was assessing his accommodation.

"Not bad. Hope they've got you on some good stuff?"

"Tramadol. I don't need to eat or use a toilet anymore, it's a real timesaver."

Coombes sat in a chair next to the bed and he allowed Lass to see him looking at his hands. He couldn't ignore them, he had to respect what Lass had gone through.

"What was he trying to get out of you?"

"Not a damn thing. He never said a word, just broke one finger after another. He was getting off on it, he had a big smile on his face. I passed out before he reached my index fingers and thumbs, so he stopped. No screaming, no fun. Wish I'd passed out earlier."

"I'm really sorry, Billy. I hope the City's paying for all this."

"Yeah. I heard Jackson himself got involved. I'm still officially on the payroll."

The Chief of Police getting involved usually meant you'd died in the line of duty, or you'd shot the wrong person. Billy Lass's hospitalization would've been a political minefield for the chief given his suspended status.

Coombes indicated a television hanging from the ceiling.

"You saw the news?"

"Yeah, I saw. You nailed that scumbag. Can't say I'm sorry about it."

Coombes nodded and stared at the floor. He'd foreseen this reaction by Lass and figured that he might not be pleased to have this view changed if it was giving him comfort.

Lass sighed. "I know that face, John. Spit it out."

"I need some clarity and figure you're in a unique position to provide it."

"You closed the case and saved the girl. What am I missing?"

"There's a bad taste in my mouth, like I got played."

Lass frowned. "News said he confessed to the whole thing."

"He did, but you know how that goes. We had twelve people do that."

"*And* told you the location of his sister?"

"I know how it looks, but it's too easy. Our killer makes no mistakes for months then suddenly we wrap the whole thing up and put him in a drawer inside 24 hours?"

"You give this guy too much credit. He had a run of good luck and then that luck ran out. That's how these cases always go; slowly then suddenly.

Everyone makes mistakes. You know, it seemed to me for a while there you suspected *I* was the Ferryman."

"Don't. I'm mortified enough about that."

"Water under the bridge. I realize how I must've looked sneaking around. To think I honestly thought I could get my badge back by solving a serial. Like that's important at all to people like Hurst. The Ferryman could have killed people like you and me all day every day and nobody would've cared, it's only money that counts in this town."

Coombes was quiet for a beat. Thinking. Listening to the sound of the hospital. It sounded like the inside of a machine. He didn't know what he wanted from Lass. Permission, maybe, to shoot himself in the foot.

"Am I trying to snatch defeat from the jaws of victory?"

Lass smiled; his bitterness forgotten.

"You've got integrity, I respect that."

"What if I'm right?"

"Just show me the picture you came here to show me."

Coombes took out his cell phone and found a photograph of Nicolas Sutton. The picture had been taken at his father's memorial service by a news agency and was pin sharp. The TV networks were using a different photograph, taken from his Facebook page. This second picture was of poorer quality, and had obviously been chosen because it showed him standing next to his sister, smiling. He held his phone where Lass could see it. He studied it carefully for thirty seconds before looking back into his eyes, his face hard.

"That ain't him."

"You're sure?"

"No, man. I'm not. It was dark and he'd hit me on the head."

"If you had to put a number on it then."

"Seventy percent."

If Billy had been convinced of Sutton's guilt, he would've let it go. Grudgingly at first, then with relief. He would've returned to his desk, filed his paperwork, then gone home for some much-needed time off. Instead, Lass had confirmed his worst fear and he couldn't be happier. It meant the Ferryman was still out there to be caught. To be put on trial.

"What jumps out at you after seeing the picture?"

"The hair. My guy had shorter hair. When I think on it, he also had a slight cleft in his chin. Face was heavier too. The two are similar looking, I guess, and around the same age." Lass smiled. "I've never been too observant with guys, it's like a blind spot."

"Right."

If Lass wanted to use humor to hide his embarrassment about being a victim, then who was he to argue? He'd probably do the same thing.

"If he's not the Ferryman, where does that leave you? I assume the shooting is under investigation?"

"Yeah. It's not ideal, but the bottom line remains the same. He pulled a gun on me and I defended myself. My partner saw the whole thing."

"Before we spoke, what made you think Sutton was innocent?"

"His confession. Half of it seemed real, half fake."

"What was fake?"

"He told me he was gay." Coombes said. He paused a second, wondering how much to tell Lass, before deciding to tell him everything. The man had been through hell, he deserved to know. "He said he'd done all of it for me. So I'd *notice* him."

He expected Lass to make an off-color joke, but instead he shook his head.

"If he's admitting to being a serial killer, why say something random like that even if it's true? What does it add?"

Coombes shrugged.

"At the time, I figured he was trying to show me that I never really knew who he was. He claimed jealousy was his motive for kidnapping his sister. Because I'd dated her back then."

"I see that, but I disagree. It's misdirection. He was hiding something."

They fell silent for a while, thinking it over. When they began to talk again, a minute or so later, the subject changed to Lass' wife and son who he'd been discouraging from visiting due to his physical appearance. The dialogue was one-sided for the most part, Coombes' thoughts caught in a loop of their previous conversation.

He knew in his heart that Lass was right. *A misdirection*. It seemed so obvious in hindsight. But what had Sutton been hiding? What would someone *bother* to hide if they were willing to admit to being a serial killer?

What secret was that big? But in a way, he knew.

The same secret that made him admit it in the first place.

"Billy, I have to hit the road. Take care of yourself, okay?"

Lass nodded wordlessly and watched him stand.

"John. Are you really not going to ask? Aren't you at least curious?"

"What?"

"You never asked what led me to the Silver Lake house."

"I assumed you were following a hunch or returning to the first suicide to find a new angle." His voice faded away as a smile broke out on his old partner's face. He knew it well; he was being mocked. He was over-thinking it. "You put a GPS tracker on Sutton's car."

"Correct."

"I don't suppose the tracker was there during the abduction?"

"Unfortunately, not," Lass said.

"Nothing's ever easy."

"You got that right, partner. Listen, any chance you could retrieve this tracker for me before it gets logged into evidence? My legal situation is already problematic and I'm stuck here. It's in the driver-side front wheel arch."

"Of his Mercedes?"

"Get a clue, John. The man drove a Porsche 911 and he drove it like an absolute lunatic. It's bright red, about 100 feet past the entrance, you can't miss it."

Coombes smiled as he walked down the corridor toward the nurse's station. He knew what a Porsche 911 looked like, everyone did. It was like a swimwear model version of a Volkswagen Beetle. It had large tilted headlights at the front, and a wing at the back. Also at the back, like the Beetle, was its engine. There was a trunk of sorts at the front, but for sure it wasn't big enough to hold Olivia Sutton.

Olivia was found in the old Mercedes and the most likely scenario was that the same vehicle was used in her abduction. She hadn't been transferred there for storage or effect. Nevertheless, he had a clear memory of the key to the old Mercedes hanging on a nail at the back door of the Silver Lake house. Despite the two decades that had passed, he imagined nothing had changed since he'd been a regular visitor.

If Nicky hadn't been using the car himself, then he figured it had been in semi-regular use by Theodore Sutton right up to the point where he took the short drop in front of the picture window. After his death, the property had remained empty and the key had doubtless remained on its nail.

Anyone at all could have taken the key.

He was still smiling as he stepped up to the nurse's station.

"Can you tell me where I can find Olivia Sutton?"

A nurse looked up. It wasn't the one he'd spoken to when he arrived yet he could tell she knew he was a cop. There was always this *understanding* that seemed to pass over someone's face when they looked at him. He'd seen it many times, even though he wore a generic suit and tie. Even, apparently, when he was smiling. Without saying anything, she typed into her computer. The head came back up.

"Olivia Sutton is not in my system."

"She came here last night, same time as Mr. Lass."

"She's not in a bed and she's not in our morgue, so I guess she went home. The hospital can only make crazy people stay."

He looked her in the eye. "No kidding."

She smiled. "You're pretty cheeky for a cop, aren't you?"

"Just the regular amount."

He took the elevator to the parking garage and got into his Charger. He sat for a moment thinking about the GPS tracker. The whole thing didn't ring true. The sheepish way Lass told him about it was not his style.

The truth was, he'd only mentioned it because he needed him to remove it before it was discovered by someone else. He'd had no reason to track Sutton when he did. The only explanation was that Lass had carpet-bombed every possible target, hoping for a Hail Mary. Coombes got out the Dodge, walked around the door, and reached into his own wheel arch.

A box the size of a computer mouse was attached inside.

38

OLIVIA SUTTON LIVED IN the Hollywood Hills on an unnamed road off Woodrow Wilson Drive. Like many homes in the area, it was entirely hidden from street level behind a high wall and a security gate. So far, no news crews had gathered outside, but that situation wouldn't last long. As both a victim and relative of the killer, Olivia was about to be consumed whole by the media.

Coombes saw an intercom unit was mounted on a post so he pulled alongside, powered down his window and pressed the button. A screen lit up showing him a live feed of his own face. The resolution was horrific. He could see every pore in his skin, every hair follicle. His eyes were bloodshot, his pupils large and dangerous. He needed a week's sleep, a shave, maybe even a couple of pints of blood.

A woman with a bored British accent answered.

"Can I help you, *sir?*"

Coombes held his badge up to the camera.

"Yeah. Open the gate. Police business."

The screen went black and a second later the gate opened out toward him on hydraulic arms. He drove through the gap then up the driveway. It was the first time he'd been here and he drank it all in. Her recent setback notwithstanding, Olivia had done all right for herself. The rich couldn't help it if they kept getting richer, it was their burden.

He parked in front of a sprawling Spanish Colonial mansion where his childhood sweetheart apparently now lived. He smiled to himself. *Police business.* He'd never used that expression before, not once. The woman's tone had triggered something inside him that he didn't know was there.

Thomas Garvy stood at the door waiting with an expression that was hard to read. He was wearing a gray three-piece-suit and a light pink shirt. The top of his shirt was open, his tie pulled down and to one side like he'd started to take it off, then changed his mind. Coombes could smell the Scotch on him from four feet away. It was ten in the morning, and Garvy was at least halfway through a bottle. He'd hoped to avoid Olivia's husband and all the baggage that went with it, but his day wasn't exactly working out the way he wanted.

"Coombes," Garvy said, dryly. "I don't think she wants to see you."

"Most people don't."

"She's in a dark place, come back another time."

"That's not how this works."

Garvy shrugged and stepped aside to let him in. A large reception room lay beyond with a black and white marble floor like a chess board. Oil paintings were spaced out along the walls. Dark rectangles with thick gold frames. Miserable people and miserable landscapes. He looked at them blankly, wondering how much they were worth. His reverie didn't last long as it was interrupted by the unmistakable sound of gunshots within the building. Coombes reached for his piece, his head snapping around to Garvy to assess his threat potential.

"Easy. It's just Olivia working through her feelings."

Garvy pointed to a door and Coombes turned toward it.

"Wait. I wanted to thank you for what you did. I'd be lost without her."

There'd always been some bad energy between him and Garvy over their shared history with Olivia, but he could see now that the conflict on the other man's face had cleared. Garvy was looking at him like nothing had gone before.

Drunk, but at peace.

Coombes nodded, then turned and went through the door and down a narrow corridor. Once again, he heard gunshots. They were in groups of three, separated by a two second pause. At the end of the corridor, he came to a doorway and he paused there to take in the scene.

It was a full-size bowling lane.

Polished maple and pine floor, automated ball return tunnel and pin reset machine. Coombes had never seen one in a private residence before. He'd heard that Clinton had one installed in the White House back in the day, and though it was probably an urban legend, he'd always chosen to believe it. A paper target was fixed to the end wall. A simple black silhouette against a white background. The drywall around the target was peppered with stray bullet holes, some as much as five feet away.

Olivia Sutton stood with her back to him dead center of the lane. She was in tight blue jeans, a white T-shirt, and wore both ear and eye protection. Her hair was pulled back behind her head into a long ponytail. She was holding an automatic in a two-handed grip. The shots were as regular as clockwork. Calm, deliberate. Controlled. Her stance was good, arms rock-steady and professional.

The shots were tearing through the already-destroyed 10-spot in the middle of the silhouette's chest. Based on this performance, it was fair to assume that the wild misses were all Garvy's. He noticed that someone had used a marker pen on the target to add the outline of some hair.

It looked like his hair.

The shots stopped, the slide locking back with a distinctive *clack*. She put the pistol down next to the spent magazines, took off her ear protection and dumped them on the table.

"You're not welcome here, Johnny. I don't want to speak to you, I don't even want to look at your face."

"For what it's worth, I'm sorry about your brother."

She turned sharply toward him. Her eyes wild with anger.

"Don't you *dare* say that. You've got no right."

"Maybe, but it's true."

She stared at her feet and removed her safety glasses. The leg of the glasses pulled at some strands of hair which fell down next to her mouth.

"I don't understand," she said, her voice dropping away. "There's no way he'd do this to me, never mind kill all those people. My brother was a good man. He wasn't...a *monster*."

Coombes thought about relatives of killers he'd spoken to before. None of them saw it coming, none of them believed it after the fact. It was how people coped, with denial. He wondered if he wasn't in his own way falling into the same trap. Nicolas Sutton wasn't family, but they'd been friends once and maybe that was affecting his judgement.

"He confessed to everything."

She nodded. "So I was told."

"He had your dad's old gun. He gave me no choice."

"Why are you here, Johnny? Why are you *really* here? Do you want my forgiveness, is that it? I'm not that person. You know what I wish? I wish you'd left me in that damn trunk. Another ten minutes the medic said. Couldn't you have done that for me? I would've died and known nothing about all this, about Nicky. But no. You had to be the big hero and *save me*. Thanks for that. I now live in hell. Go get your medal and leave me alone."

He'd known she wouldn't be happy to see him, but this was worse than he'd expected. She wished she was dead.

"I'm sorry. The truth is, I don't believe it myself. It doesn't smell right. You know what it is? It's like a movie where the killer has been right in front of the detective all along. You know how often that happens? Never. It's bullshit."

Olivia turned to face him properly.

"Thank you for saying that."

It was the first time he'd had a proper look at her face since he'd arrived and it scared him a little. She looked destroyed, and he supposed it was him that had done that to her. It made him uncomfortable and he reached into the breast pocket of his suit jacket for his notebook and deliberately took a moment to find a blank page.

"You saw nothing of the person that abducted you?"

"Nothing. I parked in my usual spot. Got out, started to walk toward the elevator and my vision goes dark. It was fast, like someone flipped a switch and the lights went out. Next thing I know I'm in the trunk of a car with a taste of flowers in my mouth and a sore head."

"Go on."

"I started screaming and the fucker opened the trunk real quick like he was standing waiting for it. He hit me with a taser. It was excruciating, my whole body seized up, I thought I was having a heart attack. Then he held that shit over my mouth again and I passed out.

"Next time I came around, there was a plastic bag over my head. I could hardly breathe the air was so thick. There was no doubt in my mind that I was going to die. I kept passing out from lack of oxygen. Finally, I woke up and you were standing over me."

Coombes said nothing for a moment and skimmed the notes he'd made in his notebook. He'd found in the past that constant eye contact could cause a victim to shut down, they needed moments of apparent privacy to recover.

"When he opened the trunk you didn't see his face?"

"All I saw was a baseball cap and sunglasses. My vision was washed out from being in the dark and suddenly getting full sunlight. It was blinding."

He nodded.

"Facial hair? Scars? Tattoos?"

Olivia shook her head.

"Did he say anything to you?"

"No, nothing."

"Did he smell of anything?"

Olivia paused. "Yeah, actually. *Gasoline*."

That figured. The killer had set her dad's house on fire. Coombes was silent for a moment. They had arrived at the moment he'd come here for and he didn't want her to dismiss it.

"Why would Nicky say he'd done it if it wasn't true?"

"I don't know, and it's all I've been able to think about. He must've thought it was the only way to save me."

"That's interesting, I hadn't considered that."

She looked at him hopefully.

"You think it's possible?"

"I do, but that's not the same as saying he didn't do it. People are not always who we think they are, everyone has secrets. Was your brother having problems with anyone, business, personal, something like that?"

"You knew Nicky. He was mercurial. Anything could set him off, but it usually meant nothing. He wasn't someone to hide how he felt, he'd just explode and get it all off his chest at once. He could be in a huge argument with someone, then see the same person again twenty minutes later, and he'd not understand why they didn't want to talk to him."

"Is it possible he had enemies?"

She sighed.

"He made a new enemy every day. Every time he opened his mouth."

Coombes recalled the way Nicky had spoken to him at his father's service. It wasn't hard for him to imagine someone taking his comments to heart. Had he simply crossed paths with the wrong person and got into an argument?

"How was Nicky's relationship with your father?"

Olivia Sutton's face soured.

"They were too much alike. They argued constantly. About the business, about nothing, about me."

"Why about you?"

"Dad thought I should work for the family business. I'm a corporate lawyer, not a realtor. What would I do in his business? It was stupid. Dad wasn't used to hearing the word no, he thought he could change anyone's mind by shouting at them for fifteen minutes. Nicky always defended me."

That about wrapped things up for him. He closed his notebook and returned it to his pocket. He noticed her chest deflate, like she'd been holding her breath and had suddenly relaxed. He'd seen the same thing many times before and it always meant something was being held back. She walked him back up through the building the way he'd come in.

He turned to her as they walked.

"I want you to understand something, Olivia. My department considers this case closed. We had a lot of pressure to solve it and nobody wants to change their minds. This is a win for them and they're going to be running the flag up. Finding this guy now is going to be difficult, I won't lie to you. He's a ghost.

"About the only advantage we have is that he thinks no one is looking for him. So do *not* mention that aspect of our conversation to anyone, not even your husband. I came by to check you were all right. That's all, okay? In the meantime, you should avoid watching television for the next couple of days. In fact, you might want to get out of town, somewhere news crews won't find you."

She nodded and was quiet for a moment.

"It wasn't Nicky, I know it wasn't."

They were in the main entrance now, with the checkerboard marble floor.

"You know what that means if it's true, don't you?"

She frowned, not understanding.

"Well," Coombes continued, his voice lowered. "If it *wasn't* him, then the person that did this is still out there. He could start all over again. It was only really chance that we noticed the killings for what they were in the first place."

"You think I'm in danger?"

"No, I don't. Coming after you would expose Nicky's innocence. He went to a lot of effort to frame your brother, so he'll want to avoid anything that could unravel all that."

They walked down the steps into the courtyard. There had always been an easy physical intimacy between them but that was gone. There was a space now, and in that space, an invisible wall now existed. He'd killed her brother; the wall would never go away. He got into his car, started the engine, and opened the window.

Her face looked blankly down at him, devoid of life.

"If that bastard comes back for me, I'll be ready."

Coombes pretended not to hear this.

"One last question. Was Nicky seeing someone?"

"You mean a therapist?"

He tilted his head.

"Was he *dating* someone."

"No."

Olivia's cheeks turned scarlet, embarrassed by her mistake. No doubt this meant that Nicky *had* been seeing a therapist. It was an interesting detail, but he knew from experience that it probably meant nothing. In the social circles Nicky moved in, seeing a therapist was as normal as visiting a dentist. It might even have been part of his court-mandated anger management program.

"Do you remember his last relationship?"

"If you're asking for her name, I don't have it. He might not have known it himself. They seemed to come and go. Probably literally. I think he met them on one of those gross hook-up apps you install on your phone. I doubt he saw any of them more than once. I haven't seen him with one of those skanks in almost a year. He had turned his life around."

Coombes nodded. It confirmed his theory. Not only was Nicky not gay, he was a serial womanizer. Until recently, it appeared.

"Maybe he met someone special?"

She smiled sadly. "I hope so."

He looked at the dark halo of her eyes and saw that they'd gone dead, like an artist's sketch.

"Olivia, I don't think you should be around guns. Get some rest."

She said nothing, and after a beat he put the car in gear and drove off leaving her standing there. He glanced in the door mirror and watched her get smaller and smaller, before the driveway twisted and she was gone.

He wondered if he'd see her alive again.

39

GRACE SATO ANSWERED HER door wearing faded blue jeans and a navy T-shirt that left a band of midriff showing. Her hair was all over the place, she had no shoes or socks on and, judging from the large neck hole on the T-shirt, no bra. Her smile was quick and natural, her eyes lighting up as they saw him.

"Johnny! Come in."

Her apartment was small, not much larger than a motel room, and he found himself looking at her bed through the open door of her bedroom. The sheets were all crumpled up, and it occurred to him that she might not be alone.

"Is now a bad time? I could come back."

She seemed to understand what he was thinking.

"Oh. There's no one else here, I'm a mess. You want a beer or something?"

Her cheeks had a rose tint spreading across them and her smile was gone.

"I'm good. Just here to pick your brains."

"I thought maybe you were here to finish our discussion."

Coombes knew what *discussion* she was talking about, and he didn't want to get into that again. Not now, not later. He looked around and saw that she had a single chair in front of her television. There wasn't even a coffee table. He turned back.

"How did it go with FID?"

"They grilled me pretty good," Coombes said. "How about you?"

"Less than an hour, not bad. You followed policy, Johnny, you'll be fine."

His face contorted awkwardly.

"I showed Lass a photograph of Sutton. He doesn't think it's our guy."

"Oh, shit. Come into my office."

She walked into her bedroom and sat on her bed. There was nowhere else in her whole apartment for them to sit together. He sat next to her. The room smelled feminine. Flowers, strawberries, and something else. It was the smell of her body, he thought. A nice smell, a fertile smell. Coming here had been a mistake.

What kind of person didn't have a spare chair?

"Is it how you imagined it?"

"What?" He asked.

"My bedroom."

"Grace, can we not do this? We're partners."

"I know you want me, Johnny. Why not admit it?"

"Whatever it is, it's my problem."

"What if we have the same problem?"

He stared at her and said nothing. It couldn't be true.

"How is this a mystery to you? That old woman in the hotel elevator saw it straight away and she's not a detective."

"It's smaller," he said eventually. "Your bedroom, I mean. I also imagined a big window with shades that never got closed, like you didn't care who saw what."

"Then you *do* know me."

"I'm not here to talk about this."

"All right, but it's not going away."

He nodded and tried to get back to where he was when he'd arrived at her apartment. It seemed to be a lifetime ago.

"I was thinking about Sutton's confession. I don't have brothers or sisters, so I wanted to ask you. If someone took one of your siblings, would you trade your life for theirs? Would you say you were a serial killer if that kept them alive?"

"I don't know. If you were trying to buy time, I guess you might."

"What would make you do what I'm suggesting, without doubt?"

She closed her eyes and took a deep breath, her head still tilted back toward him. Sato stayed like that for a while, thinking. He wanted to kiss her, and plenty more besides.

"A child. If I was a mother and someone took my kid, I'd do anything."

It was perfect. Missing piece of a puzzle perfect. Only, the missing piece came from a different puzzle and, even knowing this, Coombes couldn't get over how well it fitted.

"Jesus. Too bad Nicky didn't have a kid."

"Right. Then there's the coins. If Nicolas Sutton *wasn't* the killer, then how else do you explain all those Ferryman coins? That part of his confession about his dad collecting the coins, that seemed legit too."

Somehow, he'd forgotten about the coins.

"Grace, you work on one thing at a time and see where it leads. Pitching in aspects that don't seem to fit isn't helpful. You can always circle back to them later once you have a narrative. Sometimes those issues resolve themselves."

"There's nothing *to* come back to later, Johnny. We're done, remember? We solved the case. The task force room has been dismantled. You didn't get the result you expected, but you got one."

Coombes turned away from her, his jaws clamped tight together.

"I know he used to be a friend, Johnny. But people change, they become damaged. The teenager you knew was not the same person that drew a gun on you. The simplest answer is usually right, no? Well, the simplest answer is that Nicky was the Ferryman. I think you just have to make peace with it."

"I guess I'm not there yet."

She studied him closely.

"When was the last time you slept?"

"It's...it's been a couple of days."

"Jesus. Lie down or go home."

"I've got an errand to run first."

"Fine, but I'm driving."

Coombes waited in her living room while she changed her clothes. He pretended not to notice that she didn't close her bedroom door as she dressed, or the occasional reflection of her on the TV.

What the hell was he going to do with her?

When she re-emerged, he told her where they were going. He had expected some resistance, but instead she just nodded, like it was what she expected.

Coombes supposed she was right about him being tired, because he fell asleep before they left her parking garage. When he woke, his head was tilted over, bouncing on her passenger door window. She glanced at him with an eyebrow raised.

"You snore like an elephant."

"Sorry."

"What about *that*, is that normal?"

He saw where she was looking and flinched.

"Your car needs new shock absorbers."

"I got to tell you, Johnny. For *that* I'd put up with the snoring."

He laughed and re-positioned his arm to cover himself. She made him feel good, and he hadn't felt this good since Monica Sullivan had pressed herself against him in that bar.

After five minutes they were back at what remained of the Sutton home in Silver Lake. A police cruiser sat at the gate and he could see three news trucks parked on the street. Reporters and camera crews doing follow-up pieces on what was rumored to be the Ferryman's last stand.

The facts were the same as the night before, only this time it was daylight and more of their audience was awake and wanting to catch up. The whole country had followed the case and the interest in it had not died with Sutton.

The lack of official confirmation had served to amplify interest, rather than subdue it.

Sato parked some way from the house and they began to walk back together in silence. It was stupid, but he hadn't anticipated the presence of the media. If the reporters saw them approaching, it was going to be chaos. The cameras would swarm around them, millions of Americans ready to feed on his train-wreck face. His memory of Olivia Sutton's gatepost camera haunted him with its resolution.

The red Porsche was right where Lass said it was, ready for a getaway. It looked fast, even when it was parked. Coombes leaned down and reached into the front wheel arch and pulled out Lass' GPS tracker. Sato made a face.

"*That's* why we're here? I thought we were doing another walk-through of the crime scene. When did you even plant that?"

"Did you know that your nose crinkles when you're mad?"

"What?!"

Coombes stood. "It's quite adorable, actually. I never noticed before."

"Johnny, this is illegal."

"Yeah, but it's not mine so cool your jets, ok?"

The tracker was dirty but he dropped it into his pocket anyway.

"*Lass*," Sato said.

He knew what she thought of his old partner and didn't want to get into it with her. Lass had his flaws, but his approach had almost worked. The tracker hadn't been on the car when it mattered, during the murders, or during Olivia's abduction. He paused for a minute on the sidewalk, unmoving. He could feel an idea forming, like the buzz before a sneeze.

What the hell was I thinking. Work it.

Car...abduction...GPS. Then he had it. Coombes turned to the Porsche and looked at the windshield. He saw what he needed almost immediately, in the top corner of the glass. A sticker for a security company called AutoTrack. Like a lot of expensive vehicles, the car was fitted with its own GPS tracker to prevent theft. Everywhere the car had been was logged somewhere, on some computer database.

"Grace, you accept Nicolas Sutton's confession at face value?"

"He was pretty convincing."

"For it to work, he had to kidnap his sister as well as kill all those people, right? Otherwise, how did he know where she was? It's all or nothing."

He had her attention now, he could see it.

"What are you thinking?"

"This is Nicky's car. Obviously, it's not the one used to abduct Olivia, but he'd have to come here to pick up the Mercedes first and I'm certain he didn't take the bus."

"And he wouldn't want to involve someone else."

"This car has a built-in GPS in case it's stolen. If it wasn't parked here the morning that Olivia was abducted, then dollars to doughnuts he didn't take her. We could also check where it was parked prior to each of the murders."

"That's hardly airtight, Johnny. He could've hired a car for example."

"If he did, it would show up on his credit card and there was nothing like that on his statement, we've seen it. Same for something like Uber, everything leaves a digital trace. In my experience, owners forget their cars have GPS most of the time. It's something they select in the showroom along with the coating to stop the paint fading. Nobody remembers, least of all when their head is as messed up as Sutton's."

"Still, though. It's weak."

"You know what's weak? A confession that relies on him having to knock his sister unconscious and dump her in the trunk of his dad's car like a piece of luggage. He could've just asked her to get into this one and driven away. Doesn't that make more sense?"

"That part always bothered me, I admit it."

"My bet? Nicky's car was somewhere else the day his sister was taken. If it was, his confession is pretty much dead in the water as far as I'm concerned."

Coombes glanced down the road at the news crews and saw a man pointing at them. They'd been spotted, it was time to leave. He walked to the back of the Porsche and took a photograph of the license plate, then walked back to her Toyota. Sato floored the throttle before he had the door fully closed. She had her jaws tight together, her face unreadable.

"If that was Curtis' car, would you give him the same benefit of the doubt?"

"Are you serious?"

"They both killed their father. They both seem like fine examples of toxic masculinity. Even their taste in cars is pretty similar. From where I'm sitting, they are practically the same person. The only difference is, Sutton confessed and drew a weapon on you. If Curtis had done half those things, we'd be sitting in a bar right now."

"You really think Olivia Sutton wouldn't recognize her own brother in a baseball cap and sunglasses?"

"No, I don't. That never made sense either. We're missing something and even if we find it, it's not going to show us who the real killer is, supposing it's not Sutton."

"Actually, we're missing a couple of things. Namely, what led the killer to frame Nicky for these murders, and why he confessed to them when he was innocent. What you said before, about the coins, I can't wish it away. The coins *were* his father's, the chance of them belonging to someone else is remote. They were Teddy's all right, from his jar in his home office. That's where they *used* to be anyway, nobody would notice them gone after the fire."

"Someone stole the coins to frame Sutton?"

"Why not? Is that so ridiculous? The house was being renovated. People coming and going all day, nobody really knowing who is who. If the killer put on a hard hat and could've walked around totally invisible like he did at the Capitol Records Building. He sees the coins, picks them up and walks out.

"Maybe he didn't know what he was going to do with them at first, it was just a joke. The story of what those coins represented to Teddy was no secret, he told everybody. So now he has the old man's coins, he's back home drinking a beer or whatever, but he's still burning up at Nicky for something and slowly the plan forms, to use the coins to implicate him in a crime."

"You think he stole the Mercedes at the same time?"

He nodded. It was perfect. Two loose ends resolved at once.

"The keys to the Mercedes hung on a hook at the back door the whole time we were friends and I'm guessing that never changed. It might look old, but that car's a classic and in pristine condition. It's probably worth a decent amount of cash. Maybe our guy swipes the keys and figures he'll return later for the car when nobody's around. Only, when he comes back, he witnesses Teddy's death through the picture window and a new plan starts to form."

"Damn, Johnny. That's good."

"Whatever it turned into, this started off personal. A grudge between two men that spiraled out of control. Nicky pissed people off like I drink coffee - all day, every day. It was like Tourette's; he couldn't help himself. But to make someone this mad, we've got to be looking at something else, right?"

Sato nodded. "Love or money."

They sat in silence for a moment with just the hiss of the air conditioning pushing through the cabin and the muted sound of traffic through the glass. Something about being in a car helped him to think. At his desk there were too many distractions.

He thought of the Sutton's real estate business.

Both the principals were now dead, and although Olivia was certainly capable of running it, he doubted she'd want to. The most likely outcome was that she'd sell the business and go on with her life. If taking control of the business had been the goal, then the suspect would certainly have killed Olivia when he'd had the chance and picked up the business from an administrator for pennies on the dollar.

The big picture didn't work, it was something smaller.

Teddy Sutton had been a shark in the business world and Coombes had a feeling his son was no different. Willing to stick it to the little guy to increase his margin. Olivia had mentioned an argument she'd overheard her father have the last time she'd seen him alive. Had they simply screwed over the *wrong* little guy? It was worth checking, but with them both dead, how could he? He turned to Sato.

"If you had to guess which it was, love or money, which would you choose?"

"Love."

She didn't even pause to think about it.

"What's your reasoning?"

"Because there's no money in this, only revenge."

40

THEY DROVE STRAIGHT BACK to the Police Administration Building. He felt refreshed from his short sleep and from their new focus in the hunt for the Ferryman. Accepting that the coins were Theodore Sutton's helped to unlock things for him, instead of fighting it. He'd convinced himself that if the coins were Teddy's, then that automatically made it a lock that Nicky was the killer and with that obstacle behind him he was free to move on.

He had Sato drop him off on the street before she parked so he could pick up two large cups of coffee. She wasn't at her desk when he got back to the detective bureau, so he left her cup next to her mouse and walked along to the task force room and unlocked the door. The laptops were gone, the whiteboard had been wiped down, the boxes of Vandenberg's mail had been removed. All that was left, was the unprocessed evidence from the day before in two cardboard boxes.

He moved the boxes over to the main table. Now that the room was quiet and empty of other people, he might actually be able to use it. He pulled on a pair of blue nitrile gloves and began to go through the first box. It was full of Sutton's clothes, carefully folded and placed in individual evidence bags. The man had pulled a gun on him, but all he felt looking at the clothes was sadness. His old friend was dead, and it was his fault.

The second box was the one he was after, Sutton's personal effects.

Watch, cell phone, wallet, fraternity ring, some loose change, a couple of pens, a Zippo lighter, and a bunch of keys. Coombes set the items out, still in their evidence bags, on the table in front of him. He picked up the watch and looked at it. It wasn't a Rolex, like the killer's from the hotel footage, it was a Timex and it was old. The watch face was small, with a thick crystal. It looked like Sutton had picked it up at a pawn shop for five dollars, but he didn't know much about watches. He put it back down on the table.

Coombes looked at all the items again.

The Zippo stuck out. Nicolas Sutton didn't smoke. Not cigarettes, not cigars. He had been a health nut; smoking would be an anathema to him. Who carried a lighter if they didn't smoke? But it wasn't that much of a mystery. The lighter wasn't Sutton's. He'd found it in the ruins of the Silver Lake house and had simply slipped it into his pocket.

The lighter belonged to the arsonist.

To the Ferryman.

Coombes picked it up and turned it over in his hands. There were scorch marks on the case, supporting his theory. A logo was printed on the front; two halves of a circle, split by a lightning bolt. He didn't recognize it. After trailing gasoline around the Silver Lake home, the killer had thrown the lighter in from the doorway to start the fire. He didn't understand how Sutton had found it and the fire marshal hadn't, but that hardly mattered.

Coombes took a close-up photograph of the lighter with his cell phone then returned it to the evidence bag and took out Sutton's wallet.

It contained five crisp 100 dollar bills, along with 385 dollars in assorted used bills. Coombes sighed. He couldn't say how much money was in his own wallet, but for sure it wasn't $885. That was a lot of walking around money in a world that was increasingly cashless. He flicked through the credit and charge cards, driver's license, membership cards.

He took a photograph of the cards in two groups of six, then returned them to the wallet. Lastly, he took out business cards. There were two for Nicolas Sutton's own firm, ready to be given out, and three he'd presumably received from others. The names on those three cards were horribly familiar.

Harry Ryan, Gordon Sellers, and Simon Keehan.

Coombes looked up at the whiteboard. Although wiped down, he could still see an imprint of what had been written on it, the names of the dead. The first three victims of the Ferryman apparently had business dealings with Sutton. For nearly two months they'd searched for a link between victims and now, when he least expected it, or wanted it, he found one.

Normally he'd conclude that this supported the narrative that Nicky was the killer and he knew Gantz and Block would assume the same thing.

It was a disaster.

He took a long drink from his coffee, focusing on the flavor, on the heat of it spreading out inside him. The evidence had not yet been catalogued, there was still time. He found an empty evidence bag and dropped the three business cards into it, then folded it up over and over to get the air out and put it in his pocket.

Was it really likely that someone would pull off so many perfect crimes and be stupid enough to walk around with their victims' business cards in his wallet? It was ridiculous and yet, he reflected, not impossible.

People liked mementos. A hotel keycard, a piece of jewelry, a tuft of hair. People in love, new parents, and serial killers. When it came to mementos, there was considerable overlap. He rejected it. The cards could've been planted, or been there for a long time, forgotten. It didn't prove anything, except possibly why they'd been selected.

Focus, he thought.

Love or money, that's what Sato had said, and she'd nailed it.

He turned his attention to Nicolas Sutton's cell phone.

It was an iPhone in a bashed polycarbonate case. A couple of years old, the same model as his own. He took it out the evidence bag and looked at the display. The screen lit up and a lock screen vibrated, detecting that he wasn't Sutton. *Face ID*. He swiped up and the keypad came up, asking for a 6-digit passcode.

Mathematically, the chances of hacking the phone were poor, but he knew a little about people. They were lazy, particularly with passwords or numbers that they had to enter all the time. The old 4-digit numbers were in a lot of ways more secure, because they were shorter and easier to remember. They could be anything. On the other hand, 6-digit codes were almost always birthdays or anniversaries.

Coombes went back to the evidence bag with Sutton's wallet and pulled out his driver's license and found the date of birth. He punched 102684 into the iPhone. The lock screen buzzed. Too obvious. He was certain that the number would be a date, but *what* date? Something significant to him, but not blindingly obvious to a potential thief.

It was pointless to keep guessing. The iPhone could erase all data after 10 incorrect passcode attempts, and before that point was reached were lockout periods. The problem was, he didn't know that much about Nicolas Sutton's recent life to begin to guess at significant dates. If it wasn't his birthday, he was pretty much all out of guesses, it was his one and only shot. He thought of Olivia. There was a half chance she might know Nicky's passcode. Coombes took out his own cell phone and opened his contacts. Even if she didn't know it, she might have an idea about significant dates. The number was ringing.

"Hello? Who's this?"

A man's voice. Thomas Garvy.

"It's Coombes. Is Olivia there?"

"Yeah, but she's asleep. She took an Ambien; she'll be out for a while."

He remembered how depressed Olivia had been last time he'd seen her.

"Ah. Well, that's probably for the best."

"Was there a message?"

His voice was calm, measured. Coombes had saved her life, that was enough for Garvy. What were the odds she'd know her brother's code anyway?

"No, sorry to bother you."

He disconnected and felt the air go out of him. Every minute that passed, the trail to the Ferryman got colder. If he'd boarded a flight he could be in Argentina by now. He shook his head and began to put everything back.

Nicolas Sutton had given up his life to save his sister. It didn't seem that way at the time, but that was the only thing that made sense. They say blood is thicker than water, and in this case, it was true. He paused thinking about it then took Sutton's cell phone back out.

One last try. Olivia was born on Valentine's Day. When you'd dated a girl who was born on the same day as the patron saint of love, you remembered it for the rest of your life.

He typed in 021487.

The home screen appeared. He was in. Coombes smiled, but the smile didn't last. The home screen wallpaper was a photograph of a woman in a bikini sitting on the front wheel arch of Sutton's Porsche, legs crossed at the angle, a foxy smile on her face.

The woman was Olivia.

He had to assume Sutton took the picture, and that her come-to-bed expression was directed at him. For sure he'd never seen Olivia look at her husband with eyes like that, she was smoldering. The picture, along with the passcode, told him everything.

He had one more call to make to confirm his hypothesis.

Sato was plugged into her computer again, the big cans of her headphones dwarfing her head. He came up behind her and looked at her screen. A long list of numbers and a map. Dates, and GPS coordinates for Sutton's Porsche. Sato worked fast.

He sat on his chair and pulled himself along the floor with his feet so that he was sitting next to her. The date she was looking at was the day of Vandenberg's death. The map showed a marker in Beverly Hills. Sato took off her headphones and placed them on her desk.

He heard classical music, a piano.

"Tell me, Grace, what's our friend been up to?"

"Shopping, eating, and working. His car wasn't at his dad's house on the day of his sister's abduction, or the night of the fire. It wasn't next to a car rental either, it was up in Malibu both times. He was there a lot, I assume he has a property there. He *was* in Silver Lake the day of his father's death, although that was never in doubt."

"Right. Tell me how it works."

"The system updates every 3 minutes in response to movement or every hour otherwise. The red dots indicate the car was stationary at the time, the green dots that it was moving. You wouldn't believe how much data this company collects. I don't want to know how much my cell carrier has about me."

He turned back to the screen. The marker in Beverly Hills was green. Supposing that it was Nicolas Sutton driving, it would be impossible for him to be in Vandenberg's hotel room.

"How far back do the records go?"

"All the way back to when he bought the car two years ago."

Coombes said nothing. Sato spoke again.

"I decided something while you were away."

"That Sutton isn't the Ferryman?"

She smiled and nodded. "That too."

"What was the other thing?"

She leaned in close.

"I decided that I don't care about your wife."

His face turned red, his cheeks burning. They looked at each other in silence. This would be where he again told her he couldn't, that he wasn't interested, that he loved his wife, that it was, at the very least, against regulations. He said nothing. The silence wasn't awkward, not in the slightest. Her eyes were dark and seemed to swallow him whole. After a moment she smiled, like something had been decided, and the spell was broken.

"What were you going to tell me? I saw you grinning."

"You remember before, what you said about a child?"

"Oh, Johnny. There was no child. It was just an example."

He smiled. "What if it *wasn't* just an example?"

Sato sat back in her seat and studied him closely. She knew him well enough to recognize his tone of voice, his smile. He had something. A break, a theory. Partners always know.

"All right."

"What if Olivia Sutton is pregnant."

Sato's mouth popped open into a little O. He tilted his head to one side, smiled and put a little sparkle in his eyes. Her voice dropped to a hoarse whisper.

"*Say it.*"

"And what if Nicky is the father."

She clenched her left hand into a small, tight fist.

"Please tell me you're not just yanking my chain, Johnny."

"The second part is pure speculation, but I know this much. She *is* pregnant, the doctor I spoke to confirmed it. Twenty-two weeks. Fetus appears healthy despite what happened to the mother during the kidnapping. A miracle."

"Or an abomination, depending on your point of view."

Coombes said nothing to that. A child couldn't control who its parents were, but for sure there were people out there who felt differently.

"My love of *Chinatown* aside," she continued, "is there any reason he actually *has* to be the father? Maybe he saved her just because she was his sister."

"That's certainly the version I intend to put in my report."

Her mouth twisted, awkwardly. "But you don't believe it?"

"When Nicky confessed, he said his father had *found out about him*. This is what I think he found out. Not about being gay, but about his relationship with Olivia, about their child. *That's* why his father was killing himself in the first place and why Nicky helped him along."

"Still, though. It could just be a coincidence."

He nodded and pulled out his phone. He hadn't planned on showing her the picture, but it looked like that was the only way she'd believe him. He brought up a picture he'd taken of Nicolas Sutton's unlocked iPhone.

"This is Nicky's cell phone wallpaper."

He turned it so that she could see and her mouth fell open.

"Oh my God! This is huge, Johnny."

"No, it's *not* huge, because nobody but you and me is ever going to know about it. The child has the right to live without this following it around for the rest of its life."

Sato studied him in silence.

"You can't control who you fall in love with, Grace, I know that better than most."

"I know it too," she said.

He decided to leave that alone.

"All right. We know why Nicky confessed, why he let his father commit suicide, the whole bit, but that gets us no closer to catching the Ferryman."

"I did say that to you before, Johnny."

They were quiet for a moment before Sato spoke again.

"What about the fingerprint on Haylee Jordan's shower?"

"Assuming Sutton was framed, we can also assume the print was planted by the killer. I figure he used modeling clay, or some kind of glue. Left it in a door handle, somewhere he knew Sutton would touch. Pour in some latex to pull a positive imprint, then dab some blood on it to make the print."

Sato smiled.

"*That's* why we had to scan the film upside-down to get a match. Making a print from print would reverse it left to right. He should've copied it again."

It was an angle he'd overlooked. He nodded.

"I missed that. *Excellent.*"

He remembered the Zippo and showed her the picture.

"Do you recognize this logo?"

"It's the symbol for the Flash, a superhero. Why? Whose lighter is this?"

"The Ferryman's. He used it to set the Silver Lake house on fire."

"Don't tell me this was in Nicolas Sutton's personal effects?" She saw the answer on his face. "How do you explain this?"

"He knew what was coming, right? That he was going to make me shoot him. I think he found this lighter at the house and saved it as a clue for me to find. To get the *real* Ferryman. He knew Olivia would only truly be safe when the killer was dealt with for good, and he was relying on me to do that. Nicky didn't smoke, he'd know I'd know that."

She looked at him like he was crazy.

"You're the best friend this piece of shit ever had. You know that?"

"It doesn't feel that way to me."

"Ok, let's think about this. Forget for a moment the Ferryman is a serial killer and a kidnapper. He's also an arsonist, so we start there. He'd need gas to set that fire, right? In containers he could carry from room to room. I figure he'd use a gas station close to the old man's house, he wouldn't want to have that much gas inside his vehicle any longer than he had to. All those places have cameras, we'll have his face, registration, and maybe even a credit card transaction."

"I like it," he said. "Let's do this."

41

THEY GOT BACK INTO Sato's Honda. The interior was hot and airless, but, like her bedroom, smelled of her perfume, her shampoo and whatever else. Sugar and spice and all things nice. Grace was about to start the car, when he reached out to stop her.

"Wait. I have something to show you and you're not going to like it."

He took out the evidence bag, unfolded it, and shook the business cards so that she could see them through the clear plastic.

"These were in Sutton's wallet?"

"Yes."

Her jaw clenched and she wordlessly started the car. She turned away from him, facing forward and pulled away fast toward the exit. The car twisted and bounced but he never took his eyes off her profile. He'd never seen it before, but he supposed this is what she looked like angry. They burst out into sunlight and onto the street.

"I'm sorry, Grace. It's not him, I swear it isn't."

"You're taking advantage of me; of the way I feel about you."

"I'm not, I'd never do that. Look, no one is going to go near that evidence box until tomorrow at the earliest. I wore gloves. If by then we don't have someone in custody I will put the cards back and let the chips fall where they may. I saw them and I reacted, that's it."

"You think that fixes what you did? I'd expect this from Lass, not you."

"I guess there's a side to me that you don't know."

They drove in silence for a while, Coombes now facing front. He couldn't take looking at her disappointment anymore.

He was like an iceberg, he thought. She only saw the top part, the best part, but below the water was this huge ugly mass. There was more of that than there was at the top. They stopped at a traffic light and he turned to see her looking back.

"Gantz wanted me to let her know if you ever showed signs that you were compromising the investigation."

He nodded. It was about what he expected.

"Oh yeah?"

"She said if that happened, Wallfisch was in charge."

Coombes laughed. His lieutenant had his back and he wouldn't forget it.

"So how am I doing so far?"

"*Peachy.*"

The first place they came to was a Chevron on Glendale Avenue. Coombes could see only one camera, and it wasn't aimed at the pumps, but at the exit. If the Ferryman had filled up here there would be no footage of it and no way to identify him. When you were minding your own business, it seemed like there were cameras everywhere but when you needed them, they were nowhere to be seen.

Sato parked and they got out. There was a small unit in the middle and a heavily tattooed Latino was visible through the glass, watching them. Coombes opened the front of his jacket to show his badge as they walked over and for a second thought the man was going to make a run for it.

Coombes pointed at the door and the man opened it nervously.

"Help you?"

"You have cameras covering the pumps?"

"Just the exit. This is a cash-free business, it's all plastic."

"Were you here last week? The Wednesday?"

"Sure. Six a.m. to six p.m."

"See a guy about my height and build fill up a bunch of gas cans?"

The Latino shook his head. "No, man."

Coombes thanked him and left.

As they got back in the car it occurred to him that pursuing this line of inquiry could take them hours and get them nowhere. It was the kind of job he would've handed off to someone in the task force, or to a uniform. Sato seemed subdued by the failure. They were going to need another plan, he thought.

She turned to him as she started the car.

"Who strikes you as an obvious suspect?"

"Thomas Garvy."

His own answer surprised him a little. Sato nodded.

"Olivia's husband, *nice*. You think he found out about the relationship?"

"When I met her in that bar, she made a big song and dance about not drinking alcohol during work hours. She ordered a water. I never thought anything about it, we hadn't seen each other socially for years. Garvy would have to notice she'd stopped drinking. He isn't stupid, he'd work out why."

Sato floored the throttle, pushing into a half-gap in the traffic.

"But you don't think it's him."

"No," he said.

"Even if he knows about the baby."

"Either he thinks it's his, or he doesn't care. He loves her, he wouldn't hurt her. Also, it has the same problem as her brother kidnapping her, she'd recognize him wearing a hat. I'm pretty sure she could recognize him from his breath alone, I know I could."

They were quiet for a moment, the traffic rolling along.

"How are things between you and Julie?"

Coombes glanced at her.

"Not good, Grace. If I could pin the Ferryman killings on her I would."

Sato laughed and didn't cover her mouth. He didn't think she'd ever done that before, he thought it was hard-wired. There was a warm blush on her cheeks and for a moment he wondered again what it would be like to kiss her. It would be wrong all the way around. When she stopped laughing her thoughts seemed to return to their previous conversation.

"You're certain about Garvy?"

"The person we're looking for was strong enough to maneuver Steve Ellis onto that catapult and take out Lass, albeit with a chickenshit blow to the back of the head. Garvy is overweight and has no obvious muscle mass. Also, the kills took time to plan therefore I believe the catalyst pre-dates Olivia's pregnancy, so that can't be considered motivation..."

His voice trailed off.

"Johnny?"

He held up his hand, fingers spread open. *Wait.*

"Olivia said that Nicky used to use a hook-up app on his phone, and that he always had a different woman on his arm. I was too busy focusing on how that impacted his claims in his confession to think about it."

"You think one of them was married?"

Coombes nodded.

"They probably all were. Let's say one decided to leave her husband or boyfriend to make herself available full-time to Nicky. That guy is going to be pretty upset. Upset enough, to start following Sutton around and back to the Silver Lake house, where everything starts to come together."

"I like it, but it could take time to unravel, time we don't have."

"Agreed," he said.

They arrived at the next target, a Shell station on the corner of Temple and Alvarado. He could see cameras everywhere and he felt his mood lift. Sato nosed the Honda around the back, away from the pumps.

The station was larger than the Chevron, and the central office had a food mart. They went inside and he badged a woman behind the counter while she finished serving a customer. The counterwoman was tall and athletic with short black hair that reminded him of women he'd known in the service. Her name tag said *Joan* and she looked like she could take care of herself.

The customer ahead of him left and he stepped forward.

"Are you here about the gas cans man?"

Coombes frowned. "The guy at Chevron called you?"

"No. I guess you could say I've been expecting you, Detective. I knew there was something off about him. He bought eight of those cans," she pointed at a display, "filled them with super and put them in the trunk of his car."

"Please tell me you got this asshole on camera."

She nodded. "Come through and I'll show you."

There was a small cramped security station at the back and the three of them squeezed themselves inside, Joan working the controls as they watched. His heart was hammering in his chest. They were close, he could feel it. He glanced at Sato and saw her eyes were lit up, and a smile was on standby.

On screen, the footage swam past on fast forward, cars coming and going. It depressed him that more and more, investigations were becoming a series of played back security clips. After a couple of minutes, the footage slowed, then reversed and began to play again. An ancient red Toyota Corolla pulled into a space on pump 5. The driver got out, walked around the car and out of shot.

Coombes recognized him immediately from somewhere but couldn't place him. The high angle of the camera flattened everything out. While the man was inside buying the fuel cans, Coombes wrote the Toyota's license plate on his left hand.

A couple of minutes passed, then the driver returned carrying plastic gas cans which he set out in a line next to the pump and opened. The twisting movement of his hand as he unfastened the caps made the bright metal bracelet of his diving watch sparkle.

The Rolex Submariner.

"Motherfucker," Coombes said.

Joan turned to him.

"He paid cash for the cans, but that's a card-only pump. With the time-stamp on the video, I can get you his name and card number, but it'll take about five minutes if you want to wait in your car."

He passed her a thumb drive.

"Drop a copy of that on here first."

If the Rolex was real, he had to assume that the car was stolen or bought for cash. It would be like an untraceable burner phone, he thought. Which left the credit card for identification. Joan returned his thumb drive and they filed back out into the shop, then he and Sato walked across to her car.

"You really think this is it, Johnny?"

"It's some coincidence if it isn't. That watch is pretty distinctive."

They stood waiting next to the Honda for her to return. Time ticked by, and he could see a line of people in the shop. After close to ten minutes, Joan came out and jogged over with a piece of paper in her hand. She handed it to him and he looked at the name she'd written on it. He angled it so that Sato could see.

Gabriel Dorsey.

"You can't imagine how important this is."

"I can guess, I recognize you from TV. If you want something official, you'll need a warrant. I could probably get in trouble for this."

He held out his card.

"If you ever tire of the gas business, Joan, the LAPD is always looking for good people. *Capable* people. I could put a word in for you if you're interested."

She glanced at the line of irate customers, then back.

"I might take you up on that, Detective."

They got back in the car and looked at each other for ten seconds, twenty seconds. The hairs on his arms stood on end. *Fuck it.* He leaned over and Sato came straight at him, her tongue pushing into his mouth, his hands going around the small of her back to pull her in close. Their seating position was awkward so the kiss didn't last long but when they broke apart, they were both breathing heavily through their mouths.

"Finally," she said.

Coombes said nothing. He was going to hell.

42

THERE WAS A MCDONALD'S across the street from the gas station and Coombes directed her toward it. They'd missed lunch and he needed fuel and caffeine if he was going to be of any use to anyone. The restaurant was almost empty, so for once they decided to skip the drive-thru lane and eat inside.

When he returned to their table with their order, Sato was working on her tablet, speed-reading text on what appeared to be a lengthy news story. He separated out the food and dumped the tray on an empty table next to theirs.

She loaded a fresh page filled with a grid of square pictures. He recognized the layout even upside down, an Instagram page. Like a teenage girl, all of Dorsey's pictures were of himself. Selfies, or pictures taken of him by someone else. Some had expensive cars in shot, others yachts or motorcycles. Dorsey lived the good life, filled with expensive goods and partially dressed women with eating disorders. Sato selected a head and shoulders portrait, and it enlarged. Not a selfie, the quality was too good.

Here he is, Coombes thought, the Ferryman in all his glory.

"What you got so far?"

"Gabriel Dorsey Junior. No middle name. Twenty-seven years old, six-foot one inch tall. I was unable to find a weight listed anywhere, but from his Facebook page, he looks about one eighty. Everything so far lining up with our suspect's description."

Coombes' mouth was full of chicken so he motioned for her to continue.

"He's a trust fund brat," she said. "His great-great grandfather owned a lot of city land and property, not to mention some oil fields. Looks like his father pissed away most of the family wealth, but Dorsey's probably still worth about $20 million."

Sato paused to drink her Coke through a straw.

He found himself staring intently at her mouth. He was in love with her, he realized. Inside, a part of him was forever hers. It was a thought he'd never had before, not with his wife, not with anyone. She glanced at him as she drank and her cheeks colored when she saw how he was looking at her. He decided to move the conversation quickly on.

"What else? Does he work?"

She paused for a beat, before continuing.

"He studied Electrical Engineering and Computer Science at Berkeley, graduating summa cum laude in the 98 percentile 2018. While he was there, he and another student set up a company building cell phone apps, which they sold for two million dollars six months later. After college, he worked at Tesla and moved fast up the food chain before leaving to create a start-up developing batteries for electric vehicles."

"The next gold rush," Coombes said, wearily.

"You're not wrong. His company is due to be listed on the Nasdaq with an IPO valuing it at four billion dollars. He currently owns almost half the company."

"Don't tell me that. I might shoot him on sight."

They ate in silence for several minutes. She had always been uncomfortable with him looking directly at her while she ate, so he alternated his eye line between his food and the parking lot through the window. His thoughts drifted first to the realization they'd finally identified the Ferryman, then the fact that he'd kissed his partner. There was a link there now that he didn't like, between his feelings for Sato and a serial killer.

"What's *really* bothering you about this guy, Johnny?"

He nodded. She knew him too well.

"All this time a part of me still thought it would be Jake Curtis."

Her face showed no surprise.

"He really got under your skin, didn't he?"

"I guess so. It was that stupid beard, like a swarm of bees."

There was another thing bothering him. He knew without doubt that he'd seen Dorsey before but he just couldn't place where. The information hovered at the edge of his mind, just out of reach. It was close, he'd have it soon but until he did, he'd be unable to concentrate fully on anything.

Coombes rubbed his face with both hands.

"Let's get real for a minute. All we've got is footage of him buying gas. That's not illegal. If we raided his home and he didn't still have the cans, that's not illegal either. It doesn't prove he's a serial killer, or that he set fire to the Sutton place."

"I know," she said. "But we've got his *name* now. That's half the battle, isn't it? Do you have any doubts that this is our guy?"

"None at all, but I guarantee Block won't feel the same way."

"What now?"

"We need to find this guy and fast, we need to have eyes on him at all times until we have enough to scoop him up. I don't want him to slip through our fingers. His access to funds makes him a definite flight risk. We have to be careful not to tip him off that we're on to him. Right now, he thinks he's in the clear, having played us all for fools."

"If you're right about Block, he's going to announce tomorrow that it's all over. I don't know if you caught the news this morning, Johnny, but Sutton's name is already out there. Which probably means we only have the rest of the day to catch Dorsey."

He sighed. Block was such a prick. She was right, and with the sequence of kills now complete, nobody would know the difference if it was pinned on Sutton. Which, he supposed, was Dorsey's intention all along. If Block knew what they were doing, he'd shut them down.

"What are you thinking, Grace?"

"Well, just that we don't have time to waste tearing up the city searching for Dorsey then babysitting his every move. If he thinks he's in the clear he's probably not preparing to leave. He's rich, he'll think he's beyond the law anyway."

He nodded. Again, she was right. Tracking where he was all day wouldn't matter if they didn't find enough to arrest him before tomorrow.

"Fine. We focus on making the case and worry about where he is later."

Dorsey was a new suspect but the evidence remained the same. The work they'd done wasn't for nothing, it was just a matter of seeing how it all fitted together. For certain Dorsey matched the physical description provided by their eyewitnesses and, to a lesser extent, the lo-res video from Haylee Jordan's parking garage. The Rolex also matched, as did the suspect's mastery of electronics. It was looking good, but there was no smoking gun. Aside from the gas station, Dorsey had been careful. The only physical evidence they had was a Zippo lighter with a laughable chain-of-evidence heritage, blurred images of a Rolex, and a shoe imprint that implicated another man.

"All right," he said. "The hospital is close, let's put some pictures of Dorsey in front of Lass, see what he thinks."

She nodded and they left the restaurant. He wanted to review the material Sato had found so he picked up her tablet and entered her passcode.

7 18 1 3 5.

"I won't ask how you know my code, Johnny."

He smiled. Her code was her first name by the letters' positions in the alphabet. It had taken him a while to work out, a process aided by frequent viewings.

"You never told me how you unlocked Sutton's cell phone."

"His code was Olivia's birthday."

She laughed as she accelerated hard into the flow of traffic.

He skimmed the articles she'd located on Gabriel Dorsey. They were mostly puff-pieces about his new business. It seemed to amuse the media that the grandson of an oil man was now involved in the green revolution. For his part, Dorsey looked happy to play along and smirk into the camera when required.

The more he read, the more he came around to the idea of putting Dorsey in prison for the rest of his life, instead of Jake Curtis. The last article showed a picture of Dorsey playing golf, the club wrapped around behind his head like a pro.

Coombes glanced at the caption underneath, stating where the picture was shot. The breath caught in his throat. He pulled out his cell phone and brought up the pictures he'd taken of Sutton's cards. He found the membership card he was looking for.

"What is it, Johnny? You got something?"

"Sutton and Dorsey were members of the same country club."

"That's our connection then, where they crossed paths."

"I guess so."

In the picture, Dorsey's chin was partially concealed by his arm and for a split-second Coombes almost had it, where he'd seen him before. He focused on the image, willing it to come back, but it was gone again.

43

Late afternoon, early evening was a busy time at the hospital, and Sato had to drive around for a couple of minutes before she found a spot to park. They hustled to the elevator and he thought ahead to their next conversation as they waited for it.

"A couple of things before we go in," he said. "I don't want anyone else to know about Nicky and Olivia's relationship and it might not take much for him to figure it out, so be careful what you say. Secondly, I don't want Lass to have Dorsey's name. If we can't get him, I don't want Billy hunting him down, and trust me, that's what he'd do."

"Okay."

He glanced back at Sato to check she was cool and she looked calmly back. When his wife said *okay*, it usually meant she was ready to hold a plastic bag over his head. The elevator doors opened and a crowd got off and they got on. He pounded on Billy's floor button, hoping to hurry it up. Everything took longer when you were against the clock.

Lass was sitting up in bed with his bandaged hands out front as before. It was like he'd stepped out the room for a minute and returned so little had changed.

"John! Two visits in one day!" The drug haze seemed to evaporate, right along with his smile. "This isn't a social call, is it? You have something on this asshole."

"I apologize, Billy, but I know you want this guy even more than I do. Let's save social calls for later. I have another photograph for you to look at."

Coombes opened Sato's tablet and brought up the Instagram page. Dorsey was grinning in most of the pictures and it took him a moment to find a shot less likely to antagonize Lass.

"You ready?"

"Just show me the picture, John."

Coombes nodded and turned the tablet around. A snarl appeared on Lass' face; his lips pulled back to show his teeth.

"Motherfucker! That's the piece of shit that did this to me."

"Give me a number, Billy."

Lass glanced at him, his eyes filled with anger.

"A hundred percent. A *thousand*. It's him."

Coombes passed the tablet back to Sato, who had taken a step behind him, hiding herself from Lass' anger. He put his hand on his former partner's hugely muscled shoulder, pushing him back against the inclined bed.

"I'm sorry, man. I had to ask."

He kept his hand where it was, waiting for Lass to calm down. It took almost a minute before the bearlike head came back up and looked at him.

"You don't have him yet, do you?"

"No."

"Why is that, if you know who he is?"

"He made a mistake. Bought gas with a credit card, that's it. Everything else lines up, but we couldn't bust him for jaywalking. He's careful. You know the kind. If it rained, the drops would all miss him, land on someone else."

Lass looked at him, then Sato.

"There's something else, isn't there?"

"My captain's going to hang his hat on Sutton first thing tomorrow."

"Even if I ID this guy?"

"It's Block. He and Hurst probably shave each other's backs. Your word wouldn't mean shit to him."

The mention of Hurst visibly upset Lass.

"After you left, I kept thinking through that scene of you with Sutton. Trying to get the angles to line up. It *bothered* me."

Coombes nodded. "We figure he did it to save his sister."

"No doubt, but that's not the part that bugs me. He gave you this dumb-ass confession, made you shoot him, then, as he's bleeding out on the floor, tells you where his sister was?"

"Pretty much."

"That makes no sense, John. If he knew where she was, why not save her himself?"

Coombes thought about it for a moment. Every time he got to the bottom of the scene with Sutton, another layer seemed to be revealed. He'd been side-tracked trying to work out Nicky's *motivation* for confessing, rather than focus on what was important.

"Sutton had to believe there was no other way of saving her. That the Ferryman had a way to kill Olivia if he didn't follow orders. A bomb or something else. Our guy's pretty good with electronics, a threat might be credible. He'd certainly proven himself as a killer."

"Do as I say or she dies, that works."

The answer seemed to satisfy Lass, but Sato shook her head.

"How would he know if Sutton *had* done what he was told? We were the only people in that room, Johnny, there was no one else there. We're missing something."

"A hidden camera. Like the one in Blackstone's Tesla."

"Yes," she said, nodding. "Our killer likes to watch."

They said nothing for a moment, then their eyes connected.

"The camera's a loose end," Coombes said. "At the very least it proves Sutton was being watched and since there will be no fire damage, the person who installed it would have to know what was going on."

Sato's face was lit up, her cheeks flushed.

"He'll have to retrieve it. Tonight, when it gets dark. We've had units on the scene all day, not to mention the news crews, it'll be the first chance he gets."

"Glad I could help," Lass said, sarcastically.

"Thanks. We've got to go."

"A quick word alone, John?"

"Is this a *testicle* thing?" Sato said. "Because it's bullshit."

When the door closed behind her, Lass looked at him with a knowing look.

"Are you crazy? Sleeping with your partner?"

"I'm not."

It sounded weak, even to him.

"John, there's a river of energy flowing between you. Don't insult me by telling me I'm *imagining it*."

"You're not imagining it, but nothing's happened."

"*Yet.*"

Coombes nodded and looked away. "I'm crazy about her."

"What about Julie?"

He didn't feel like getting matrimonial advice from a lug nut like Billy Lass, or sharing the poor state of his relationship with his wife.

"Anything else? We have to get going if we're going to catch this guy."

Lass looked at him the way a person always looked at someone determined to make a mistake, with an equal mix of pity and disbelief.

"Yeah. I want you to give this prick a message from me."

44

THEY RETURNED TO SATO'S apartment to change her ancient Honda for his official vehicle before heading back to the Sutton home in Silver Lake. All the other members of the task force had been brought up to speed and would be arriving as soon as they could to strengthen their perimeter. Gantz was frosty about how long he'd kept her in the dark, but approved the trap with some reservations.

"What did I say, John?"

"No shitshow."

"I'm concerned that maybe you haven't heard me. I don't want another situation like last year in the L.A. River. I am still getting paperwork for that."

"You mean when I saved a nine-year-old girl?"

"*No explosions!* Are we clear?"

"It's my mantra every day, I swear."

Gantz was quiet for a beat and Coombes heard a television in the background. The sound poured out of the Dodge's dashboard somewhere. His lieutenant was watching a Tom Hanks movie, he recognized the actor's voice.

"Good luck, John."

She disconnected and he turned to Sato.

"You blow up *one* semi full of gas and people lose their minds."

Sato smiled and her nose wrinkled. Goddamn that was cute.

"She's just mad that she wasn't there to see it."

"You're not wrong."

Overhead, a traffic light turned green but they had to wait for some old derelict to finish crossing the street before he could pull away. The homeless man turned to look at them, unfazed. He was ready for death; it was there in his eyes. *Just do it, you'd be doing me a favor.* Coombes found himself thinking about Dorsey, something about this man-

Then they were moving again, five minutes out.

His thoughts shifted to the task in hand.

If Dorsey had planted a camera in the room with the big picture window to monitor the shoot-out, then it stood to reason that another camera was positioned to cover the car where Olivia was held captive. Olivia had been his leverage; he couldn't risk losing that. The setup required two cameras minimum. But where there were two, there could be more.

Dorsey would check the feeds before he arrived, to see if it was safe. The Ferryman was careful. He got in, he got out. No one saw him, and he left no evidence behind. More than two cameras meant extra time installing, then removing. He'd want to limit that, as well as the possibility of the cameras being seen.

Two cameras then, the minimum needed to get the job done.

Coombes parked on Berkeley Avenue and saw that the rest of the task force was already there. The six of them hustled up the street toward the Sutton house, then after a nod to the cop parked outside, walked up the driveway. The patrol car pulled away and they were left in the shadows.

It was full dark, the moon no more than a fingernail clipping in the sky. He set out where he wanted each of the task force positioned around the property and to avoid at all costs the room of the shoot-out and anywhere near where the Mercedes sat as there were likely to be cameras in those areas.

"You better be right about this. I'm missing time with my girl to be here with you."

He turned to Wallfisch.

"When we catch our serial killer, I'll be sure to tell him about the nine to five, Monday to Friday hours that you prefer."

"We already caught him, Coombes, remember? He's in the morgue."

"Why are you here, Wallfisch?"

"If you're wrong, I get to see you fail, if you're right I get a piece of the action."

Coombes shook his head.

"You can teach a pig to hunt, but that won't make him a dog."

Wallfisch came at him, but stopped himself the last second.

"What you say to me?"

"I didn't choose you for this task force, Wallfisch. I have *suits* with more experience than you. Right now, is the longest I've seen you standing in three years. Now get the fuck upstairs and watch for this guy like I told you and try not to let your fat ass fall through the floor."

Wallfisch's breath hissed out, like he had a slow puncture.

Just when Coombes thought he'd have to tell him again, Wallfisch turned and walked away into the darkness, toward the stairs. Falling through the floor was a real possibility for Wallfisch, the fire damage was extensive. Show over, the rest of the team moved into position, leaving him alone with Sato.

"I thought he was going to hit you," she said softly.

She was standing right in front of him in the darkness looking up into his eyes. Her lean abdominal muscles pressed against his groin in a way that didn't feel accidental. She moved against him like a cat.

"What are you doing, Grace?"

"Helping you stay awake."

Coombes thought about what Lass had said about the energy that flowed between him and Sato. He was right, and it was getting worse with every passing second. They were going to have to get real and put an end to it before there was any fallout. He moved away from her and sensed her face falling.

"We need to focus."

Silence grew between them. The darkness was almost total and although there was now a space between them, it still felt intimate. Minutes passed. The image of the homeless man on the street came back to him. The man had wild hair and a beard that trailed over a filthy white T-shirt. He was nothing like Dorsey, he didn't even look like Jake Curtis, who at least had the beard. It was where he was standing in front of his Dodge.

He had it then, what he'd been trying to remember.

The man who stood in the middle of the street photographing them after their visit to the Capitol Records Building was Gabriel Dorsey. Coombes wanted to scream, he'd been right there in front of them and they'd had no idea. Was that the only time, or had there been other close calls?

How many chances had he missed?

Not far away, he heard the soft whoosh of someone shutting a car door. Not slamming it shut, being careful. Quiet. The darkness shifted next to him; Sato had heard it too. Coombes took out his Glock. This was his own weapon, his LAPD-issued Glock was elsewhere, awaiting a verdict on his shooting of Nicolas Sutton.

There was no street light outside, the only light came from the moon above and the glow of Los Angeles below. A figure walked up the drive and a flashlight snapped on. It was angled low, with a narrow cone. After the darkness, the light was incredibly bright. He heard it then. Dorsey whistling to himself, a happy tuneless rasp.

Twenty feet away, he turned to the side, following the driveway around to where the Mercedes had sat. This was not a surprise to Coombes, yet he found that he hadn't thought through what he would do if Dorsey grabbed that camera first. The best potential capture point was inside the house and it was where he'd positioned his team.

He forced himself to stay still, and wait.

Dorsey wasn't long. Less than a minute later, the flashlight reappeared, the whistling back in Coombes' ears. Soon he would walk through the doorway and turn to the right, toward the room where the second camera had to be. There was no front door, everything wood had been destroyed by the fire Dorsey himself had started.

Dorsey stood in the doorway and the whistling stopped.

The flashlight swept around the room, shadows stretching out into the black. Coombes and Sato were to one side, pressed into the space of a doorless closet. If the flashlight landed on them, it was all over. He hadn't thought about Dorsey using a flashlight, a ridiculous oversight.

Dorsey remained in the doorway. Had something tipped him off?

The flashlight went out.

The darkness rushed back in, only this time Coombes' vision was blown out by the after images from the flashlight. He heard nothing. He couldn't tell if Dorsey was still standing in the doorway. It was impossible to remain in a cover position that prevented him from seeing his quarry. He eased himself around on his right foot like a door opening and brought his Glock and Maglite up, both of his hands together, ready to turn on his flashlight.

He heard a creak far over to his left and he turned toward it. There was another creak and Coombes moved out from the closet space, toward the sound. Purple shapes swam in his vision, he could see nothing, not even if Dorsey was still in the room.

It had to be twenty or thirty seconds since the light had gone out, he couldn't risk Dorsey getting away. Their whole case against him relied on catching him red-handed.

A flashlight came on at a high angle, filling the room.

The sounds hadn't been Dorsey, they'd been Wallfisch coming down the stairs. The room was empty in front of him. Coombes swung his head back to the doorway and saw Dorsey lunge at Sato. He grabbed her by the throat and lifted her up like a shield in front of him. He had a silver revolver in his left hand and he pressed it against her temple.

"Drop the guns or I'll kill her. You know I'll do it."

"Easy. Let her go."

"I won't tell you again, Coombes."

Sato's hands were empty, she must have dropped her gun. Then he noticed her fingers change, tucking them in, one at a time. Ten, nine, eight. Coombes held up his hands.

"Okay, don't shoot."

The fingers continued their countdown. When the last finger folded in, Sato arched back and smashed her head into Dorsey's face. He let go of her and Coombes changed his grip from dropping his gun and fired it just over Dorsey's head. He couldn't afford to hit Sato, so had missed deliberately. Dorsey spun to the side and fired his revolver into the room, hitting nothing. Wallfisch's flashlight was blinding him.

Then he was gone, and running, disappearing into the darkness beyond. Coombes chased after him, Wallfisch trailing him down the stairs.

He expected to see Dorsey on the driveway in front of him running toward his vehicle, but instead saw him go around the side return, back toward where he'd picked up the first camera. He set off after him, his own flashlight now on. There was no way out in that direction, the driveway ended in a fence and Dorsey had to know that from the number of times he'd been there.

As he came around the side there was a bright flash in front of him and another round whistled past his ear. He ducked back into cover, before he realized it was a wild shot, intended to buy Dorsey time to escape. He cursed himself and began his pursuit again, his flashlight next picking Dorsey out at the top of the fence as he moved onto the low roof of the property next door.

There *was* a way out, Coombes saw, through the neighbor's property, onto the next street over. As he got up on the neighbor's roof, Dorsey dropped down, out of sight.

He ran across the roof alone.

Wallfisch wouldn't get over the fence, and the others would move to phase two, picking up the camera left behind in the room with the picture window.

He got to the end of the roof and heard yelling out on the street. He dropped to the ground and was in time to see Dorsey pull a man out of a blue Mustang, then get in and race off down the street.

No shitshow, his lieutenant had said.

He was pretty sure this qualified.

45

Coombes ran after the car, ignoring the owner of the Mustang, who was still on his ass after being car-jacked. The night air was cool and dry, but beads of sweat soon formed on his forehead, neck, and back. He wasn't as fit as he wanted to be, and he made a silent deal with himself to get into better shape as soon as possible.

At the bottom of the road, he saw Dorsey turn right.

Back in his car, he hit the gas, heading after the Mustang. The other man had a two-minute lead and there was no way he'd be able to make up the lost ground on his own. Fortunately, he *wasn't* on his own. He called in a description of the car and Dorsey, requesting an airship and every available unit in the area.

He reached Scott Avenue and turned right toward Silver Lake Boulevard. The junction was on the crest of a hill, and he took the turn fast. His Charger rose up high on its suspension, wheels close to leaving the asphalt, before crashing down again.

He flashed past a junction without seeing what it was, or checking the cross street for the Mustang. He figured Dorsey would've done the same thing, keen to put in some quick distance. A school scrolled by on the right, like a prison with bees painted on the walls. He slowed for the next left junction and was treated to a millisecond glimpse of tail lights turning west again at the end of the street.

He turned down Coronado after them. He couldn't swear it was the Mustang, or if he just *wanted* it to be the Mustang so much, his eyes were filling in the detail. He hit the gas hard, pushing his Dodge to catch up. Speed humps were built into the road and this time his wheels left the surface, once, twice, by the time he got to the third hump, he wasn't even lifting his foot off the gas anymore.

If the suspension was trashed, they could *bill* him.

He got to Reservoir Street and plunged down the steep grade. At the top of the next hill he saw the Mustang with its distinctive tail lights and the back of the Shelby racing stripes. He flashed through a stop sign then the road angled up again and he pushed the Dodge's engine hard to close the gap.

Ahead of him Dorsey braked dramatically, the back of the Mustang swinging over to the left as the car turned sharply to the right, off a side street. When the car cleared, Coombes saw two LAPD SUVs blocking the street in a nose-together wedge. He followed the Mustang's path with less of a skid, and powered north up McCollum. The street was lined with tall palms and was immediately familiar to Coombes. He'd been here before.

Dorsey floored the throttle, leaving him far behind.

It was like a camera zooming out, the Mustang was in a different league. The road they were on was taking them back toward where the chase had started, they'd only be a couple of blocks from the Sutton house. By the time he got to the top of the road, the Mustang was gone. He looked both ways on the cross street and could see no sign of the tail lights.

Coombes opened his window and listened. He heard the big V8 breathing somewhere, like a lion panting. It was close. He rolled across the junction and turned left again, which was still McCollum, but with a dogleg. His headlights swept over a darkened Mustang ahead. The headlights snapped back on and the car took off. They were thirty feet apart now. His closer distance pushed Dorsey straight across the next junction at Berkeley. The road became narrow, with a thickly vegetated island on the left that prevented U-turns.

The road widened out and a gatehouse sat in the middle of the road, a stubby barrier extending three feet into the road. Dorsey drove through the barrier without lifting his foot off the throttle, tuning the last foot of the barrier into dust.

Once past the gatehouse, Coombes fell back and stopped at a four-way junction. No matter how it looked on a GPS unit, there was no exit ahead. It was a dead end. This was a gated community, and the people who lived here didn't want outsiders coming and going all day. Steel barriers had been installed, cyclone fencing. A situation Dorsey was no doubt familiar with from his own property in Brentwood.

The Mustang got to the end of the road, swung around a turning circle and stopped, pointing back the way it came. Coombes smiled. He was at the other end of the street, yet he still felt the anger and frustration in the way Dorsey revved the V8.

A minute passed and nothing happened.

That was okay by Coombes. It was better to let a criminal realize for themselves that it was hopeless to continue than to force the realization on them. Dorsey had to have prepared in some way for this moment. Nobody killed nine people without thinking about what would happen if they got caught, it just wasn't possible.

The two Interceptor Utility SUVs rolled up behind Coombes like tanks, high beams blazing, strobes pulsing. One drove past, blocking the road to the left, the second lining up in the lane next to him. Four cops emptied out fast, spreading out across the street, guns drawn, bristling with intent. Coombes sighed. The show of force blew any calm acceptance that had been building in Dorsey. The uniforms gave him something to fight against.

There would be no peaceful surrender now, only a last stand.

A quarter mile away, a police helicopter directed its searchlight in their direction, and the street lit up in ghostly white light. One of the uniformed cops began working his way toward Dorsey, a shotgun pressed into his shoulder, the long barrel aimed down at the asphalt. Part way, the cop dropped onto one knee and leveled the shotgun at the Mustang.

"Get out of the vehicle and lie face down on the road."

"Oh, Jesus," Coombes said.

The Mustang's rear wheels spun, brakes still on. Smoke poured out, the screech of the tires tearing at the asphalt audible to Coombes through his windshield. He pictured the scene from above, like a chess board. The uniforms were spread out with no cover from a speeding car. Once he'd plowed through them, Dorsey would simply mount the footpath, drive around the blockade, and back down the hill to the gatehouse.

Escape was still possible.

Dorsey released the brake and the Mustang shot forward toward the cop with the shotgun. Coombes hit the gas and raced to meet the oncoming car, forcing it to line up with him, not the cop. Dorsey's face was caught in his headlights. He was grinning, his eyes wide. Time seemed to elongate as the two cars headed toward each other. He didn't know what he was doing. It was stupid, like something that would happen in a Pacific Pictures movie. Dorsey's crazy face would be the last thing he saw before he died.

He flashed back to Sato's cheeks turning red in McDonald's.

It was something he wanted to see again.

There was something between them, something worthwhile.

At the last second, he turned the wheel hard to the left, away from the impact. Dorsey flashed past, a bright blur. Coombes stamped on the brakes as he approached a tree, but he was going too fast to stop. The front of his Dodge crumpled up and his airbag deployed into his face, his seatbelt yanking him backward.

A second passed, then another.

He heard nothing but a high-pitched tone.

Coombes patted the huge gray pillow of the airbag out of the way and got the door open. Dust filled the air inside the car's cabin. He stumbled out onto the street and saw no sign of the Mustang. The high-pitched sound continued. The cop with the shotgun approached.

"Are you OK? I think you just saved my ass."

Coombes nodded. "Where did he go?"

His voice sounded distant, through a thick carpet. The cop turned and pointed.

"Through that hedge."

There were no tire marks on the road to indicate that Dorsey had attempted to brake or turn away from the head-on collision. Instead, the Mustang had continued straight and punched right through a 12-foot-high hedge.

Coombes drew his gun and ran across the street. The uniformed officer moved with him, covering his flank.

He stopped at the boundary and turned to the cop.

"If that prick comes back out here without me, put him down."

"That works for me."

46

COOMBES STEPPED THROUGH THE gap in the hedge into the yard beyond. The destroyed hedge lay all around but there was no sign of the Mustang. He moved forward, his finger resting on the trigger of his Glock. He resisted the urge to move quickly and risk getting blindsided by Dorsey in the shadows.

There was a light in the black ahead.

He followed it up a raised bank of earth. At the top of the rise he saw a large swimming pool in the yard below. The water glowed. A smile spread across his face. The Mustang was at the bottom. After clearing the raised bank, the Ford had hit the water and been dragged down by the weight of the engine.

Coombes ran to the edge of the pool and looked into the water. If Dorsey could've got out on his own he would've done so by now. He hadn't. The doors were shut and a silver bubble of air still remained in the cabin. He put his gun away.

He took off his suit jacket, tie, gun holster, and shoes, then jumped into the water. The cold gripped his chest tight, knocking the air out of him. He took several deep breaths, then ducked under the surface, pushing himself down. Without goggles or a face mask, his vision was poor. The water, and whatever chemicals were in it, moved directly over his eyes.

He drew level with the passenger door window and grabbed the Mustang's door handle to hold himself in place. He saw Dorsey inside the cabin. The internal dome light was on and he could see water pushing in through the air vents in thick jets. The water was halfway up Dorsey's chest. The other man turned and saw him through the glass.

The big crazy smile was gone, replaced by panic.

Coombes tugged on the handle, but the door wouldn't open. Water pressure was holding it shut. Either he'd have to wait until the pressure equalized, or he'd have to break the glass.

He thought of Nicolas Sutton and Billy Lass.

Maybe he didn't have to do anything.

The helicopter crew had seen him dive in. He'd tried his best. Who, later, would know any different? All he had to do was wait it out. With a bit of luck, the monster would die right in front of him. Not what he'd had in mind, but he could live with it. For sure Olivia could live with it, maybe all the victims' families could.

The water level was just below Dorsey's shoulders now. At this rate, it would only take a couple of minutes to completely fill with water. He held up a finger to indicate he'd be back in a minute, then kicked off the floor of the pool and rose back to the surface.

He took an urgent breath of air. It stung him deep inside, like the air was poison. Coombes swam to the edge of the pool and let his forearms rest on the side. He was a strong swimmer and a half-decent diver, but he was exhausted and the water was cold.

All he wanted was to be warm, and asleep.

Lights were coming on in the house next to the pool, the owners finally realizing that something was happening in their yard. Sirens were approaching, he wouldn't have the scene to himself for much longer.

He rapidly inhaled and exhaled, flooding his blood with oxygen, then ducked down under the water. Swimming down to the car took more out of him this time, the water pushing him back like it was getting paid for it. When he reached the window, he saw that the cabin was nearly full, the water now up to the top of Dorsey's neck.

The rapid progress of the water surprised him; the pressure would almost be equalized. If it occurred to him, Dorsey would soon be able to open the door and swim out on his own. But it looked like something had happened to Gabriel Dorsey while he'd been up at the surface. Like he'd been screaming into the shrinking bubble of air that was keeping him alive.

Like he'd lost his mind.

The water became bright as day. The searchlight was directly overhead.

Coombes tapped the glass to get his attention. Dorsey's head spun around, eyes wide, the water briefly covering his mouth and nose. In about thirty seconds, he'd have to tilt his head back to suck his last air off the ceiling. Coombes smiled at him and waved. Dorsey lost the last ounce of his sanity. His arms pumped the water with fury, his teeth biting together.

Then, just as suddenly, a calm seemed to sweep over Dorsey and his eyes became focused and hard. He reached into his jacket and pulled something out. It took Coombes a second to make it out.

The silver revolver.

He kicked himself backward through the water until he hit the side wall of the pool. A shockwave bubble formed around Dorsey's revolver and a narrow cone of gas instantly appeared in front of him.

Coombes flinched, but nothing hit him.

Three more shockwaves appeared within the Mustang as Dorsey emptied his weapon at him. With the passenger window now gone, the rounds got within a foot of his chest before stopping. The water had stopped them dead. He thought of the tank at the lab where they test-fired handguns to recover rounds. Instinctively, he'd used the water to protect himself.

Relief gave way to anger.

He surged forward and caught Dorsey as he came through the destroyed window. Coombes punched him on the nose and a pink cloud of blood surrounded his face. They grabbed at each other and fought as they floated to the surface.

He took a deep breath, then another.

The helicopter was directly on top of them now, fifty feet off the deck. The surface was choppy, water spraying in all directions. It was going in his mouth and up his nose. His arms and legs felt heavy and Dorsey easily got out of his grip and swam to the edge of the pool. He raced after him, limbs aching. Dorsey hadn't spent the last two minutes holding his breath, fighting his own buoyancy in the water, he was fresh.

Coombes' suit jacket and shoes sat in a small pile in front of him. He remembered his firearm underneath and the thought gave him a burst of energy, enough to lever himself up out of the pool and onto his feet.

He gagged uncontrollably and almost a pint of water emptied out of his throat. His eyes streamed. Dorsey slammed into his side and they rolled together on the concrete apron next to the pool.

Blows rained on his head and neck before he could respond. He punched Dorsey in the side of his body, the first part of him that he could reach. He was lucky, he felt a *crunch* from one of Dorsey's ribs. He hit him again and again in the same spot until he felt the rib snap and break free.

Dorsey collapsed in pain and roared.

Coombes pushed him off his chest, spun him around and cuffed him, hands behind his back. Once Dorsey was secured, he got him in a seated position. He leaned in close to Dorsey's ear.

"I have a *message* from a friend of mine," he said.

He reached down to Dorsey's hands and yanked his right index finger to the side, snapping it.

Dorsey screamed, but the prop wash of the helicopter sucked it away like it never happened. He fought to free himself, but against steel handcuffs he was wasting his time.

Coombes gripped his shoulder one handed and held him in place while he waited for Dorsey to calm himself. The veins and tendons in his neck stood out like he was about to explode.

"You son of a bitch!"

Dorsey continued to rant and Coombes filtered it out by moving his head two inches closer to the rotor blades above him. He had no sympathy for Dorsey, not after what he'd done. As far as he was concerned, the man in front of him was no man at all, he wasn't even human. He was a monster and deserved to be treated as such. Soon enough, the vitriol came to an end and he leaned in close once again.

"My friend's message has *five more parts*. Mention this to anyone and I'll make sure you get it. Do you understand? Every cop in this city wants you dead. LAPD, Sheriff's, even the Highway Patrol. I put the word in the right ear, it's done."

"How do you expect me to hide this?"

"You were in a car accident, genius."

Dorsey said nothing, his teeth clenched hard together. Red and blue lights strobed through the trees beyond the raised bank and across the side of the house. Doors were slamming. They were about to have company.

Coombes grabbed the next finger.

"Do we have a deal, or do you want the rest of the message?"

"We have a deal! We have a deal! Jesus!"

A moment later, he saw close to a dozen figures moving toward them, one of them was Grace Sato. He smiled; it was impossible not to. Now that backup had arrived, the helicopter pulled up to about three hundred feet, the searchlight expanding to encompass everything around them. The sound of the rotor blades died back and it was a relief to be free of it.

Sato smiled at him. "Wow, you look terrible."

"Thanks, Grace."

She circled around behind him and looked at Dorsey's hands. If she noticed the broken finger, she didn't say anything.

"Johnny. *The watch.*"

He hadn't noticed it in their struggle, but Dorsey was wearing the Rolex Submariner he'd been wearing in the hotel video. Coombes nodded.

"Good catch. We should bag it before he gets booked in case it…goes missing. Check his pockets for the camera. I assume you got the other one?"

"You bet. Right where we thought it would be."

She pulled on gloves while he and Becker pulled Dorsey to his feet. The watch was in front of the handcuffs, so she was able to remove it without uncuffing him. Dorsey turned toward her, face twisted with pain and anger.

"I'm going to want that back, *bitch*."

Coombes flicked his hand casually against Dorsey's broken finger, causing the other man to yelp. Sato glanced at him, a question in her eye, then turned back to Dorsey and emptied his pockets. A camera and a transmitter unit were in his left pocket. She took the opportunity to bag up his cell phone, and keys. When she was done, he read Dorsey his rights then two muscular uniformed cops took an elbow each and dragged him away.

Coombes tagged along. He wasn't ready for it to be over.

They went up the raised bank and down the other side, through the hole in the hedge. One of the SUVs lay waiting, back door open. The cops launched Dorsey inside like he was a bag of soiled laundry and were about to slam the door closed when Coombes arrived.

"Guys? A minute?"

They shrugged and left him to it. He leaned inside the SUV.

"You made this personal to me. *That* was your mistake."

He got a flash of the earlier arrogance, the sneer.

"Those cameras were transmitting video, Coombes. I uploaded it all online two hours ago. Sutton's confession, you shooting him, the sister in the trunk. No one's going to believe I did what he's already admitted to. I'll be released before you've changed your shirt."

Coombes shrugged like that was possible, like it was none of his concern.

"Then you have nothing to lose by telling me."

"Telling you *what?*"

"Why you killed all those people. I need to understand. It's just you and me here. A couple of coyotes, separated from the pack."

Dorsey smirked.

"They were my investors. They owned 51% of my company and they were trying to force me out before the IPO. They'd get billions, I'd get pocket change. It was *my* company, Coombes, *my* invention. These people were nothing but corporate vampires. *Thieves*. They got what was coming to them."

"*This was all for money?*"

The question irritated Dorsey, like he was talking to a child.

"That's how it started...after a while it was just too much fun to stop. Vandenberg was the last investor; the others were just people that annoyed me. As long as there were coins left, I had to keep going. I can't explain it, it was like they called to me. I *was* the Ferryman."

They'd been trying to find a link between kills when half of them were irrelevant. It explained a lot, particularly Haylee Jordan whose death always defied explanation. None of it surprised Coombes. Oftentimes, a question raised by an investigation was more interesting than the answer. Truth could be random, disappointing.

"And Nicolas Sutton?"

"Stole my girl for a one-night stand. Destroying him was an utter pleasure. Something you're going to understand very soon."

"What's that supposed to mean?"

"You drove straight home from that hotel. The Metro Grand. That was pretty stupid, Coombes. I was able to follow you all the way there, no problem. I could have killed you or your wife any time I wanted. You're alive because I didn't."

"I'm not some fat industrialist that you can sneak up on and knock over the back of the head."

Dorsey nodded.

"Maybe, but your wife would've been easy pickings. I went back to your home the next day after you were gone. Sat in my car across the street thinking about how to kill her. Something special, so you'd know it was me. That you'd got her killed. While I was waiting for the muse to strike, a big guy in an expensive suit turned up. She answered the door in a robe. Didn't look like there was much underneath it. She was *very* pleased to see him."

Coombes said nothing, his face frozen like a mask.

"You already knew, huh?"

There was a tonal difference between how Dorsey had told him about the cameras, and how he'd told him about his wife. One was true, the other was a lie. He didn't need to examine it too much to know which was which. There would be no video of the shoot-out with Sutton, of that he was certain.

Coombes waved over the uniformed cops.

"Take this garbage away before I do something I regret."

47

THE NEXT DAY THERE was only one thing left to do, and that was to lay it all out to the public who paid for the whole show. It was considered good policy to highlight success because there seemed to be a never-ending tide of anti-police narrative in the press that needed to be offset. It amounted to feeding the same beast that was trying to eat you and hoping it would give you a break in return. To him, talking to the press was a chore. He took no pleasure in it, and anyone who did was a politician to him, not a cop.

Coombes gave a carefully-worded summary of the capture and arrest of Gabriel Dorsey. The pending trial limited what he could say, beyond the list of charges facing Dorsey, which was substantial and took several minutes to go through. Not on the list, was the death of Nicolas Sutton, or the kidnapping of Olivia. It was a tough pill to swallow; but there wasn't enough evidence to make either case. This didn't prevent him from closing up by stating that Sutton had given his life to save his sister and should be considered the final victim of the Ferryman.

When he turned to hand over to Gantz to finish up, he instead saw the captain approaching with a smile on his face. From day one, Block had done nothing more than file his nails, but now that there was good news, he had appeared out of nowhere to take credit. Coombes pretended not to see him and swung his shoulders wide, forcing the captain to step hastily to the side to let him past on the narrow stage.

Out in the press pack, a woman laughed.

The laugh was sharp and clear. It seemed to bounce around the walls like a goofy machine-gun, and it caused a ripple of follow-on laughter from other members of the press. He'd turned Block's moment of glory into something comical, and he knew there'd be some form of payback coming.

Out of politeness, he stood at the back next to Becker and Sato to watch Block fumble his way through a speech. It was about as interesting as watching paint dry, and he let his eyes move around the room.

After a moment, he saw Sullivan. She was looking back at him, a big smile on her face.

It was the first time he'd seen the journalist since he'd fed her the line about the coins. The mundane truth of the coins had still to come out, but he didn't think she'd mind when it did. By the time the trial came around, her position at the *Times* would be secure and she'd be all set for the main crime seat when it became available.

Coombes thought again of Dorsey's claim that he'd uploaded the Sutton shooting footage to the internet. The claim hung over him like a cloud. If it was true, he was in a lot of trouble and the case against Dorsey would be substantially weakened. Sutton's confession might convince a lot of jurors who wouldn't care much about why it was being recorded or Sutton's motivation for admitting it.

It had been ten hours now. If the footage was out there, he thought it would have been found by now, while people were still actively looking for Ferryman content. In any case, there was no point worrying about something he could do nothing about. He was certain it was no more than a worn-out play by a sick killer who had no more moves left.

They had located Dorsey's red Toyota Corolla on the street outside Teddy Sutton's home earlier that morning. As he had surmised, it was still registered to the previous owner, but it looked like that was where Dorsey's precautions had ended. His fingerprints were all over the vehicle. The passenger side footwell contained the real prize; the rare Nikes with a treasure-trove of DNA evidence on them.

Dorsey's luck had finally run out.

Block finished up and closed down press questions due to the trial that still lay ahead, then turned and walked away from the podium. He shot Coombes a foul look but said nothing.

The room was already half empty. Some had left while Block was still speaking, knowing it was going nowhere. The members of the task force left the stage and walked down steps at the side to where the press was clearing out. He wasn't surprised to see Sullivan waiting for him.

"Congratulations, Coombes. I wasn't sure you had it in you."

"Thanks," he said.

She stepped closer and messed his hair up with her fingers.

"I told you that you'd suit it short."

He saw Sato watching closely.

"You have a loud laugh, Sullivan. I think the whole of America heard."

"I make all kinds of loud noises once you get to know me." She glanced at Sato. "Don't worry, honey. I don't mean to stand on your toes, I'm just shooting the shit."

Sato gasped and walked away, her face scarlet.

"Thanks a lot. I'm going to be fighting fires all day now."

"She likes you, Coombes. Maybe as much as I do."

He wasn't sure what to say to that and she laughed at his expression.

"Here's my card. *Call me*. We can get another drink."

She put a card in the front pocket of his suit jacket, winked and walked off. He turned to watch her go, and again she looked back and caught him. A captain with six 5-year service stripes on her sleeve approached. He knew what she was going to say before she opened her mouth.

"Chief wants to see you."

He knew better than to ask *when*.

———

COOMBES HAD NEVER MET the Chief of Police before and had managed to live his life just fine. When he got to his outer office, he was told to take a seat and wait. It was only when he sat that he wondered why the Chief wanted to see him. It couldn't be for making his captain look like an idiot on national television, that wouldn't be handled by anyone but by Block himself. If not that, then what?

The video of Sutton's confession and death?

The minutes ticked by and he resisted looking at his watch. The more time that passed, the safer he figured he was. If the video had landed there would be no delay, Jackson would have him in front of him as soon as possible. Almost twenty minutes passed before he was told to go into Jackson's office.

The Chief was standing in front of the plate glass window that made up one wall of his office. He had his jacket off, and his shirtsleeves were rolled up to the elbow. As he turned to face Coombes, he took a hands-free cell phone headset off his ear.

"That was some fine work, Coombes."

"Very much a team effort, sir."

"That's too bad, there's only Scotch for you and Sato."

He indicated wrapped packages on one of the chairs.

"It was all us, Chief. Everyone else just got in our way."

Jackson smiled and walked back to his desk.

"Adapts quickly. Funny. I have a good feeling about you."

Coombes nodded and smiled back.

Even the least expensive Scotch was worth a moment's courtesy. More than the gift itself, was the implied closer relationship between them which could prove useful in the shark-infested waters of RHD. Of course, someone like Jackson would have a whole collection of gifts for any situation. There'd be a closet somewhere full of them, perhaps a whole room. Paid for by the city, chosen by someone else.

He knew this, and didn't care.

What *did* bother him, was that Sato had been excluded from their conversation. It indicated to him that Jackson wanted something and that maybe the gift was to soften him up.

"Was there something in my report that you wanted to ask me about?"

"In fact, it was something that was *not* in the report."

"Shoot."

"Olivia Sutton. The two of you are close?"

He felt himself relax. Jackson hadn't seen a video of Nicolas Sutton's confession, and if he hadn't seen it, no one had. If that clip had landed anywhere online it wouldn't take long for it to find its way to the 10th floor.

"We dated as teenagers. I've seen her maybe five times since."

"How well did you know her brother?"

"I met Olivia through him, he and I were at school together. We were friends until I dated his sister. He didn't like that."

Jackson nodded. "You crossed the line."

"It was worth it."

A smile flickered at the corners of Jackson's mouth.

"Let me put my question simply, Detective. Your report states that despite earlier reservations, you finally believed Theodore Sutton's suicide was genuine. Given your relationship with the family, I wanted to know if there was something else there."

Coombes made a face before he could stop it.

"The report is accurate, but not complete. Nicky was at the scene. His father hanged himself in front of him on purpose. It was a brutal thing to witness and it traumatized him. He froze up. He could've saved his father, but he didn't. I left it out of my report because it added nothing. They are both dead now and I thought Olivia had been through enough."

Jackson said nothing for a moment.

"I guess I can live with that. You showed discretion and respect for the dead. In future, I expect you to keep me in the loop regardless as to what appears in your report. Don't leave it to me to read between the lines to get the full picture. Understood?"

"Yes, sir."

"Have a good New Year, Coombes. You've earned it."

Jackson turned to his computer, their business apparently at an end. Coombes picked up the two packages of Scotch from the seat in front of him then walked to the door. As he reached for the handle he paused and withdrew his hand. It was no use; it wasn't in his nature to turn the other cheek. He had to try.

He walked back to where he'd been standing before.

"Was there something else, Detective?"

"I was hoping you could do something for Billy Lass. We wouldn't have gotten to the end of this one without him, Chief."

Jackson sat back in his chair, a sour look on his face.

"Lass is damaged goods, Coombes. You'd do well to avoid getting some of his shit on your shoes right when your career is taking off. Do you follow?"

"He's certainly damaged now. Six broken fingers, two broken ribs, a broken nose, and a concussion. That has to offset his beef with Hurst."

"He shouldn't have been there, he was suspended. It wasn't his case."

He felt his chest fill with anger. Lass was no angel, but to throw him under the bus to save a useless piece of skin like Hurst was too much. For a moment he said nothing and dipped his head so he was looking at Jackson's desk. It looked unused, like a prop in a movie.

"I can appreciate your loyalty to your former partner, Coombes, but striking a superior officer is a big deal and is clearly grounds for dismissal."

"I understand Hurst isn't pressing charges."

"That's not the point and you know it."

"He isn't pressing charges because he knows if he did the whole truth would come out and it would be him eating the grenade, not Lass."

Jackson took a deep breath and looked out the window.

"I know all about the captain and his...views on race. The problem is that almost a hundred people, myself included, saw Lass kick Hurst while he was already on the ground. That's assault with a deadly weapon, Detective. It's only because of me that he isn't currently in lockup awaiting trial. Any person that could've helped him fight this was probably at that charity function. No one is going to get involved. I couldn't get him a job anywhere in Los Angeles, not even in animal control. He's done."

Coombes straightened.

"What about *outside* Los Angeles?"

Jackson tilted his head over. "A transfer?"

The idea seemed to amuse him, like he was washing his hands of a problem and passing it down the line.

Coombes had a good feeling.

"San Francisco. He loves that city, he'd accept that. Get the IA boys to clean his slate. There's no departmental blowback if he's leaving anyway, right? Consider the optics. He was defending his pregnant wife from a known racist. That's not a story you want coming out."

"His wife was *pregnant?*"

"She gave birth two weeks later."

Jackson sighed. "Leave it with me."

"Thanks, Chief."

Coombes left the room and closed the door softly behind him. He'd pushed his luck with Jackson and knew well enough to get gone while the going was good.

48

COOMBES PARKED HIS PERSONAL vehicle across the street from Sato's apartment and glanced up at her windows. Grace had reacted badly to Sullivan's joking around and had taken off without saying goodbye. The journalist was an outrageous flirt, it was how she got her information. It meant nothing, she probably barely realized she was doing it. He knew it like the sun was shining, yet when he was on the receiving end, he'd enjoyed it just the same.

Sullivan had made Sato feel foolish and he couldn't let that stand. They were off rotation now for three weeks. He couldn't leave the situation until they returned to work, he had to fix it before it became unfixable.

What was needed here was a light touch.

He fanned the fingers of his right hand and moved them back and forth over the vent of his air conditioning. Light touches were not part of his skillset. If he said the wrong thing, he stood only to make the situation worse. She needed to be reassured; to know that nothing between them had changed. Sato's windows were black, with no reflection or light inside.

His cell phone rang. A restricted number. He sighed, half his calls were from restricted numbers.

"Coombes."

"This is Detective Harrison, West Bureau. We were given your name by someone we just arrested. Said he'd only speak to you."

"Oh yeah? What's this character's name?"

"Walter Ford. He walked into Hollywood station two hours ago wearing a quart of blood and a big happy smile. If it's human blood, we're looking for at least one homicide."

He pictured the lumbering giant the day he'd confessed. Ford wanted to be famous, to be *seen* in a world full of celebrities and reality stars. Fakes with Photoshopped faces and perfect lives. It was the new American Dream; he saw it everywhere he went. Ford had admired the Ferryman and wanted to be part of it, why else involve him? But the answer was obvious.

Ford hadn't seen the press conference.

He didn't know it was all over.

Either he would again claim to be the Ferryman, using a real kill to sell it; or he had taken his advice to help other people in a new direction, by doing what the task force couldn't.

"Did you notice if Ford had any dog bites?"

Harrison paused. "Yeah. On his hands, arms, and face. How did you know?"

"I think your victim is Jake Curtis, 2041 Desford Drive, off North Beverly."

He heard Harrison's cheap ballpoint scratch the name and address down.

"Are you Sherlock Holmes or something?"

"I guess we'll see."

But he didn't need to see, he already knew. In the pit of his stomach, where he always knew something was true before it was confirmed. He thought about how he'd left things with Curtis and sighed. As much as he disliked the writer, he didn't want him dead.

"Are you going to come speak with Ford?"

He looked again at Sato's window and saw she was watching him through the glass. Their eyes connected and she waved. Friendly. Happy. She wasn't mad with him, far from it. He acknowledged her wave with his left hand. She was smiling so hard her face shone.

"It looks like I'm going to be tied up here for a couple of hours."

"Understood. This guy's going nowhere anyway."

Coombes disconnected.

He killed the engine, then picked up one of the packages sitting on his passenger seat. Her gift from the Chief. He crossed over the street, a cool breeze pushing through his hair. His mind was blank and at peace as it always was at the end of a case.

Her apartment was on the second floor of the building, and he took the stairs three at a time. In his hand, he felt the Scotch move inside the bottle. When he got to her door, she was standing waiting for him with one hand propped up on her hip, like he'd kept her waiting. They stood on the threshold for a moment, looking into each other's eyes. *I could still leave*, he thought. *It's not too late.* His gaze dipped to her mouth and he knew that wasn't remotely true.

Grace opened the door wide and he walked inside.

NEXT IN SERIES:

The Scapegoat (Johnny Coombes #2)

About the Author

I live on the outskirts of Edinburgh with my fiancée and young son. I would like to thank my family for their support and encouragement, it means the world to me. I am the author of Night Passenger, The Dark Halo, and The Scapegoat.

If you enjoyed The Dark Halo, please consider writing a quick review, it would be greatly appreciated. To stay up-to-date on new releases, click Follow on my Amazon author page.

f facebook.com/dstanleyauthor

y twitter.com/davidjstanley

instagram.com/dstanleyauthor/

g goodreads.com/stanleyd

Printed in Great Britain
by Amazon

43817209R00192